MURDER ON A KIBBUTZ

MURDER ON A KIBBUTZ

A COMMUNAL CASE

BATYA GUR

**TRANSLATED FROM THE HEBREW
BY DALYA BILU**

HarperPerennial
A Division of HarperCollins*Publishers*

The Library of Congress has catalogued the hardcover edition as follows:

Gur, Batya.
    [Linah meshutefet. English]
    Murder on a kibbutz: a communal case/Batya Gur.—1st ed.
       p. cm.
    ISBN 0-06-019026-4
    1. Ohayon, Michael (Fictitious character)—Fiction. 2. Police—Israel—Fiction. 3. Kibbutzim—Fiction. I. Title.
PJ5054.G637L5613   1994
892.4'36—dc20   94-26642

ISBN 0-06-092654-6 (pbk.)

95 96 97 98 99 ❖/RRD 10 9 8 7 6 5 4 3 2 1

To Amos

MURDER ON A KIBBUTZ

In the open field next to the kibbutz entrance they had stacked the big bales of hay into a broad, high golden wall. The spaces between the bales were filled with massed bunches of flowers. Someone had gone to a lot of trouble to make it look as if the flowers were growing there of their own accord. Strips of blue, cloudless sky peeped through other apertures in the wall.

Aaron smiled as he imagined the battle that Srulke must have put up over every single flower. Srulke's lips tightening in his lined, sunburnt face, hiding his pride and exposing his objection to waste, his back bent and his expression resentful at the demand for this floral tribute. For a moment Aaron wondered whom they had sent to extract the tribute from him this time. In the past they had always sent Estie, but after seeing her, hard and shriveled, in the dining hall today and remembering with a pang the delicate silhouette, the winsome grace that had once been capable of influencing Srulke, he knew that by now they were sending someone else. Every few years they would change the delegate, but it was always some- one of whom Srulke would say, "She's a sweet, refined girl, not like your sabras," and then he would cut the flowers for her.

Aaron saw the splendor of the big roses, distinguished the yellow and red of the gerberas, the purple of the snapdragons, the modest white of the daisies, but as always a dusty earth brown dominated the colors of the flowers, and it seemed that the golden shade of the hay only made it more pronounced. Briefly Aaron felt the rare delight of encountering himself, as he suddenly noticed in the flowers and their colors the changing seasons of the year. There was a moment when he saw things as they were, and it seemed to him that his better part, the part that had forgotten for a moment to be cautious and calculating, anxious about every word he said, the part that could even sometimes be poetic, had come alive.

Moish was already standing at the microphone on the platform that had been erected in front of the wall of hay and was looking at the gathering crowd. Assembled in a distant corner of the field were the groups bearing the first fruits. The kibbutz choir, four men and three women in blue and white, stood, song sheets in hand, at another microphone. The whole kibbutz was there. They had begun streaming to the site just before the ceremony was due to begin, after the hour set aside for coffee and cakes baked specially for the holiday. Already at lunch he had heard Matilda complaining in her aggrieved tone that there wasn't a single package of margarine left in the big dining-hall refrigerator, and later in the afternoon the smell of cheesecake rose from all the "rooms," as the kibbutz members' small houses were still called. Even Matilda had to admit—he had just overheard her as he walked past her room—she was pleased that the young scatterbrains had used her recipe book to bake the holiday cakes.

Gradually the area next to the water tower filled up with kibbutz members and their children, as well as the many guests who could be recognized by their elegant clothes, so unsuitable for sitting on the dry ground that raised brown dust with every step. The dust clung to everything. For hours afterward Aaron would still feel it in his nostrils, and he remembered how when he returned from roaming the fields in summer the smell of the dust would go on clinging to his body, even after he had taken a shower. He looked at the tractors parked at the side of the field. Children were clambering over the big chains of the D6, the yellow Caterpillar, which had been decorated with red and pink geraniums, and fathers lifted toddlers in the air to let them touch the top of the cotton picker. Like a big slumbering animal, the cotton picker stood at the head of the line of tractors, crowned with garlands of yellow, pink, and purple zinnias looking like the flowers the kindergarten children diligently draw, gravely coloring in one petal after the other. Tractors of the old generation were there as well, Aaron saw— two big, green John Deeres whose wheels had been polished and decorated with enormous yellow roses, the ones Srulke particularly cherished.

The crowd didn't quiet down even when Moish intoned into the mike, "One, two, three, testing." It was only when the little choir began to sing, softly at first and then louder, "Baskets on Our Shoulders, Garlands on Our Heads" that people began hushing their children, and the old women standing in the first row said "Shhhhh," not in rebuke but with satisfaction.

Aaron stood on one side and looked at their wrinkled faces, their thin, wispy hair, the floral dresses that seemed cut so as deliberately to blur the lines of their figures, and at the old men who had begun by standing next to them and afterward settled down at their feet. He looked at Zeev HaCohen, whose tall body seemed to have shrunk with the years but who still, despite his striking thinness, looked impressive with his mane of white hair. Srulke's voice echoed in his ears, as it always did when he saw HaCohen: "That politician," Srulke had called him angrily, vigorously soaping an empty coffee cup. This was an image from many years ago, Srulke in a gray undershirt standing at the sink, Miriam sitting at the table, which was covered by an oilcloth, stiff at the corners and sticky to the touch and decorated with brown flowers on a beige background. "You shouldn't talk about him like that," he remembered her saying, her voice alarmed and pleading, and their sudden silence when they noticed Aaron standing in the doorway.

Zeev HaCohen was now sitting at the feet of Matilda, the kitchen-complex manager who also ran the kibbutz minimarket; a small boy sat on the floor next to him playing with the buckle of his brown biblical sandal. One of his grandchildren, the son of one of his children by who knows which of his wives, thought Aaron, vaguely remembering what he had heard from Moish about the complex domestic life of the acknowledged leading intellectual and philosopher of this kibbutz as well as others of its kind. "How old is he now?" Aaron had asked Moish when they arrived together at the scene of the celebration. "I don't know exactly," Moish had said absentmindedly, lifting his child off his shoulders and heading for the platform. "Maybe seventy-five. No, definitely more than seventy-five."

The kibbutz itself was now fifty years old. A half century had passed since the oldest members had settled on this land. It was not the oldest kibbutz in Israel, but it was certainly well established. The atmosphere today was festive, but at the same time it was clear that nobody was taking the celebration too seriously. Only the children looked excited, but they were drawn to the lineup of agricultural machinery, and none of them paid any attention to the platform and the little choir standing on it. And apart from the members of the choir, hardly anyone was wearing blue and white. Not even the kindergarten children, Aaron noticed with a trace of disappointment that then amused him, and there was no sign anywhere of the national flag. He would have to ask Moish about that too. And at the same moment he thought of the nostalgia that would overcome him on national holidays, and of the excitement with which he would look forward to Shevuoth, the Festival of Weeks, in particular, the feeling of participation in great and important events that had really and truly pervaded him then.

He could not entirely suppress the feeling that once you took away the blue and white and the flags on the Caterpillar, the whole ceremony seemed archaic and foreign, as if it were taking place on a collective farm in Soviet Russia. And yet, he thought, chewing a straw reflectively, he felt that time had stood still, as if he were watching documentary footage from a movie about early Zionist history. But now it was the farce of an agricultural ceremony in a place where agriculture was almost bankrupt—a kibbutz, a Zionist agricultural commune, that derived its income from an industrial plant that, of all things, manufactured cosmetics, having given its name to an international patent for a face cream that abolished wrinkles and rejuvenated skin cells and was advertised in all the newspapers with two photographs of the same woman captioned "Before" and "After." No one else seemed to be showing any recognition of the absurdity of celebrating an agricultural rite where only the manufacture and sale of face cream made it possible to go on working the land. It could, he thought, be why Srulke hadn't appeared. When Aaron had looked for him in vain in the dining hall in order to greet him, Moish had assured him that he would show up for the ceremony, "if only," he said, grinning, "to inspect what they've done with his flowers."

As he looked around, ostensibly keeping an eye out for Srulke but actually trying to catch a glimpse of Osnat, Aaron concluded that at least one sector of the kibbutz economy was blooming: There were so many children that a stranger might be excused for wondering how anybody had time for anything else. The products of this intensive reproductive activity scampered about, and the apparent contentedness and good humor of the large families gave him a pang of vague longings. But his other voice nipped them in the bud. The little devil inside him immediately scoffed at his wish to belong, and the skeptical inner voices that had grown louder over the years now asserted themselves and conjured up the image of a herd of placid Dutch cows, spoiling his sense of festivity beyond recovery. He tried to suppress the feeling that there was something stupefying about the tranquility here, recalling the rage that would seize hold of him in the past and that had attacked him today too, on his way to the dining hall with Moish for lunch.

It was only a short distance from Moish's room to the dining hall, but it had taken a long time to get there, what with having to greet everyone they met and with Moish's delaying them by remembering one little chore after another, stopping at the children's houses to see if a dripping faucet had been repaired and the sandbox in the kindergarten refilled with fresh sand, and then at the secretariat to find out whether someone who was supposed to phone had phoned, and only after he had studied the notices on the bulletin board, extracted the newspaper from his pigeonhole and read all the notes he also found there, and answered the phone ringing in the big lobby on the ground floor—only then did the two of them climb the stairs to the building's second floor, to the dining hall itself.

At the door, Moish lingered to take in the scene, and an eternity seemed to pass before he picked up a tray. As they stood before the trolley holding the trays, Aaron suddenly felt fatigued and impatient with the waste of time, the idleness. He summed it up for himself: The minute you walk into the door of the dining hall, your oxygen supply drops, your productivity declines; that phlegmatic calm, that slowness, they're enough to drive a person crazy. He retreated behind the protection of the guessing game: who was who, who belonged to whom. He succeeded in identifying members of three and even four generations standing together in groups, the youngest children on their fathers' shoulders. Which of the adults had been born on the kibbutz and which had married into it he couldn't guess, but he could tell at a glance which of them were guests like himself.

The ceremony began. He still hadn't seen Osnat, but he didn't dare look for her openly. The first to be called up to the platform were the orchard and vegetable-garden workers. Two children and two men in dark blue work clothes laid their offerings in two big straw baskets next to the wall of hay and stood in front of the microphone. In a short declamation about the fruits of the year, they mentioned such exotica as mangoes, avocados, and kiwi, even star fruit and pineapples, but not grapes or apricots. Once more Aaron felt betrayed. The brimming baskets looked as if they had been brought straight from the display window of a fancy fruit shop in Tel Aviv's Ben Yehuda Street or like a fruit arrangement in a hotel room. "What good are these things," he said to himself, thinking of the anachronism of the big straw baskets, so like those in the posters of the old pioneers, "with that kind of stuff inside them?"

Then came the cotton workers, and after them the workers from the sewing shop and the clothes factory, "dressed in our latest models," announced Moish, pointing to Fanya, the elderly head of the sewing shop, who was standing to one side, at some distance from the microphone. The field-crop workers came next to last, followed by the landscape gardeners. Srulke was not among these, and again Aaron asked himself where he could be, for despite his age nobody had yet dared to challenge his status as the kibbutz's father of horticulture. But his question was quickly thrust aside by the big basket containing giant pots of face cream, one of which, in a transparent plastic box decorated with a gold ribbon, was held aloft by Moish, who announced, "Eternal Dew!" This was the uninspired name of the face cream that had earned the kibbutz hundreds of thousands of dollars in recent years. The basket was decorated with the cactus from which the cosmetic was produced, and Aaron stared in bemusement at the dull, ordinary-looking thick-stemmed green plant.

Before the big tractors began rolling in formation around the area, the children who looked after the animals in the little menagerie marched by, escorting a brown foal and a month-old donkey with a garland of carnations around his neck. A little girl in a white dress held a fluffy white rabbit on her shoulder, and a boy and a girl carried a chicken in a big straw basket.

Finally eleven young women paraded in front of the flowery wall holding their babies born that year, and the audience again applauded, perfunctorily, with the general noise continuing unabated. Then the tractor parade started, with the young girls on the slowly moving floats scattering confetti and silver stardust in all directions.

It was hot but not muggy, with the dry heat characteristic of the northern Negev. Although it was already six in the evening, the sun still seemed near its zenith, and the children rushed about excitedly in the clouds of dust raised by the big machines. Everyone stood up and moved back, grabbing hold of the little ones to stop them from getting too close. The children of the various agricultural managers sat in the drivers' cabins with their fathers. At the wheel of the big cotton picker sat an adolescent boy with a bare, bronzed chest, his expression blank, almost indifferent, as if he were unaware of the impression he was making on the kibbutz children and the teenage girls, some of whom wore white dresses, emphasizing their youthful blooming health and beauty.

"Our barns are packed with wheat, our vats are brimming with wine. Our homes are full of babies," sang the choir, and Aaron thought that the words had never been so apt as they were here. Everything proclaimed abundance. The economic difficulties of the kibbutz movement, which had recently made headline news and been discussed in the Knesset as a whole and in its Education Committee, were unrecognizable here. The profits of the cosmetics factory were so high, as Moish had explained to him on their way to the ceremony, that they subsidized everything, including some other kibbutzim that were sunk in debt. Here members could still afford to go on trips abroad, and the projected change to family housing, with the children to sleep at their parents' rather than in the traditional children's houses, had been rejected not because of budgetary problems but because of a decision by the Kibbutz Artzi, the national council of the most ideologically traditional wing of the kibbutz movement, to which they belonged.

Aaron, who had been scanning the crowd for Osnat, now suddenly noticed Dvorka standing not far from him and shading her eyes with her hand. A small child, perhaps five years old, held her other hand. With a shock Aaron realized that this must be Osnat's son, Dvorka's youngest grandchild. Even from a distance he could see that she was more stooped than he remembered her. "She must be over seventy by now," he had remarked to Moish at lunch, and Moish had nodded: "Seventy-two. But still a bulldozer. You should hear her at the *sicha*,"* he said, smiling. "Still the same voice, the same energy. She's a holy terror."

Almost eight years had passed since Aaron's last visit to the kibbutz. And now too, when he accepted the invitation to attend the double celebration of Shevuoth and the kibbutz's jubilee, he had thought of Osnat. It was years since he had seen her. How many years exactly, he asked himself, carefully calculating and wondering whether Arnon had already been born when he was here last, and then dimly remembering that Dafna had still been pregnant at the time. But it wasn't only because of Osnat that he had kept away. Even after becoming a public figure, even after becoming an M.K., a member of the Knesset, he was flooded with uneasiness whenever he remembered the kibbutz. In his autobiographical references he frequently mentioned that he had once been a kibbutz member, and some newspapers had made much of his having been a child from outside who had been successfully absorbed by the kibbutz and left after completing his studies. Someone had even written in so many words that he had studied at the expense of the kibbutz and then left it behind. "One of the great disappointments of the kibbutz movement," a well-known journalist had once called him, explaining in psychological terms "M.K. Meroz's indignant objection to the demand to alleviate the debts burdening the kibbutz movement."

The fear of feeling ill at ease, the sense of oppression that descended on him whenever he drove thorough the gate, prevented him from visit-

---

*Discussion; plural: *sichot*. Term used in the Kibbutz Artzi kibbutzim for the weekly general meeting at which issues are discussed and decisions voted on.

ing. Each time the visits became more difficult, "instead of the other way around," he had thought to himself on his way here this morning, trying to shake off the heaviness taking hold of him. On the phone Moish had said to him, "Have a heart, fifty years, it doesn't happen every day—can't you make an effort?" He didn't have to make too much of an effort. He could even have given it an official justification, made it into a public relations exercise, but somehow—presumably it had something to do with Osnat, he thought now as he looked around again in the hope of seeing her—he had preferred to keep the visit private and told nobody but his daughter where he was going, and to her too he had said "maybe." He had set up a meeting with the head of the Education Department in the Ashkelon municipality first, and when it was over, without coming to any conscious decision (on the phone he had said to Moish, "I'll try, but I can't promise; you know how it is"), he had turned the steering wheel sharply at the last minute, and the car had driven him into the kibbutz.

This time he drove through the gate feeling like a conquering hero returning to his old home. On his last visit he was already a successful lawyer, but his fame had not reached the kibbutz; now not even they would be able to ignore his visiting card. But together with the sense of triumph he went on feeling the old oppression and malaise. He tried to shake off upsetting pictures from the past, sorrow, loneliness, shame. Mainly shame. Vividly the first images rose before his eyes, together with the nagging pain in his left arm, the pain that had made him stop smoking.

When he parked his car next to the "Daffodil" quarters where Moish lived, he noticed two youngsters talking to each other and looking at him with casual, idle curiosity. They were wearing dark blue work clothes, and one of them was holding a big drill. Aaron was sure that they must have recognized him from his pictures in the press and his television appearances—lately his face had frequently been seen on the screen—but they didn't say anything, and he didn't know whether their silence was because they had recognized him or that they were too busy with their own affairs to take any notice of him.

When he had gone over to Dvorka in the dining hall at lunch, his newfound self-confidence covering up the old malaise that attacked him whenever he thought of her, he was astonished to see the hesitant expression on her face. For a moment he suspected that she had failed to recognize him. Although she nodded and shook his hand—hers was hard and callous—her grip was rather limp, and she didn't smile. Before turning away she said, "How are you?" in a tone that did not invite a response, and when he said something about the jubilee celebration, she nodded mechanically and looked around as if she were busily searching for someone. Aaron cleared his throat and said, "I'll see you later, I hope; there are a few things I'd like to consult with you about." It was only then that she looked at him with the bright, piercing look he remembered, the look that immediately made him feel like a child again, completely transparent.

For a few seconds she looked at him like this, and then, as if she had summed up everything she had seen inside him, she said, "I'll expect you this evening, if you're staying here tonight." And Aaron promised to drop in. "After the artistic program," said Dvorka, "after supper. We've got a lot to talk about."

Aaron nodded obediently and swallowed his saliva. They were standing, trays in hand, in front of the main-course counter, and in order to shake her hand Aaron had to set his tray down, and by now there was a queue forming behind them. Moish was standing at the juice dispenser in a corner of the dining hall, and Aaron saw him out of the corner of his eye filling a jug with juice while bending over a woman to whom he was listening attentively. "You haven't been to see us for a long time," said Froike, who stood behind the counter serving the main course. "Kitchen duty today," he added apologetically, or perhaps he wasn't apologizing but only stating a fact, and it was Aaron who read the apology into his words.

Dvorka had been Aaron's first teacher on the kibbutz. She was the sixth-grade homeroom teacher, and Aaron remembered the hair scraped back into a bun, white threads in the dark coiled braid, the smell of soap rising from her hands, the dark clothes, the tall body, and the voice full of passion. He remembered the kindly way she corrected him when he called her "Miss," and the precision with which she pronounced her name, "Dvorka," with the stress on the last syllable. Even now, seeing her in the dining hall at the height of summer, he could still hear the shuffle of her steps in her black rubber boots on those cold, rainy mornings, could hear the voice full of vitality with which she read the poems of Rachel aloud to them. And when he shook her hand he was flooded by vivid memories of the misery of the communal showers, of the embarrassment of boys and girls dressing and undressing together. Of the assurance with which Hadas would, in the summer, push her bronzed legs into the short blue pants with the elastic bottoms, bloomers made of a material as hard as tarpaulin, and in the winter, into the long blue pants. The laundry would come back to the children's house in one big pile, which included the few items of clothing that Aaron had brought with him to the kibbutz. Sometimes Uri would wear Aaron's checked shirt. Gradually the boundaries blurred, and he began taking clothes from the pile of laundry like everyone else, without looking for the things that had once been his own.

The year his father died, during the Passover holiday, his big sister, who was already in the army, serving in a Nahal* unit attached to the kibbutz, had brought him to the secretariat, and taking no notice of the ingratiating looks with which he pleaded not to be left alone there, she had handed him over to Dvorka and gone away. Moish's family had adopted him. After school and work he would go to the room of Srulke and Miriam, Moish's parents. Even now he had only to think of Srulke to be flooded with awe and uneasiness, a muffled feeling of strangeness and uncertainty, as if he still had to fulfill certain expectations as a condition of acceptance. Even today he didn't know what those expectations were and what sense of belonging he yearned for, but Srulke, like Dvorka, gave rise in him to feelings of sin and shame, anger and oppression. In those days on the kibbutz Aaron thought of himself as the most miserable child in the world, and with all her pedagogical sensitivity, all her efforts, Dvorka had been unable to blur the boundaries clearly drawn between himself and the kibbutz children.

Now in the dining hall Dvorka said not a word about his political career, as usual showing neither interest nor admiration. One look into her eyes was enough to wipe out the sense of triumph and pride with which he had arrived on the kibbutz. In Moish's room too, where they had coffee after lunch, that old feeling of uneasiness came back, as if he

*Acronym of Noar Halutzi Lohem (Pioneering Fighting Youth), an organization of the Israeli Defense Forces that combines military service with agricultural work on communal settlements.

were still a child from outside who had only been accepted as a favor to his sister.

When he left the kibbutz he had been regarded as a traitor. What that journalist had written was, of course, a lie. He had never studied at the expense of the kibbutz, and at one of his recent press conferences he had even found an opportunity to say something to that effect. But in public life there was no point in issuing denials, or so the experts told him. The truth of the matter was that he had left because he wanted to study law, but the higher-education committee had recommended that he wait his turn and in the meantime study "something we need on the kibbutz," such as economics or agriculture. And at the *sicha* too the members had told him to wait his turn, and "then we'll see."

The vote was almost unanimous against his request, and Yocheved, one of the oldest members, had folded her arms on her huge bosom and loudly said, "What's your hurry? Education isn't everything in life. First of all, you need to spend a few years working on the kibbutz, that's the most important thing." And Matilda had come out with the crushing remark: "We haven't even sent our own children, who were born here, to the university yet." Dvorka had silenced her angrily, and Zeev HaCohen had protested, and even Yehuda Harel, Dvorka's husband, who was on the kibbutz that day—he spent most of his time in the city, as external secretary responsible for contacts with the outside world—said, "That's completely irrelevant: Aaron is a son of the kibbutz and a member just like everyone else." But Aaron knew that he was going to leave in any case. The possibilities there seemed so limited, almost determined in advance, and he couldn't live with such a narrow vision of the future.

When he notified the secretariat of his intention, they sent him to talk to Dvorka. He remembered every detail of their conversation and of what preceded it. She had come up to him in the dining hall at lunchtime and said, "Why don't you drop in later for a talk?" He remembered that he had knocked hesitantly on the door of her room, and the efficiency with which she had made the coffee and removed it from the flame without letting it boil over, and the sure hand with which she had poured it out and sliced the marble cake and set the cups and plates on the embroidered cloth covering the rectangular table the kibbutz had distributed to all senior members as living room furniture. He remembered her sharp, all-knowing look when he mumbled something about needing to get away and being unable to wait for two or three years until his turn came around, and her remark about short-term sacrifices that would justify the meaning of his actions in the long term.

He didn't understand what she was talking about then, but in the past few years, running from one meeting to the other, taking a bite of a tasteless pita or a gulp of Nescafé and powdered milk, hurrying to a meeting with one or another regional inspector of schools or lunching with some reporter on educational matters, he would sometimes remember the clarity of the intuition in this sentence of hers and try to console himself with the thought that he had been a successful law student and was now a successful lawyer, and to remind himself of his large apartment in Ramat Aviv, the result of making the right financial calculations, and his new, air-conditioned car, which he was now parking next to Moish's room. He noted each of these achievements, among others, on a mental balance sheet against the members of the kibbutz, including Dvorka, for not having sufficiently appreciated his potential.

And anyway, when he left, Osnat had already moved into a small house with Dvorka's son, Yuvik, something Dvorka hadn't even seen fit to mention. Dvorka didn't concern herself with details, but even so it was clear that she must have known how much Osnat's affair with Yuvik had broken his heart. The whole kibbutz talked of nothing else for days. He saw their pitying, sympathetic looks and how quickly they dropped their eyes when they encountered his own—and he was grateful to Dvorka for not treating him with the insensitive gentleness that would have exposed him to her in all his weakness.

Only at the end of the conversation, after she had risen to her feet, holding the two coffee cups in her hands and almost bending over him, she had said with hesitant warmth, "Unless personal matters are involved in your decision, and solutions have been found for those too in the past . . . " But he had ignored this remark and risen to his feet, feeling clumsy and awkward, and then she had added, "In any case, not everybody is made manager of the field crops at your age. You don't seem to appreciate the importance of that position here." And again

Aaron heard behind her words the comment that he wasn't really a son of the kibbutz, that he had come from outside and nevertheless had climbed so high, the echo of a claim that he had been singled out for special, favored treatment. At that he had succeeded in mobilizing the anger necessary to square his shoulders and say, "I'll think about it; I haven't actually decided yet."

Sometimes, when he was driving home from Jerusalem, he would ask himself where he would have been today if he had shared his life with Osnat, if she hadn't chosen Yuvik, if he had remained on the kibbutz. Would he have sunk with her into a life of calm, peaceful child rearing, of heated debates at kibbutz meetings? But he had never succeeded in picturing it to the end; his mind would always stop at the moment when they were left alone together in their room, after putting the children to bed (Osnat and Yuvik had four children—how many would she have had if she had lived with him?). Here the picture would disintegrate, because the anger, still acute and fully alive, would come back and again overwhelm him.

The ceremony came to an end. Watching the people who began moving slowly in the direction of the dining hall, Aaron waited for Moish, who was talking to the person disconnecting the mikes. He remembered the Shevuoth holiday celebrations thirty years ago. There were no face creams or exotic tropical fruits then, and none of the placid apathy he now saw on the faces around him either. Everything was more intense, nobody smiled forgivingly, and the happiness was different too, full of tension. In those days, everyone had taken their roles so seriously that the preparations had taken ages. In his second year on the kibbutz, he had led the baby donkey from the menagerie. Aaron saw himself standing then somewhere in the middle of the line and remembered the back of Hadas's neck as she carried the loaf of bread the children had baked. He remembered her braid. Today she was in the United States. She had left years ago, following her husband.

For a long time now the members had not lived in "rooms" but in two- or three-room houses, depending on their needs, and these little houses were now furnished with everything a house required—refrigerators and gas stoves, coffee grinders and mixers and blenders. And on the closed-circuit television they showed late-night movies and also specially recorded programs, mainly the Saturday-night ones, so that people could come to the weekly kibbutz meetings and watch the shows later. "It's hard to compete with television," said Moish, and then he mentioned that the *sicha* was televised too. "Right from the start we bought two video cameras, for the sake of a few older members who physically couldn't make it to the meetings, and naturally some people took advantage and preferred to watch it at home instead of attending." He sighed. "What can you do, there are always some people who go for a free ride."

Now Aaron was walking next to Moish's wife, Havaleh, who was holding her small son's sticky hand. Another little boy toddled behind them, while the older children, a boy and a girl, made off in the direction of the kibbutz war monument, in memory of members killed in the wars, from where shouting and laughter could be heard. Aaron looked at Havaleh and thought with astonishment that she would soon be a grandmother. The satisfaction he saw in her eyes when she looked at her adolescent children as they walked away almost completely overshadowed the sourness of the expression he had noticed when he was having coffee with her and Moish in their room. There was resentment in her voice too, before Moish put an end with a warning look to the argument that had broken out between them.

They were walking in the direction of the rooms where the youngsters lived, a row of huts that had once housed the founders of the kibbutz. Aaron could still remember the day when Srulke and Miriam had moved from their hut into a stone building. Today the boys and girls serving in the army lived there, along with single members before they moved into family houses. Moish was now standing and talking to Amit, his second son, at the entrance to his room. Amit was doing his national service in the army but was on leave thanks to the policy announced in a newspaper clipping Moish had shown Aaron: "All commanding officers are requested to allow members of the kibbutz to attend the jubilee celebrations." Aaron looked at the young soldier and remembered what Moish had said. "He's in Nahal, but the unit's stationed in Hebron now. I don't know how to cope with it. You and your National Unity Government . . . " That was the only reference he had made to Aaron's position. "Son," Moish called Amit whenever he addressed him, and Aaron felt inferior again.

He had only two children from a failed marriage, a marriage that from the beginning had been the result of circumstance rather than choice. Arnon was only seven, Pazit was ten, and—he had to admit—she lacked the lazy grace of the little girls here. Havaleh had given birth to six children, and she was still walking around the room in short pants, and at the kibbutz pool she wore a bikini, as he noticed in the family photograph (an enlargement of a snapshot taken by Amit before his conscription, as Moish explained) that shone forth from its frame on top of the TV set in the little family house. Havaleh and Moish, members of Aaron's own generation, were still living here like a young couple, each with a secure place in the world. Moish was general director of the kibbutz, and Havaleh, on study leave, was taking refresher courses in music education. That he himself was a member of the Knesset Education Committee was not even mentioned. His political career did not impress Havaleh, who suppressed a gigantic yawn after the first curious glance she gave him.

At lunch too the family ate together in the dining hall, and when Aaron saw Amit slicing a large cucumber, he remembered the dexterity with which the kibbutz members had prepared salads for themselves at supper. On the rare occasions when the the children had accompanied Srulke to the dining hall Aaron would marvel at the punctilious slicing of these salads. First came the slow peeling, as thinly as possible, of a cucumber, then cutting it into tiny cubes, together with an onion and a tomato, then the search for the oil and, among connoisseurs, for a lemon too. After the frustration and feelings of clumsy failure that had accompanied his own unsuccessful attempts to cut the vegetables small and thin (only half the flesh of the cucumber would remain, and the tomato was almost always crushed), he would be seized with fury at the ritual itself, which he later discovered in the literature to be one of the characteristics of the communal kibbutz meal. Individualism blossomed here when it came to cutting up the salad, he had thought to himself on his previous visit too. All the individual energy that found no expression elsewhere was channeled into the preparation, with slow, maddening concentration, of this personal salad. In this they were all special. But in the past he hadn't known how to translate his rage into words; he couldn't call it by its name.

And then the children would eat in the dining nook of the children's house, except for Friday nights, when there was only chicken soup and tasteless boiled chicken (hummus, tahini, and the savory cheese-stuffed pastries called *burekas,* such as they had eaten at lunch today, were unheard of then). In those days, when Moish came to town with him, he would greedily devour the Popsicles Aaron bought him, and once when they spent a two-day vacation with Aaron's mother in town, Moish had demanded to be taken to the movies three times. Today they had videotaped movies, and an air-conditioned bus waited to take anyone who signed up to a rock concert in the open-air amphitheater at the neighboring kibbutz. Today, said Moish, kibbutzniks saw more shows a year than anyone who lived in town. "Things aren't what they used to be"—this statement, full of satisfaction, was repeated whenever Aaron remarked on some change.

In fact, nothing was the same as it used to be. The old dining hall had been converted into a clubhouse and replaced by this splendid new building. But as they stood outside the entrance, Moish said warningly, with sudden vehemence, "Just don't think it's paradise." And staring at the festive holiday meal, Aaron noticed the look in Moish's eye as he surveyed the hall and heard the sigh that bore witness to the fact that not everything was perfect here. As if to confirm this thought, Moish said, "It's not simple. There's a price for progress." But then he shook himself, and with a renewed burst of organizational energy, announced, "We're starting early."

The dining room was decorated and festive, its long tables covered with white cloths. They sat down at a table bearing a card that said "Ayal family."

"What's this?" asked Aaron. "Reserved places?"

"They have to know how many people to expect," said Havaleh calmly. "There are so many members and visitors you can't take it for granted that there'll be enough room anymore." With a decisive movement she seated Asaf and Ben on either side of her and sat down herself. Aaron reached for a dish and took a few sticky dates. An orange stain spread next to the bottle of orangeade standing next to the dates. He looked at the variety of soft drinks, at the bottles of wine, at the decorated paper plates, at the dozens of people entering the dining hall in a leisurely stream. At the end of the spacious room they had set up a platform decorated with the seven species of grains and fruits and equipped with microphones, and Aaron recalled that before they ate there would be an artistic program. A group of older members began to file onto the platform.

"I have to go up," said Moish, energetically pushing his chair back, and a few seconds later he was standing on the platform saying, "Good evening, everybody," in a calm, authoritative tone, and then: "Happy Holiday. Let us begin. The serious part of the evening will precede the meal. After we've eaten we'll stay together for the lighter part of the program."

Aaron looked around again for Osnat. He didn't dare ask about her. And again he wondered why Srulke wasn't there, but before he had time to ask Havaleh about her father-in-law's absence, his attention was caught by Moish, who was performing his role as master of ceremonies with a calm confidence that aroused his admiration and surprise. After silencing a few noisy children, who immediately sat down submissively, and waiting for everyone else to stop talking, he read out the blessing, then stood next to the choir, all seven of them in white shirts, and sang "Fields of Wheat" along with them.

The atmosphere in the hall was one of relaxed attention, occasionally disturbed by the noise of a crying child. Aaron looked at Moish, at the formerly brown curls that were now gray, at the arms whose tan was thrown into relief by the white shirt, and wondered for the thousandth time, as he did whenever he visited the kibbutz, why he wasn't living here in this harmonious peacefulness, rearing children and working the land and celebrating the seasonal festivals, enveloped by this all-embracing feeling of belonging and togetherness. They were at home, as always; it was their home, and he was the child from outside again, despite the friendly looks he encountered in the faces around him, and whenever he took a bite of the pickled cucumber and red pepper, he did so stealthily, as if he had no right, for after all, he had not worked to provide this food. And the fact that he was the guest of the kibbutz general director didn't help either, nor did the moments of discord he picked up here and there, like the argument he had witnessed after lunch. Moish had been making Turkish coffee, and Havaleh had said, "And if I don't want to take a trip abroad, and what I do want is a big refrigerator, and my mother said she'd give me the money, what do you care?" And Moish's hard voice from where he was standing in front of the gas burner: "When the kibbutz decides to buy big refrigerators for everyone, then you'll have a big refrigerator, and not before, never mind what your mother says or doesn't say," and Havaleh had said in an ominous tone, "We'll see."

Nor did his discovery in their bathroom bring him any comfort. He still felt embarrassed at the thought of the curiosity with which he had opened the medicine chest. Next to the pink plastic jars that Lina, still the kibbutz beautician, had labeled "EYE CREAM HAVA A." and "HAND CREAM HAVA A." stood a box labeled "TAGAMET" and a bottle full of a milky liquid labeled "ALUMAG." On the Tagamet box the name "Moshe Ayal" was written, and quickly reading the instructions, Aaron realized that his childhood friend who had turned into this calm, gray-haired, broad-shouldered man had an ulcer. And together with his astonishment, a strange, wild hilarity seized hold of him. So it was only skin-deep, all that equanimity displayed at lunch in the dining hall, during the ceremony outside in the field, and that would doubtless be on display as well at the festive evening meal.

Behind the microphone on the platform in the dining hall, Dvorka now stood reading from the Bible. The members turned the pages of the mimeographed program booklets for the Festival of Shevuoth in the kibbutz jubilee year. Her voice, still impressive, was filled with feeling, and every now and then it broke, as if there was too much to contain. She read from the Book of Ruth, and Aaron asked himself if she too was thinking now of Osnat, the girl from outside who had gone with her mother-in-law to a foreign land. He himself was alarmed by the association ("How can you call it a foreign land?" he asked himself), and his thoughts returned to Dvorka.

She's changed, he thought; there was something bitter about her. "It began even before Yuvik was killed," Moish had said when Aaron asked him about her; "she's getting old, and it's hard. First Yehuda died on her, and then that business with Yuvik in Lebanon. He should never have been there in the first place, at his age. One year later and he would have been released from reserve duty altogether. The only thing that keeps her going now is the grandchildren and Osnat." Aaron had felt himself blushing, but Moish, who was busy washing the coffee cups, hadn't noticed, and went on: "Yes, it's her relationship with Osnat that saves Dvorka. Only now Osnat's got that bee in her bonnet about the kids sleeping with their parents, and she can't think about anything else, she quarrels with everybody about it all the time."

"Is Dvorka for or against?" Aaron had asked, even though the mention of Osnat's name had pushed every other thought out of his mind.

"Against. Of course she's against it. What did you think?" Moish had muttered. "Don't you know Dvorka's opinions by now?"

"Yes, but I thought she was flexible about things like that. After all, all the kibbutzim are going over to it now."

Slowly and solemnly Dvorka closed the little Bible, removed her reading glasses, and stepped stiffly off the platform. For a moment or two Aaron looked at the stooped shoulders, the bun that seemed to have grown sparser and was completely silver by now, and watched her walk toward the kitchen. Then he turned his attention again to the platform.

A group of small children were standing there, dressed in blue and white. "Those are the 'Bambis,'" said Havaleh. "Grade two," she explained before he could ask. He looked at the children radiant with health and listened to them excitedly chorusing the recitation they had composed themselves, noting the solemn gravity with which they pronounced the words and the proud smiles spreading over some of their faces, exposing the gaps of the missing baby teeth, when everybody applauded. Even the memories, and the knowledge that things weren't so simple, together with the boredom that began spreading through his limbs and making them limp and heavy, did not succeed in banishing the feeling that here lay true peace, for both body and mind, and the gloom of knowing that he was an outsider and had no chance of ever becoming a part of this whole and happy life. As Havaleh had said back in the room, with the indifference that characterized all her remarks of this nature, "You would never have stuck it out here. As far as I remember, you always had difficulties with the group. You're not the type to accept the supremacy of the *sicha*." This was the expression she used—"the supremacy of the *sicha*"—an expression that sounded out of place coming from her lips, as if she were declaiming something traditional, archaic, and weird.

"How many years have you been the general director?" Aaron asked Moish when they began dishing out the first courses.

"Eat, it's a kind of egg roll, it's delicious," said Havaleh as she set it before him.

"This is the fourth year," said Moish wearily, "and I hope they find somebody else this year, because I don't know how long I can keep it up. I'm dying to get back to the cotton."

"Tell me," said Aaron, looking at the bottle of white wine standing next to him and the red wine in the glasses they were now all being asked to raise, "your economic situation seems okay. How did you manage to come out so well in that business with the bank shares?"

"Yes, we're in relatively good shape," said Moish.

Havaleh, who didn't miss a word in spite of her constant preoccupation with Asaf and Ben, who kept overturning and dropping things, said proudly, "It's all thanks to Jojo; he knew when to get out." And as if to make sure that Aaron understood what she was talking about, she added, "To get out of the stock market and sell the bank shares before they collapsed. We got out in time and made a profit. And now we've only got to help the other kibbutzim who're really in trouble." This was uttered in a tone of complaint, as if she were protesting some general injustice.

The second course arrived. The paper plates from the first course were collected and thrown into the big bins standing under the tables. Aaron placed a portion of chicken on his plate and refused the roast meat offered by Havaleh. She bit into the meat and said, "Wonderful meat! Who did the roast today?" And long before she had finished what was on her plate, she heaped it with more slices of roast meat, and then cut the chicken she put on Asaf's plate into tiny pieces. Moish drew the dish of pickles toward him, eating everything with his habitual calm and thoroughness, including the ring of fat around the roast.

"Take off the skin for me, take off the skin," yelled Asaf, and Moish bent over the child's plate and removed the pieces he referred to as "skin."

"Everything that isn't brown and smooth he calls skin," Moish said with a tolerant smile.

"This is the first holiday the little ones have been included in the general celebrations. Before this we never brought them along," said Moish, pouring Aaron more wine. "Because of that business of family sleeping that's being discussed, people are beginning to behave as if it's already in the cards, and you can see the changes everywhere. In the kibbutz movement in general we're already an anachronism, the last kibbutz that still hasn't decided to go over to family sleeping."

"Why, have all the kibbutzim in the country already gone over?" asked Aaron in surprise.

"Maybe not all. No, definitely not all of them, but they've all decided in favor. Implementing the decision is an economic problem at the moment, because of all the additional building that's needed. The absurdity is"—and Moish suddenly smiled, as if it had only just occurred to him—"that as far as we're concerned it wouldn't be such a problem technically, although of course it depends on the movement's decision. Now they're talking about freezing all construction until the kibbutzim recover financially, but theoretically we could do it. The absurdity is that here of all places we haven't even yet reached the stage of deciding—"

Someone fat and bespectacled came up to Moish, bent down, and asked him something about the next day's work mobilization. He looked at Aaron with curiosity. Aaron didn't remember him. Moish asked the man, "Don't you remember Aaron Meroz? He was an outside child adopted by us, and a member too until twenty-two years ago, right? Until he was . . . how old were you when you left?"

"Twenty-four," replied Aaron uneasily, feeling the pain in his left arm returning. He had also felt it yesterday, but had decided not to go for a checkup anyway.

"But you've been here since then," said the man, and Aaron nodded. "That's it. I thought you looked familiar, but I couldn't place you," said the other apologetically.

"Maybe from the television," said Havaleh, and the man nodded and said, "That's it, you're the party faction secretary, right?" and then repeated his question about the next day's mobilization. Moish replied in a few brief sentences and concluded, "Look at the table on the bulletin board; it gives the quota points."

"What quota points?" asked Aaron when the man had left.

"What do you think? That people volunteer like they used to?" grumbled Moish. "The member in charge of the work-placement roster's sick, and in any case she can't cope with the job. So every time there's a work mobilization I go out of my mind, because nowadays we get quota points for picking mobilizations, and bonuses, and all kinds of stuff like that, and I shouldn't have to deal with it at all. Let them go and ask Osnat."

"Osnat?" asked Aaron, feeling an unexpected punch in his stomach.

"Didn't I tell you? Osnat's the kibbutz secretary now," said Moish, then he smiled. "We've grown up, eh? We're proper people now." Then he turned his head and said in a worried tone, "There's such a racket here, I don't know how they're going to put on the skits." He looked at the stage, where preparations for the second part of the program had begun. "How many years is it since you last saw a kibbutz skit?"

Aaron shrugged. "I don't think I've seen one since the last time I took part myself," he said slowly, "and there weren't so many children then." He tried not to think about the nagging pain in his arm.

"There were," said Moish, "but only from the first grade up. Under that age they didn't come to parties. You can see the changes and the sociological influences already. Because they bring the toddlers we have to start early. Before, we never began a party until half past nine, ten, after everyone had put their kids to bed. And there won't be any dancing either, as you'll see. Maybe the youngsters, but not us, we'll leave early to put the kids to bed." He chewed another pickle and stood up.

Then Havaleh said, "I can't see Srulke anywhere, and I'm beginning to worry."

"Where is he?" asked Aaron. "Why didn't he come with you?"

"He said he had to go to his room for a minute and he'd be back right away," said Havaleh, looking around. "I forgot all about it." Moish stood near them, nodding as he listened to a very old woman.

"Can't you see that the place is too small to hold everybody at once?" the woman protested. "We're not built for parties like this in the dining hall, and you can't hear anything or sit comfortably—"

"Take it easy, Menucha," said Moish. "If need be, we'll somehow find a way to solve the problem. You can't stop the processes. We'll discuss it later." He steered her to her place, gently holding her by the shoulder.

The sixth-grade children, the "Daisies," as Havaleh called them, were putting on a dance. Her own daughter was among the dancers, her ponytail bouncing with every step. Moish sat down and looked around him. "I don't see Srulke," he said to nobody in particular. "Hasn't he arrived yet?"

"Maybe he's tired from all the commotion this afternoon," said Havaleh with a clouded look, while Aaron bristled again as he heard Moish refer to his father by his first name. He had never been able to understand this habit that was so characteristic of kibbutz children; there was something so alienating about it.

"But he wasn't there this afternoon," Aaron wanted to say, but he kept quiet because everyone had turned away to listen to the skit written by Yoopie. Panic gripped him as he tried unsuccessfully to remember Yoopie's real name. Now, he knew, the effort to remember would not let him be; it would keep on bothering him like some pesky fly until he remembered. It was a kind of game he played with himself, and he couldn't simply ask Moish. But the question of Yoopie's real name prevented him from listening to the skit, which previous experience as well as the bursts of laughter from the audience told him would be venomous, studded with inside jokes and plays on words. Aaron looked at Havaleh, at Ben who had fallen asleep in her arms, at Asaf who was staring, worn out, at the stage, crumbling a piece of pita in his hand and nibbling at it from time to time, and at Moish, who was looking at the stage and smiling. And then Moish glanced at his watch and looked around him, his face clouded with concern. "If he doesn't show up in a minute, I'm going to go to see what's up."

Aaron was about to say something reassuring, but then someone sitting nearby looked at him and made a snide remark about politicians, and as he raised his eyes to reply with the good-humored smile he always adopted for such occasions, he saw Osnat.

Her green eyes narrowed in the expression of concentration he knew so well, and the power of the current that ran through his body astonished him. In the eight years that had passed since he had last seen her she had hardly changed. She still looked the same as she had looked then. She reminded him of a panther, with her yellow hair and brown skin and slanting eyes whose radiance in the dark he remembered now too as he looked into them. They looked back at him calmly, with smiling curiosity, a reflective look from where she was standing on the other side of the table. She leaned over to say something to the young man sitting next to Havaleh, and in the middle of the sentence she stopped talking and held out an unembarrassed hand to Aaron and asked him how he was in a measured, serious tone.

He knew very well that she had been following his rapid advancement over the past years. When Yuvik was killed he had written her a letter of condolence. He had worked on it for hours, trying to make it warm but not seductive, intimate but not exaggeratedly so. Yuvik's death had only complicated matters, and this was something that Aaron did not want to think about. The details of the complications, their implications, were too threatening. Osnat too, he was certain, avoided thinking about it. From her point of view the threat was even more concrete.

"I'm going to see what's happened to Srulke," said Moish decisively, standing up, and Aaron followed suit.

"I'll come with you," he said hesitantly, and Moish made no attempt to stop him. So it happened that Aaron was next to Moish when they found Srulke lying on the flower bed next to his room in Founders' Quarters A, and for the first time he heard Moish say "Father."

"What's wrong, Father?" he said after shouting, "Srulke, Srulke, get up! What's the matter with you?" Aaron was so shocked by the violence of Moish's reaction, by his loss of control, that at first he didn't even register the fact that Srulke, whose face in the yellow light of the lamp at the building entrance appeared frozen in an expression of terrible pain, was dead.

An eternity seemed to pass before Aaron recovered and said, "I'll run to get the doctor." He left Moish there and hurried back to the dining hall, at a pace that brought the pain back to his left arm, and as he ran he remembered that there were telephones in the rooms. He thought of going back and phoning for an ambulance, and for a moment he stopped, but then the need to do something concrete and energetic, however illogical, prevailed, and he reached the dining hall out of breath and asked the member sitting nearest the door where the doctor was. The member looked at him in blank surprise and curiosity and pointed to one of the tables at the back of the hall, and Aaron squeezed through the chairs and bumped into Fanya from the sewing shop, who gave him a look of alarm, and finally he managed to catch the attention of the young doctor, who jumped over the long table. Aaron drew him aside with the thought of not creating a panic now uppermost in his mind and whispered that Srulke was lying unconscious in the flower bed next to his room.

The young doctor's face immediately grew grave, and he quickened his step. When they reached the dining room door he touched the shoulder of a youngster standing there and said, "Find Rickie right away and tell her to bring the resuscitation kit from the clinic to Srulke's room. It's urgent. And don't talk to anyone, you hear?"

The youngster nodded in alarm and disappeared into the dining hall. The doctor began to run, and Aaron ran behind him, and on the way he asked the doctor whether Srulke had been having any problems with his health lately. "Not as far as I know," the doctor said, "but I haven't examined him." He turned to look at Aaron, who was falling behind and breathing heavily. "But at his age you can never know, he's not a youngster anymore."

Then they reached Founders' Quarters A and the path leading to the second building in the block, where Srulke had been living alone since Miriam's death eight years before. Moish was leaning helplessly over Srulke as he lay sprawled out on the ground, and there was something horrifying about the expression on his face. "Bring me a towel from the room," the doctor ordered, and Aaron went into the room, where he was suddenly assailed by the smell of the oilcloth. On his way to the bathroom he found himself touching it and wondering if it was the same oilcloth, but there was a smell of roses too and of damp earth, an uncharacteristic smell for an old man's room.

When he emerged from the room Moish was standing next to the doctor, who was trying to give Srulke artificial respiration and hitting his broad chest, which was completely covered with gray hair. His white shirt was torn and stained, and Moish kept repeating, "His hands were wet. He must have been opening or closing the sprinkler, I don't know, but his hands were wet, and I dried them on his shirt."

The doctor didn't react. He went on hitting Srulke's chest and pressing his mouth to his, as Aaron had seen people doing on television. All around he could hear the buzzing of fluorescent lights and the chirping of crickets, as well as the distant echo of community singing. The sky was full of stars, and Aaron felt very small on the path between the flower beds and the rows of houses, which seemed tiny in comparison to the great expanses of sky and land stretching out interminably around them.

"How long will it take for your resuscitation kit to arrive?" Aaron asked in order to dispel this physical sense of tininess, in order to hear the sound of his mature, responsible voice. The doctor didn't reply. "Don't we need an ambulance?" Again the doctor didn't reply. "How come there's no ambulance on the kibbutz?' he asked Moish.

"There is one," Moish explained. "But the starter's gone. They only told me today, and by the time we get a mechanic now . . . They only told me this afternoon that the starter was gone, and I forgot to tell Chilik to have a look at it because nobody's due to give birth this week . . . " Moish sniffled. His voice was choked as he repeated, "I forgot to tell Chilik."

"It doesn't matter, we wouldn't have been in time anyway," said the doctor. "Even if we phoned for an ambulance, by the time we reached Ashkelon . . . " He didn't finish the sentence, turning his attention to the sounds of running feet and panting coming from the end of the path. "Rickie?" called the doctor, and when a young woman emerged from the darkness, gasping for breath, he said, "Quick, let's have the injection first of all." She took out a big needle and stuck it in Srulke's arm, while the doctor stuck a tube in Srulke's neck. Aaron turned his head away. "Now the respirator, quick," said the doctor, and Rickie handed him the instrument; they worked with great concentration, and from time to time the doctor muttered that the muscles were very constricted. After a long time, when the body lay without moving, the doctor raised his head, looked at Moish, and shook his head.

Moish sat down, his knees trembling, on one of the stones bordering the flower bed and stroked his father's shriveled head. "Do you want us to transfer him to the hospital?" asked the doctor, and Moish looked at him in bewilderment.

"What for? Will it do any good?"

The doctor cleared his throat before replying in a low voice, "No. But we won't know what happened otherwise, without an autopsy."

"No," said Moish firmly. "What for? What good will it do anyone?" And after a short silence he said, "What was it—his heart?"

The doctor nodded and said, "That's what it looks like, cardiac arrest."

"From the procedural point of view, is it possible not to move him anywhere?" asked Aaron.

The doctor replied, "Yes, of course, I can sign a . . . "—he looked at Moish and then continued—"I can sign a death certificate . . . at his age . . . "

Then Aaron and the doctor lifted Srulke's body and carried it into the room and laid it on the double bed in the bedroom. The doctor closed his eyes and covered him with the white starched sheet that was lying neatly folded at the foot of the bed.

They buried Srulke on the holiday, in the afternoon. "There's no alternative," Zeev HaCohen explained to Yocheved, who had protested on behalf of Ruthie's elderly parents. A few years earlier they had come to live on the kibbutz, and here too they kept a kosher kitchen and observed the other practices of Jewish tradition. They had complained about the violation of conducting a funeral on a religious holiday. "We haven't got the facilities to keep him here," whispered Zeev HaCohen, glancing nervously in Moish's direction to see if he had overheard. He touched Yocheved's shoulder. "We'll just have to explain to them that we don't mean any harm by it. Tell them I'll drop in to see them this afternoon. I'll talk to them," he said in the authoritative and reassuring tone he reserved for crisis situations.

Aaron remained on the kibbutz until after the funeral. He didn't actually say anything about Osnat to himself, but he had hopes. Nor did he make, in his mind, the connection between death and desire, but the funeral here on the kibbutz, Havaleh's phlegmatic face and Amit's serious one, the sound of Moish's coughing after he had vomited during the night, the heavy silence of Dvorka, who had spent the morning sitting beside the body and whose eyes were red, gave rise to a storm of feelings in him and to an anxiety he tried to suppress. He didn't really understand the meaning of these emotions. Srulke's death should have left him with a feeling of relief. He had always regarded him as a witness to the humiliations of the past.

As a child he had been in awe of this man who worked so hard and successfully, covering the kibbutz with carpets of lawn dotted with dozens of varieties of flowers, which to this day gave the kibbutz its look of unreality, of a little Garden of Eden surrounded by shades of yellow and brown. In the photograph exhibition that had been hung in the dining-hall lobby in honor of the jubilee celebration there were a few old black-and-white snapshots of barren fields with an occasional tamarisk tree in the uncultivated soil. Next to them was a large color photograph of the landscaping in front of the dining hall, and underneath the caption read "Then . . . and Now." Under photos of Srulke's greenhouse, which was begun as an experimental hobby in a small structure next to the toolshed and had grown into a professional greenhouse and place of pilgrimage for all the kibbutzim in the area, the caption quoted Herzl's words: "If you wish it, it is no legend."

Srulke had been a taciturn man who never took the trouble, if only with a smile or a word, to make life more pleasant for those around him. Nor did he try to make things difficult for anyone. He seemed completely unaware of his influence on his surroundings. When he returned to the room after the day's work, he would ask the children what they had done all day, concentrating on where they had worked rather than what they had studied, and after a shower and changing into a clean gray undershirt and dark blue trousers, he would go into the garden next to the house and bend over his flowers, touching the petals of the giant roses, examining the rows of potted fuchsias—dozens of different varieties with their branches bowed beneath cascades of red and pink and purple blooms—and only then, after bending down to smell the yellow jasmine, would he sit down and unfold his copy of *Al Hamishmar*.* And when darkness began to fall Srulke would sigh, neatly refold the newspaper, look around, and then get up to turn on the sprinkler, move the hose, or merely touch a leaf.

*The newspaper of the left-wing MAPAM party with which the Kibbutz Artzi Movement is affiliated.

The older Aaron grew the more it amazed him to see that Moish was not in the least afraid of his father. And the older he grew the more he realized that Moish dearly loved his father, and that this man who so often paralyzed him simply by the fact of his industrious presence did not threaten his son at all. The truth, thought Aaron, was that he had always hoped to hear a kind word from Srulke, something warm and appreciative of his talents, but when he was a child there had scarcely been a relationship between them. Srulke had hardly ever addressed him directly, and he couldn't remember a single occasion when the two of them had been alone together.

It now occurred to Aaron for the first time that Srulke had been a very shy man, and that he had hardly ever spoken to him because he couldn't find anything to say without appearing to be making a deliberate effort to relate to him. He must have sensed intuitively that any overture toward Aaron would be false and hypocritical. With a pang he thought that it had been easier for Srulke with Osnat. He hadn't talked to her either, but for her he had warm, mute smiles. Aaron could still see the intent concentration on Srulke's face listening to Osnat telling Miriam about her day as they sat on the lawn in front of the room on late summer afternoons.

Aaron walked in the funeral procession without feeling either relief or sorrow, only the obligation to stay next to Moish. He couldn't stop thinking about the meaning of his presence on the kibbutz at precisely the hour of Srulke's death. Eight years ago, when he had been here last, they had buried Miriam, Moish's mother, who had died after great suffering. It was then that he had gone to bed with Osnat for the first and only time, the night after the funeral, in the room they gave him after he had failed to start his car. Osnat had accompanied him to the room, which was at the end of the prefab cabin quarters, carrying clean bed linen. It was winter, and the weather forecast warned of the danger of frost in sensitive areas. He clearly remembered the talk of the avocado harvest. On the way to the cemetery people had discussed it in whispers. Osnat took a little electric heater out of the closet and switched it on.

"Whose room is this?" asked Aaron.

"Dave's," Osnat replied. "You don't know him. A middle-aged bachelor. He came here as a volunteer from Canada, and we accepted him as a member a year ago. Now we've sent him to an ideological seminar at Givat Haviva."

"To find him a wife?" Aaron said with a laugh.

"It's not so funny. Do you think it's fun being on your own here?"

"Better than in the city, surely?"

"I wouldn't be so sure," said Osnat coldly as she put the clean sheets down on the narrow single bed and began pulling apart the starched hems. She was wearing a black sweater, and her eyes narrowed as she sat down on the edge of the bed and paged slowly through the book that had been lying at its foot.

"Gurdjieff," Aaron read hesitantly. "What's it about?" he asked, sitting down beside her.

"I don't know, something mystical. Once he tried to explain it to me and even gave me something to read, but I'm no good at that kind of thing."

"Is he one of those types who's trying to find himself?" said Aaron, smiling. Osnat shrugged her shoulders.

"Tell me," he suddenly found himself saying to her then, "did you really love Miriam?"

Osnat didn't reply immediately. Finally she said, "So-so. I love Srulke more. She wasn't anything special . . . "

"But she was good to us when we were children," protested Aaron.

"What do you mean, good?" Osnat pressed him. "You mean that they told her to take two outside kids, and she took care of them? What was so good about her? You couldn't talk to her about anything, and she always paid more attention to Moish and Shula than to us. And even though people called her a warm woman—did she ever kiss you?"

Aaron was silent. Finally he admitted, "I don't remember."

"You see?" said Osnat. "If she had, you would have remembered. Besides, I always had the feeling that she was afraid of me."

"You know, it's only in the last few years that I've begun to realize how hard it was for me then. It must have been the same for you. We never talked about it."

"Talking wasn't your strong point then, was it?" said Osnat, standing up to spread the woollen blanket on the bed.

"And is it Yuvik's?" Aaron heard the bitterness in his voice, and Osnat didn't answer. He looked at the fair curls gathered with a rubber band into a kind of topknot that exposed her beautiful, unmade-up face, broad like a Slav peasant's, with full, clearly drawn lips. When he examined each feature separately, the flaws were apparent—the nose too sharp, the cheekbones too broad, the eyes clouded, tiny blemishes on the dark skin—but the face had a savage, sensual beauty that was not at all compatible with the stern expression it wore now as she concentrated on making the bed. "What's it really like, being married to Yuvik, the kibbutz stud?" he asked with a burst of crudeness that took even him by surprise.

Biting her lip, she looked at him with a mixture of anger and sorrow and finally said, "Will you please stop?"

He was embarrassed and ashamed. "I'm sorry," he said. "I apologize, it just came out. We've never talked about it. But I really want to know how you are."

Osnat looked at him very seriously, the corners of her mouth straightened, her eyes narrowed again, and she said, "Fine, I'm just fine. At the moment I'm absorbed in my studies."

He didn't know what made him sense that if he drew her toward him, she wouldn't resist. When a feeling of sorrow and bereavement and loneliness flooded him, he took her soft hand in his and laced his fingers in hers, and then, when she turned her face to him, he saw the familiar expression of seriousness there, the one that tried to cover up the signals of abandonment and loss, the one that had always touched his heart, the one that said she was his sister in distress. Their two hands now resting together on the gray woolen trousers he had bought himself in London on his last trip abroad suddenly changed into two little hands scratched from a long day of picking grapes. He saw themselves as a boy and a girl sitting on a bed in the children's house, remembering how he had longed to touch her little hand. It was the year of his bar mitzvah, a few months before they overheard the conversation between Alex and Riva. Until that evening he had never dared to touch her.

Little by little the sentences beginning "Do you remember . . . ?" began to flow, and for a long time they relived their moments of loneliness and hatred for their peer group and for the kibbutz as a whole.

And it was only natural for Aaron suddenly to say, without any embarrassment, "I didn't even know myself how much I wanted you then," and Osnat replied hesitantly, "But I couldn't. I don't know if I wanted to or not, but I couldn't." And like someone taking what he's entitled to, in an extraordinary burst of confidence such as he had never felt before in his life, he drew her toward him and embraced her tightly, and what had seemed impossible in the past seemed natural and self-evident then, the night after Miriam's funeral.

At two in the morning Osnat got out of bed and dressed quickly and quietly. She ignored his hesitant smile, and when she stood at the door and he asked her if they could meet again, she said, "What for? What can come of it? Not like this."

"What does that mean?" asked Aaron, and he sat up in bed and wrapped himself in the woollen blanket, which felt prickly and unpleasant to the touch.

"It means that I don't want to meet you like this."

"But you'll be going to study in Tel Aviv, you'll be in town and—"

"I don't want to," said Osnat in a hard voice. "If you come here, we'll see each other, and if you don't, we won't."

Aaron sighed and looked at her in silence. And then she said, "And don't think I usually do this kind of thing."

"Come on," he protested impatiently, "give it a rest. I'm not a stranger."

"No," she said, narrowing her eyes in a suspicious, hostile look. "I want you to know that it's against my principles. I don't intend doing it again. I don't know what got into me. I must have been mad."

"I understand that Yuvik's conscience isn't as highly developed as yours. Just today I heard about him and that volun—"

Osnat interrupted him in a low voice that emphasized her anger: "Yuvik and I aren't the same thing." And before she slammed the door, she turned to him and added, "And you should be ashamed of yourself."

It was a repeat performance of a long-ago quarrel neither of them had ever mentioned. Not even during their reminiscences on the night they slept together after Miriam's funeral. A terrible argument had broken out between them, before the affair with Yuvik began, the evening he told her about his desire to leave the kibbutz. He'd never forgotten the accusations she had hurled at him about his opportunism and adventurism; she herself was free, truly free, precisely because, unlike him, she didn't yearn for the superficial freedoms and petty adventures on the outside: Only life on the kibbutz could insure true freedom, the security of belonging.

"You're talking as if you're seventy years old—look at yourself!" he remembered saying.

"I'm looking; you're the one who can't see anything!" she had yelled at him in reply.

Now she walked at the head of the column next to Havaleh and Moish and his sister, Shula, who had arrived from Beersheba with her husband and children. Unlike Aaron, Osnat had always felt at home here, and until today he had never known how much he envied her. He had never been jealous, not even when it seemed to him that Miriam—about Srulke there was no doubt—loved Osnat more than she loved him.

Aaron was at the end of the column, far from Moish and Havaleh and Ronit, and as he walked he heard Fanya from the sewing shop talking to herself. He couldn't catch the words, but he knew the tone: cruel and resentful, on the verge of a hysterical outburst, the tone in which terrible things are said, when the speaker is so intent on ridding herself of a burden of bitterness carried for years that she doesn't care if everything around her is poisoned. Fatal words that fester in the mind and can never be forgotten, as Dvorka said to Fanya afterward. But now there was no stopping her, and Aaron registered the excitement glittering in the eyes of Bruria from the laundry, who smelled the onset of a sensational scene, and saw the shocked faces of Shmiel and Rella from the poultry section. Everyone stopped, even though most of the cortege was still outside the little kibbutz cemetery. There was a sense in the air of impending sacrilege.

It was only when they started moving again and he approached the grave that Aaron could hear the words. "I suppose you're satisfied now," shrieked Fanya. "You killed him with your ideas, with all your fine words about quality of life and family sleeping and old-age homes!"

"Shhh," someone said, and Fanya yelled, "I won't shut up, and nobody will say 'shhh' to me—it's all because of the family sleeping and the old-age home, because you can't stand keeping things the way they were once."

"Where's her sister, where's Guta?" someone asked in a whisper, and someone else answered, "She's not here. She doesn't go to funerals." Finally Osnat went over to Fanya and took her arm. Aaron was stunned. He had never heard Fanya uttering such long sentences before. She always muttered to herself in half-words, half-syllables. Nobody ever took any notice of the resentful noises coming from her at *sichot*. She had never badmouthed anyone either, and standing next to the open grave, Aaron thought that she had broken all the stereotypes about kibbutz seamstresses. This kibbutz sewing shop was not a hotbed of gossip. The women who worked there were frightened to death of her. And just as she never said anything bad about her fellow kibbutzniks, neither did she ever say anything good. Fanya was an excellent seamstress. Everyone praised her magic touch. "She's a wizard with scissors," he had once heard Rella say.

And now he remembered an image: Ronit and Osnat standing at the door of the room on the evening of some kibbutz celebration while Miriam exclaimed admiringly, "Look how beautifully Fanya sews, how she thinks about every detail, how she takes advantage of the material, and what an original idea to make your class wear red checks! Girls, aren't the dresses pretty?"

And Osnat, Aaron remembered, kept her hands in the pockets of her party dress and said, "She only made two patterns."

"And what did you want? For her to make twelve?" Miriam laughed good-naturedly. "That's what's so clever about it, that she managed to make something to suit everyone even with only two patterns, something that brings out everyone's good points." And when she noticed Osnat pouting, she added, with the same stupid, kindly benevolence that characterized her relations with the world in general, "What does it matter? At your age you look pretty whatever you wear."

And Aaron, who had been sitting in the corner of the room paging through old volumes of *Al Hamishmar*'s children's supplement but not missing a word, could still hear, absolutely distinctly, the sound of the little girl's voice as she swallowed her disappointment and said with dignified restraint, "Dvorka says more than that, she says that the inner beauty of each one of us shines out even when we're wearing our working clothes."

And even though Aaron didn't understand exactly what was going on, he sensed that Miriam had missed something of Osnat's meaning when she nodded enthusiastically and cried, "And she's right, Dvorka's absolutely right!" The anger behind Osnat's ostensibly innocent words had completely passed her by.

What would Miriam have said, he asked himself now, if she had known that the most profitable section of the kibbutz economy would come to be a factory that made cosmetics from cactuses grown on the old orchard grounds from which the plum trees had been uprooted? And what did Dvorka herself say about it? he asked himself, almost smiling openly as he thought about Dvorka's philosophy of life and her sermons about simplicity. Now everything here, all the prosperity he had seen yesterday at the ceremony and at the festive meal, was based on a cosmetics factory that exported its products to the entire world. Where was Dvorka's inner beauty now? And how did the women of the founders' generation—with faces that had been weather-beaten and wrinkled by the time they were Osnat's age—how did they feel when they saw the women of the middle generation, looking, most of them, as fresh and smooth as if they'd never spent a day working in the fields?

In the dining hall the evening before, Moish had told him about how hard it was for Fanya to accept the decline of the sewing shop that she had founded. The cosmetics plant had pushed it into the background, and she refused to make any changes. When he had offered her the chance to transform the old sewing shop into a big modern factory, to bring experts and professional cutters in from outside, and promised her that she would still be in charge, she had gone berserk and thrown a temper tantrum that had paralyzed the whole kibbutz and resulted in the shelving of the plan.

Moish also told him that the older she got, the wilder and more futuristic her designs became, the more difficult to turn into patterns or to imagine anyone wanting to wear them. "All kinds of low necklines," said Moish in an embarrassed voice, "all kinds of crazy things. I don't know anything about women's clothes myself, but people talked about it, and Havaleh told me." Finally, he said, they had been obliged to order patterns from outside, and now a lot of the women members preferred buying their clothes outside, and the sewing shop produced mainly work clothes and clothes for children. "And there too she designs weird things, God knows where she gets them from. For example," said Moish, laughing, "she designed a white safari suit for the bar mitzvah boys, we didn't know what the hell to do with it, she wanted to make them all into little English lords in the colonies."

Then he grew serious again and said in almost a whisper, "She couldn't cope with the changes, not when we went over to mass production. And it was impossible to pull the wool over her eyes. When we tried to make her responsible for a kind of exclusive boutique, she wasn't having any. And after that, when we talked to her about setting up a doll factory, don't ask what a scene she made. Personally, I think she's gone off her head."

Osnat put her arm around Fanya's shoulders, and the broken words and snatches of phrases gave way for a moment to the sound of low sobbing. And then Fanya shook off Osnat's supporting arm and repeated over and over, "It's an old-age home, it's an old-age home." And then she said, "You want to put us into an old-age home, that's why he died. What do you think, we did your dirty work, and now you don't need us anymore? Eskimos . . . savages . . . barbarians . . . " And the unintelligible muttering began again.

The procession advanced despite the people clustering around Fanya attempting—appalled and hesitantly, since the blue number tattooed on her arm made them shrink from touching her—to calm her down. Then too, everyone was afraid of both Fanya and her sister, even though Guta seemed less frightening, sometimes even laughing and telling stories. When Aaron was a child the two sisters had filled him with dread, and his eyes had always come to rest on the blue tattoos on their arms with the feeling that everything was permitted them, everything would be forgiven.

Both women were exemplary models of the kibbutz work ethic: No one could deny their capacity for hard work. Once, when Aaron was in the twelfth grade and taking part in a peach-picking mobilization, he had found himself working next to Guta. She worked like one possessed, not stopping for a minute, the crates near her filling up with dizzying speed. It was the second crop of the season, and the trees were big with pink fruit hanging from their branches. The picking took place early in the morning, before the heat set in, and when it was over they all went to the dining hall for breakfast, and here, too, he couldn't take his eyes off Guta. Slowly and thoroughly, withdrawn into herself, with the same expression of dedication and concentration she had worn during the fruit-picking, Guta ate every particle on her heaped plate. This frightened him.

"What do you expect, after what they've been through?" Miriam would say whenever anybody complained after working in Guta's milking barn that she had driven them mercilessly and found fault with everything they did. Guta's dairy herd was famous throughout the Negev. In the skits Yoopie wrote for kibbutz celebrations he would joke about Guta's relationship with her cows, each of whom she knew by name and character. But in private people said, without joking, that her cows were dearer to her than her own children, whom she would put to bed in the children's house only after inspecting the evening milking shift in the barn. One morning Aaron woke up late and arrived there panting and panic-stricken for his shift. Guta didn't say a word, didn't even raise her head from the pail over which she was bending, but when he went to get the hay she said, "Never mind, I've done it already. You think I've got all the time in the world to wait until you decide to arrive?"

Fanya was worse than Guta, and so he was even more frightened of her. Drawing kitchen duty at the same time as Fanya was nothing short of hell. She never spoke to him at all, only giving out those obscure mutterings, and she too worked like a lunatic, without stopping to breathe. When breakfast was over and after washing the dining-hall floor, the kitchen workers of the day would finally be able to sit down to have coffee. She never joined them, always finding some work to do, such as scrubbing and polishing obscure corners, and the sounds she emitted as she worked with clenched teeth were daunting. The dining hall would fill with noise, everyone raising their voices in order to drown out Fanya's Yiddish gruntings as she polished the window frames.

Like her sister, she had two children. The daughter, who left the kibbutz to live in Haifa, rarely came back to visit, mainly on holidays, with her husband and children. Then Fanya would fill with pride and when she took them to the dining hall would heap their plates with mountains of food and look around her defiantly and aggressively, as if daring anybody to challenge her right to offer hospitality to her family.

People spoke of Yankele, her son, as a "problem." Aaron had seen him at the ceremony, looking slender and boyish, much younger than his age—Yankele was only a year younger than Moish and he—and still smiling his perpetual smile, a contortion of the lips that seemed to have frozen on his face and had nothing to do with his feelings or his mood. Yankele lived alone in the singles' quarters on the fringes of the kibbutz, next to the foreign volunteers, and worked permanently in the cosmetics factory, which everybody called "the complex." "It's the best solution for him; with that kind of work he's fine," Moish had said with a sigh the night before. Aaron didn't ask him what he meant by the word "solution." Moish's remark, together with the sight of Yankele's smile, made him shudder and brought back a vivid memory of Moish limping to the kibbutz clinic with Aaron's support, to dress the wound made by Yankele's teeth in his calf.

Nobody knew why Yankele had attacked Moish then. Moish and Aaron were on their way back from laying irrigation pipes in the fields, many years before the introduction of modern irrigation methods, which had no doubt put an end to such romantic nocturnal journeys by jeep and the rare sense of tough male confidence they had afforded him. As they were heading back to the jeep, joking and panting, Yankele had pounced on Moish and clamped his teeth into his calf. He had loomed up suddenly, as if springing out of the ground on which he had been lying among the cotton plants. To this day Aaron didn't know whether he had fallen asleep there or had been waiting for them.

The bite was deep and had torn the flesh. Blood streamed from Moish's leg, but after the first cry of pain he said nothing. Aaron could still feel the cramp in his muscles when he remembered the strength he had needed to drag Yankele off the bare leg and throw him aside. He didn't even hit him. For some reason they didn't tell anyone the truth about what had happened, not even the nurse, Riva, even though the teeth marks were clearly visible and she had kept repeating, "Maybe it was a jackal; you need a tetanus shot." But Moish had insisted: "No, it's from the fence, I tell you. It's not a bite, it's from the barbed-wire fence." Even while she gave him the tetanus shot he went on talking about barbed wire. Ever since then Aaron couldn't look at Yankele and that smile of his without shuddering.

Fanya behaved as if nothing was wrong. She never admitted, by word or deed, that Yankele was deviant. She never referred to his condition, let alone allowing any explicit discussion of the subject. She put his exemption from military service down to the asthma attacks from which he had suffered as a child and expressed her obvious relief in the pride with which she dragged him behind her to the dining hall and in the care with which she piled the food on his plate, choosing the ripest tomato and the youngest cucumber and urging him with vehement movements to eat a lot of vegetables.

Zacharia, his father, didn't talk about Yankele either, but then Zacharia didn't talk about anything. Small and meek, he did his work in the poultry section alongside Rella, and in the evenings he would follow Fanya and her sister to the dining hall, and even if only by the way he walked, you could tell that all he wanted was to disappear, not to be seen or heard.

In the kindergarten, Aaron remembered, the children had treated Yankele with kid gloves, as if he were sick or handicapped. Once when Aaron was walking past the menagerie, he remembered, and the kindergarten children had come to see the newborn lamb, Yankele, who was hanging around inside the compound, started throwing dry twigs at the big rabbit cage in the corner, and Rinat had reprimanded him, putting her hands on her hips and saying, just like her mother, Lotte, "That's not nice, that's not the way to behave." Aaron remembered that even then—he was twelve and Rinat was four—he had laughed to himself because he recognized Lotte's tone when she rebuked them for leaving mud on the shower floor, and he also remembered how Yocheved's little boy, Oded, had whispered to Rinat, "Speak to him nicely, otherwise Fanya will give you a bad time."

"She won't give me a bad time," said Rinat confidently, "Lotte'll tell her."

"But she'll frighten you at night because she's the night watcher," said Oded fearfully. "I know she is, because when she's the night watcher I don't sleep in the children's house."

"You can't do that," said Rinat with supreme certainty. "Yes, I can," Oded assured her. "Yocheved said so."

"She didn't say so," said Rinat, "and anyway, she doesn't decide. Mothers don't decide."

Even Oded interpreted the decisiveness of her tone as hesitation. "Yes, Yocheved said that I could sleep with her and my father tonight, 'cause when Fanya's the night watcher I'm afraid to go to sleep. She never comes when I cry, never!"

Aaron asked himself what on earth had made him recall that long-ago dialogue—a dialogue he hadn't even known he remembered. He looked at Fanya, who couldn't stop sniffing. "If the children are all she's got," he had once asked, "how come she lets them stay with the group instead of sleeping in the room with her?" And Osnat, without any hesitation, remarked that for Fanya it was a given, a fact of life that was taken for granted with no questions asked. She had come to the kibbutz as a young woman, her children were what she proudly called "sabras," and the fact that the children slept together in the children's house and not with their parents was a dictate from on high, an act of God, like the fact that her daughter, Nehama, had gone with her husband to live in Haifa—with not a word of protest from Fanya.

Like a wild animal showing its claws, Fanya defended her children against insults or harsh words, and they sheltered under the heavy shade of her arms. The problem of separation at night she solved by volunteering for night-watch duty at the children's house, thereby instilling terror in the hearts of the other kibbutz children, even though she was actually always nice to them. It was partly their parents' fear, which had been transmitted to the children through snatches of overheard conversation and casual remarks, and in particular it was the fear of Fanya's sounds as she walked along the kibbutz paths, a babble of incoherent grunts and mutterings in Polish and Yiddish.

Dvorka didn't cry at the open grave, and neither did the other old people. Srulke's friends, Bezalel and Shmiel and other survivors of the founders' generation, stood together close to the grave. Aaron looked at the gravestones around him. Srulke was being buried next to Miriam, where the bunch of gerberas he had left there the day before, just before he died, was still lying. Aaron felt an overpowering urge to cover himself with these very clods of earth, a kind of certainty that this was where he wanted to lie, between the tall cypress trees, in the silence where only the singing of the birds was heard.

Dvorka eulogized Srulke, and then Zeev HaCohen also said a few words in his memory. The ceremony was secular, but nevertheless full of mystery and awe, and Aaron, who had attended a number of Tel Aviv funerals at the cemeteries in Holon and at Kiryat Shaul during the past few years, and in Jerusalem as well, felt that justice had been done to Srulke, who had died instantly, without knowing what was happening, and while he was still doing the work he loved. And it was with this thought that he tried to console Moish too. "The kiss of death in a bed of flowers," said Osnat when everybody gathered in the room after the funeral. "Everybody" meant Moish and Havaleh and the children, and Osnat, and Bezalel from the field crops, and Shmiel and Zeev HaCohen. Dvorka went to her room, her back more bowed than it had been the day before.

The silence in the room was hard to bear. Aaron paged through the kibbutz weekly bulletins stacked on the shelf underneath the television set and glanced through the minutes of the *sichot*. He was ready to leave and was only waiting for the right moment to do so. In the news sheets he found articles by Osnat, who had been the kibbutz secretary for a year now and before that had run the regional kibbutz high school and also represented the kibbutz at the ideological seminar at Givat Haviva, all as part of her aspirations "to fulfill herself and change the face of the kibbutz in our day," as she told him. Articles by Dvorka were also there. In the silence while Bezalel was filling the electric teapot, simply for the sake of saying something, even something disagreeable, Aaron asked, "What happened to Fanya?"

The silence continued, as if nobody had heard his question, until Moish, uncomfortable under Aaron's expectant gaze, finally said, "It's hard for her. She was attached to Srulke; he brought her and Guta here after the war."

"I had no idea," said Aaron.

"Srulke wasn't a great talker."

"How did he bring her?" asked Aaron. "Where from?"

"There was a D.P. camp in Milan where the refugees waited for certificates to come to Eretz Israel," said Shmiel. "We were both there working for the Bericha—you know, the underground rescue organization set up by the Haganah and the Jewish Agency and the Joint Distribution Committee to bring illegal immigrants here. Never mind the details now, it's a long story. They were terrible to look at. And we got them certificates and brought them here—Shmuel and Rocheleh were with them too, and some others that we took to different places in the country."

"How old were they?" asked Aaron, relieved that a conversation had been struck up.

"Maybe eighteen, twenty, twenty-something. I don't remember exactly, but young, very young. And Fanya was sick, she had TB. And Guta was so hungry all the time, and so frightened of not having anything to eat that she hid everything we gave her under her blanket and hoarded it. It was terrible. When you look at them today, you'd never believe what they've been through."

"No. But what was all that about the old-age home?" persisted Aaron.

"Nonsense," said Shmiel angrily. "Just nonsense. A lot of silly ideas that nothing will come of. There are some people who prefer talking to working," he said, stealing an anxious look at Osnat.

"First of all," said Osnat with calm authority, "it's not an old-age home, and second, it's certainly not nonsense"

"So what is it if it's not an old-age home?" said Bezalel furiously. "You're talking nonsense, and it won't happen. And don't bring those dreadful ideas here. What's wrong with the way we live now? Why do you have to change things all the time? Where are you running to, that's what I can't understand."

"It's an entire concept," said Osnat in the same confident tone, "and we're talking about saving lives. Look at the neighboring kibbutzim—can you grow old with dignity in Maayanoth, for example? We're only thinking about what's best for everybody, and in the end you'll see that you'll agree with us."

"We'll see about that," Shmiel threatened. "We'll see how the vote goes. Not everyone thinks like you do, thank God."

Osnat didn't reply, and Zeev HaCohen said in a soothing tone, "It's not necessarily such a terrible thing. You just have to overcome your prejudices."

"And you'll have new housing," Havaleh suddenly interjected, "and there'll be an end to all that talk about the cottages our generation built for ourselves while your rooms were only renovated."

"What is this old-age home? What is he calling an old-age home?" Aaron asked again.

Osnat coughed and then sat up straight in her armchair and said, "First of all, change your terminology. We're not talking about an old-age home. We're talking about a regional institution, on the principle of the regional kibbutz school, which will be like a center for the older generation, to be established in partnership with a few neighboring kibbutzim, with a plant of its own and so on. The proposal hasn't been properly formulated yet, all we want to vote on now is the question of setting up a planning committee, and afterward everyone will have a chance to vote on the plans it submits. Nothing's decided yet"—she directed a reassuring yet also a warning look at Shmiel—"but in principle the concept will be of communal housing and work in the plant we set up there, a kind of kibbutz for the golden age." She folded her arms and looked around her with a serious expression on her face.

"But what on earth for?" asked Aaron in surprise. "That's what's so nice here, everybody living together, the old side by side with the young. What do you need it for?"

"It's complicated, it's very complicated to explain," said Osnat, "but believe me that in the Kibbutz Artzi they don't think it's such a bad idea. The concept stems from the economic difficulties of the kibbutz movement and the structural rigidities that have to be changed. I can't go into it now. I'm only prepared to tell you that there are already kibbutzim where people can't grow old with dignity, there are kibbutzim in the area that have collapsed. Don't you know that the United Kibbutz Movement has already decided to sell apartments in such centers to people from town?"

Aaron shook his head.

"So we can still count our blessings here," said Bezalel with a sour smile.

"We're not interested in profits," said Osnat, "and we're not in the business of selling apartments to senior citizens. But," she said, turning to Aaron, "the idea did come up, and if you're interested, I can give you material to read about the whole project."

"I'm interested," said Aaron without knowing why he said it. His mother was now living in a retirement home in Ramat Aviv and seemed very satisfied there, but nevertheless he was shocked. He thought about Srulke. "How did Srulke really feel about the idea?" he asked quietly.

"He didn't say anything," said Osnat. "You know Srulke."

"Srulke was an angel," said Shmiel loudly. "A *lamed-vavnik,* one of the thirty-six just men of his generation. But you don't know what he really felt. No one will ever know what he thought. Especially not after Miriam died."

Havaleh pulled an impatient face and said, "I'm going to make coffee. Who else wants some?" Nobody answered her.

"It's because we're spoiling their plans, because of the way we vote," Shmiel burst out. "Even that, they think we don't understand."

Osnat turned to Aaron and said quietly, "So shall I send you the material?"

"Why don't you give it to me now," said Aaron hesitantly, thinking about the opportunity to be alone with her.

"No, I have to prepare it first," said Osnat with the serious expression he remembered so well, the expression she wore during the activities organized by the class cultural committee, or later on, when she was responsible for the new Nahal unit on the kibbutz.

When he stood up and murmured something about previous engagements and having to get back home, he hoped that Osnat would see him out, but it was Moish who rose to his feet, looking as if he had recovered, and accompanied him to his car. When they were nearly there, Moish said, "I just want to tell you that you helped me a lot." Aaron looked at the gray curls, the suffering face, the uncharacteristically gentle expression in the gray eyes, the big tanned feet in their open sandals, at the health radiated by his whole person. He thought about the Alumag he'd seen in the bathroom, and the Tagamet tablets, and he wanted to say something about that, but he didn't want to betray the fact that he had peeped into the medicine chest, and so he said nothing.

He sensed the sharp pain piercing his left arm as he waved it and said, "Nonsense, it's natural. I'm glad I was here to help. I owe Srulke something, no?" And he immediately felt that there was something out of place in his words, but he didn't know what it was. He couldn't think of Moish as a brother or a friend, and he certainly couldn't think of Srulke as a father. He couldn't have said anything warmer without sounding false in his own ears.

When he arrived home it was already half past seven in the evening, and the pain in his arm was still bothering him. The apartment was empty, and he couldn't stop thinking about Osnat and the fact that he hadn't exchanged a single personal word with her. On a sudden impulse he couldn't control he dialed the number of her room, which he had copied from the internal phone directory lying next to Srulke's telephone. When he heard her clear voice, he replaced the receiver without a word.

3

In the weeks following Srulke's death, Aaron returned to the kibbutz a number of times. He would park his car just inside the back gate, behind the cottonseed barn, in the hope that no one would see him. Without saying it in so many words, Osnat made the need for discretion plain. He would usually arrive at nightfall on Thursdays, when there were no meetings of the Knesset Education Committee or the kibbutz higher education committee or the kibbutz development committee, the latter the group responsible for planning the family-sleeping project. Twice she wasn't home when he got there, but he knew where the key was hidden, and he waited for her inside the room. They would have supper there, and then he would stay the night.

Both of them were hesitantly trying for the possibility of reviving something other than adolescent erotic excitement, something rather like the close intimacy of their silent walks long ago back to the children's house from Srulke's and Miriam's room. Their early-morning good-byes were studiedly casual, and Aaron carefully avoided any hint of an attempt to schedule their next meeting, sensing that she would feel threatened and refuse to commit herself. He would leave the kibbutz before sunrise, through the same back gate, which was supposed to be locked but never was. Arriving or departing, he would find the heavy steel chain hanging loose on the closed gate. He would leave the car to push the gate open, then drive through and get out again to push the gate shut.

Trying to sound casual, Osnat asked him, the first time he came, whether he thought anyone had seen him. Uneasily he remembered the silhouette that had loomed up behind the row of houses, but he shook his head. In any case, nobody could have recognized him in the dim light of the single lamp on the post at the end of the path. He himself did not feel the need to be particularly careful when he came to the kibbutz—he could always say he had come to visit Moish—but the shadow that popped up behind the buildings whenever his solitary footsteps sounded on the cement-paved path made him feel uneasy nevertheless. Once, on his fourth visit, he even caught sight of a slender, boyish figure in short trousers running away at the bottom of the path. He didn't know whether it was the same figure or not, and he never said anything about it to Osnat. He didn't want to arouse the fears she obscurely and carefully signaled by continuing to ask him, with would-be indifference, whether anyone had seen him when he arrived. He didn't ask for an explanation, because she had always guarded her privacy fanatically. Even in the children's house she had always opted for the side room, the corner bed.

Now she drew the heavy curtains, closed the windows, and switched on the air conditioner so that its noise would disguise what was happening in the room. She was always careful to lock the door. Even Moish, he had noted with surprise on his Shevuoth visit to the kibbutz, had locked his room when they left to go to the jubilee festivities. Moish had responded to his questioning look with a shrug of his shoulders, saying, "There've been some burglaries here, people from outside," and an unpleasant look had crossed his face as he pushed the key under a stone in the low wall surrounding the little garden in front of the house. Yet, before they had left the room, several people had lightly knocked on the door and opened it without waiting for Moish to say, "Come in." Moish showed none of Osnat's anxiety about guarding privacy.

Aaron well remembered her in the children's house trailing for days after Yedidya, the maintenance man, begging for "a little cabinet with a key." Next to the toolshed Yedidya collected all kinds of junk that he restored and made into wonderful things. When Osnat eventually got what she wanted and the little brown cabinet stood next to her bed, Hadas had demanded a class discussion on the subject. They were only twelve years old, Aaron remembered with a smile, but she was already emulating the adults at their *sichot*. In the discussion Hadas had insisted on mutual trust. "Osnat suspects everybody, she doesn't trust anybody," Aaron remembered Hadas saying accusingly, tossing back her long braid as she spoke. He couldn't remember anything else that was said, except for Dvorka's firm and supportive appeal to Osnat, with the warm look she gave her when she asked her to explain herself to the group, and Osnat's stubborn silence as she sat staring at the floor. And only after a long pause with eleven pairs of eyes fixed on her, she had merely said, defiantly but also desperately, "I need it." A commotion broke out, and Osnat's ostracism was ordered—an order he alone ignored, causing further class discussions.

Then one night the cabinet was broken into and its contents scattered around the room: handwritten pages, yellowing photographs, a dried flower, a little bottle of scent, a broken bracelet with links of light silvery metal, which Osnat had never worn, black-and-white pictures of American tourist sites in yellowing plastic frames, a miniature bar of blue soap of the kind he would later see in hotel bathrooms, and above all, the little bra, a strip of pink material that had been suspended like a flag from one of her bedposts. Naturally, there had been soul-searching, an ultimatum from Dvorka, and Lotte, the class housemother, had walked around for days with a tragic expression on her face, but the culprit had never been discovered. Before the event had melted away and apparently been forgotten, Osnat had agreed to leave her cabinet unlocked, and Miriam had offered her a corner of her own in the family room—this carried a whiff of Dvorka's pedagogical advice, for Miriam would never have been capable of such a thought on her own.

His visits to Osnat always began with a discussion about the transformation of kibbutz society. To their first meeting, some two weeks after Srulke's death, he brought the sheaf of papers she had sent him concerning the changes taking place in the kibbutz movement in general and on this kibbutz in particular. Without actually saying so to himself, he realized that it would be easier for him to meet her if he showed an interest in the debate about what she called "the new concept." The fanatical gleam that appeared in her eye whenever she spoke about family sleeping and other proposed changes in kibbutz institutions made him uncomfortable, but he didn't dare say anything about it. Taking advantage of his position as a member of the Knesset Education Committee, she asked him to bring her scholarly journals and copies of articles on family structure published abroad. She read these thoroughly and then spoke to him about what she had learned and with renewed urgency about the need to change the kibbutz and transform it into a model of the new kibbutz society.

Aaron never scoffed at her or dismissed what she said. Although he himself was not interested in the subject, he couldn't mock her earnestness, not even to himself. There was something touchingly naive in the way she gathered her hair into her hand and bent over the journals he brought her and in the enthusiasm with which she responded to his suggestions. He knew exactly what was going on inside her, as if she were transparent. He thought of all the ways in which she had struggled to overcome the image of frivolity that had attached itself to her because of her animallike beauty, which she had deliberately ignored all her life, of which she had never taken advantage, which she saw as an obstacle. Everyone was always waiting for her to slip up, to prove that she was only cut out for making love, and she, ever since he remembered her, had insisted on being an organizer.

Defiantly she had buried herself in her books, avoided small talk and gossip. He remembered nights when she was knocking herself out preparing for the matriculation exams, the patience with which she had gritted her teeth and waited for the kibbutz to send her off to study. He had learned from Moish, on one of their rare meetings in Jerusalem, of her victory in the struggle against the decision to send her to the teacher-training college instead of to the university. There she had studied educational administration and sociology and later applied what she had learned in her work at the regional kibbutz high school.

The cautiousness of his secret arrivals, the uneasiness that flooded him at the sight of the mysterious figure looming up at the end of the path as if it were waiting for him there, the patience with which he pretended to listen to Osnat's lectures on the future of the kibbutz—all these things invaded his lovemaking. Aaron did not see himself as a great expert on the female sex. It had been years since he had contemplated the possibility of a steady sexual relationship with any woman, and he had never been attracted to short-term flirtations. Soon after his marriage he realized, as he had known instinctively even before, that it wasn't going to work. He watched his wife, Dafna, gradually growing away from him and for some reason didn't even try to counter this. During the recent years of the marriage their sexual relationship had almost ceased to exist, and when he was elected to the Knesset he welcomed the prospect of having to sleep over in Jerusalem. Whenever the opportunity of a sexual adventure came his way, he felt that he had "nothing to offer in that area."

In two cases only had he responded to the advances initiated by women, more out of an embarrassed fear of turning them down than out of any real need. He had never been uninhibited, had always felt constrained, uncomfortable in his body, fearful and uncertain as to what was expected of him. He had always felt heavy and clumsy, and he saw his thinning hair as part of a process leading inevitably, among other things, to a final renunciation of sex. He never exercised, his body felt flabby, and he avoided looking at it in the mirror. Nor did he like the reflection of his face, with its expression of obstinate passivity. On the rare occasions when romantic fantasies entered his mind he dismissed them by making an effort to think of other things. He didn't try to remember his dreams.

During his first years in Dafna's father's law firm, he was so tense before every court appearance that he didn't have time to think about anything else. He was actually grateful to Dafna for being so undemanding. He grew accustomed to seeing himself as a man with minimal needs, and the only desire he had left was an almost abstract yearning for Osnat, symbolized by the image of two helpless little pairs of hands. He longed for the melancholy loneliness that united them when they were children, for the sense of sharing the same fate, which he had never felt with anyone but her. Now, whenever he emerged from her room at dawn, after a sleepless night (he was too tense to sleep), he felt the flat taste of missed opportunity. A kind of sourness would well up inside him, rising from the pit of his stomach, because he had not found what he was looking for. Exactly what he was looking for Aaron could not have said, could not have given a name. But he knew that this was not the way things should have happened, that the relationship he had hoped for should not include so much caution. He wanted to feel at home and not be on guard in case he said the wrong thing.

The first time he arrived, he was so excited he could hardly breathe. When he parked his car out of sight, not knowing why, he was in fact obeying her instructions. She had told him to come late. "How late?" he had asked her.

"If we don't want to be disturbed, you'd better come after ten, otherwise you'll have to wait for me."

And he had come early and waited for her. He found the key where she had told him it would be and went inside and sat down. He remained frozen in his chair, not daring to get up and look around or take a book down from the shelves. There were back volumes of the kibbutz-movement cultural magazine, *Shdemot,* in a straw basket on the floor next to him, and he paged through these.

When Osnat arrived he clearly saw fatigue and tension on her face, along with signs of age. For a long time she lectured him on plans to transform the kibbutz. Expressions he heard frequently in the Knesset Education Committee, like "keeping up with the times," "economic means," "anachronism," emerged earnestly from her lips. She spoke of "emphasis on the individual" as the condition for the continued existence of the kibbutz in the twenty-first century. "The vision of the new kibbutz," she quoted from a seminar in which she had participated at Givat Haviva, "is egalitarian elitism." She spoke of "new values" and several times repeated the word "concept."

Aaron was tired, and as time went on he grew more and more bored. In their first meetings he tried to persuade her not to go ahead with the old-folks project, which she called the "supraregional kibbutz," but he soon gave up the attempt. "There's nothing to talk about," she said. "I'll get a majority, and not only of our age group. Some of the senior members are delighted by the idea. In any case, it's a question of survival. It's impossible to implement change with such a large number of people wanting to preserve the past. There are three hundred and twenty-seven members here and a hundred and forty old people among them! In order to reach a decision about a matter of principle like family sleeping you need a two-thirds majority, and most of the old folks are against it. And some of the young people are against it too, on all kinds of peculiar grounds. You can't imagine how narrow-minded people can be, how filled with stereotypes!"

Aaron tried to dismiss the uneasy feeling that overcame him at the sound of her determined voice. There was something cruel in her arguments about the forces opposed to progress, a cruelty whose sources were crystal-clear to him. Knowing and understanding its origins, he was embarrassed by its manifestations, but at the same time he couldn't help being moved by her power, by the passion with which she believed in her vision of the future. Hours went by before he finally dared to touch her hand. He was determined to sleep with her that very night. But the thought of the awkward movement he would have to make to reach her from the other side of the table stopped him from making a move.

Finally, innocent of any sexual intentions, she came to sit down next to him on the sofa, in order to show him a table giving the kibbutz figures for per-capita financial outlay. He gazed at the nape of her neck as she bent over the news sheet in which the table had appeared and finally took her hand. The hand did not respond, lying in his, dry and frozen. With an effort he suppressed the urge to ask her what she wanted him to do next. He himself had no idea, all he wanted was to feel that old intimacy again, to know what she was really thinking. It was hard for him to believe the source of all her emotional energy lay in kibbutz ideology (she hardly mentioned her children).

As he stroked her arm he thought of her beauty and of the years she had spent alone since Yuvik was killed. By the time he began stroking her head he already knew that he himself was not exactly burning with desire. Above all, he was afraid of her. And of the possibility that what happened next might rob him even of his fantasies. You couldn't say that she was unresponsive. She even turned her head and body toward him to respond to his embrace, offering him her lips. But her movements lacked vitality and warmth. He stood up and led her to the bedroom, where the air conditioner was humming noisily, and she let him undress her, which he did clumsily and with an embarrassed smile. Here too his instincts warned him not to joke about his failure.

In the end she helped him with efficient movements. She didn't actually fold the clothes, but she put them at the foot of the bed without a hint of anything wild or impulsive, as if she were going through the motions of a familiar scenario. Embarrassed, he undressed quickly, conscious of the paleness of his skin, of his flabbiness, of the fact that he hadn't taken a shower; he left his underpants on. They didn't exchange a word. The scent of her body was strange to him, and he was paralyzed by the fear that at any minute she would come to her senses and suddenly recoil.

Even when they had finished he didn't dare say anything to her. She got up and he heard the water running in the shower, and when she came back, wrapped in a big towel, he asked her, "Did you enjoy it?"

She nodded faintly and looked at him quietly and directly. The same thing that prevented him from driving through the front entrance of the kibbutz, from stopping the affair before it could begin, from running away before the last of his fantasies died, prevented him now from trying to talk to her about what had happened. He tried to convince himself that he had to give her time, to be patient, to see what would happen next time, and conjured up various other consolations of whose emptiness he was well aware. He was always left with this disappointment; on all their subsequent meetings too there was something missing in their lovemaking. Their continuing silence, he thought, was a kind of tax paid by both of them to justify his continued visits. He himself didn't understand why he kept phoning her, why he repeated these nocturnal journeys and closed the back gate soundlessly behind him. He didn't admit it to himself in so many words, but he recognized the inability to let go of the hope against hope that he would again feel for Osnat what he had felt for her for so many years.

He knew of course that Osnat had chosen Yuvik, upon his return to the kibbutz after an absence of three years, because he was Dvorka's son, because he was tanned and his hair was a mop of curls, and because he had completed the ship-officer's course with distinction. That Aaron had the important position of field-crops manager on the kibbutz didn't help. She had to consolidate her position by marrying Dvorka's son, the child of the kibbutz's backbone. He often wondered whether she herself was aware of her motives, to what extent, if at all, her moves were calculated. And something told him that she wasn't really conscious of her wish for revenge, that she didn't even taste the sweetness of her victory.

But during the course of the years, after he had left the kibbutz and after the insult had faded, he had sometimes asked himself whether her marriage to Yuvik had indeed brought her the inner peace and security she longed for so desperately, without even knowing it. More than that, he asked himself if she was still motivated by hatred and rage, by the insults whose causes and expressions he had known so intimately ever since they were children together. And when he went to bed with her for the first time, after Miriam's funeral, when she was already the mother of two children, he knew that nothing had changed. Underneath her calm, efficient expression, the hatred went on simmering, and the rumors he heard from Havaleh about Yuvik's affairs with volunteers from abroad and young girls from Nahal units stationed on the kibbutz obviously did nothing to strengthen the tenuous feeling of belonging she was so intent on demonstrating, even when they were alone together.

And even if she had managed to acquire a measure of security, thought Aaron, it must have been badly shaken by the death of Yuvik, whose tanned legs shone through the glass covering the big photograph standing on the television set. When he heard about the birth of their first son, some two months after they were married, he knew that from the moment she had chosen Yuvik, whose rumored return had been the main topic of conversation on the kibbutz for weeks before he actually arrived, she had been thinking about children, her children who would be Dvorka's grandchildren. She had always lived in terror of being thrown out. Now her children were Dvorka's grandchildren. And now she had integrated the serious expression, the decisive tone she had adopted over the years, into a total view of the world, and when she spoke about the changes that were necessary to "adapt the system to what's happening in the world today," she was filled with the passion that was absent in her lovemaking.

Every now and then he would momentarily feel the old closeness, especially on the rare occasions when she mentioned her children, or when she told him one evening about the attempts of various well-known personalities on the kibbutz to approach her sexually, both before and after Yuvik's death, and about how she had rejected their advances. And when she told him about the scene made by Tova, Zeev HaCohen's daughter by his second marriage to Hannah Shpitzer (who hanged herself when he left her, upon which he was sent by the kibbutz on a mission to Marseilles), he saw the hunted, desperate look in her eyes, which he remembered from the days when Dvorka used to lecture her about personal commitment and the need for individual sacrifice to smooth the path of communal living. Once when he asked Osnat, with a smile spreading over his face, what Dvorka had thought of her when she was the high school principal, she said gravely, "Why are you smiling? Do you think nothing has happened to me since I was seventeen? That Dvorka still thinks I'm as empty-headed as she once suspected? Let me tell you that nobody thinks that anymore. She's known for years now that I'm nothing like what they thought I'd turn out to be."

Despite his request (he only dared to ask once, and she had said, "Why, what on earth for?"), Osnat did not disconnect the phone when he was there. People often called her on public matters, and he listened disbelievingly to the tone of voice she adopted in these conversations—judicious and reasonable, filled with unshakable confidence in her own rightness. And when he realized that public needs had consumed the last vestiges of her vitality, he felt extremely depressed and pessimistic about retrieving the wordless intimacy between the two outsiders pretending to believe that they were both part of the same big family, while a millimeter beneath the skin both of them were really feeling that nobody had forgotten for a moment where they came from.

On their third or fourth meeting she asked him if he was considering the possibility of returning to the kibbutz, and he said no. Cautiously feeling his way, he asked if she could ever consider living outside the kibbutz, and to his astonishment she did not dismiss the possibility out of hand. "In any case," she said during that conversation, "Dvorka would never let me take the children." When Aaron said that the children were hers, she replied, averting her eyes, "You don't know what you're talking about. She managed to take over the first two almost by force, and—as you can see for yourself—she puts the little ones to bed every night. I always have the feeling that she doesn't trust me to give them the right values. She'll never let me take them out of the kibbutz. And do me a favor, if she finds out about us and tries to talk to you, please tell me."

She did not respond to the overtures either of the divorced or of the married men on the kibbutz. And when Tova, Zeev HaCohen's daughter, had made that scene in front of everyone in the dining hall, she had felt—so he understood—all her desperate attempts over the years to free herself of the image of the frivolous beauty going up in smoke. "He really did come by a few times, and his intentions were clear, but what she said wasn't true. I wasn't interested at all. I've never fooled around with married men on the kibbutz, I've never fooled around with anyone," she said angrily. "But even though they knew there was nothing to it, the scandal, the suspicion itself, was enough to ruin everything." She didn't go into details about what she meant by the phrase "ruin everything," but he knew without her telling him.

He had stood beside her that evening outside Alex's room, when they were about fourteen. They weren't holding hands anymore, they were about to go in to talk to him about the program for hosting eighth-graders from a Tel Aviv labor-movement school and the need to put off a group from the Hashomer Hatzair youth movement, which wanted to come on the same weekend. There were technical problems about the sleeping arrangements and questions about co-opting the visitors to pick peaches in the general mobilization that Saturday. He vividly remembered the room in the cabin where the kibbutz-born soldiers now lived, with khaki uniforms hanging on the clothesline outside the door. In those days it was Alex and Riva's room. Alex was in charge of the work roster, and Riva was the kibbutz nurse.

Before Aaron and Osnat reached the front door, they had gone around the back, passing the wide-open windows. It was hot, and the wooden cabin gave off the heat it had soaked up during the day; the walls creaked as he and Osnat stood next to the doum palm growing under the window, which had since been cut down because its roots had rotted, and Osnat put a trembling finger on his lips and held his arm more and more tightly as Riva talked in the same pleasant, soothing voice she used when she was giving shots or when she had bandaged the terrible boil that had erupted on Aaron's inner thigh the summer before, preventing him from taking part in the hike to Haifa and the Galilee—the hike in whose wake Lotte, the class housemother, had discovered fleas, and all their mattresses had to be burned and all their clothes disinfected with kerosene, and he was the only one who was spared these purification rites.

In that same gentle, reassuring voice, Riva was saying, "And of course Osnat will have to be watched. With the background she comes from it won't be easy for her to fit in. I spoke to that mother of hers, and I'm telling you, the girl will have to be watched because that kind of thing is genetic, and one day when it comes out it'll be too late, and the look in her eye is already just like her mother's."

And he remembered Alex's voice saying something he didn't catch in a quiet, reasonable tone, and Osnat's rapid, heavy breathing at his side, and he sensed her rage in her painful grip on his arm, and he could still feel the pain now, more than thirty years later, as she told him about the scene Tova had made in the dining room. "Next to the trays, in front of everyone, without any restraint, any pity, and it didn't help when people went up to her and tried to shut her up, it only made things worse, and she screamed, 'Whore, home-breaker, just like your mother, that's what you are,' and it didn't make any difference that nothing had happened. You could see that anyone who didn't know yet, the kids from the Nahal unit, for example, would soon get all the information on my mother."

And then the feeling of pain came back to the arm into which Osnat had dug her fingertips some thirty years before; the nails bitten to the quick had prevented scratching, but the next day there were bruises on his arm, bruises made when Riva said in the pleasant voice clearly audible outside the room, "What can you expect from the daughter of a nymphomaniac? Her mother's a sick woman, don't you understand? It's a disease, I've read about it, and we learned about it in a course, too. Don't you understand that it's in her genes, she's already at the right age, and if we don't keep a tight rein on her, she'll soon be seducing all the boys on the kibbutz, and after that breaking up families. You talk as if we've never seen things like that before!"

Osnat didn't run away immediately. She stood there for a long time, and Aaron was afraid that the harsh sound of her heavy breathing would be heard in the brightly lit room from which the pungent aroma of freshly made coffee and the tinkling of glasses wafted toward them. Then she sat down on the lawn next to the tree without saying anything. She let go of his arm only when she got up, and she didn't ask him to accompany her. She said nothing as she began to walk with uncharacteristically slow steps toward the water tower at the entrance to the kibbutz, and he, who wanted so badly to comfort her, to say, "Never mind, it doesn't matter, don't take any notice," didn't dare utter a sound.

He walked behind her without talking, without touching her delicate bare shoulder or her wild hair, and until they reached the water tower she said nothing to him; she appeared to not even notice his presence. There, at the foot of the tower, she sat down, and he sat down next to her, and finally, when he was unable to bear the silence any longer, he discovered that his vocal cords were paralyzed and refused to produce a word, and besides, he was afraid that she would burst out crying if he said anything. He touched her arm timidly with a clammy, sticky hand, and she, who had been staring ahead of her without saying a word all this time, shook it off violently and looked at him, and then he kissed her and her lips tasted sweet, and even though it was a kiss on the lips there wasn't a trace of lust in it, only a tremendous wish to console her, to connect with her in some mysterious way without spoiling anything with words. At first she understood this, he knew, but after a few seconds, as if she were hearing Riva's words again, she recoiled from him and said, "I'll show them. I'll stay a virgin till I marry. See if I don't!" And she stood up and said, "Let's go back now," in a hard, choked voice. On the way back she said in a tight voice, filled with restraint, "And I don't intend to leave either. I haven't got anywhere to go, and I like it here." And after a pause, breathing deeply, she added, "And if I'm not yet happy here now, one day I will be, and they'll be sorry."

Now, as he waited in her room, examining the delicate charcoal sketches covering the walls and the vase of flowers standing on the television set next to a large photograph of Yuvik, he thought of her restraint. Of the almost ascetic atmosphere in the room, which opened at one end into the kitchen alcove. There was no big refrigerator here like the one Havaleh had spoken of yearningly to Moish, there wasn't even a coffee grinder. He thought of the austere taste she had developed over the years, the standard furniture—a three-seated brown sofa and two brown armchairs on either side of the brown table and a small beige rug, and the absolute cleanliness of the place, as if there hadn't been any children playing here in the afternoon. And then he remembered that afternoons the children usually went to Dvorka's room, where they were joined by Osnat.

The stainless steel sink gleamed, and he could see his swollen, distorted reflection in the electric teakettle when he filled it to make himself a cup of coffee, and he knew that Osnat still kept to her daily ritual floor-washing with the same rage that had led Lotte to say when she was a girl, "On the days when Osnat cleans the children's house you can eat off the floor." And he thought sorrowfully of the severity of the taste she had cultivated in the clothes she wore, when he saw her appear on the television screen when he automatically turned on the set and the dining hall came on with the members seated in rows, and he remembered Moish telling him that they showed the *sichot* on closed-circuit television for those who couldn't make it to the hall.

On the screen Moish's face was pale and gray, and Aaron thought of the times he himself had appeared on the TV news during the teachers' strike, and then the students' strike, when the minister was abroad and nobody else was available, and how they had made him up beforehand so that he wouldn't look sick, as they explained it to him.

There was apparently something wrong with the sound: Moish's voice was barely audible. Aaron turned up the volume as far as it would go, and he heard Osnat saying in a clear, official voice, "I'm putting it to the vote: All in favor of setting up the committee, please raise your hands." He recalled that she was the person in charge of the agenda for the *sichot*. The television set made protesting noises, as if the question were too difficult to answer. Sitting in a semicircle were the members of the secretariat; besides Moish and Osnat, Aaron recognized Alex, who had shrunk over the years and was now completely bald, and Jojo, who had been kibbutz treasurer for the past few years. He didn't recognize the other members of the secretariat, but he saw Dvorka sitting off in a corner, her face sealed; the camera caught her bun from the side, and Aaron contemplated the profile of this woman with her inexhaustible reserves of strength, who in spite of her widowhood and bereavement was still taking part in the public life of the community.

Facing the secretariat sat the members of the kibbutz. The dining hall was not full, and Aaron smiled to himself as he caught sight of Fanya still sitting in the same place—in the row before last, on the chair nearest the windows—she had occupied more than thirty years ago. She sat in the same part of the room, as always rapidly and angrily knitting an unidentifiable garment, even though it wasn't the same dining hall but rather the grand new building with the ice-water drinking fountain on the ground floor and the patterned tiles in the toilets, with a special ramp for baby carriages and wheelchairs, broad stairs leading up to the second floor, and decorative wall hangings next to the windows.

Moish counted the raised hands and whispered to Osnat, and she wrote something down on the piece of paper in front of her. "Thirty-one in favor," said Moish. "Those opposed?" Again hands were raised. "Twenty-three opposed. Abstentions?" he asked mechanically, and his lips moved soundlessly as he counted hands. "Eight abstentions," he said at last. And then he raised his head and repeated the results. "It's important to understand," Moish said quietly, "that this is only the beginning of a process. The final vote will be structured differently. Then we'll need a majority of at least two-thirds in order to implement the plan. None of the other kibbutzim went over to family sleeping before they had a two-thirds majority in favor, even without the special facility for the older members, and naturally the same thing applies to us, and even more so, with the tremendous project we're talking about here."

A hand went up in the first row, and Aaron heard the elderly voice without being able to identify the woman who said, "I just want to say for the record that we should think about other people too, not only about ourselves. And if some people, and I won't mention any names, people who spoke here tonight, would think of others too, they would realize that the changes are only for the good. It may be hard to get used to, but it's important to think of the common good. I don't want to repeat what Zeev said, I just want to say that not everybody agrees with some of the members who spoke here tonight."

"All right, Haviva, it's on the record," said Moish, looking at his watch. Then he turned to Osnat, who said, "We've only got a short time left to discuss two far-from-simple questions. The first item is on the agenda: The higher-education committee has turned down Zvikie's request to take a course in London, but he refuses to accept its recommendation and demands that the matter be brought before the *sicha*. May Zvikie go ahead and present the problem?"

Osnat turned hesitantly to Zeev HaCohen, who was sitting in the corner. HaCohen suggested that he wished to explain the committee's position first, and then Zvikie could present his point of view.

"Why complicate matters with presentations and points of view," shouted one of the secretariat members whom Aaron didn't know. "Zvikie simply asked for something completely outrageous . . . "

"Just a minute, wait until you get permission to speak," said Zeev HaCohen. "There's no need to get excited. We won't settle anything by shouting. There's been quite enough shouting for one day." Aaron looked with amusement at Fanya, who was muttering obscurely to herself. "The word *outrageous* is uncalled for," continued Zeev HaCohen. "The question is whether a member who's completed one stage of a course here in Israel can continue his studies abroad, and the decision is a matter of principle. We thought that since this is the third course Zvikie's requested during the past three years, he can at least put it off for a couple of years."

"What course is it this time?" asked Hayuta impatiently. Aaron congratulated himself on recognizing her; she was only three years older than he and looked like a grandmother.

"Courses shmourses," said Guta in a clear, loud voice; she was sitting, as she had in the past, next to Fanya. "First let them work, first let everybody do their work. And you say that there's no money to keep us here!" she shouted, as Fanya pursed her lips and bent over her knitting.

Zeev HaCohen held up his hand for silence, and Guta turned to him and said angrily, "You won't shut me up. On the one hand you talk about efficiency and saving, and on the other—"

That was apparently the moment when Aaron fell asleep. It was the pain in his arm that woke him up, and the time on his watch was two o'clock in the morning when he found himself lying on the short sofa, covered with a pique blanket that Osnat must have put there. The first thought that came into his head was that he must stop coming here. There was no point to it, he said to himself as he stood up and went into the bedroom. Osnat was there in bed, sleeping. He touched her shoulder, and she made vague noises. "Why didn't you wake me up?" he asked, trying to smother his anger and wondering why he was whispering.

"You were so exhausted that you didn't even hear me come in; I felt sorry for you," said Osnat, sitting up in bed, now completely awake.

"Your hand's so warm," said Aaron, fully intending to say good-bye and set off immediately for home, and taken aback by the tenderness in his voice.

"It was a difficult meeting tonight, and besides, I think I've got a fever," said Osnat. He put his hand on her forehead. It was burning.

"Where's your thermometer?" he asked, then came back from the bathroom holding it in his hand. "It's a hundred and three and a half," he said with alarm. "Shouldn't I call someone?" She shook her head stubbornly. But she did swallow the two aspirin with the glass of water he obediently brought her. When she drank the lemon tea he made her, her teeth chattered on the rim of the glass cup, and she shivered as she said, "Perhaps you should leave now. I don't know what's the matter with me, and it might be catching. Anyway, it's late and I want to sleep."

Aaron nodded, asked if he should make her another cup of tea, touched her forehead, still burning hot, and finally said doubtfully, "All right, then, good-bye for now. I'll give you a ring tomorrow. Go and see the doctor." Then he left the room.

The clear summer sky was full of stars, but they didn't shed enough light to illuminate the path. The lamp was off, and he almost tripped on the stone border as he turned off in the direction of the back gate. And when the figure in short trousers sprang up again from behind the building, as if it had been standing under Osnat's window, his heart missed a beat. Suddenly he realized that the figure might have been hiding there all the time, under the window. For a moment he wondered if he should chase him—now he was sure that the figure was that of a man, a tallish man—but the pain in his arm brought him up short, and his distaste for drama made him unwilling to give chase. Instead, he walked quickly in the direction of his car.

4

Until the problem with her son Mottie began, Simcha had been able to cope with everything. And if anyone had used the term "underprivileged" in her hearing, she would have looked at him with astonishment, unable to understand what he was talking about. Despite the fact that she had brought up six children by herself and had been the sole breadwinner too ever since Albert's accident at work, when his back had begun to give him such trouble that he spent most of his time in bed, aside from his monthly visit to the national insurance offices to collect his meager disability checks and his daily visits to the center of town, where he went to meet people and drink Turkish coffee and sometimes arak diluted with water. Despite the fact that she worked long hours outside the house, after cleaning and tidying and cooking at home, and despite the fact that almost every day, when she came home from work, she looked after the neighbors' children when they asked her and listened to her brothers-in-law and sisters-in-law and her younger sister's children who came to complain about their troubles, despite all this Simcha always radiated a kind of acceptance of her lot combined with an expression of contentment and even gratification.

Except for her mother's funeral and the birth of her third, stillborn child, there was only one other time when she nearly cried. This was when they removed the plaster cast from her left hand, which she had broken running after one of the neighbors' children, and the hand was stiff and they told her that she would need physiotherapy. The doctor at the Sick Fund clinic who spoke to her about it asked her, "Where do you work, Mrs. Malul?" and after she told him, he asked about her husband's occupation, about her children, and finally, directly, how she made ends meet. She described her daily routine, and when she had finished he looked at her and sighed, and she said, "What can I do?" and then she said, "It's hard, Doctor, it's hard," and she felt the tears coming, not because of the difficulties of life but because of the look he gave her, which was filled with compassion and helplessness. If she had been asked, she would not have been able to say what it was about this look that had given rise to the tears that she didn't even know were there inside her. She could only have said that instead of this young doctor with his blue eyes she would have preferred Dr. Ben Zakkan, who would give her a cursory examination and write out a prescription without asking any questions. But Dr. Ben Zakkan was on vacation, and instead there was this new doctor, who gave her a note for a month's sick leave.

But she didn't use the note, because she was afraid that they would get someone to replace her, because how long could they leave the other home-care aides in charge of the kibbutz infirmary without her? After years of cleaning work, at first in private houses in Kiryat Malahi and then in the hospital in Ashkelon, where the work was easier but the nurses were strict and the patients suffered so much and the bus journeys wore her out, she had done something she had never done in her life before: With the encouragement of the head nurse of the internal-diseases ward where she was working, she had applied for a home-care nursing-aide course. It lasted for six months, and when she completed it, two years ago, she got the job on the kibbutz.

And now, at the age of forty-nine, a grandmother of five, she could sometimes even rest at her place of work. But for the business with Mottie, she could be living in peace, because somehow she managed with the money and with only eating chicken on Fridays and on the other days improvising with vegetable patties and thick soups, and knowing how to make wonderful pancakes with the chicken wings from Friday's soup. But the problem with Mottie made peace and quiet impossible.

Mottie was only twelve, but Simcha knew that if she didn't do something quickly to get him out of the neighborhood, he would be lost. Mottie was the youngest of her children, and the only other one still left at home was thirteen-year-old Limor, a good-natured, obedient girl who did what she was supposed to and helped at home as well. Simcha had recognized the signs in Mottie immediately: She had seen the same things in a lot of other neighborhood children, and she had always been able to tell, right from the beginning. She knew all about the visits from the police at night, the shouting, the ruined families, the stolen money, and she knew the youngsters too, who spent all day hanging around the shopping center with nothing to do but pull the levers of the gambling machines, or lying on their backs at home with blank, staring eyes. More than once she had been called to Jeannette Abukasi's house to help her confront her oldest boy when he came to demand money. She didn't try to understand the reasons, not even to herself, although somewhere inside her she knew that Mottie's situation had something to do with Albert's behavior, and with her own weakness too, for the passing of the years seemed to have sapped her strength. She could no longer insist that Mottie do his homework with the same persistence as before, and when she scolded him for missing school, her voice no longer held the authority it had possessed with his older siblings.

The actual word *drugs* had never passed her lips. She had listened with her head bowed and nodding in agreement with the counselor who had invited her to come to the school for a talk. Although she was tempted to, not even once had she helplessly said, as she had heard other mothers say, "What can I do?" When the counselor, who was wearing an elegant blue headdress for religious reasons, finished talking, Simcha sat there silently and finally said, "I understand"; she had even felt superior to the counselor, who failed to understand the true gravity of the problem. Because the counselor, who kept uneasily pushing a lock of hair back inside the headdress, surely did not know how to recognize them, those youngsters Simcha in her heart called "the damned"; Mottie was not yet irrevocably damned, if only she could get him out of the little town.

Simcha talked it over with her elder brother a couple of times, and finally, after a number of failed attempts to talk to Mottie, who looked straight at him without saying a word, he told her to send him to the kibbutz. The despair on her brother's face after his attempts to talk to Mottie she understood only too well. She knew the picture, because on the occasions when she herself had tried to talk to him she too had been driven to despair by his withdrawal. As she spoke she would hear the passion fading from her words, and she would feel him slipping farther and farther out of her hands. When she tried to say anything to him on days when he played hookey from school, when she would meet his blank eyes looking straight into hers without seeing her at all, images would come into her head of the plump baby who had never cried at night and of the toddler, tied to her apron strings, whose happiest moments were when she came home from work. When she looked now into his empty eyes, she was overwhelmed by a feeling of failure such as she had never known before.

"What's the problem," said her brother. "You work there on that kibbutz, you can fix him up there." And she thought about it for a long time.

Every morning, after making the sandwiches and sending the two children off to school, Simcha would run to catch the 8:10 bus from Kiryat Malachi, getting off at a stop on the highway and from there walking for twenty minutes along the narrow road to the kibbutz. Sometimes, if she was lucky, a car would pass and give her a lift. At 8:45 she would arrive at the infirmary to take over from the night home-care aide. Usually Dr. Reimer would drop in when she took over her shift and listen with her to whatever the night aide had to report. His second visit would not be until the late afternoon, when Simcha had already left for the day.

Whenever the doctor arrived, she intended to ask him about fixing Mottie up on the kibbutz, but at the last minute shame would prevent her from doing so. Right from the start, when she began working on the kibbutz, bringing her references from the last family she had worked for, she had thought of Mottie. Even though the signs of what was to develop in the future were not clear then, she had already sensed a peculiar weakness in him, a kind of lack of what a more educated person might have called ambition. She didn't call it anything but kept an anxious eye on his actions and behavior and the friends he chose for himself.

Now she was determined to act, and just as she had not known before how to ask Dr. Reimer what to do, she knew now that she had to apply to the kibbutz secretariat, quieting her fear and shame by thoughts of the kibbutz members' politeness toward her. In the two years she had been working there, no one had ever reprimanded her, and the more time passed, the more their appreciation of her grew, finding expression in friendly looks and explicit words of praise, in gifts of fruit and presents for the holidays. The nurse, Rickie, and the patients and their families had nothing but good to say of her. Sometimes she received gifts from the patients themselves and from the sons and daughters of old people in the infirmary.

Waking up that morning worrying about Mottie, she thought about all this and concluded that the only problem now was taking the first step. How, she asked herself in despair, was she going to get to the secretariat office when she had to be in the infirmary by 9:00 in the morning and in the afternoon had to run to catch the 3:30 bus or wait three and a half hours for the next one, which would mean leaving the children home alone until so late? Not to speak of the two grandchildren she was supposed to look after that afternoon while her daughter and son-in-law went to a wedding in Kiryat Shemonah. And during the day she was alone in the infirmary, and it was forbidden—she had never broken this rule—to leave the patients alone. This had been made clear to her from the outset, and so she never left the building until she left to take the bus at the end of her shift.

The work itself was not difficult. Usually there were only a few patients in the infirmary, several infectious ones in quarantine, and the old people. Occasionally there were ill soldiers who preferred to remain on the kibbutz rather than going to the military hospital. The infirmary had never yet been empty, which gave her a feeling of security, the confidence that things would continue like this forever and she would never have to worry about finding new families in need of home help.

Ever since she began at the infirmary, at least one old person had been hospitalized there. Some would be there for months, and Simcha, looking now at Felix and wondering how she was going to wake him so that she could wash him, thought about the sadness of lying there like that until you died, of waiting patiently, without any struggle, for death, just like her grandmother, who had died a few years after the family immigrated to Israel from Morocco, spending the last two years of her life in bed.

"Poor things," she said aloud to herself as she prepared the basin of warm water. She thought of how Felix's daughter, Zahara, came to see him twice a day but he didn't speak to her at all, as if he didn't even recognize her. His grandchildren came sometimes too. They had taken care of him for a long time in his own room, the doctor had told her, but now he needed round-the-clock supervision.

At the moment there were only two old people in the infirmary, and Simcha looked after both of them. Physically it was not particularly difficult; only washing them sometimes tired her. Especially Felix, who had to be firmly coaxed. Like an obstinate baby, he refused to cooperate. From her experience she knew that his days were numbered. Whenever she force-fed him through the nose, a furious despair flared in his eyes, and she knew that this was one of the signs of the end. After it there was only total surrender. This despair, together with the yellowish-gray color of his face and the skin that hung in folds on his dry bones, showed that the end was near. But naturally she didn't say anything. When she looked at Felix, she thought of Mottie, and she knew that she wouldn't have the courage to ask the doctor's advice. Especially since the doctor was always so brisk and harassed, in a hurry to go somewhere else.

This very day, she decided, she would go to that secretariat office. Even if she missed the bus back, she would go to the office to talk to them about taking Mottie. Or perhaps she would leave before the end of her shift, she thought, frightening herself with the thought, before the afternoon home help came to take over from her.

Simcha liked her work. The feeling of satisfaction that filled her when she saw the dirty sheets from the night piled in the corner and the patient, clean after his morning wash, lying on clean, starched ones was like the contented fatigue she felt on Friday nights, in the moments of well-being when everybody sat around the table in the freshly cleaned house. Now, as she dipped the soft cloth in the warm water in the blue plastic basin, she couldn't stop herself from clucking and sighing. Felix was growing increasingly remote, cooperating less and less, resisting more and more.

"You'll get bedsores, washing is important because of the hygiene," she repeated to the old man, who lay in the fetal position and refused to move. "It will make you feel better, you'll see how nice you'll feel," she said, pulling the sheet off his shoulders. "Zahara will be coming soon to bring you the newspaper, and later the children will come too. Aren't you ashamed for them to see you like this?" she murmured as she wrung the cloth out into the basin. "Aren't you ashamed?" she repeated, and she couldn't get the word *ashamed* out of her mind, even though she was no longer thinking of cleanliness but of the shame of being so old and helpless. It wasn't her business to consider other solutions, and she received the doctor's instructions about the force-feeding unquestioningly, but sometimes, when she saw the despairing look in the old man's eyes as she carefully poured the gruel into the tube, she felt a terrible sorrow, and a powerful desire not to see him in his disgrace.

After Felix it was Bracha's turn. Bracha was more amenable, even though she too did not speak. They lay in the infirmary's two adjoining rooms, which were separated by a big pair of wooden folding doors that were closed only when there was a very bad situation in one room or the other. When there were more than two old people there, they were put two to a room, although the original intention had been to give each their privacy, though Simcha sometimes wondered what they needed this privacy for, since they were unaware of their surroundings, withdrawn into themselves in the most private of all worlds.

A third room, smaller and isolated, was intended for patients in quarantine. Now, after a soldier who had been there with infectious hepatitis had recovered and returned to duty, the isolation room was empty. How much noise there had been, Simcha thought, during the week he was in the infirmary! People going in and out all the time, and music. But there was really something nice about it, and now silence would reign until they again brought in someone young.

Simcha warmed up Bracha's gruel, dipped a finger into the bowl to test it, and only when the temperature was just right sat her up against the big pillow, spread the clean towel over the blanket, and fed her. Carefully she collected the dribbles of gruel from the corners of her mouth, and she talked to her all the time. In the home-help course they were taught to talk to the patients. Even if the patients didn't appear to react, it was important for them to feel human contact. And Simcha carried out the instructions obediently and talked to Bracha, and it wasn't difficult because on the whole she liked her. Afterward she cleaned the floor and the kitchen cupboard, and when she looked up at the big clock hanging on the wall, it was already twelve o'clock and she knew that soon they would bring lunch, and after lunch, she reminded herself, she would go to the secretariat.

Then she heard noises, not the usual noise of the food trolley but people's voices, and Dr. Reimer came in with the nurse, Rickie, bringing a new patient, a young woman. When Simcha looked at her she recognized the beautiful blond woman who had been talking on the telephone in the office on the day they had interviewed her for the job. Her beauty was obvious even now, when she was so pale and her eyes were closed. They took her, half-carrying her, to the isolation room. Simcha stood to one side, ready to help, and she wondered if it was hepatitis again, but she didn't say anything, waiting patiently for the lunch trolley.

When the trolley arrived, Dr. Reimer and Nurse Rickie were still in the isolation room, and Simcha busied herself so with the food— warming it up and separating Felix and Bracha's portions—that she hardly heard anything from the isolation room. Finally the doctor came out and said, "Look, Simcha, we've just brought Osnat, she'll be here for a few days. She's got severe pneumonia, and I want her to stay in the infirmary. All you have to do is see to it that she has plenty to drink, take her temperature, and help her to wash, if she wants you to. She's very weak now, but in a day or two she'll feel better and be able to go outside. In a minute Rickie will give her an injection." Simcha nodded and asked about lunch, and the doctor said that she certainly wouldn't want anything to eat, but it was important to see that she had a lot to drink. "Maybe the juice from the plum compote?" suggested Simcha hesitantly, and the doctor nodded and said, "Anything, as long as she drinks. She's conscious and you can ask her."

Then the two of them went away, and the silence returned. Simcha went quietly into the isolation room. The woman was not as young as she had seemed at first, but she wasn't old either. And really very beautiful. She seemed to be dozing. The doctor had said that Rickie would be back immediately with the injection. Simcha decided to ask her for permission to go to the secretariat, and perhaps Rickie would agree to take her place for a few minutes. When Rickie returned Simcha was busy washing the lunch dishes with her eyes constantly on the clock. Rickie went into the isolation room, and Simcha heard murmurs and snatches of sentences without trying to understand what was being said. She couldn't stop thinking about Mottie and the counselor and the question that Limor had asked that morning: "Where are you going to get the money to pay Victor at the grocery store? He says he's not going to give us anything more until we pay the bill."

Rickie came out of the isolation room and said, "That's it, she's had her penicillin shot for today. I'll drop in again this afternoon, and when Yaffa comes to take over from you, don't forget to tell her to give her a lot to drink."

Simcha said, "Yes, yes, of course," and she didn't dare say another word. Rickie left. The two old people dozed off, and Simcha peeped into the isolation room where Osnat was lying with her eyes closed. She stood hesitating for a minute, looking at the clock and the woman lying in the bed, and finally she went up to her and put her hand on her forehead. Osnat opened her eyes and smiled, and Simcha smiled back and asked her if she could give her something to drink. And only after she had fed her a few teaspoons of Bracha's compote juice and Osnat closed her eyes and said with difficulty that she would like to sleep now did Simcha lay the compote dish on the white bedside cupboard, remove her gown, and leave the little building. She ran almost all the way—the secretariat was on the other side of the kibbutz—and when she arrived the door was shut and there was a note stuck to it saying something about a meeting in the clubhouse.

She sighed and retraced her footsteps. In all the time she had worked here she had never looked around her, not even on the way to the bus, but now, when she was in such a hurry, she suddenly noticed the buildings and the flowers and the quiet, and heard the birds singing, and she thought about the contentment of life here and what a good thing it would be for Mottie if he could grow up on the kibbutz, not only Mottie but everybody.

She hurried back to the infirmary as quickly as she could, but she couldn't walk very fast, and when she entered the small, white building and looked at the big clock, she saw that it was already two o'clock and she had been gone for about half an hour. But when she looked away from the clock and got her breath back, and recovered from her panic, she saw immediately that the door to the old people's rooms was closed, and when she opened it she saw too that somebody had closed the wooden door that divided the two adjoining rooms, and her heart pounded at the thought that something had happened in her absence. But when she opened it she saw that both old people were sleeping as usual and there was nobody else there. The door to the isolation room was closed too, and Simcha asked herself in alarm, putting on the gown she had left on a chair in the kitchen, if she had closed it herself before she went out, and while she was standing hesitating in front of the closed door, strangely alert to the sound of the birds outside, she heard groans and went inside.

The patient's head had slipped off the bed, and she was breathing rapidly, with a hoarse, whistling sound. As Simcha stood paralyzed in the doorway, trying to make up her mind whether to run and phone the clinic, she saw that the patient was about to slip off the bed, and she ran to Osnat and lifted her up, and with a great effort managed to say, "There we go, dear, easy does it," and then Osnat began to vomit, and Simcha held her head. The sick woman's eyes were closed, and it was impossible to tell whether she was semiconscious or completely unconscious. She supported the head with a steady hand, heard the rattling breath, and caught the spasms of vomiting in her lap. When Osnat appeared to have finished vomiting, Simcha stroked her head, pushed away the hair sticking to her forehead, and was about to go for towels and water. But then Osnat let out a kind of grunt and her head fell back.

Simcha had already seen more than enough dead people, and although she refused to believe it, she knew without the shadow of a doubt that the woman had died. For a moment she froze and tried to make out whether she was breathing, but her lips, twisted in an expression of pain, didn't move, and when Simcha put her ear close to the distorted face, she couldn't hear anything.

She knew what she had to do. She went quickly to the telephone and dialed the number of the clinic on the other side of the kibbutz, where Rickie was busy dishing out medicine and bandaging wounds and doing all the other things she did when the doctor was away from the kibbutz. Rickie arrived puffing and panting and behind her came a man who ran into the isolation room when Rickie called, "Moish, Moish, come here!"

Simcha stood in the doorway watching Nurse Rickie giving mouth-to-mouth resuscitation and massaging the chest of the patient, whom Simcha was already thinking of as "the deceased" or "the poor thing," because it was obvious to her that there was no way of bringing her back to life, although they had brought the butcher Ben Yaakov's wife back to life after banging on her chest like Rickie was doing now to this poor woman, but with Ben Yaakov's wife it was after she drowned in the sea and not after she was sick with a fever of maybe 104 degrees.

In the meantime, the man Nurse Rickie called Moish left the room to phone, and she heard him shout, "Mordie, bring the ambulance here on the double, Osnat's in a bad way!" and afterward, "No, no, Eli Reimer's already on his way to the hospital, he left a quarter of an hour ago, we can't possibly get hold of him!" The ambulance arrived immediately, and they transferred Osnat to it. At the last moment Nurse Rickie came back to the isolation room, looked inside the little litter bin, and took out the ampule and syringe she had used for the injection. "Give me a plastic bag," she said to Simcha. Then she ran outside and got into the ambulance, whose wheels squealed on the narrow road, and suddenly there was absolute silence, and only then it struck Simcha that she should have told them she had left the infirmary, and because it was clear to her that Osnat was completely dead and nothing in the world would bring her back to life, she would be blamed, because maybe if she had been there all the time, she could have called Nurse Rickie in time to do something to save her. If only she had stayed there and reported to the nurse immediately, the minute Osnat began to feel bad. She was seized by panic at the thought that she should have confessed to going to the secretariat and leaving the patients alone, and once she had done that she could have said goodbye to her job on the kibbutz and any chance of fixing Mottie up there.

She looked at Felix, who went on lying there as if nothing had happened, his wide-open eyes staring at the wall next to his bed, in the same fetal position in which he had been lying for the whole of the past month. Bracha, on the other hand, was sleeping peacefully, as she always did after lunch, and Simcha knew that she wouldn't wake up before the next home help came to take over from her, and since nobody in the world knew that she had gone out, maybe she needn't say anything about it, and she wouldn't have to lose everything.

She wiped her face, took off the blue gown soiled with vomit, and went into the third room, and with all the strength stemming from her anxiety she ripped the bedclothes off the bed, washed the vomit from them and from her gown, and threw them into the laundry basket. Then she scrubbed the mattress and turned it over, remade the bed with clean, fragrant sheets, and washed the floor twice. And when she was done and the room looked as clean as it had been before it all began, she felt relieved. Her anxiety subsided, and she said to herself that in any case she couldn't have helped Osnat, even if she had been there all the time, because what could Nurse Rickie, even if she had been summoned in time, have done? But other voices told her that this wasn't necessarily true. She cleaned the traces of vomit that had soiled her dress despite the gown, and a profound uneasiness filled her heart and made her legs tremble as she sprayed the room with bathroom spray to rid it of the remnants of the bad smell. She sat down next to the little table in the kitchen, put her head on her arms, closed her eyes, and waited.

5

Michael Ohayon shifted constantly in his chair. Sometimes he folded his hands, sometimes he put them on the table in front of him. But neither the cigarettes he chain-smoked nor the restraint of Emanuel Shorer, head of the Criminal Investigations Division, succeeded in relaxing the tension and the anger being radiated by Inspector Machluf Levy. Levy, who was in uniform, kept smoothing an invisible crease in his trousers, and from time to time he wiped his forehead with a handkerchief he removed ceremoniously from his pocket—an exercise that required him to raise himself slightly from his chair—after which he folded it neatly and replaced it in his pocket. Whenever he began speaking he looked down at a point on the floor, at the same time twisting the thick gold ring he wore on the slender, manicured little finger of his right hand, tapped the ash compulsively from his cigarette into the glass ashtray next to him, and only then raised his eyes to the man sitting opposite him.

Michael Ohayon shook his ash into his empty coffee cup, into the muddy dregs where one after the other he had dropped the stubs that spluttered out as they touched the bottom.

Brigadier General Yehuda Nahari, the head of NUSCI, the National Unit for Serious Crimes Investigation, was the only person in the room who appeared indifferent to the fate of the case, as if the whole thing had nothing to do with him. At moments he even looked bored, and the longer the meeting lasted, the shorter the intervals grew between his glances at his watch, and finally he even began a nervous, rhythmic drumming of his fingers on the edge of the table, which only ceased when he propped his elbow on the table and cupped his chin in his hand.

When Michael permitted himself to sigh aloud, releasing the air compressed inside him with the sound of a small explosion, Shorer said, "As I've already said, there are two possibilities, and as I also said before, it wasn't my decision to transfer the case to NUSCI, but the commissioner's, so there's nothing to argue about. However, there's also the possibility, in my opinion the optimal one, of co-opting someone from the Lachish Subdistrict onto the team, if you agree."

For the fourth time during the meeting Levy made his voice heard, saying in a deferential tone filled with injured pride and suppressed anger: "All this is because of that letter? Even though there's nothing incriminating in it?"

Shorer said nothing.

"You all know it's not just the letter," said Levy, raising his voice for the first time. "If we were talking about a case here in Ashkelon, you wouldn't have handed it over to NUSCI even if there were two letters. What's this bullshit all about? Never mind who gets the case, but let's at least be honest."

Michael refrained from responding to the offended look and fixed his eyes on Shorer like a loyal, obedient pupil.

"You don't have to take it so personally," said Shorer placatingly.

"So how should I take it? Tell me how I should take it, go on, tell me," Levy protested, banging his gold lighter on the table. "What do you think, that apart from NUSCI nobody understands police work here? There are important cases and unimportant cases, and we're supposed to stick to the pushers and burglars and whores all our lives? What is this crap? It's not because of the letter—it's because of the kibbutz. Tell the truth at least."

The main advantage of this outburst, thought Michael Ohayon, taking care to keep his eyes fixed on the wall opposite him and not to look directly into Levy's pale eyes so as to prevent the rage from being directed at him—its main advantage was that all the subterranean currents that had been seething since the beginning of the meeting had now found their way to the surface. Machluf Levy had the guts to call a spade a spade and make it impossible for them to ignore him. The outburst they had just witnessed was a rare spectacle in this forum. The disparities in rank and the venue in the national police headquarters might have been expected to restrain him.

"I don't understand you," said Shorer, trying another angle. "You're talking as if we've already decided that the case warrants a special investigation team. We haven't decided anything yet. And if we do decide that a crime has been committed, have you got any idea what it's like to conduct an investigation inside a kibbutz?"

"What's the matter?" bristled Levy. "What's the big deal? When it was a question of investigating the thefts and burglaries in Kibbutz Maayanot, we were good enough? When there was that business with the drugs, we knew how to investigate it? All of a sudden we're not good enough to conduct an internal investigation? What's going on here? And if you'll pardon me, sir, with all due respect, we know the ground a lot better than anyone else here. The Lachish Subdistrict is our home ground, and we weren't born yesterday either. And I'd just like to know when was the last time that NUSCI went into a kibbutz?" He looked around him with a triumphant expression, still riding on the wave of his initial boldness.

But Shorer was silent, his face expressionless, and Levy dropped his eyes. Nahari sighed and looked despairingly at the ceiling, and Commander Shmerling, Investigations Division officer of the Southern District, looked wearily at Machluf Levy and was opening his mouth to say something when Shorer repeated, "The decision was not ours, and in any case it doesn't look like headline news to me. If you want my honest opinion, the case looks to me like a loser, and if I were you, I'd be glad to have it taken away from me. The commissioner's decision was made after you reported on the letter, as you know very well, and NUSCI exists precisely for contingencies like these. I don't understand you," he said gently, as if to a child, "you know perfectly well that whenever a case comes up involving the so-called public interest, if there's an M.K. or some other kind of public figure involved, and there's no knowing what can of worms we might be getting into, we call in NUSCI. You've already been congratulated for the swift action you took, for your identification of that letter, and you definitely deserve a lot of credit for it."

Machluf Levy didn't seem to have heard the compliments. Instead, he looked like someone who knew when he was beaten and was determined to make the best of it. His expression was one of a man calling on his reason to master his feelings. He sighed. "Okay, I'll transfer everything to them," he said, "but you should realize that we don't like it when we're treated like second-class citizens. We can work with Forensics too, we've got lab technicians too, we've got everything it takes. Just remember that." And with sudden animation he added, "But we haven't even concluded yet if it's a murder case or merely a case of unnatural death—why on earth should they take on a U.D.?"

"I don't know what you mean by 'concluded,'" said Nahari. "It will take time to conclude any such thing. In a few hours we'll get the pathologist's report, and then we'll know the cause of death. We're only on alert here, and if it turns out that she died of pneumonia, the whole thing's a false alarm. So what are we playing at? Why make waves if we don't even know which way things are going to develop? What's all this sensitivity about? What do you care if Ohayon goes with you or instead of you to the Pathological Institute? Haven't we got anything else to worry about besides smoothing ruffled feathers?"

He turned to Shorer, who was again looking through the papers in front of him. Shorer shook his head and removed his tiny reading glasses, a new acquisition that had brought an astonished smile to Michael Ohayon's face when he saw them for the first time that morning on Shorer's nose. The rectangular gold frame was lost on Shorer's broad face, and he said apologetically, "What are you laughing at? They cost me four dollars in Hong Kong, and I've got three pairs." Now he took them off and said, "I can't see any objections, I'm sure it will only help. As far as I'm concerned we can get to work."

"Can we have some more coffee first?" asked Michael as he opened the cardboard file in front of him. Shorer looked inquiringly at the others.

Nahari said, "I'd prefer something cold. It's hot here in Jerusalem, no better than Petah Tikva, if you ask me."

"But at least it's dry here, not like on the coastal plain," remarked Shmerling. "It's more like the Negev here, you don't sweat like you do in Tel Aviv," he added, looking to Levy for confirmation. But Levy went on turning his ring round and round, and only nodded and said, "Yes, please," when Shorer asked him whether he wanted something cold to drink.

By the time the coffee and bottles of juice arrived, everyone was absorbed in the printed pages inside the cardboard files. Shorer offered milk and sugar. He himself poured three teaspoons into Michael Ohayon's black coffee and stirred it pedantically before handing him the cup with an expression of disgust, saying, "Here's your poison, I don't know how anyone can drink such syrup." For the next few minutes the only sounds were of sipping, cups clattering, and pages being turned. The air conditioning was out of order, and the fan revolving in the corner of the room did not cool the increasingly stuffy room, merely making a humming noise and blowing fitful blasts of warm air onto the people sitting around the table.

Shorer set the file down in front of him and snapped in two a burned matchstick he had taken out of Michael's matchbox. "Machluf," he said, "why don't you take us through the story again? We know the facts, but we've never heard them in this forum, and you might say that from now on this forum is beginning to work as a team. Where are we? Today's the seventh of July? And it happened two days ago, right?" He looked at Nahari, who nodded as he drank the last of the juice in his glass.

"Okay, so give me a cigarette," said Nahari to Michael Ohayon, who reached over the long table to hand him the Noblesse pack and immediately afterward offered the burning match to Machluf Levy, who settled down in his chair in preparation for a long speech.

The expression of concentration on Machluf Levy's face showed a combination of effort and pain, and Michael felt embarrassed at witnessing the feelings it reflected. Only after the meeting, when he became aware of the cramps in his leg muscles, did he realize that, more than embarrassment, he had felt complete identification with the tensions displayed by Inspector Machluf Levy, who despite being from the provincial backwater of the Lachish Subdistrict, had not yet conformed to a single one of Nahari's expectations of him as an investigator. Levy's brows met in a frown over his pale gray eyes. He dropped his eyes and then raised them to the ceiling, puffed out his cheeks as he breathed in noisily, blew the air out ceremoniously through his narrow lips, and only then laid his hands on the table in front of him and began to speak.

Michael wondered whether everyone else in the room felt as tense as he did, but a careful examination of their faces betrayed no signs of embarrassment and suspense comparable to his own. He prepared himself to listen attentively and tried to ignore the way his heart beat whenever he looked at Levy's face and saw the astonishing resemblance to his uncle, his mother's younger brother, who had died suddenly of a stroke while on an intelligence mission in Brussels. Michael had been very attached to him. He was the one he turned to whenever he was in trouble. Now too he almost smiled when he remembered their conversation on the eve of his marriage to Nira, and then, later, some of the jokes Jacques had told him to relieve his tension before the divorce.

Jacques was a bachelor whose prowess with women was a family myth. He himself never boasted of it. He would come to family dinners or to other festive occasions bringing a different woman every time, and he never even permitted himself a wink when he introduced her to everyone as if she were the first woman he had ever brought with him. It was from him that Michael had learned to bend over a woman and look into her eyes with the yearning that melted hearts. ("But you have to really want her," warned Jacques. "It's not an act, it's maybe only shamelessness.") And whenever Michael started a new affair, even a casual one, when he opened a door for a woman or listened attentively to what she was saying to him, certain sentences of Jacques's would echo in his ears. "The cleverest thing I ever heard," Jacques would say, quoting a popular Israeli entertainer: "'Be a man, humble yourself.' Stick to that advice, Michael, and you won't go wrong. With those eyes and that lean body and that pretty mouth you inherited from your father, you'll go far. Just learn how to humble yourself, but not too much." And here Jacques would laugh his unrestrained laugh, and in this, Michael now decided, he was completely different from Machluf Levy, in whose eyes there was no mischievous twinkle and who had not laughed freely even once. "Humbling yourself means not taking yourself seriously, at least not all the time," Jacques had explained to Michael on more than one occasion.

Jacques too had worn a gold ring on the pinkie of his right hand, and he would turn it mainly when he was reading the riot act to Michael. Michael's father had died when he was a child, and his mother would call on her brother to fill his place on those rare occasions when it was necessary to make the boy toe the line—as when he refused to eat for weeks after his father's death, or when he insisted on going to the boarding school in Jerusalem, or when he disappeared for two days and had gone as far away as Eilat.

Jacques died a year after Michael's divorce. Throughout his marriage they had met once a month, just the two of them, at a Jaffa fish restaurant where Jacques was an habitué. Jacques had never criticized Nira, and he treated her parents, Yuzek and Fela, with polite respect. He had conquered Fela's heart on their first meeting, when he sang the praises of her gefilte fish with a completely serious expression on his face and asked for a second helping of the compote of which she was so proud. But what really won the hearts of Yuzek and Fela—who had their doubts about their son-in-law, was the feeling of ease Jacques radiated, his lack of embarrassment, and his perfect manners. From the very first time he visited their house he behaved as if he had dined on innumerable occasions in the houses of rich diamond dealers of Polish origin. And when he came to visit Michael and Nira when Yuval was born, four months after the wedding, he treated Nira as if he had a particularly soft spot for her. Jacques was the only member of Michael's family who could make Nira smile in delight and sometimes even blush. He would flirt with her shamelessly in his subtle way, he never came without flowers, and he never stayed too long.

He lived alone in his bachelor apartment in the center of Tel Aviv, leaving from there on his secret journeys. Michael's mother feared for his safety—Uncle Jacques was only sixteen years older than he—and even now, years after her death, he could still hear her lamentations for her little brother "who doesn't have a wife to look after him." Michael loved him and was proud of him.

Yuval was seven when Jacques died, and whenever he was sad he asked his father to tell him more about Uncle Jacques. Sometimes the boy would say, "Let's remember Uncle Jacques" and take the photo album from the bureau in the bedroom, page through it, and cry happily, "Here's Uncle Jacques when you went to ski on Mount Hermon, and here he is on a wind-surfer, and here . . . " Sometimes Yuval would burst into the tears imprisoned in his depths, using Uncle Jacques as the reason that made it all right for him to cry.

Once, when Yuval was fourteen and he was making fun of his maternal grandfather, Yuzek, to Michael, he said, "But you know, even he doesn't have a bad word to say about Jacques. And he doesn't sigh when he talks about him either. He even smiles." Yuval sighed and looked at the black-and-white photo of Michael sitting on the backseat of a heavy motorbike, his arms around his uncle's waist and his eyes shining with the happy light reflected in his broad smile. "It's a pity he's dead," said Yuval sadly, bending over the photograph. "I've never seen you so happy as you were with him," he reflected aloud, looking at his father appraisingly.

"I really did love him," Michael said to his son, "but I love you too," he added quickly in the same breath, returning his look guiltily.

Jacques was the only person who never made fun of Michael's anxieties about his son. A few days after Yuval was born, Jacques appeared with a big, fluffy teddy bear. "That's something I never dared to do, have a child," he whispered to Michael as they stood side by side over the cradle looking at the baby. "For that I didn't have the guts. I don't understand how you can keep them safe. It seems to me a great miracle." He gently touched the baby's exposed foot. "Take care of him," he said when he stood at the door, and then he disappeared.

Now too, looking at Machluf Levy's tense hands, Michael heard the tenderness in his voice and decided that the resemblance between the policeman and his uncle was exceedingly faint. Jacques was also the only person who supported him in his decision to leave the university, to forfeit the scholarship to Cambridge, to reject the brilliant academic career everyone predicted for him, so that he could be near Yuval after the divorce. And he was the one who introduced Michael to Shorer. "A very good friend of mine," he said to Michael as he shook the hand of the head of the Criminal Investigations Division. And for the affection Shorer showed his junior officer, the special relationship that was the envy of all his colleagues, Michael Ohayon knew that he had his Uncle Jacques to thank.

When Michael Ohayon was transferred a few weeks earlier to the Serious Crimes Unit and began traveling to Petah Tikva every day, he never dreamed that the first case he would be given to investigate would be a murder on a kibbutz. When the suspicion of murder was first brought to his attention, his initial reaction was astonishment. "Has there ever been a murder on a kibbutz?" he asked.

Nahari had made a face and replied, "There have been two cases, but not like this one. There was one not long ago, of murder during a fit of insanity, and another one in the fifties. But that was just a weird case of attempted murder," he said, looking at his notes. "Some poor woman went off her head and tried to kill somebody who hadn't done her any harm. Here, read the verdict for yourself," he said, handing Michael a photocopy of the judges' verdict.

Michael began reading to himself: "The petitioner against the Attorney General and the counterappeal in the High Court of Justice sitting as a Court of Criminal Appeals." For ten days in the month of March 1957 the judges had deliberated the case of the accused woman, who had been sentenced to sixteen months' imprisonment, and the appeal of the attorney general against the leniency of the sentence. When Michael considered that thirty years had passed since then, he felt that he was holding a historic document in his hands. After a few lines he forgot about Nahari and became absorbed in reading the verdict:

The appellant, a woman who was formerly a member of Kibbutz M., was present one evening in the dining hall of the kibbutz. At the time in question a teacher on the kibbutz, Mr. A., was dining alone there, the other members having not yet assembled. When he concluded his meal, the appellant approached him and offered him a cup of chocolate pudding. Mr. A. was surprised at this on a number of counts: firstly, he was surprised at the presence of the appellant in the dining hall at this time since she had concluded her work there in the early hours of the afternoon. . . .

Nahari's voice startled him: "I didn't mean for you to sit and read the whole thing now; you can take it with you. I just wanted to show you that such things have happened before." Michael folded the document and put it in his shirt pocket. He intended to read it even if the case were not transferred to him. He thought about the paper now again, as Machluf Levy began reciting the facts everyone present already knew.

"On the date of the fifth of the present month," said Machluf in an official voice that embarrassed Michael for his sake—Machluf was far from being a fool, but he was completely unaware of the gap, so predictable as to be almost stereotypical, between him and the others revealed by his movements and manner of speaking—"we received a telephone call at the Ashkelon police station from Dr. Gilboa of the Barzilai Hospital. The call was answered by—"

"Never mind all those details," Nahari cut in impatiently. "Get straight to the main facts." Machluf Levy blushed at the undisguised insult, while Michael berated himself for having seen any resemblance between this man and his Uncle Jacques.

"Let him tell it at his own pace," said Shorer, sparing Machluf the need to protest. "So what if it takes a few minutes longer? We might as well hear the whole story once." And then he turned to address the speaker. "Go on at your own pace, with all the details," he said with the authority Michael knew well but which nevertheless surprised him time and again because it always appeared at unexpected moments.

"So anyway, to cut a long story short, Sergeant Kochava Strauss and I went out to the hospital, and she, that's to say Dr. Gilboa, explained the whole thing to us. Which was, that they had brought in the body of a woman of forty-five, Osnat Harel, who had apparently died as a reaction to a penicillin injection she received on the kibbutz. And the kibbutz nurse brought her there in an ambulance when she was already dead, and there was nothing for them to do except ascertain the cause of death. And there was a big fuss in the emergency ward because they tried to resuscitate her, but they saw it was a lost cause, and then the doctor in charge of the emergency ward, Dr. Gilboa, quite a young woman but a very good doctor," Machluf Levy assured them, "I've seen her on the job a few times now," he said, and perhaps it even crossed his mind to go into details to prove the professional competence of Dr. Gilboa to them, but one look at Nahari's face and his fingers drumming with obvious impatience on the table nipped any such thought in the bud.

"Anyway," he continued, "she explained to the family, and to the kibbutz general director, that they had to do an autopsy on the body, and for that they had to transfer it to the Institute of Pathological Medicine in Abu Kabir."

"Just remind us again," said Shorer in a paternal tone, "and try to be precise, what the problem was, why they couldn't confirm that the cause of death was the reaction to the penicillin. Ohayon hasn't heard it from you yet, only what's written here in your report." He looked threateningly at Nahari, who stopped drumming on the table, studied his fingers carefully, cracked their joints one by one, and finally rested his chin on his palm.

"It's like this," said Machluf Levy, looking straight at Michael, who lit another cigarette without taking his eyes off the speaker. "It begins with the kibbutz nurse, a hired nurse. The kibbutz girls don't want to become nurses, it's out of fashion, so when the last one left they had to hire someone from outside, the first position they ever filled with a hired person, and some of the older people there said it would be the beginning of the end of the kibbutz. This hired nurse is leaving soon, at the end of the month, she's a thirty-four-year-old woman named Rifka Maimoni who everybody calls Rickie. She's an experienced nurse—she used to work at Barzilai Hospital, and she knows the whole staff there. So this nurse described what happened there like this: She said that the deceased had severe pneumonia, which was diagnosed by the kibbutz doctor, Dr. Reimer, who also works at the Soroka Hospital in Beersheba but lives on the kibbutz as a salaried doctor. This pneumonia that he diagnosed the night before, on Sunday, was severe, and he wanted to hospitalize her on Monday, but she objected."

"Who objected?" asked Michael. "The patient?"

Machluf Levy nodded and then corrected: "The deceased, the late Osnat Harel, objected to being hospitalized. The nurse, Rickie, told me that she was a stubborn woman with a will of her own, the type who doesn't like being told what to do. And he, the doctor, didn't know what kind of pneumonia it was—there are two kinds, one's infectious and the other one isn't, I forget the names," he said apologetically and looked at Michael, who shrugged as if to say, "Don't ask me."

"Viral and bacterial," said Nahari in a tired voice, "and the problem isn't whether or not it's infectious but whether treatment with antibiotics could have helped or not. Never mind, go on."

"They put her to bed in the kibbutz infirmary, and the nurse, on the doctor's instructions, gave her a shot of penicillin, like it says here in the report in the file."

"Procaine penicillin six hundred thousand units," said Nahari, scratching his smooth-shaven, pointed chin. "Why didn't she give her pills?"

"It was the doctor's decision, how should I know?" said Machluf Levy, shrugging his shoulders. "That's the treatment he decided on—he's the doctor, right?"

Nahari nodded, but it was obvious to everyone that something was bothering him. These vibrations now increased a tension that had seemed somewhat to have subsided. Anyone else might have let it go, but not Emanuel Shorer. With his characteristic directness and impatience with nuances he sharply asked, "What exactly is your problem?" Michael was afraid that he was going to explode and take Nahari to task for his transparent need to know better than everybody else.

"My problem is that as far as I know, if my memory doesn't deceive me," said Nahari with a false modesty that didn't deceive anybody, "that for two or three years now it hasn't been normal practice to give penicillin injections for pneumonia, and the preferred treatment is in tablet form. So I'd like to know what exactly happened here."

"Okay, so I didn't clarify that point and Dr. Gilboa didn't say anything about it," said Machluf Levy aggressively.

"Make a note to find out about it," Nahari instructed Michael, who unwillingly started writing a note with the new yellow pencil that had been lying next to the file, and which he had begun to chew a minute or two before, to check out the matter of the medication.

"Just a minute," said Nahari. "Before we go on, I want to understand something. The kibbutz doctor, the one who prescribed the injection—you didn't talk to him?"

"No," said Machluf Levy, "it didn't work out, he was on call at the hospital until the night after, and then he went straight to his army reserve duty, and I couldn't get ahold of him."

The expression on Nahari's face bordered on disgust, but there was also a faint note of triumph in his voice, as if his expectations had been confirmed. Inspector Machluf Levy had slipped up.

"The army isn't on the moon," he said indifferently, raising his eyes to the ceiling, then dropping them and giving Shorer an amused look.

"Can I go on?" said Machluf Levy, lighting a new cigarette and putting the lighter down next to the cardboard file into which he glanced from time to time.

"Go on, go on," Shorer encouraged him.

"So they gave her the shot, and Nurse Rickie sat with her for about twenty minutes, and everything was okay. And then she went away, because she had to be at the clinic on the other side of the kibbutz."

"And where was the doctor then?" asked Michael, and Machluf Levy replied, "That's it, he was in a big hurry, because he was on call at the hospital in Beersheba. That's what I said, that he works at Soroka."

"They left her alone in the infirmary?" asked Shorer in surprise.

"No, sir," Machluf Levy corrected him, "not alone, they've got home-care helps there in the infirmary, hired workers from outside the kibbutz. They've got shifts twenty-four hours a day, because there are two old people in the infirmary who can't take care of themselves. So they bring in the home helps for them, because over there they don't send their people to old-age homes or nursing homes."

"So she stayed there with the old people and the home help," said Nahari. "And then?"

"As far as the old people go," Machluf Levy said with a sigh, "you can't get a thing out of them, they're on their way out." He paused for a moment, as if for private reflection, sighed again, and said, "They're both out of it. You talk to them and they don't answer you. The old woman talks, but not to the point, and the old guy simply doesn't answer. So at about three o'clock, according to the home help, she heard noises coming from the room where the deceased was lying, and she went in, and the deceased was vomiting and choking, and then she let out a rattle and died."

"Who's this home help?" asked Shorer, paging through the file, and then said as if to himself, "Here we are, I see her signed statement." He rapidly read the document. "According to what it says here," he said slowly to his colleagues, who were also paging through their files, "she then telephoned the nurse, and the nurse came from the clinic and tried to resuscitate her and then called an ambulance. Go on, please," he said, turning to Machluf Levy, who took a deep breath and resumed his report.

"So they brought her to Barzilai Hospital, and from there they phoned us at the station in Ashkelon, and I arrived with Sergeant Kochava Strauss, and there they told us the facts, and Dr. Gilboa told me they needed an autopsy order to ascertain the cause of death."

Machluf Levy took a swallow of the juice in the bottle in front of him and listened to Nahari with an expression of concentration. "I understand that Dr. Gilboa's problem was the time?" Nahari asked rhetorically, and Levy nodded with his mouth still to the bottle and raised his eyes. "Yes," he confirmed when the bottle was empty, "she said that in her experience, and it was a well-known fact, an allergic reaction to penicillin appears immediately, not two hours later, like it did in this case."

"So what did she think?" asked Nahari in a gentler tone.

"She thought that it couldn't be an allergy to penicillin. That's what she said, like it says here in the report."

"And what was her guess in the matter?"

"That's just it, she didn't know; she said the body had to be transferred to Abu Kabir. And Nurse Rickie was standing there all the time saying they had to have the body transferred immediately, because she didn't want it on her conscience, she didn't want people to say that the deceased died on account of the injection she gave her and so on."

"So the situation is now that the body's in Abu Kabir and you have to go there to witness the autopsy. Why did it take so long for it to get there?" asked Shorer, paging through the file. "What did they waste half a day on?"

"Okay," said Machluf Levy, "you see how it is. Her mother-in-law was there in the hospital, an old woman, and her daughter, the deceased's daughter, a young girl of twenty-two, and the director of their kibbutz, and with people like that you can't just tell them what to do. They didn't agree. It took time to persuade them nicely. I wanted that order issued pronto, and in my experience," he said, looking challengingly at Nahari, "if you can persuade the family, and there's a more friendly atmosphere, you get cooperation, and the judge gives the order on the spot. And that's just what happened."

"Why didn't they agree?" asked Michael.

"Because the daughter said that she wanted to talk to her brother, who's in the army on a regimental exercise, and the old woman said that you had to let a person die in peace, and only the nurse, Rickie, and the kibbutz director thought that the autopsy should be performed right away. The family . . . it takes time to persuade them nicely. When all's said and done, you're dealing here with a family, and they've had a bad shock," he said apologetically. "But in the end they didn't have a choice; they're intelligent people, after all."

"But what happened is that in the meantime you found the letter?" said Michael.

"Yes, that's why I talked to Commander Shmerling, and he talked to the commissioner, and that's why the order for the postmortem was issued in Petah Tikva, on your turf." The latter part of the sentence was uttered in a glum, complaining tone.

"Okay, go on, what happened next?" asked Nahari. "I see that the nurse brought the syringe and ampule with her to the hospital and that you sent them to Forensics right away. And everything was in order—the syringe, the drug, there was nothing suspicious?"

Machluf Levy confirmed this. "No, and we praised the nurse for putting it all into a plastic bag and bringing it with the deceased to the hospital, and then after we talked to the family and all that, we drove to the scene of the event." He examined the gold ring on his finger closely and said, "The only pity is that we couldn't get hold of a sample of the vomit there in the infirmary. We tried everything, but the home help had done a really thorough job. She washed her gown that the deceased had vomited on and cleaned up the whole room. But we sent everything to be examined anyway, even the floor rag, over here to your lab."

"What made you decide to look for traces of the vomit?" asked Shmerling, the C.I.D. Southern District officer.

"Well, that's obvious, isn't it?" Machluf Levy said, waving his hand in the air. "We went there with a lab technician right away; the woman vomited, didn't she?"

"I wasn't complaining, I was just surprised."

"Why, wouldn't you have done the same?" protested Machluf Levy.

"I would, certainly," said Shmerling. "That's not the question, it's just—"

"It's just that you're waiting for me to screw up," Levy whispered defiantly. "Waiting for me to screw up," he repeated.

"Do me a favor, Machluf," said Shorer despairingly.

"Anyway," said Machluf Levy in a low voice, "obviously it would have saved trouble if there had been traces of the vomit, but they've got the stomach contents, so it doesn't matter all that much."

"And when and how did you discover the letter?" asked Nahari, looking at Levy with new interest, as if he had discovered something he hadn't expected in him.

Machluf Levy, busy with his own reflections, didn't notice the subtle change, the shadow of something new evident in Nahari's voice, and he said, "No, first of all, we were in the infirmary, and we didn't find anything incriminating there, at the actual scene of the event."

"Excuse me a minute," intervened Michael Ohayon, "but I'm still at the infirmary. When you came and began your examination there, you didn't find anything? Not the contents of a glass, a plate, nothing at all?"

"Nothing. Absolutely nothing. Everything was clean as a baby's bottom, and all the fingerprints were of people with legitimate access."

"Okay," said Nahari, "that's the problem with a kibbutz; everybody's got legitimate access there."

"No, I mean that when we compared them, we saw that all the fingerprints belonged to the people we'd seen there, the home help, the old people's relatives, and so on."

"And who was there in the infirmary?" asked Nahari, pushing his chair back and clasping his hands behind his neck.

"When? At the time of the event?"

"I don't know when; before the death, was there anyone there?"

"That's what I said before," said Machluf Levy. "The home help says that they brought her to the infirmary with the doctor and the nurse, and afterward the doctor left, and after that the nurse stayed and gave her the shot, and after that she left too. And after that, like I said before, the home help heard noises and . . . "

"And how did she reach the infirmary?" asked Michael.

"What do you mean, how?" asked Levy with a baffled expression on his face.

"What are the procedures there? When did she start feeling ill?"

"She had a fever on Saturday night and she went to bed, and on Sunday she was supposed to go on a trip somewhere, to Givat Haviva, I think, but she didn't have the strength to get up, and on Sunday afternoon she stayed in bed too, and her daughter took care of her and her two small children were with their grandmother, and on Monday morning when the doctor was there she phoned him, and he came to see her and removed her right away to the infirmary."

"And who knew that she was there?" asked Michael Ohayon, examining the yellow pencil in his hand.

"What do you mean?" Levy asked in bewilderment.

"Quite simply, who knew apart from the doctor and the nurse that she was in the infirmary?"

"I really don't know," Levy said, looking helplessly at Michael, who wrote something down in the margin of the paper in the file in front of him.

"Okay, when did you find the letter?" asked Nahari, looking at his watch. "We haven't got the rest of our lives to sit here listening to the whole story from the beginning. It's already twelve o'clock. We've been here for three and a half hours already, and we've reached nowhere."

Levy counterattacked: "You asked me, sir," he said, stressing each word separately. "I only told you what you wanted to know."

"Enough already of this childish squabbling," Shorer scolded. "Go on, Machluf." And Machluf Levy went on to recount at length, in exhaustive detail, how they had searched the deceased woman's house, and how they had found nothing suspicious, how he had gone with Moish to the dining hall, where the kibbutz director had pointed out Osnat's mailbox to him, and how, among all the other mail, they had come across the letter in question, and the director had identified the handwriting, the name, everything. And that was how it had come to light, the involvement of Member of the Knesset Aaron Meroz, member of the Education Committee and party faction secretary, and his intimate relations with Osnat, which had aroused the astonishment of Moish, who was quoted by Machluf Levy as saying, "What a pity, what a pity."

"So where do we stand now?" asked Shorer, turning first to Michael and then looking at Nahari.

"We have to be very clear," Nahari said. "I suggest we go into a couple of basic questions first and then send for Ohayon's team from our unit, and from here Ohayon goes to Abu Kabir, with or without Machluf Levy, and then we'll see from the results that the whole thing is a teapot tempest, with the cause of death the illness itself."

"Who dies of pneumonia these days?" protested Shmerling. "Nobody!"

"Maybe it wasn't pneumonia," said Shorer, closing the cardboard file. "Maybe the diagnosis was wrong. There are all kinds of viruses. There isn't much we can do until we get the autopsy report, and we have to talk to that home help again—what's her name?"

"Simcha Malul," said Machluf Levy.

"Did she have any kind of relationship with Osnat Harel?"

"She met her for the first time in the infirmary that day. They didn't know each other before," said Machluf Levy, adding after some thought, "And I didn't get the impression that we're talking about suicide here. The deceased was the kibbutz secretary, and her room was full of projects for the future, notes and ideas, and I talked to people too. Nobody said anything about any changes recently, except that nobody knew about her affair with M.K. Meroz."

"Didn't know, or didn't say?" muttered Nahari.

"Didn't say they knew." As he said this, Machluf Levy smiled for the first time that morning, a smile that made him look younger and less vulnerable. And now he looked like Uncle Jacques again. It seemed to Michael that Machluf Levy was recovering and getting back his orientation, that his sense of grievance was fading and that it would be possible to work with him. And, in fact, Michael now had no doubt that he would be a useful member of his team.

"There are no secrets on a kibbutz," Nahari announced, looking around for confirmation.

"That goes without saying," said Machluf Levy slowly, in a philosophical tone. "And the truth is there aren't any secrets anywhere, if you work hard enough. Even in a skyscraper in a big city there aren't any secrets. The only question is how long it takes to find them out." He twisted the gold ring around on his pinkie.

"What I meant was, how long can you keep an affair like that secret on a kibbutz? I know, I was a kibbutz member once. All you need is one visit to the laundry; what they don't tell you in the laundry they'll tell you in the sewing shop, and what they don't know in the sewing shop, if such a thing is possible," said Nahari, rolling his eyes, "you'll hear from the kibbutz nurse. A couple of conversations with the kibbutz nurse and you'll know everything there is to know."

"Not in this case," said Machluf Levy, and Michael wondered if he was imagining the crow of victory in his voice or if it was really there.

"You just have to know who to ask," Nahari insisted.

"Excuse me," protested Machluf Levy, "but in this case the nurse has no interest in hiding anything. First of all, she wants to leave. She's been planning it for a long time already, and they're just waiting to find a replacement. And even though she cooperated, she didn't have anything to tell me. Apart from which, she wants her name cleared. And to me it seems that she's in the clear. There's no motive. Apart from the fact that the deceased was very active, and the secretary of the kibbutz, and a war widow, from the Lebanon War, there aren't any stories about her. Even though she was such a looker, or that's what everybody says."

"So where did she meet him, M.K. Meroz?" inquired Shmerling.

"First of all, as far as I understand, they grew up together, as outside boarders on the kibbutz, so they met a long time ago," explained Machluf Levy. "She was originally from the Tel Aviv area, father unknown and the mother a shady character, it's not important now, and M.K. Meroz ended up there, on the kibbutz, after his father died, and he left—"

"Okay, okay, never mind all that now," said Nahari impatiently. "We'll get the details later, from the horse's mouth. So we've decided that Ohayon's going down to Abu Kabir and you're working on it together as of now, okay?"

"Yes, that's about it," said Shorer. "Michael, haven't you got anything to say?"

Michael nodded. "No problem," he said, "there's no problem," he said again, as if to convince himself.

"So what's the problem?" asked Shorer, the hint of a smile appearing at the corners of his lips.

Michael Ohayon stood up, gathered his papers and his car keys, smiled in return, and said nothing.

Shorer caught up with him in the broad corridor. He waved the miniature eyeglasses and then put them in his pocket. "Listen," he said to Michael, "I have to ask you something."

Michael sighed. He guessed the question. "Yes," he said to Shorer, "I saw."

"You saw how much he resembles him?" asked Shorer. "I thought I was going crazy." And then Shorer touched Michael's arm. "I was very attached to him, your uncle. He loved you very much," he said as he turned to go. "I've never told you this before, but he was always talking about you, long before I met you."

"Actually," said Michael to himself, "he doesn't look like him, not really. Only the smile."

6

"So you're with NUSCI now?" asked the secretary of the director of the Institute of Pathological Medicine with open admiration. "And you've already made chief superintendent? It's a pity you don't wear a uniform, it would suit you," she said smirking as she buzzed the director.

"A very good day to you, sir," said the director as he emerged from his office. "And how is His Honor today? We've got something to tell you."

"Have you finished?" asked Michael.

"Of course we've finished," said Dr. Hirsh, "but let's call Andre Kestenbaum, he did the autopsy."

"Are you trying to keep me in suspense?" asked Michael. "What is this, an educational exercise of some kind?"

"Coffee?" inquired Hirsh.

"First I want to know if I've got a case," said Michael, "and I've never worked with Andre Kestenbaum. I hardly know what he looks like."

"You've never worked with him because you haven't got agricultural districts in Jerusalem, but Kestenbaum's an expert on agriculture. Wait till you hear. And I don't understand why you're so tense." And then Hirsh smiled and said, "Your first case with NUSCI? What exactly is your status now? What are you, a section head? To this day I still don't understand the way things are structured there, exactly how it works."

"There's nothing to understand. Yes, I'm a section head, and if you've got any questions, you can ask Nahari—he's here every other day," said Michael, sitting down and stretching his legs out in front of him.

"Well, you know how it is, we're stuck here with the corpses," said Hirsh, smiling, "far away from all your troubles. And the good thing about the dead is that they don't talk. You people talk a lot, and now that you're a section head you can always send someone else here in your place. You've got twelve people under you there—how come you're doing us the honor in person?"

Michael smiled. "I didn't know that the rumor had reached you."

"What, that you don't like coming here? To watch us at work on the stiffs? Come off it!"

Michael smiled and said nothing.

"So it's a serious unit, NUSCI, only cases that aren't funny?" Hirsh looked at him with amusement and then said, "Don't take any notice, I'm just letting off steam. It's godawful work here, and there aren't too many people here I can laugh with."

"If we're already talking about cases, what about this one? When do you intend telling me?"

"In a second," said Hirsh, his face growing serious. "I really do want you to hear it from Kestenbaum, because the credit belongs to him."

Michael looked around the big, simply furnished room. Bookshelves made of light wood lined the walls, and there were three long tables, in addition to the desk behind which Dr. Hirsh was now sitting, the telephone receiver in his hand, ordering coffee and asking for Dr. Kestenbaum to be sent to his office. The barred window behind the desk overlooked a big lawn that separated the little white building from the busy road beyond.

The slender man who entered the room even before the coffee was brought in wore a gold ring too, on his ring finger rather than his pinkie, and not as thick as Machluf Levy's. Michael remembered having seen him a couple of times at meetings, where he always sat quietly in a corner.

"I'll be leaving you now," said Hirsh. "I've got another postmortem to perform. Give him the diagnosis," he said, smiling at Kestenbaum. "He doesn't know what he's in for."

They sat on either side of Hirsh's desk, and Andre Kestenbaum put the long package of Kent Lights and the slender black lighter down on it between them.

At the top of his white gown the collar of a blue nylon shirt and a tie peeped out, and his hands playing with the lighter on the desk were covered with liver spots, betraying the fact that he was quite an old man in spite of his deceptively supple movements. His face too was covered with brown blotches, and his scant hair, combed back like that of the actors in old American movies, exposed a high, lined forehead, giving his face an expression that combined surprise with disapproval. There was something touching about his eagerness to talk. He began talking as soon as he sat down, and he didn't stop except to listen to the few questions Michael succeeded in slipping into his monologue.

He began, "Abroad I was not only pathologist, but investigating doctor, both, how to put it, both doctor and detective."

Michael nodded and asked politely where he came from. "Transylvania," replied Kestenbaum. "Eight years I am here, but I am working in the police in Hungary before." Michael waited. "Before I give you the findings," said Kestenbaum, "please to hear what I have to say about the method of investigation in general." And then came a long lecture about how abroad, not like in Israel, the body was not transferred from the scene of the crime to the Institute of Forensic Medicine, but the investigating doctor was summoned to the crime scene, and nothing was touched until the real boss, the investigating doctor, arrived.

Despite the heavy Rumanian-Hungarian accent, despite the awkward Hebrew, despite the details that were irrelevant to this or any other subject, Michael Ohayon was determined not to miss a single word, and he placed the tape recorder on the desk between them. Dr. Andre Kestenbaum made no objections, but with an ostensibly indifferent shrug of his shoulders made his pleasure at being the center of attention abundantly clear to Michael, who was painfully aware, through his tense anticipation, of how rarely in Kestenbaum's life he had the satisfaction of knowing that his words had real significance in the ears of his listener.

"Okay," said Michael, "so could you tell me, please, what she died of?"

"Parathion," replied the pathologist, looking intently at Michael. "But I have not been able yet to write the report."

"Parathion?" repeated Michael, startled. "Are you sure?"

"I have examined contents of the stomach, the liver, the bones. I have found parathion."

"Yes, I understand," said Michael, bewildered. "But what on earth made you look for parathion? Why should anyone . . . " He recovered his composure, brought his voice under control, and continued in a more deliberate tone. "As far as I know, you only find parathion if you look for it. What made you think of looking for it in the first place?"

"This I explain, if you wish," promised Kestenbaum in a more animated tone.

"Of course I wish," protested Michael. "It's lucky you found it, no? Were there any symptoms that indicated the possibility of parathion poisoning?"

Kestenbaum shook his head several times. "No symptoms if you do not look for it. In any case, she arrived here too late." This led to another lecture on the investigating methods abroad, and then Kestenbaum wiped his forehead and said, "This is question of experience. I have much experience of death in agricultural districts, this is the reason I look for parathion. And also I have once a similar case, before many years."

They were both silent, and then Kestenbaum said, gazing at the tips of his shoes in false modesty, "I have also written a book on this matter, the textbook studied in Faculty of Law."

"Is that so?" said Michael.

"Yes, yes," said Kestenbaum firmly, "in Hungary, to say the truth."

"How did the parathion get into her system? Can you tell at all?"

"Naturally," said Kestenbaum, waving Michael's anxiety aside, "so, there are number of ways. I don't think through skin, because if parathion is placed on skin, in the right amount, you can die instantaneous. But it is also in stomach. I think by drinking, maybe eating plums."

"Are you talking about suicide?" asked Michael, touching the knob of the tape recorder, which Kestenbaum regarded complacently.

"All will be written in report we shall write soon," he promised. "I don't know if suicide, or accident, or murder. This is already your work with data."

"You said you had a similar story in the past?" asked Michael. "Could that help me?"

Kestenbaum shrugged his shoulders with an ingenuous expression on his face. "I have many stories, oho, how many stories! But once I have the case with pneumonia, I can tell you this case."

"Please do," said Michael, and Kestenbaum took a long drag on his cigarette and then said, with a warning look, "I shall tell like narration, yes?" and he began without even waiting for confirmation from Michael, who nodded wordlessly, folded his arms, leaned back in his chair, and stretched his legs out in front of him without taking his eyes off the narrator.

"One day at end of month of December, I received telephone as forensic doctor, that child age three has died during treatment with penicillin at public clinic, for diagnosis of pneumonia. The mother brings the child age almost three to clinic for injection of penicillin by nurse on duty there, only she is there because of date which is twenty-fifth December, the birthday of Jesus," and here he looked uncertainly at Michael and asked hesitantly, "Yes? You say it so?" and Michael said, "Yes, yes," in a reassuring, encouraging tone, and Kestenbaum's face resumed the dramatic expression it had worn at the beginning of his story.

"And even though it is not the official holiday, still it is holiday. After twenty-five minutes from the penicillin injection, while the mother is sitting and speaking all kinds of nonsense with the nurse, they hear noise outside and find child in stage of dying, and after few minutes the child dies in the government clinic." Here Kestenbaum paused for a moment, as if to allow his audience to digest the facts, and Michael felt the need to utter an "Aha" of simultaneous confirmation and thanks in order to maintain some pretense of a dialogue. "The problem now arises," continued Kestenbaum, "if the child died of anaphylactic shock from penicillin. And this diagnosis is job of forensic doctor, to prepare report if it is shock or not."

Here Kestenbaum took a deep breath, turned his face aside, and explained to the corner of the desk, "I tell you now little details only, but I have written on this subject entire book."

Michael nodded and said, "Yes, yes, I remember."

The pathologist lowered his eyes modestly again and continued, "I get a telephone from the district attorney to go to the scene, for as I am already telling you, we never move body to Institute of Forensic Medicine first, because moving body can cause all kinds of other things too. Now—" the pathologist straightened up and waved the hand holding his cigarette, "I . . . the story . . . " he hesitated, "I tell true story now: I say to the attorney that according to story which they tell, that child died about thirty minutes after penicillin injection, this is one hundred percent not case of anaphylactic shock, because such shock comes few minutes after injection! Cause of death must be pneumonia or something else, but not penicillin injection. Since death occurred in government institution the attorney decides there will be examination of forensic doctor only. I went to perform autopsy."

The tape recorder whispered, and the pathologist took a deep breath. "I went to perform autopsy in framework of state clinic where he died. I found no signs of anaphylactic shock to penicillin. I found no signs of violence which can explain cause of death, however . . . " Michael suppressed a smile; the curious mixture of acquired figures of speech such as the the word *however* side by side with the crude mistakes and other peculiarities gave Kestenbaum's speech an inimitably eccentric quality and betrayed the fact that Hebrew was not and would never be his language. "However," continued Kestenbaum, unsuspectingly convinced that he was speaking fluent Hebrew, "in stomach contents I found mud containing chocolate at initial stages of digestion. Among other samples I took, among all kinds of things what we take for examination," he said absentmindedly, as if there was no point in troubling the listener with scientific details he would not understand, "I took also stomach contents, because I thought from the beginning that the chocolate found in stomach contents they bought it in the countryside, and I know that in such places there are many mices in the food and there are instructions to kill the mices with pesticides, and so I thought that maybe the mices with their feet go in this powder, and then leave some poison on the chocolate. Maybe, maybe, maybe"—with every "maybe" the doubt increased, the wishful note grew more pronounced—"maybe the child died from this."

When Michael listened and relistened to the tape later, he heard in that thrice-repeated "maybe" the entire spectrum of feelings he knew so well in his own work. It was all there—the prayer for a solution, at least for a lead, the pride at the intuition itself, the willingness to follow every lead however insubstantial, and above all, the familiar mixture of enormous pride in hitting on the right solution and the doubt lurking in wait for that pride. It wasn't false modesty, but the doubt a man casts on his own intuition, the inability to believe that it could lead to the truth—all this was contained in that "maybe, maybe, maybe." And in the intonation of the repetition there was also a kind of musical climax after which Kestenbaum appeared to be calling himself to order and returned to a normal speaking voice.

He lowered his eyes to the desk again and went on with his story. "The toxicological tests performed day after the autopsy showed that the chocolate contained pesticide by name of parathion. Parathion is phospho-organic substance. One gram of parathion can cause death of five people weighing sixty kilos minimum. A child that age, three years old, a few milligrams is enough to kill him. As soon I knew that cause of death was the pesticide parathion that was in the chocolate, I went immediately to scene of the event, before they bury the body." And here he mentioned the fact that "abroad they bury the dead only after two, three days after he dies." Michael nodded.

"I asked mother where they buy chocolate for child in question from. It was Christian holidays, and they buy chocolate for childrens only on holidays. I tell nobody except attorney investigating cause of death my suspicion. So mother tells me that she got chocolate in mail from first girlfriend of ex-husband, which sent a little parcel with all kinds sweets, altogether one pound maximum, and she gives me address. And she tells me that her ex-husband was with this woman together two years, from the same village, and on Sunday at some folks-dancing in the village hall, now called Palace of Youth and Culture, suddenly the husband leaves girlfriend and goes to dance with present wife, and he whispers in her ear, 'Do you want to marry me, because next week I have to marry that other woman and I don't want her, I want you.' She agreed, and the same day that he had to marry the first woman he married her. On the wedding day the first woman left the village in disgrace and went to live in another village far away. Fruit of the marriage—present child, now deceased."

Dr. Kestenbaum leaned back and breathed deeply. Then he leaned forward and resumed talking. Michael was spellbound, hypnotized, as caught up in the story as a small child, like Yuval when once in a blue moon he would tell him a really spooky story and the boy would hold his breath not only in fear—Michael would hold his hand in the dark bedroom—but also in suspense.

"Since the marriage they had no contact with the first woman. Before one year since child's death, the husband has left her too, gone to town, where at present resides with woman having ten years older than him. Occupation in town, bus driver. This third woman, from economic point of view, very well-to-do. On receipt of parcel for son from first woman, she, the mother, thinks first woman still in love with husband, and for this reason sends parcel to husband's son. I, as forensic doctor and detective, immediately request remains of parcel, and she hands over small cardboard box containing two wafers in shape of triangle, name of Delta, three little bars of chocolate, name of Rom."

"Rum?" asked Michael.

"Yes, yes, Rom," repeated Kestenbaum. "And six sweets in cellophane which is put on pine tree."

"You mean fir tree?"

"Yes, the tree for Christmas holiday," explained Kestenbaum, and once again his music began, softly at first and then building up to a crescendo. "The cardboard box was covered with very thin paper, of yellow color, today they make this paper of white color, last time it was used maybe ten years before. On this paper is written name of expediter—you say sender?" Michael nodded. "That's it, the name is written there. That same night I knocked on door of this sender, and to my astonishment she says she never sent any parcel and since more than three years she has no contact whatsoever with village, and especially not with that family, which she hates to death." The last word was pronounced with all the venom in which it had apparently been originally uttered.

"After interrogation lasting more than three hours, I conclude that it really wasn't her which sent that parcel. I returned the same night—" he grimaced, exposing his teeth in a kind of smile, and corrected himself: "the same morning—" another grimace was followed by the final version: "The same night-morning I returned to the mother and requested address of her husband. The husband was bus driver in exact same town where I work myself. To house of this person I went the same day. He already knows of death of son, he is too upset to answer our questions. Please to come back after funeral. After few days I obtain search warrant for his house. We go there and question the husband and his mistress. No, they sent no parcel whatsoever, they know nothing about it, he only pays alimonies for the child and the wife for more than one year now, and above the alimonies he sends nothing. After conducting search of premises, I find same yellow paper which is no longer made for years, I find this paper there, in little room—" here Kestenbaum took a deep breath, crushed his cigarette stub and lit a new one, and suddenly looking sharply at Michael, asked, "You were born here in country or abroad?"

"Abroad," replied Michael, wondering what this was leading to.

"But not in Eastern Europe," stated Kestenbaum.

"No, no," said Michael, "in Morocco."

"Aha, so you don't know. I explain. There in Hungary, or Rumania, or Poland, there is no refrigerator, only little room."

"A pantry?" inquired Michael.

"What?" said Kestenbaum. "How do you say it?" He repeated the word with some effort, and then took up his story again, in the tone of someone providing unimportant information in parentheses. "And together with all the pencils, pens, inks, I took this too, I made inventory of everything. In police laboratory we compare ink with ink of address on parcel and result—negative!"

Michael raised his eyebrows and made a clucking noise, and Kestenbaum smiled as if to a child and said, "One moment, this is not the end."

"So what did you do then?" asked Michael.

"We took more than thirty schoolgirls who know the family, because we know, from psychological point of view, the address is written by young girl, not man. Over there," he leaned forward, and with a sly, contemptuous expression he said, "Over there investigations are conducted differently," and with this he concluded his criticism of the Institute of Pathological Medicine, and the country as a whole, for the day, and without waiting for Michael's reaction he went on: "With each one we wrote thirty times the address with the same letters. From the graphological point of view, none of them matched."

He put his cigarette down on the edge of the ashtray in order to free his hand to thump on the glass plate covering the desktop with a gesture that said, "That's it, it looked as if everything was lost." Immediately he raised his eyes to Michael's attentive and concentrated face, and when he was satisfied that the latter was listening with the proper curiosity, he went on to say, "In meantime I sent paper I found in— how you say?—panty?"

"Pantry," corrected Michael, and Kestenbaum nodded. "To make examination with edges of paper on parcel." Here he took a piece of paper from the corner of the desk, tore it in two, and demonstrated the manner in which the two sides matched each other. "Good," he said, "you know these examinations, when they make microscopic photographs of these things, very difficult work."

Michael's knowing nod was lost on Kestenbaum, who kept his eyes on the paper and went on talking. "After two weeks I receive results that edges of paper which I found matches one hundred percent to paper which was on parcel, so now we know parcel was sent from house of husband." Kestenbaum sighed as if he had delivered himself of the crux of the matter. Michael lit a cigarette and offered the pack to the man sitting opposite him, who glanced at it contemptuously and said, "Since strike at Dubek cigarette factory I smoke only import."

"What happened next?" asked Michael.

Kestenbaum sighed. "From legal point of view to prove they sent the parcel was impossible. But we already knew wrapping paper of parcel came from there. Our last card to prove in court they sent parcel was only psychological card. But now comes main, basic problem—how do I know that chocolate which he ate came from that parcel? Maybe there was other chocolate also. Mother told us after injection she said to child, 'If you let nurse give you injection, I give you chocolate.' In toxicological laboratory of Institute of Forensic Medicine, of three bars of Rom chocolate I took from parcel I gave mices one bar. The mices ate it up—nothing happened. I gave them all the wafers and all the Christmas-tree sweets to other group of mices—the mices live. Only two bars of chocolate remain in original wrapping." He paused for a moment, looked at Michael with open enjoyment, and then continued, stressing every word: "In presence of attorney I give group of seven mices one bar, we wait three hours—mices hundred percent healthy. One bar remains. I say to the attorney, 'Let's try this one.' He gives a good look at wrapping, which is so original as if nobody ever opened it, and he says to me, why wait three hours for mices, I eat it now myself."

Kestenbaum smiled slyly at Michael, and Michael smiled back. "I open the outside paper. I see chocolate covered with original silver paper. After I remove this too, on upper surface of chocolate, where is written Rom, I see gray stripe, the rest is shiny. We give a bit of gray stripe to one mice, the mice dies on the spot. We give the rest of mices more of chocolate remaining—all the mices die. In examination of blood of dead mices we find parathion. In examination of traces of substance on chocolate—parathion. So now everybody knows that chocolate with parathion is sent by husband," concluded Kestenbaum with the triumphant expression of one writing Q.E.D. at the end of a theorem.

Michael nodded and said, "Nice work, congratulations." Kestenbaum lowered his eyes demurely, as if he hadn't heard, and said, "Wait, that isn't the end."

"I imagine so," said Michael, folding his arms and stretching out his legs.

"The next day, I know he is driving the bus. I know what stations he stops. Together with director of bus station, at exactly two o'clock I get on bus and take him off, I put him in jeep, and we bring him to courthouse where prosecuting attorney waits. Before this we arrest the mistress which we put in the corridor, and when we lead him down the corridor he sees her there between two policemen, under arrest."

"Hmm," said Michael reflectively.

"In first interrogation conducted in prosecuting attorney's office we say, 'Listen here, your mistress has told us everything. If you want to be state witness, you can get less time—she already told us everything.' And then he said, 'For that bitch I killed my child.'"

Kestenbaum's tone now became almost indifferent, as if from now on he was recounting the dull part of the story. As in a detective story, thought Michael. The thrilling part is the process and not the predictable end. "And he says that this woman wants to kick him outside because of his wages he has to give one-third for alimonies for child. What can he do—only kill child. So then she tells him how to kill child. She talked to expert laboratory technician of pesticide spraying, she knew how much required to cause death. That same night they went to this technician, she put with a pipette the parathion in that two chocolates of the Rom, and also this young technician wrote the address. In opposite room another team already tells to mistress the same story: 'If you confess, et cetera.' We arrest the technician."

"Why did the technician help them?" asked Michael, and Kestenbaum looked at him in bewilderment and said, as if nothing could be more obvious, "For money, of course." After which he went on as if there had been no interruption. "After about four hours there was clear case against all three for causing death by parathion. The husband got nineteen years. The mistress got eighteen years, the technician got six years."

"Congratulations, nice work," repeated Michael, shaking his head to emphasize his admiration.

"I tell you something," said the pathologist, ignoring this praise. "Before eight years I come here, there was no standard. But now too I see the work here is dry, very dry. Over there we are investigators. When I come here and meet the people from Pathological Medicine Institute, I tell them, we have to be on the scene of crime. And this is just one little, little story. I have others, many, ah, how many stories I have! For days I can tell you."

"I'm sure," said Michael, glancing at his watch. "I'd really like to hear them. Maybe we can meet one day, if you're willing."

"Why not?" said Kestenbaum with an indifference that did not succeed in disguising his eagerness, and Michael felt guilty about his own professional success, about his relative youth, about his undisputed belonging to this country and its culture, about the easiness of his life, and he almost had to suppress an impulse to put out his hand and touch Dr. Kestenbaum—even though he had already shown him as much appreciation as he could without exaggerating, without sounding ironic (and the pathologist's eccentric Hebrew, together with his self-important expression, had certainly invited irony). But why should he feel guilty and pampered vis-à-vis this man, who was a senior pathologist at the institute? In order to relieve the oppressive feeling to which his guilt gave rise, and also because he really wanted to know, he asked for an explanation of the way parathion operated.

"I explain, I explain everything," said Kestenbaum like an impatient child. "I also show you everything immediately," he promised, raising his eyes to the ceiling and saying rapidly, "Parathion is poison of chemical cholinesterase, used for chemical warfares worldwide. Acetylcholine, causing action of muscles including breathing and heart muscles, affected central nervous system depressed and death following. Come with me, I show you." He stood up, and Michael rose too and followed him down the wide corridors to a side room, where Kestenbaum took a little key hanging from a wooden board and turned into another room, with Michael obediently following him.

In the second room the pathologist stood in front of a gray metal cupboard with a large lock on its door, opened the lock with the little key, and pointed to the shelf, saying, "Here, here you have everything." On the shelf stood jars and bottles, and in the room there was an unpleasant smell of mice and chemicals. Kestenbaum leaned against the wall. "Please," he said, "please, you can see everything, what it says on bottles, everything." From the next room they heard somebody call, "Who took the key?"

"I, here, I took it, don't worry," said Kestenbaum, and he whispered to Michael, "Doctor Cassuto, our toxicologist." A couple of seconds later a man in a white gown appeared, not young but younger than Kestenbaum. Cassuto remembered Michael's rank and the purpose of his visit but not his name.

Michael introduced himself to the toxicologist and said, "So show me where the parathion is in all this treasure trove you've got here."

"Here you are," said Dr. Cassuto in a sabra accent, and he took out a silvery metal bottle and held it in his hand. "Even holding it like this is dangerous," he warned.

Kestenbaum, who was standing to one side, nodded and said, "Oho!" Michael, looking at the bottle and reading with interest the writing on the label—"FOLIDOL E 605. 45.7%"—sensed Dr. Andre

Kestenbaum shrinking, standing in the corner like a timid child trying to take up as little room as possible.

"And is that what it looks like on the market?" asked Michael. "Do they sell it in a bottle like that?"

"The bottle's manufactured in Germany," said Cassuto in an indifferent, self-confident voice. "This is the undiluted substance. For agricultural use it's diluted. It has to be dissolved too. In a special substance—it doesn't dissolve in water. And here in Israel it's supposed to be prohibited to market it without a special license."

"Nonsense," exclaimed Kestenbaum from the corner. "In territories you can find this everywhere."

"Yes," Cassuto agreed, "it's available in the territories, and it's also misused there. They use parathion for all the murders to do with family honor and other internal matters, but I was talking about the prohibition against using it."

"That is also not correct," protested Kestenbaum, "not correct at all. You don't remember the case of the girl with the kerosene?"

He turned to Cassuto rebukingly, and Cassuto, momentarily defeated, said, "Yes, that was a terrible case, of a girl who washed her hair with kerosene, to get rid of head lice, and the kerosene was mixed with parathion, and she never made it out of the bath. She died instantly."

"And the grandmother? What about the grandmother?" demanded Kestenbaum.

"Yes, there was a case of a grandmother who was treating her little grandson for lice, the same story. Kerosene mixed with parathion, and instant death."

"There are plenty stories," said Kestenbaum in a slightly contemptuous tone, "plenty, so many as you want. Only yesterday colleague here told me he wants to spray hedge against—never mind—against something, and his wife brings him spray from pharmacy and he looks on label, at back, where it says composition, and what does he see? What does he see?" He addressed Cassuto with an expression of open rebuke: "He sees it says there parathion!" he said triumphantly. "So what does it mean against the law?"

"I never said it was illegal. I never said parathion was banned in Israel; all I said was that the Ministry of Agriculture has stopped using it," replied Cassuto indifferently.

"Don't hold it like that!" Kestenbaum cried suddenly and gingerly took the bottle away from Michael, who was turning it around in his hands.

"How dangerous can a bottle like this be—it's hermetically closed, no?" said Michael apologetically, and the two men looked at him with pity.

Kestenbaum returned the bottle to its place on the metal shelf in the metal cupboard and said chidingly, "You know how it is strong? Three drops of this on skin, and you are in another world!"

"It's undiluted, see, we get it in a concentrated form of almost fifty percent," said Cassuto. "It has to be diluted and dissolved for use."

"You remember story I told you with blanket?" Kestenbaum asked the toxicologist. "Tell him."

"Yes," said Cassuto with a bored expression, "he can tell you about death as a result of contact with a woolen blanket that was formerly on a horse treated with parathion against fleas. And the man who used the blanket to cover himself afterward died."

"And how he died!" said Kestenbaum gaily. "He was in the middle to make love and suddenly—dead!" He smiled to himself and then grew grave. "Also that is case I investigated abroad."

"Sorry, I didn't know," Michael apologized, and then he asked, "What's parathion's l.d.?"

"Twenty milligrams to sixty kilos lethal dose," said Kestenbaum confidently.

"I'm not sure that's the exact dosage," said Cassuto doubtfully.

Kestenbaum flushed and raised his voice: "I tell you so, I know."

"Why do we have to know when we can look it up and calculate it exactly?" asked Cassuto, locking the cupboard and checking the lock before returning with them to the other room, where after hanging the key in its place he pulled a thick volume from the bookshelf, paged through it muttering "parathion, parathion," and turned to Michael, asking, "Can you read German?"

"No, to my regret," replied Michael.

"That's a pity, otherwise I could have given you a lot of stuff to read," Cassuto said and went on leafing through the book.

"A waste of time," muttered Kestenbaum, "I tell you already, twenty to sixty kilos. Why you don't believe me?"

"We'll see in a minute, let's see what's written here," said Cassuto with unruffled calm, and then he called, "Here, I found it. Parathion, lethal dose: one-third of a milligram, per kilo, that is."

"Twenty milligram to sixty kilos, like I said, no?"

"A teaspoon is five cc, in other words, less than a quarter of a tea-spoon," pronounced Cassuto, ignoring the cry of triumph uttered by Kestenbaum, who looked at him with undisguised hatred, almost tak-ing Michael's hand as he said, "We finished here, yes?"

"Yes," Michael said. He glanced at his watch, which told him it was six o'clock in the evening. "So," he said to Kestenbaum as the lat-ter accompanied him to the roofed parking lot, where only two cars were now parked, "on the kibbutzim, do they still use parathion?"

"Not officially. Officially no, but agronomists of older generation like this poison for spray. Maybe they have some there, why not? You can get it from Germany."

Before starting the car, Michael shook the hand again extended to him by Kestenbaum, who stood next to the window and said in a low voice, his eyes on the ground, "Only if you have opportunity, please to mention that it was I who found—"

"Of course, what a question! You'll get all the credit," said Michael, and he started the Ford Fiesta.

7

"So how long have you been with NUSCI?" asked Machluf Levy as they turned off the highway onto the road leading to the kibbutz.

"Not long, two months," said Michael uncomfortably.

"You made it in record time, that's what I heard anyway," remarked Inspector Levy, resting his arm on the open window.

Michael said nothing.

"They could have sent you here, to be the Lachish Subdistrict C.O.," Levy continued pensively.

"Yes, but they decided on the Serious Crimes Unit," said Michael, looking at the green-and-gold expanses stretching out on both sides of the narrow road. Cliches about pastoral peace and quiet, about the quality of this dusk light on these rolling fields passed through his mind. He was tense and thought about his brother-in-law Ami, his older sister Yvette's husband, who had done his reserve duty during the Lebanon War in the regional military headquarters office.

He had been on a team consisting of one other officer and a doctor, and together they had functioned as what since the Yom Kippur War had been known as a "death squad," notifying the families of those killed in action. During the whole time he had come home evenings and without saying a word to anyone, without eating or taking a shower, had gone straight to the bedroom, where he shut himself in and lay on the bed for hours staring at the wall. When he was discharged he had ceased to function. He would go to the garage he owned in partnership with his younger brother and sit behind the desk in the office, staring at the invoices and accounts.

In one of her moments of despair Yvette had left the children with her mother-in-law and gone to meet Michael for lunch in Jerusalem. So rare were such meetings between them that Michael had spent two entire days choosing the right place. When he was finally sitting opposite her in the Chinese restaurant on Helene Hamalka Street, with the spareribs he had ordered in front of her, she had told him, choking with tears, the story of this past year of her marriage. She told him about his nightmares, about his black humor with its macabre jokes, about his total lack of interest in her and the children, and she had also hinted, with great embarrassment, at their lack of any sex life.

"Talk to him," she had begged. "Somebody has to talk to him." And later, pushing the dish of Chinese vegetables aside—and Yvette was a lover of Chinese food—she said, "Even though you're ten years younger than he is, he respects you. I don't know why he thinks so much of you, but you've got to talk to him." And she began to cry again.

Michael, who had completely lost his appetite, paid the check and took her for a walk in the direction of Mea Shearim. She continued talking all the way, and he quietly listened. From time to time he put a comforting arm around her shoulder, and finally, when she fell silent, he sat down with her in a little café and said, "Of course I'll talk to him if you want me to. But he needs professional counseling of some kind; you realize that one talk won't solve anything, don't you?"

"You don't know what it's like," said Ami when they met the next day. "The worst are the stiff-upper-lips, the Ashkenazis, the ones with style. They don't scream, they don't say anything. One night I was sitting in the car with the doctor waiting for it to get light, before the announcement on the news. You sit in a car and look at the house and wait for it to get light, for it to be five o'clock in the morning, and you know that inside that house people are sleeping peacefully, and you know that you're sitting there like the Angel of Death and you're about to destroy their lives." And Ami had covered his face with his big hands.

Machluf Levy broke into Michael's thoughts: "And how are you doing?" he inquired.

"It seems okay, no problems," replied Michael, turning the steering wheel sharply to avoid a big stone in the middle of the road. "What's this? Has the Intifada reached here too?" he asked in order to change the subject.

"Well, we're not so far from Gaza here—of course there are problems. And with that business in Ashdod, and all the searches for the kidnapped soldier, it isn't easy. There's no lack of work, I can tell you."

"I've got a son in the army now," said Michael without knowing why.

"Really?" Levy asked with interest. "Where?"

"In Nahal. Now his unit is in the territories, in Bethlehem. It'll take a while until he gets out, because he started a year late," Michael volunteered.

"Why a year late?" asked Machluf Levy suspiciously.

"Because he spent a year with his group in Beit Shean first," said Michael apologetically, "and then he signed on with the regular army, so it works out to a long term of service. He's just turned twenty."

"I've got two sons in the army," said Machluf Levy with a sigh. "One in the Golani Brigade and the other one's stationed here in Julis, near home. Have you got any other kids?"

Michael shook his head. "Only the one," he said.

"It's no good being an only child, it's hard on them. I've got five. A full house."

"All boys?" asked Michael as they reached the big metal gate of the kibbutz.

"Four boys and a girl," said Machluf Levy, leaning out of the window as Michael drew up next to the guard. "We're here to see the kibbutz general director," he said and pulled his ID out of his pocket. The guard, a young man in dark blue work clothes and army boots, looked at the car and nodded wordlessly. He pressed a button, and the electric gate slowly opened.

"Is there always a guard here?" asked Michael.

"Always," Levy absentmindedly replied, "but they don't always shut the gate when it's still light, only at night. Now, because of . . . because of the situation, they're stricter." He sighed.

"The Intifada," said Michael, again feeling the weight of responsibility for the imminent disruption of the pastoral peace of this place, with its soft, fresh, green lawns, its white-roofed houses with their curtains waving in the pure air, its people on the neat paths—among them two old women driving golf carts who had stopped to converse loudly—while a police car made its way slowly toward the kibbutz secretary's office. Everything will be destroyed in an instant, thought Michael, it will all crack and collapse after the Pandora's box is opened. Then he shook himself and again reminded himself that perhaps they were only dealing with a suicide, and for that there were more than a few precedents in the kibbutz movement.

"Yes, of course, the Intifada," said Inspector Levy. "Here you turn right—here, park here," he called out, smoothing an invisible wrinkle in his uniform trousers.

Michael looked at the man who rose to greet them as they entered the office. His face was tanned, but its expression was anguished. "Do you want something to drink? Coffee? Something cold?" he asked, looking at Machluf Levy, whom he had already met.

"Something cold," Levy said and looked at Michael, who nodded and watched the man's neat movements as he poured juice into glasses from a plastic jug he had taken out of a little refrigerator in the corner of the room.

"Where are the others?" asked Machluf Levy. "We want to talk to the family too."

"Yes, I've told them. We'll go there in a minute," the man promised, and Levy now remembered to say, "This is Chief Superintendent Michael Ohayon of the National Unit for the Investigation of Serious Crimes, who is heading the SIT."

"SIT?"

"Special Investigation Team. They've brought in reinforcements because of . . . never mind. And this," he turned to Michael, "is Moshe Ayal, the general director of the kibbutz. But everybody calls him Moish," he added with a smile, and Michael shook the hand extended to him. Then Moish turned to the desk, which was piled with papers, sat down with a sigh, and pointed to the chairs opposite him.

"Sit down," he said in a lifeless voice. He turned to Machluf Levy. "And what's this unit for investigating serious crimes? It's not part of your outfit?"

Machluf Levy replied with a negative cluck of his tongue. "They're out in Petah Tikva," he added, pursing his lips in a contemptuous expression.

"NUSCI is a unit that investigates cases that are of ostensible public interest," said Michael, hearing echoes of Nahari behind the "ostensible."

"Yes?" asked Moish. "What public interest? And who's talking about an investigation anyway?" The second question had a note of open alarm.

"The public interest stems from the involvement of M.K. Aaron Meroz," Michael slowly replied, "and as far as the investigation is concerned, there always is one in a case of unnatural death, and there are a number of possibilities arising from the pathological examination."

"You didn't say anything about this to me," Moish burst out with alarm in Machluf Levy's direction. "What possibilities are you talking about?"

"I couldn't have known before the autopsy," Levy apologized. "We only got the final results this morning."

"We now think," said Michael, "that there are a number of possibilities to explain the . . . the death of Osnat Harel. The first, most simple explanation, is that it was an accident, but as you'll soon see, this is extremely unlikely. And suicide is a possibility too. But we also have to take the possibility of murder into account."

"Murder? What murder?" whispered Moish. "Where? Murder— here? Osnat? Tell me," now the anticipated anger began to seethe in his voice, "have you got any idea of what the word *kibbutz* means?" And without waiting for a response, he announced, "You don't know what you're talking about. You can eliminate murder right away. There's never been a murder here, and there never will be!" With a trembling hand he moved a piece of paper that was lying on a corner of the desk. "It's just not possible. I don't understand, what did Osnat d— die of? What did they find in the autopsy?" he finally shouted, when neither of them replied immediately.

Michael searched for a soothing tone and said quietly, "Of parathion poisoning."

Machluf Levy opened his mouth in astonishment and stared at Michael, who avoided his eyes. "That's privileged," he whispered to the room at large. "How could you tell him like that?" he protested in alarm, wiping his forehead.

Moish buried his face in his hands. When he looked up, his face was white as a sheet. He put his hand on his stomach. "Just a minute, excuse me," he said. He stood up quickly, bent over a brown leather briefcase standing between the chair and the window, took out a big bottle, and swallowed a mouthful of a white liquid that left its traces around his lips. Then he said, "Just a minute, just a minute," and left the room.

"Why did you tell him about the parathion? How can they polygraph him now?" complained Machluf Levy.

"I'll explain afterward." Michael replied. "But don't forget that this is a kibbutz; there's no other way of getting through to them." From the toilet next door they heard sounds of throat-clearing and coughing.

"He's vomiting," announced Machluf Levy. Michael was silent. "So are you going to tell him everything?" asked Levy in a panic. "Why? Isn't he a suspect? Do you know what Forensics is going to say? And Nahari! What's gotten into you? I don't understand it at all!"

Michael stared at the desk and said nothing.

When Moish returned his face was grayish white and his hands, which he placed on the desk in front of him, were trembling. But his voice was completely under control when he said, "Explain it to me, I don't understand."

"Tests ruled out the possibility of an allergy to penicillin, and the pathological examination discovered a lethal amount of parathion in her blood and stomach contents. There is no doubt that her death was caused by parathion. Since the dead woman had no contact with agricultural crops or spraying, and there was no realistic possibility of it being an accident, the only possibilities remaining are those of unnatural death as a result of murder or suicide. This is what we're here to investigate now," Michael explained.

"You're out of your minds," whispered Moish, then added in a throttled voice, "Osnat didn't commit suicide; why on earth should she commit suicide? And how did she come by the parathion, that's what I'd like to know—where could she have known about parathion from in the first place?" he asked in despair, as if trying to explain something that there was no chance of explaining. And then he repeated, "Sorry, but you're out of your minds."

Machluf Levy dropped his eyes and turned the gold ring around his finger in a movement Michael had come to recognize as a cover for anxiety or embarrassment. Moish turned to Michael with a questioning look. His clear eyes were moist, and they stood out in his pale face. His hands shook uncontrollably, and he clasped his fingers together.

Michael kept quiet for a long time. "The Institute of Pathological Medicine didn't invent the parathion," said Machluf Levy. "If it wasn't there, they wouldn't have found it."

Moish looked at Michael imploringly. "Do you understand what you're saying to me?" he asked.

Michael nodded. "Of course I understand," he said finally, "but I can't change the facts. And you too, with all the pain and the fear, should want to know what happened here."

"I still can't grasp the fact that she's not here, and it was only a month ago that my father died. What do you think, that I'm made of iron? Throwing it at me like that."

Michael was silent. What was the point, he thought, in explaining that it made no difference how he told him—the panic that had seized hold of Moish stemmed from the facts. There was no point.

"Let's examine the less frightening possibility first," said Michael, "the question of suicide."

"Who says that's less frightening?" said Moish bitterly. "Maybe it frightens you less, but not me. I grew up with her. She's like my sister," and then corrected himself, "was."

"I understand that she grew up in your family," said Michael.

"Yes. We, my parents, were her adoptive family. She arrived here when she was seven."

"So she lived with you?" inquired Levy.

"No, not lived. We lived in the children's house, and every day at four o'clock we went to my parents' room. Aaron Meroz the M.K.

too. We grew up together, and they were like my brother and sister."

"What was her background?" asked Michael. Levy took notes in the orange notebook he had whipped out of his pocket.

"Her background," repeated Moish. He stood up, went over to the refrigerator, took out a blue plastic jug, and poured himself a glass of water. "Her background was shit," he finally said in a voice filled with rage. Machluf Levy raised his eyes from the orange notebook in surprise.

"She arrived in this country as a baby of three, I think, with her mother, from Hungary. Her father was apparently dead, and maybe she never had a father. Her name was Anna, and we changed it to Osnat. She didn't have a father, and if you saw her mother, you'd understand what I'm saying."

"I thought," said Michael in surprise, "that she had no family outside the kibbutz."

"She didn't. She didn't have so much as a dog. Her mother died when she was fourteen, but by then of course she was already here with us. And the way she died, too. In a car accident. She was run over. She crossed the road without looking. Outside Netanya. But they didn't tell Osnat at the time. They didn't tell me she was run over either. My father only told me a few years ago."

"Uncles? Aunts? Other relatives?" asked Michael.

"Nothing," said Moish, sniffing. "They all died in the Holocaust." The color began to come back to his face. "The only family she's got is here. This is her home."

"I understand," said Michael gently, "that she was a war widow, too."

"Yes. That too. Yuvik was killed . . . how many years is it since Lebanon?"

"Three," calculated Machluf Levy.

"Three years," Michael confirmed.

"So she's been a widow for four and a half years," said Moish. "She was married to Yuvik Harel. Maybe you've heard of him." He looked at Michael, who nodded.

"The lieutenant colonel?" Michael asked to make sure.

"Yes."

"The one from the navy," said Levy.

Moish again confirmed, "Yes."

"Four kids," said Moish, "and Dvorka, Yuvik's mother, is a widow too. And you're telling me that suicide's less appalling?"

"In the long run, taking the circumstances here into consideration."

Moish was silent.

"We'd like," said Michael gently, "to discount the possibility of suicide first. And in any case," he added, looking directly at Moish, who was staring at the wall—for a moment Michael wasn't sure that he had heard him—"in any case," he stressed, "we have to know everything there is to know about her, and you'll have to help us."

Moish was silent.

"You understand," said Michael, "that we'll have to talk to the family and friends and everyone who had any contact with her, and everyone will know what's going on anyway."

Moish was silent.

"How many members have you got here?" asked Michael.

"Three hundred and twenty-seven," said Moish unthinkingly in a hoarse voice.

"Adults?" asked Michael.

"Members. Three hundred and twenty-seven members; you asked about members. Apart from children and hired workers and parents."

"A big kibbutz," said Levy admiringly, but nobody reacted to his remark.

"Okay," said Michael finally. "I'm afraid there's no alternative. We can't escape talking to the family,"

"I don't want to be there," said Moish, his voice breaking.

"You don't have to be there," said Michael, "but before I get to them, there are a few questions I'd like to ask you."

Moish said nothing and put his hands on his stomach. His face contorted in pain, and Michael asked, "Are you all right?"

Moish nodded and said, "It'll pass in a minute," and again he bent over the brown leather briefcase, took out the bottle of white liquid, and swallowed another mouthful.

"What is that stuff?" asked Levy as Moish returned the bottle to the bag.

Moish ignored his question. "What do you want to know?" he asked Michael.

"Everything. We have to know her. And first of all, to examine the possibility of suicide with you."

"Suicide's out. I know Osnat like . . . like I don't know what, like myself. Suicide's out of the question, it just doesn't figure. I know everything there is to know about her. She'd never kill herself."

"Did you know about her affair with Aaron Meroz, too?" asked Michael.

Moish was silent. A hesitant look came into his eyes, and finally he said, "Let's say I didn't know, but I'm not surprised. I know where it began. I know him like the palm of my hand too."

"So what was there between them?" asked Michael.

"They were like brother and sister, always together. Until . . . until Yuvik came back from the navy, and then Osnat moved in with him, and Aaron left the kibbutz. In my opinion, that's why he left, but he claims it was because he wanted to study."

"Did they keep in touch over the years?"

"I don't think so . . . " Moish hesitated, "no, I'm sure they didn't. He didn't even know what she was doing. He didn't even come when Yuvik was killed."

"So how did it begin again?"

Moish shrugged his shoulders. "How should I know? It began. He was here on Shevuoth, exactly when my father died, of a heart attack."

"Why didn't she tell you? You were close, weren't you?"

Moish was silent and looked at his fingernails. He shifted in the chair and finally said, "We were close, but it depends on what you call close. We never talked about things like that."

"Like what?" asked Michael.

"Like that," said Moish stubbornly. "We never talked about personal matters."

"What did you talk about?"

"Everything except that. About, I don't know, about plans and work and stuff."

"So you don't know much about her in that area," persevered Michael.

"Why?" said Moish angrily. "You think if people don't talk, they don't know? I know a lot of things without anybody telling me, and

I'm telling you, she . . . she had plans. She built herself up here, step by step . . . she didn't kill herself, no way."

"Supposing, just for a minute," said Michael, ignoring Moish's impatient gesture, "supposing that she did kill herself; would she have left a note?"

"Yes, of course, Osnat's a responsible person." Something like a smile rose to his lips at the sound of his own words. "But she wouldn't have committed suicide. She's got four children, who're already fatherless. It's out of the question. Apart from which, she'd just begun a project that she herself told me was the most important thing she'd ever done in her life."

"What project?" asked Michael curiously.

"It's complicated," said Moish unwillingly. "Something to do with the structure of the kibbutz, moving over to family sleeping and things like that,"

"Why, haven't you got family sleeping already?" said Machluf Levy in surprise.

Moish shook his head. "No, not yet."

"That's funny," said Machluf Levy, "you're not short of money here, and all the other kibbutzim around here have already—"

"Yes, we're the last," said Moish. "And Osnat had a real bee in her bonnet about it. Just the night before she . . . before she died we spoke about it. And anyway he," Moish said, looking at Machluf Levy, "searched. He turned the whole place upside down. And what did you find there? Nothing. Except a bunch of old letters."

"What was her status on the kibbutz?" asked Michael.

"What kind of a question is that? I told you, she was the kibbutz secretary. Her status was fine. Everyone liked her."

"Everyone?" asked Michael.

"Everyone," Moish stated firmly. "Definitely everyone," he repeated confidently, and then he put his hands on the desk in front of him and a trace of hesitation crept into his voice. "Well, you know, there's always—"

"What is there always?" asked Michael.

"Things. Jealousy and things like that."

"Jealousy of what?"

"Well, she was so beautiful, and so many guys wanted her, and she had principles, and her kids were all fine. I remember when we built the cottages and she was one of the first to move in, there was a lot of talk . . . "

"Who in particular was jealous of her?" asked Michael.

Moish looked at him in horror. "What are you getting at? I'm not talking about anything out of the way, it's the kind of thing that exists on every kibbutz. What do you think, that—"

"When was the last time you saw her?" asked Michael.

"On Monday morning, before they came to take her to the infirmary. I dropped in to see her because I knew she was sick, and she had this tendency to ignore the physical side of things, to neglect herself, not to eat if she was busy. So I dropped in to see her in the morning, and she was really weak, and I forced her to go to the doctor, to Eli Reimer, and after that I had to run off because I had things to do, and after that . . . " his voice broke, "after that it was already too late."

"And in the morning did you talk to her? Did she seem okay?"

"What do you mean okay? She was really sick, but she wasn't unconscious or anything. Yes, she was okay."

"Who else knew that she was sick?"

"I suppose everyone knew, because on Sunday evening Dvorka, her mother-in-law, told me she was sick and she couldn't go to the seminar at Givat Haviva, and we went to the dining hall to look for someone to take her place. And in the secretariat office they knew too. Everyone must have known."

"And who knew that she was in the infirmary?" asked Michael, stressing every word.

Moish paused to think before he replied. "A lot of people must have known, because people were talking about it at lunch. Eli Reimer, the doctor, dropped into the dining hall on his way to the hospital. I knew and Dvorka knew and a lot of other people. But why? Why do you ask?"

Michael was silent.

"This whole conversation sounds absolutely crazy to me," said Moish, and he buried his face in his hands.

"When did she actually get sick?" asked Michael.

"I think she already had a fever on Saturday night. She said at the *sicha* that she felt cold, and believe me, even with the air conditioning on it was hot in the dining hall. So I think she was already sick then."

"Who were the people close to her here? Who can we talk to?" asked Michael.

Moish said through his hands, "You're talking to me. What's close?"

"Friends, intimate girlfriends. You know, the kind women have. Women always have some close girlfriend they confide in."

Moish removed his hands from his face and wiped his eyes. "I don't know," he said in confusion.

"One close girlfriend?" insisted Michael.

"There's no such thing here," Moish said finally, with the confused expression still on his face.

"What do you mean, no such thing? In general, or as far as Osnat was concerned?"

Moish looked around him. "There's no such thing here. We work together and live together and know everything about each other, but there's no such thing as whispering together. There are people you sit with in the dining hall, or on committees, but not . . . " he paused to reflect, as if he were reexamining basic concepts, "not the kind of friends you talk to."

"Okay, then, who came to visit her, dropped in for coffee, that kind of thing?"

Moish looked perplexed, as if he were being forced to think about things he had never thought about before. "Well, there are some—how should I put it?—cliques, people you work with more closely, or who were with you here and there, or let's say in a study circle with you, but people don't actually spend much time visiting each other, and Osnat was a busy person, all kinds of people dropped in, because of her position, too. If you're the kibbutz secretary . . . anyway, that's the way it is here." And then, as if talking to himself, "There's loneliness here, I can't say there isn't. There are people here whose rooms I've never been in." And apologetically: "Like I said, there are little groups, cliques, who visit in the afternoon. And apart from that, you get married and have children and you spend the whole afternoon with them, and then you go and put them to bed, and by the time you've finished, say you've got three kids, which is the average here, by the time you've finished, it's eight o'clock, and then you go to the dining hall, or have supper in your room. And then there's a lot to do, committees, cultural activities, I don't know . . . " His voice gradually faded away.

"So there are people here who never go to each other's houses? Never visit and so on?" Machluf Levy asked with astonishment.

"Yes, of course, they go to ask something, say, and then they sit down for a bit too, no question, but let's say the older members, the singles, no . . . not like in town. I guess."

"But if somebody wants to talk to someone about an intimate problem—I don't know—a crisis in their marriage, let's say, presumably that happens here too," said Michael, and Moish nodded, "who does he go to? Who does he talk to?"

"Now that you ask," said Moish with increasing embarrassment, "I don't know what to say. They talk to Dvorka, or sometimes they come to me, or somebody else. They go to the nurse, I don't know. When we were young we used to go to the kibbutz nurse with our problems. There's a psychologist, but he doesn't live on the kibbutz, I really don't know . . . " His voice had died down, but then he ended by saying, "But everybody knows everything about everybody."

"How?" asked Michael. "How do they know? You mean they see what's going on, or what?"

"I don't know how. Gossip, how should I know? People live side by side, they see everything, they've known each other since they were babies, they know everything."

"So you don't know who was close to her? Apart from yourself? Your family?" Michael asked again.

Moish shook his head steadily and finally said, "But Osnat was particularly reserved. It was hard to get to know her. She never talked about herself at all."

"Terrific," said Michael to himself. And to Moish he said, "So who should I talk to apart from the family?"

"Well, there are the people involved in education who worked with her. I can give you their names, no problem, and you can ask me whatever you want. I'll tell you everything I know, I've got nothing to hide."

"Okay, so before we go talk to the family, maybe you can tell me if she had any enemies here," said Michael, "and before you blow your top, do me a favor and think about it," he added when Moish's mouth opened in protest.

"Okay, look," Moish hesitated. "Osnat, I think, was the most . . . she was very beautiful, and that's hard to take. And she married Yuvik. And Dvorka's her mother-in-law, and everyone here admires Dvorka, so that's another source of envy. I don't know," he said, his hand again clutching his stomach, "there's a lot of spite in kibbutz society, here too. There's ill will," he said, his face twisted. "I'm not saying there isn't." He withdrew into himself again.

"Can you give me names?"

"What for?" asked Moish suspiciously, and then he said firmly, "I'm not prepared to go along with that line at all. You're crazy, I'm telling you. You want me to give you names of people who—what? Who wanted to kill her?"

Michael said nothing.

"There's no such thing and there never was," declared Moish, "and there never will be either! I'm telling you that you don't understand the meaning of the word *kibbutz*. It's like one big family. How can you say such a thing?"

"You yourself said that there was a lot of spite here," Michael reminded him tactfully.

"Spite, yes. Of course there's spite, we're talking about human beings. But there's no violence. And certainly not the kind you're talking about."

"Okay, so let's try another angle," suggested Michael, "with regard to the parathion."

"What about the parathion?" asked Moish in a calmer voice.

"I understand that the Ministry of Agriculture has banned the use of parathion," stated Michael.

Moish nodded, and then for the first time since they had met, he smiled. It was a small one, but it exposed two rows of even white teeth and illuminated his agonized face like a ray of sunlight on a rainy day. Michael thought about people's astonishing resilience in the short term, about the speed with which his interlocutor had recovered and produced this spontaneous smile, with even the hint of a sly twinkle in his eye.

"Yes, that's right," said Moish apologetically, "and we shouldn't have needed them to ban it, because we actually had an accident with parathion here, in fact it was with Aaron Meroz, when he was in charge of the field crops. At that stage we were spraying with parathion in gas masks—I'm talking about thirty years ago, no, twenty-something—and he had a hole in his mask, or the valve fell off or something, I don't remember the details, but he got a severe case of parathion poisoning. He lay there in the field—he told me about it later, much later—and he saw death. He was sure it was the end. But a few hours later he got up and it went away, the giddiness and the nausea and everything, and then he went to Srulke." The sly twinkle as well as the smile now faded and died.

"Srulke was my father, he was responsible for the landscape gardening," he explained, "and he told him the whole story, and Srulke got into a big panic. He was usually a quiet kind of a guy, but this put him into a tearing panic, and he ran with Aaron to the nurse, Riva was the nurse then, she's dead now. And my father's dead too," Moish sighed and covered his face with his hands. "So anyway, he didn't need any treatment because it went away by itself, but ever since then they stopped using parathion for the cotton spraying. But . . . " he stopped talking and looked down at the desk.

"But what?" asked Michael.

"But Srulke, my father, kept a few bottles of parathion for the rose leaves and so on. He said there was nothing as good as parathion."

"Where did he keep it?" asked Michael, and he heard the nib of Machluf Levy's pen squeaking as he diligently wrote down every word, and the pages rustling as he wet his finger and turned them over, oblivious to the tiny tape recorder in Michael's pocket.

"Locked up in the poison shed, in a safe place. Because of the kids, and to prevent accidents in general," explained Moish.

"Where is this shed?" asked Michael.

"I can show you. Close to the edge of the kibbutz, not far from the cottonseed barn. That's why it's kept so securely locked, because the kids like sliding down the grain. There's a big pile of grain stored there in the barn until they come and take it away, and the kids have a lot of fun jumping off the gallery onto the cottonseed."

"And who has access to the shed? Who's responsible for it?"

"Yoopie's responsible for it, he's got the key, he's in charge of EfCro now."

"EfCro?" asked Michael.

"Field crops," explained Moish. "Barley, cotton, sunflowers, and so on. But," he added with a note of animation, "my father had a key too, and Jojo's got one now because he's temporarily in charge of landscape gardening."

"And which of them had any dealings with Osnat?"

"My father most of all, but she was in contact with Jojo too, because as the internal secretary she . . . never mind, it doesn't matter. She had contact with Yoopie too, but nothing to write home about. She didn't like his sense of humor. He's an unusual character altogether."

"And Osnat herself didn't have a key?"

"No, why should she?" protested Moish. "With all due respect, she didn't know the first thing about crops. She worked in education for years, and apart from mobilizations and shifts at the height of the season, let's say with the apricots or the peaches, she never went into the fields. She never even took care of her own private garden; my father did it for her."

"And did your father keep parathion at home?" asked Michael with sudden interest.

"No, I don't think so," said Moish. "Why would he keep parathion at home? He was very careful, you could even say pedantic. I never saw any, but I can check. I'll take you to the shed after"—his face clouded—"after you talk to Dvorka and Shlomit and Yoav, they're with her now in the room, waiting, and I don't want to . . . Come on, I'll take you there." He sighed deeply.

Michael felt a growing tension, which became more acute as they approached Dvorka's "room." It was a two-room house in a relatively new quarter of the kibbutz. On the way they saw even newer ones. "Senior members' housing," explained Moish when asked who lived there. "We built them about ten years ago, and later on, when we built the new houses for our own generation, over there, in the Ficuses," he said, pointing toward the corner of the kibbutz on the right, "these were already out of date."

"And where's the block where Osnat lived?" asked Michael.

"In the Ficuses."

"You've got names for the different quarters," remarked Michael.

Moish replied without smiling, "Yes, it begins with a landmark, and then it turns into a name. The kibbutz is quite a big place by now. Maybe they should do research on that too," he commented bitterly. "They've researched everything else. And here we are at Dvorka's room." He strode on ahead of them.

"Dvorka's room" was the last house in a row of five interconnected structures. The garden in front of the building was so colorful that even Michael, tense as he was, came to a halt in front of the flower beds and gazed at them admiringly while he waited to be called inside. Moish knocked on the door and went in. A couple of minutes passed until he came out again and motioned to Michael with his head. Machluf Levy followed him in with his head bowed.

Despite her age, the woman sitting there made a profound impression on Michael. She reminded him of someone, he couldn't remember who. The deeply lined face possessed great power. Her dark blue eyes, the whites bloodshot, turned toward him with a penetrating look, and her wide mouth, whose thin lips curved downward, twisted for a moment. Her hair, gathered into a bun, was completely white. She was wearing gray trousers and a man's white shirt, and she looked like a gray-white stain against the bright background of the armchair. The girl sitting on the sofa next to her, who was introduced as Shlomit, Osnat's daughter, had her grandmother's large, wide mouth, but her eyes were green and narrow. Yoav, her brother, who looked about Yuval's age, was in army uniform, and his eyes too were narrow and green, standing out against his brown skin. "Healthy Israeli beauty," Michael immediately dubbed the young man's striking good looks. They looked at him as if they had been sitting for hours without moving, waiting only for him to come.

"Where are the little ones?" asked Moish.

"Hagit took them," Shlomit replied. Dvorka looked at Machluf Levy and nodded but said nothing.

"They're from the police," said Moish. "This is . . . remind me," he said in embarrassment, "what your name is."

"Michael Ohayon."

"He's from the Serious Crimes Unit. And this is Inspector Levy, whom we've already met," said Moish, and the three people looked at them in tense anticipation. Michael recognized the signs of fear on Shlomit's face. Dvorka's face was as blank as a plaster mask.

"Have you got the results of the examination?" asked Shlomit, and they all waited as Michael nodded.

"It was parathion," Moish burst out, "parathion, can you believe it?" Machluf Levy shook his head and gave Michael a look of rebuke.

"What do you mean, parathion?" demanded Shlomit with an expression of incomprehension and disbelief, and all three of them raised stunned eyes to Michael as he repeated what he had already told Moish. Dvorka's intense, blue-red eyes filled him with awe. Despite the strong attraction he felt, he avoided looking at them and focused his eyes on the youngsters first. Only then did he dare to look at her. Her lips were clamped, and she looked as if she hadn't heard a word that had been said.

"That woman, just think," said Moish when they left the room, "she's like Job. I can't understand how her heart's not broken. Sometimes I think I can hear the snap of it breaking."

But Michael, walking behind Moish on their way to the poison shed, withdrawn into himself, scarcely taking in the scenes around him, remembering the notices on the big trees only later, seeing and not seeing the broad lawns, could only think about the sentence Dvorka had spoken at the end of the conversation: "Anyone who has never lived on a kibbutz," she said without looking at him or at Machluf Levy, as if they were one indefinable entity that did not merit being taken into consideration, "doesn't understand the first thing about it. It's impossible to understand from the outside, and this whole investigation of yours is pointless. You're wasting your time."

8

Nahari didn't raise his voice. He pronounced each word clearly, stressing the ends of the sentences. "Here we work as a team," he said several times from his place behind the table. And in the same cold, authoritative tone, but speaking more quietly, he added, "You don't even give anyone a chance to discuss the wisdom or otherwise of your moves, you act alone like . . . like a cat or something. This isn't the Jerusalem Subdistrict, you know; we've got intelligent, creative people here. And the dynamics, as they say, are different."

Michael looked at him in silence.

"I don't really understand why you felt you had to go behind the backs of Pathology and sabotage their work like that. We could have coordinated with them in advance . . . " His voice gradually subsided. "Haven't you got anything to say?" After a few seconds of silence he burst out suddenly, "You've got nothing to say about interfering with the course of the investigation? About bringing up the parathion before we were ready?"

"I've already said what I have to say, for a quarter of an hour, to be exact," Michael reminded him, "and we've already agreed that there was no precedent for the situation I found myself in. I had no other way of getting through to them. They needed shock treatment."

"And what are they going to do in the polygraph now that you've already let the cat out of the bag? Haven't you ever heard of confidentiality in an ongoing investigation?"

Michael too heard the handle creaking, and he turned his head toward the door. "They've arrived," said Nahari without enthusiasm. "We can begin. The damage is done, and you'll be the one to suffer for it in the end." Then he turned his attention to the people entering the room.

At the rectangular table in the big conference room in the Petah Tikva building, Machluf Levy sat at the far corner from Nahari, and Sarit, the coordinator of the Special Investigation Team, sat opposite Nahari. Benny, a member of Michael's section who had only been co-opted onto the SIT that morning and had not yet managed to "go over the file in depth," as he put it, sat next to Michael. Michael was on Nahari's left and Avigail on his right, across the table from Michael. Despite the oppressive heat outside the air-conditioned building, she was wearing her usual long-sleeved man's shirt, with the cuffs buttoned tightly at her wrists. Everyone studied the photographs passed around by Sarit, and from time to time someone raised his eyes.

"So you didn't see anything interesting at the funeral?" inquired Nahari, looking at Avigail and then at Michael, who said something about shadows still lacking flesh and concluded, "You know how it is, things will only fall into place and link up with what we saw at the funeral later. We're talking about too many people here, and a lot of tiny threads."

Nahari said nothing as he paged through the file. The others also leafed through the files that Sarit had placed before them.

"But you could tell who the people were who were most affected," said Sarit. Michael looked at Avigail. He was still learning to read her face. The right corner of her mouth dropped as Sarit spoke. He could read her thoughts. But she didn't say anything. Not even a general remark about different ways of expressing sorrow. At all their meetings Avigail hardly ever spoke.

"There was one woman who started talking, and they shut her up," recalled Levy.

"Yes," said Michael, "but it turns out that she's been doing that a lot lately. Moish told me that she did the same thing at his father's funeral. Here she is," he said, holding one of the photos and pointing at a short woman standing near the open grave with her mouth open. "Her name's Fanya, and she's in charge of the sewing shop, or she used to be." Nahari took the picture from Michael, looked at it, and put it down outside the file.

"Okay," he said finally, "so what's new?"

"The main thing is that there turns out to be a rational explanation for a number of events," said Michael, "and I think Avigail should tell you herself about what she found out last night." They all turned to look at Avigail, who gripped her elbow and wiped her forehead. Michael looked at her curiously, thinking that to him she was still a closed book. On his first day at work here, at a small celebration in this conference room to introduce him to the members of the section he was to head, Nahari had said to Michael, as he handed Avigail her little paper cup of wine, "Watch out with her: still waters," and Avigail had narrowed her eyes and given a small, critical smile.

"About the home help," Michael now prompted.

Avigail pushed the fringe of hair off her forehead, bit her upper lip, and then said in a quiet, hesitant voice, choosing her words carefully, "She did leave the infirmary; she was apparently away for about twenty minutes."

Nahari stiffened. "When?" he asked.

"At lunchtime, about one-thirty. Apart from that, everything happened as she said."

"Could you give us more details?" asked Benny.

"That's the important thing," said Avigail, holding her right elbow. "I've told you the relevant thing."

Michael put his cigarette down in the glass ashtray in front of him and said with a gentleness whose source he himself did not understand, "We don't need to hear the tape, but there's a transcript of the interview right here, on page four—Avigail's interview with Simcha Malul, and her signed statement. The details are all there, but perhaps you could enlarge a little anyway, tell us what happened, fill us in on the things that aren't written."

Avigail's slender fingers locked themselves around an empty plastic glass. "What's there to tell?" she said unwillingly. "It's all written down here. She lives in Kiryat Malachi, and she's been working as a home help in the kibbutz infirmary for some time. They're very pleased with her work. She mainly looks after the old people, they've always got at least one geriatric case in the infirmary because they've got a problem with an aging population there." Avigail swallowed. "Never mind that, I spoke to her and we hit it off, and what turns out is that after Osnat received the injection, somewhere around half past one, she went to the kibbutz secretariat to arrange something; she didn't know that Osnat was the internal secretary," she explained, and Michael realized that above all Avigail wanted to protect Simcha Malul from some unknown threat.

"Why did she go to the secretariat?" he asked. "And why, as a matter of fact, didn't you mention the reason in your report?"

"To fix something up," said Avigail with an absentmindedness that did not deceive him.

"To fix what up?" he insisted, and he felt the impatience welling up in him and regretted not having spoken to Avigail before the meeting. She said nothing and squirmed uneasily in her chair.

"To fix what up?" Nahari echoed. "What business did she have in the secretariat?"

He looked at Avigail, and she bit her lip and then shot words out like rounds of ammunition: "She's got six kids and she's got problems with the youngest. She wanted to ask the kibbutz to take him."

"What problems?" asked Michael. "You can't pick and choose with the facts. We have to have the whole picture before we can decide what's important and what isn't, what's relevant to the case and what's irrelevant."

As Michael spoke, he noticed Nahari looking at her suspiciously; then he broke in impatiently: "Go on, spit it out, what's your problem? Who are you trying to protect here?"

Avigail kept cool. She crossed her arms, her hands on both elbows, and began speaking in an expressionless tone, "Since you insist, here's the whole story, which I sweated blood to get out of her, and which I promised her I wouldn't tell a soul."

"We've heard that before; promises don't cost anything around here," said Nahari, taking a long, fat cigar out of the table drawer and removing the cellophane wrapper without taking his eyes off Avigail's face.

"Her youngest son is twelve years old, and he's apparently begun to get involved with drugs, and she wanted to put him on the kibbutz in order to get him out of the neighborhood." Avigail stared at a point on the wall and said, "What's the wonder? When you see her house, the overcrowding, that husband of hers who does nothing all day, and the way she keeps everything so neat and clean . . . And she's a simple sort of woman, but with a lot of strength. There isn't much left to her but self-respect."

Nahari sighed.

"What you're saying," said Michael, "is that she was away from the infirmary because she went to the secretariat, right?" Avigail nodded. "And she doesn't know exactly how long she was away?"

"I understood from her that it was twenty minutes, a quarter of an hour. She waited there for a while. It's on the other side of the kibbutz, she says. You probably know better than I do, because I haven't been there. And she says that she ran, but she doesn't look as if she could run very fast, she's not a child anymore."

"No shit!" said Benny, stroking his bald head. "No shit!" he repeated. "Half an hour would be enough."

"So maybe she found the parathion too?" asked Nahari.

"No, I asked her about that," said Avigail confidently; "I asked her several times. What she did say, though, is that she left a dish of plum compote in the infirmary, and when she came back it wasn't there. But I only got that out of her after hours of talking."

"Compote? Was that part of their lunch that day?" asked Nahari, stiffening in his seat. "Or did somebody specially—"

"I asked her that," Avigail assured him; "she didn't know. But as a rule, she said, the old people and the patients got special food, which was also served in the dining hall to people on special diets and so on." And then she sat up. "What difference does it make anyway? Were there any other cases of poisoning on the kibbutz?"

"Not that we know of," said Michael, "but we'll have to check."

"You would have heard by now if there were," said Avigail. "I think we can discount that possibility. No, it's something that had to be in that particular dish of compote, if at all."

"What else?" asked Michael, and she looked at him questioningly. "What else was different when she returned?"

"Ah, the doors were closed. But that's in the file."

"What doors?" inquired Nahari.

"The folding doors between the adjoining rooms," explained Avigail. "I don't know exactly, because I haven't been there."

Michael leafed through the file and muttered something about a sketch of the kibbutz. And then he took the paper napkin out from under the sandwich he hadn't as yet had a chance to eat and, with the yellow pencil lying in front of Nahari, made a rough sketch of the infirmary.

"And Simcha Malul swore to me on the lives of her children that she didn't close them."

"So where did the dish of compote disappear to?" asked Benny.

Avigail shrugged. "She didn't find it, but she didn't look, because she was busy with Osnat, who began vomiting and everything as soon as she returned. But we already know that." And after a short silence she said, "And she was busy cleaning up."

"And she didn't see anybody leaving the infirmary?" asked Nahari.

Avigail replied, "Really, have a heart, do you think I wouldn't have told you something like that?"

"You know that there are some things you didn't tell us," remarked Nahari, rolling his fat cigar between his fingers.

Sarit gave vent to a long, drawn-out sigh and said, "So everything was cleaned up, there's no parathion, no compote, and she didn't see anybody either."

"Not a soul," confirmed Avigail. "And that's the thing I talked to her about most of all. She didn't see anybody except for the people we know were there."

"Terrific," said Nahari, giving Michael a look that made him wonder again if the whole thing wasn't a trap. "What with Uri abroad," Nahari had said when he handed him the file at the Serious Crimes section-heads meeting, "and the other section heads occupied with other cases, I think you're our man." At the time Michael couldn't help suspecting that it was a cunning scheme to trip him up. "They'll be waiting for you to screw up," Shorer had warned him. NUSCI, the National Unit for Serious Crimes Investigation, the "jewel in the crown," as his old chief had called it when he set out the options for his promotion, was "a whole new ball game," as he put it to himself when he tried to account for the feeling of alienation aroused in him by his new surroundings.

There were none of the open tensions, the conflicting feelings he used to have in the Criminal Investigations Division when he began on a new case. There was always something threatening and exciting about every case over there, but here he felt as if he were in a foreign country. Nahari's behavior displayed a style very different from the outbursts of the Jerusalem Subdivision chief, Ariyeh Levy. Here there were no open tensions, and it was impossible merely to make a face and dismiss undercurrents in the various relationships with such words as "he's having his period today." Nor was there anything approaching the intimacy he had felt with Eli and Tzilla. If anyone had told him that the day would come when he would feel homesick even for Danny Balilty's disappearances and other irregularities, for his protruding stomach and sloppy appearance, he would have been amazed. But here the efficiency, the intelligence-data terminal, and even the little section in charge of investigating Nazi crimes made him feel ill at ease and as if he were being tested.

He felt insulted by the very need to prove himself, and this, in turn, made him careful about what he said. He spent no time outside the building with the dozen people under his command, except in the course of their duties, and in the evenings he longed for the old sessions in Meir's restaurant, for the little corner café where he would sit on a stool opposite Emanuel Shorer, during hours that went unaccounted for, without the knowledge of Ariyeh Levy, who never disguised his anger at the special relationship between them.

Here nobody was angry with him, but nobody showed him any undue respect either. "A jackal's head or a lion's tail," Shorer had said, laughing, when Michael came home after one of his first days here and wordlessly requested comfort from the man who had brought this trouble on his head. "You'll get used to it," Shorer had said to him; "don't start losing your nerve on me. I'm counting on your becoming police commissioner one day, the first with an M.A. It's lucky you're not an Ashkenazi. If you were, you would never have been promoted like this, not in investigations anyway. It's time you realized that you've got what you've got, and nobody can take it away from you. And Nahari may be a royal pain in the neck, but at least you've got people you can talk to there. They're professionals, they've got style." Shorer, as always, had formulated with brutal frankness what Michael had only transmitted wordlessly: his fear of being "out of his element," of the alienation that caused the tension he felt every morning upon awakening, an acute, undefinable, unfocused anxiety, which also produced the insomnia characteristic of the periods when he was working on a particularly difficult case.

"So who's your fifth column over there? Doesn't Nahari have a secretary?" Shorer had asked, and Michael had laughed. But the laughter died as he began to speak, surprising even himself with his vehemence.

"The whole place reeks of Tel Aviv, it's entirely different territory. I don't understand them, they're built differently. He does have a secretary, and she looks as if she's just stepped out of the hairdresser's, her hair stands straight up. Yuval tells me there's a kind of gel you can stick on your hair, according to him it's the latest fashion. The last thing you would say to look at her is that she works for the police. Anywhere else—the theater, a café—but not the police. I can't stand all that sophistication, it gets on my nerves. I don't know," he said, sighing, "it's a far cry from Ariyeh Levy's Gila sitting with a bagel and painting her nails; it's something else entirely."

"Stop talking nonsense," Shorer had said. "I'm not worried about you. You'll get used to it. At any rate, that's not what really worries me." Michael hadn't asked what he meant. The things that worried Shorer were the things they didn't talk about. Like the fact that at the age of forty-four Michael was still on his own. It had been fourteen years since his divorce, and for seven of them his clandestine life with Maya had fulfilled all his romantic desires. He had never spoken of this to Shorer, although the older man suspected that Michael was having an affair with a married woman, and once he had even asked him, but Michael had refused to answer. Ever since he had split up with Maya, there had been no one else. Once Shorer had looked at him critically and said, "A man needs a wife. Who do you think you are, Sherlock

Holmes? You haven't even got a violin. I know that detectives aren't supposed to fall in love, but you don't have to be such a perfectionist. It's months since I've seen you with a girl." And Michael had smiled in embarrassment.

For the first time in his life the only feeling aroused in him by a new case was simply that of the bloodhound. He himself wondered at the energy that filled him from the very first time Nahari spoke to him about Osnat Harel's death, but he knew that this was simply the flip side of his sense of alienation, this lack of sadness or regret nothing but the will to prove something. What it was that he had to prove and who it was who gave rise in him to this need he found impossible to put into words. Vaguely he felt that a new kind of respect was at stake here, as at the beginning of his career. But this time the fear of failure was connected not only to himself but also to something that he represented, and despite the inner pressure, he refused to deal with it.

"Playing away from your home ground is no picnic," Shorer had said, "but it has advantages, you'll see." The familiar signs of weariness, of despair and fear, that assailed him whenever he was put in charge of a complicated case were now translated into a crude, anxiety-fueled determination not to fail the test. Nahari, with his B.A. in economics and business administration from Tel Aviv University, did not of course use the sentence, "This isn't a university here," so beloved of Ariyeh Levy, his boss in the Jerusalem Subdistrict, but Michael sensed that Nahari felt threatened nevertheless—by his reputation, his rapid promotion, and especially by the rumors of his special relationship with the head of the Criminal Investigations Division, Emanuel Shorer.

And something else threatened him too, which dawned on Michael when he noticed that Nahari was careful always to talk to him sitting down. Nahari was a very short man, not fat but solid, with a square build. During the course of the years, Michael had learned to recognize the body language of short men who expressed their uneasiness in his presence by taking pains to speak to him sitting down, by asking him to sit down the moment he entered a room. Nahari's appearance proclaimed his narcissistic attitude toward his body. The bright green T-shirt that emphasized his biceps, the desperate attempt to preserve a youthful appearance, made him look pathetic in Michael's eyes, especially since his fifty-three years were only too evident on his face and on the white hairs sticking out the neck of the T-shirt.

The word *diet* too was mentioned today, when somebody brought a bag of *burekas* into the room. And the short "Roman" cut of Nahari's white hair and his deep tan embarrassed Michael because both betrayed the amount of energy he invested in maintaining them: "Exercise and swimming every morning, jogging on the beach," Benny told him admiringly, without a trace of irony. "At six o'clock in the morning, Saturdays, holidays—he hasn't missed a day for twenty years."

Shorer had put it in a nutshell: "He takes good care of his ass. And don't think he's just an overcompensating shrimp. He's like an athlete in training, and he never lets up."

Michael looked at the square skull, at the macho gestures, the cigar Nahari licked with his tongue before lighting it; he noted the way he ignored Sarit's demonstrative coughing as he held the cigar between his teeth like an actor in an American movie, and the frozen, lusterless look in his light, almost transparent eyes, as they came to rest on Michael in a way that gave him gooseflesh and convinced him for a panicky moment that Nahari was simply trying to trip him up, until he pulled himself together and heard his new boss say again, "Terrific." This time Nahari's eyes came to rest on Machluf Levy, who was sitting at the corner of the long table and looking as if he had long ago given up any idea of asserting himself or saving his self-respect.

"Well, did you find the compote dish?" he asked.

Levy replied deliberately, "No, I didn't, but I didn't look for it either, because how was I supposed to know that it was there in the first place?"

"I thought," said Nahari slowly, calmly puffing on his cigar, "that you had already spoken to what's-her-name, Simcha Malul."

Levy looked at him apprehensively. Then he said, "But I didn't get it out of her that she'd left the scene." He turned his hostile and anxious eyes toward Avigail, and she bowed her head and looked at the glass plate covering the table. "Sometimes," he said defensively, "it takes a woman to get things out of another woman."

Michael, who even before the meeting began had hauled himself over the coals for falling into his standard pattern of rushing to the defense of the underdog, couldn't stop himself from covering up Machluf Levy's embarrassment. "In any case," he said, "it seems to me that it rules out the possibility of suicide. It's a little difficult for someone with severe pneumonia to get up and take a swig of parathion, and then to hide the bottle outside her sick room. Not to mention a dish of compote."

Nahari asked about the search. In a few sentences Michael described the hours he had spent in the poison shed, and as he dryly gave them the facts, he saw before his eyes the image of Moish at the moment when he shook his head in despair and said, "It isn't here." Both of them stood stooping in the shed with the picture of a skull on its door and the explicit warning: POISON—KEEP OUT above the flimsy old lock.

And Jojo, who had let them in, introducing himself with the words "I'm Elhanan, but everybody calls me Jojo," had said, "There was only one bottle here. I know because Srulke," he looked with embarrassment at Moish, "took it out for his rosebushes; they were infested with aphids. And I remember he said that we had to order more because it was the best thing for aphids."

"When was this?" asked Michael.

"I don't remember exactly," said Jojo, scratching his head; "a few days before he died, two or three days before, we dropped in here for something, and he took the bottle."

"And he didn't bring it back?" asked Michael.

"What can I say, he usually brought things back, but maybe with all the hullabaloo about the jubilee celebrations and Shevuoth he got confused."

The three of them—Michael, Moish, and Jojo—had remained silent. Michael examined the lock, which showed no signs of having been forced open, bagged it mechanically, with the unenthusiastic air of one who had no illusions about it leading anywhere, listened again to the names of the people who had keys to the shed, and followed his companions to the neighboring cottonseed barn. He stood next to Moish and kicked the gray seeds that looked hard, but when he sat down on a pile of them—following Moish, who held his stomach, saying, "This ulcer is killing me"—he sensed the softness and felt as if he were sinking into it. He remembered that Moish had described the place as a favorite haunt of the kibbutz children, who would stand on the high gallery and jump onto the mountain of seeds, sinking into it as if it were a pile of soft white sea sand.

"They love it so much," Moish said to Michael, "even the big kids, the teenagers, that last week, when we had a Children's Day as part of the jubilee celebrations, the main event, the treasure hunt, ended right here, with the treasure hidden in the seed pile. You should have seen what went on here." Michael was sifting the grains through his fingers and digging his hand into the unfinished pile in an attempt to reach the bottom, wondering whether someone might have hidden the bottle in it, but it was pointless—the barn was huge, and in order to conduct a thorough search, they would have to clear out all the seeds.

"The place should be systematically searched," he said now, having mentioned the cottonseed barn, "but it's impossible as long as we have any intention of keeping it a secret."

"What secret?" snorted Nahari. "You can't keep a secret on a kibbutz!"

Michael looked skeptical and said, "I don't know, I had a word with Aaron Meroz at the funeral. It seems to me that he succeeded in paying quite a few visits without anyone knowing."

"That's what he thinks," said Nahari, smiling. "That's what he thinks. Anyone familiar with kibbutz life knows otherwise. He may think nobody knows, but I can promise you that someone like her . . . " He pointed to one of the women standing near the edge of the grave in the enlarged photograph.

Michael said, "Her name's Matilda; she's the kitchen manager."

"Have you got a memory for details, or did you talk to her?" asked Nahari, writing something on a piece of paper.

"I didn't talk to her," Michael replied and in the same breath went on to describe the search they had conducted in Srulke's living quarters. He spoke sparely, again seeing the image of what Moish referred to as "Srulke's room," a two-room house resembling Dvorka's, but in another row of houses. It had been unlocked, and looked—but for the dust covering the surfaces and Moish sighing and saying, "I really should clean it out, but I don't have the heart"—as if the person who lived there had just gone out for a moment.

"To sum up," he said, "we searched wherever we could under the circumstances, and we didn't find anything."

"There are three top functionaries on a kibbutz," Nahari said to the room at large. "Osnat Harel was the secretary. Do you know what the function of the secretary of a kibbutz is?" he asked Michael, and without waiting for an answer, he said, "On some kibbutzim the internal secretary is the most important person on the kibbutz, on others it's the kibbutz general director who's top dog. The secretary is involved in the day-to-day running of the kibbutz, on the social side of things; he never has a minute to himself. There are committees for everything, but when the members don't agree with a committee's decision, who do you think they go to? To the secretary. The director is concerned more with general policy questions—economic policy and so on. But in the last analysis," he said, and a shrewd look crept into his eyes as he studied the file cover in front of him, "the dynamic is determined the same way it always is, by the particular personality of the person fulfilling the function. That's what determines the dominance."

Nahari was silent for a moment and then went on talking quickly, as if he were losing his patience. "What's-his-name, Moish, is the general director. The third top function is treasurer. Who's the treasurer there? Do you know?" He turned to Michael, who pointed silently at the figure in the photograph standing next to Moish and his wife. "Him?" said Nahari with surprise. "Isn't that the same guy, Jojo?" He turned irritably to Sarit. "Why are your pictures so blurred? You'd better get the camera looked at."

"I don't think it was the camera," said Sarit, shaking her curls. "I think my hand was shaking. That whole scene, murder on a kibbutz, it really got to me, the very possibility of something like that happening. I was upset. It's not like an ordinary funeral. And everyone looks at you, and you can see them asking themselves what the stranger's doing there."

"Do me a favor, keep your feelings out of it. I've got enough on my plate as it is, without sentimental melodramas about what's happening to us and what's the country coming to."

"He's been the treasurer there for the past six years," said Michael.

Levy asked, "What difference does it make?"

"I'll explain in a minute," promised Nahari. "But before I forget, who's in charge of the work roster there now?"

"Some woman called Shula," replied Michael.

"Okay," said Nahari, "I want all four of them, including the new secretary, here this afternoon. We'll put them in the picture, and they can organize the search for us."

Michael cleared his throat and said, "Excuse me, but I don't think that's a good idea."

Nahari straightened up in his chair. "Why not?" he asked, his tone too provocative to ignore.

"I think we should leave the search to the people who already know what's going on and try to be as discreet as possible about the whole thing for the time being, without letting the whole kibbutz in on it." He looked straight at Nahari, who waved his cigar in the air, dropping ash on the glass tabletop as he answered.

"You've already sabotaged any hope of that yourself." He studied his fingernails, then raised his eyes and added, "In any case, you can forget about discretion. You can't keep anything secret on a kibbutz."

"Someone did," said Michael.

"When are you meeting him?" asked Nahari.

"Who?" asked Benny. "Who's he meeting?"

"Meroz," said Sarit.

"This afternoon, at the Hilton," said Michael.

"Which Hilton?" asked Nahari.

"The Jerusalem Hilton," said Michael. "That's where he stays when he's in Jerusalem."

"I wouldn't mind changing places with him," sighed Sarit, pulling her T-shirt tight over her breasts.

"You could at least have arranged to meet him in Tel Aviv," grumbled Nahari. "What does the pathologist say about the time lapse between the poisoning and the death?"

"Half an hour at most," replied Michael, looking for the pathologist's report in the file.

Avigail raised her head from the photographs she had been studying as if she weren't listening to a word, and with uncharacteristic authority she said, "No more than fifteen minutes."

"How do you know?" asked Nahari suspiciously.

"I know."

"How?" insisted Nahari.

"I thought you had read the dossiers on the people who came to work here," she said dryly.

"I read it. So what?" said Nahari impatiently.

She bit the yellow pencil in her hand and again stared down at the photographs on the table.

"Avigail!" shouted Nahari. "How do you know about the fifteen minutes?"

"I was a nurse for ten years. I worked as a nurse on a kibbutz for six months. I know. I've seen cases after parathion spraying. It doesn't take more than fifteen minutes."

"A nurse? You're a registered nurse?" asked Michael. She nodded and then sank back into herself.

"Now, about the search," said Nahari.

"Zero. Nothing at all," Levy piped up. "We were at it again all day yesterday, me and my men. We looked everywhere, the poison shed, the infirmary again, that guy's—Moish's father's place, and her house of course, Osnat Harel, and we didn't find a thing. We'll have to search the whole kibbutz, go through all the rooms, and last night we started doing it, but discreetly; nobody knows what we were looking for."

He looked at Michael for confirmation, and Michael said again, "It's important to put off publicizing the cause of death as long as possible. I know it's impossible to conduct an investigation and keep it under wraps at the same time, but at least until we're sure that the parathion's disappeared, although I must say I don't think the bottle would be so easy to get rid of; it's made of metal." He looked at his watch. "They'll be here soon."

"Who?" said Nahari.

"The family and Moish and Jojo, and the kibbutz nurse, the doctor, everyone who's already involved anyway. And I thought, as long as it's possible, we could ask them to conduct the search themselves. I don't want the rest of the kibbutz to know we're talking about parathion."

"Don't you think you should establish their alibis first?" said Nahari, his eyes colder than ever.

"We've already done that," Machluf Levy intervened. "It's on the second page, before the photographs." He pointed to the open file in front of him.

"The son was in the army," said Benny, in the tone of one who had done his homework, "and the daughter was in Tel Aviv—she's studying there. Dvorka, the mother-in-law, was in the dining hall, and from there she went to her room to rest. She's still working, that old woman," he said in amazement; "she's a teacher there."

"The Bible," said Machluf Levy reverently. "She teaches the Bible, and she also directs study circles for Bible lovers."

"Oh, God, save me from those kibbutz study circles," sighed Nahari. "So on the face of it she wasn't there at all? In the infirmary?"

"No," stated Levy firmly. "We asked her specifically. It's hot there in the middle of the day; she was planning to go later in the afternoon, to 'drop in on her,' like it says right there."

"And the treasurer, this Jojo? With his access to the poison shed?"

"He was in the secretariat, in the cotton fields, in the factory, all over the place, and there was someone with him all the time. We checked it out," Levy assured him.

"He could have set it up in advance. I'm not sure we can write him off," muttered Nahari.

"You have to start with someone," said Benny hesitantly. "If it's one of them, we've really had it."

"Has anyone from the kibbutz seen you?" Michael asked Avigail.

She thought for a moment and shook her head. "No, how could they have? I've never been there. I interviewed Simcha Malul at home, and also here after they spoke to her in Ashkelon."

"Good," said Michael. "Very good. I want you to stay out of the picture."

They all looked at him, but he kept quiet. An icy light glittered for an instant in Nahari's cold eyes, and he said calmly but firmly, grinding his cigar into the ashtray, "Forget it. Forget it completely."

Michael didn't react. There was silence in the room. A brief eye battle took place, at the end of which Nahari repeated, "It's out of the question. There'll be such a scandal that you won't know what's hit you. In any case, they won't let you do it, so just forget it."

"What are you talking about?" inquired Benny, and Avigail bowed her head and seemed to shrink in her chair.

She held her elbows as Nahari said, "He's thinking of planting her there."

Almost a full minute passed before Avigail broke the silence by saying quietly, "You should ask me first if I agree, no?"

"Why shouldn't you agree?" asked Michael.

"Because I didn't stop being a nurse and come here in order to go back to being a nurse again," said Avigail, looking at the glass plate and rubbing an invisible mark with her finger.

"There's nothing to discuss," Nahari said, waving his arm dismissively. "It makes no difference if you agree or not. We'd have a second Watergate on our hands if it ever came to light. Undercover police on a kibbutz? Who'd be crazy enough to authorize it?" And after a brief pause, "Not me, for one. I'm not sticking my neck out on this one. Don't expect me to back you up. I say no. And the commissioner . . . " He left the sentence unfinished and smiled. Only the corners of his lips moved, exposing even, white teeth.

"But how?" Machluf Levy asked hoarsely. "How?"

"Instead of the nurse, Rickie, who's leaving," Benny explained. "She wants to leave, remember?"

"So you want to let her in on it?" asked Nahari.

Michael replied, "I don't know yet, we'll see how things develop. But two things are clear to me: One, we'll never find out anything without somebody inside, and two, we have to find the bottle and delay the explosion on the kibbutz for as long as possible."

"What about bugging a few phones first? Have you thought of that?" asked Nahari.

"Impossible," said Michael quietly. They've got an automatic switchboard there; we'd have to bug every phone in the place, and there's a phone in every room. It's impossible. I've checked it out, and it just won't work."

Nahari threw his body back, leaned it against the black imitation leather of the office chair, folded his arms, and said, "I'm not giving you my permission. You can apply to the head of the CID, of course. Go ahead. If he's prepared to take the responsibility for what happens afterward, I won't make any difficulties. But I'm telling you right now that I intend putting it on record that in my opinion the whole thing will blow up in our faces."

As far as Michael was concerned, the challenge was clear, and he felt as if the contest had now become public.

The telephone rang, and Nahari bent down, picked up the instrument, which was on the floor next to him, and put it down at the edge of the table. As he did so he waved his other hand at Michael, and before speaking into the receiver he warned him, "In writing. I want to see permission in writing, so there won't be any arguments about who said what later." Then he growled into the phone, "Let them wait, we'll be ready in a minute." Turning to Michael, he asked, "How do you want to do it? One by one? All together? They're here, all the people you invited. How long have you got before you have to leave for Jerusalem to keep your appointment with Meroz?"

Michael looked at his watch. "They're early," he said. "That's good; it gives us a bit of time." And then, after a bit of reflection, he said in an authoritative tone, "I want them together in my office, and I'm inviting you to talk to them if you want to be present."

"Thanks," said Nahari, "but I've got other things to do. This case isn't the main event in my life, you know. You can manage them on your own."

With his hand on the door, Michael said, "Avigail, you remain here until they're in my office. And Sarit, you and Benny come with me. Don't worry," he turned to Nahari, "I won't do it without authorization."

"We'll see," threatened Nahari, and he stood up and stretched.

"And what about me?" asked Machluf Levy. "Where do I fit in?"

Nahari ignored his question. Michael glanced at his watch in embarrassment and then said, "You can come along too, but you can go back to Ashkelon now if you're needed there."

"I'll come with you," said Machluf Levy firmly. "You can never tell how things might develop."

9

As Michael described the facts in a quiet, measured voice, he examined their faces and the subtle changes in their skin color and body movements. After announcing that "suicide has to be ruled out for technical reasons," he began to explain the need for secrecy. When he asked for their help in searching for the bottle of parathion, he still spoke quietly, avoiding dramatics and careful not to betray any emotion. Nobody said anything, except for the nurse, Rickie, who let out a smothered cry, and no one protested. Moish bent over and sat bowed in his chair, and Shlomit tugged nervously and rhythmically at her curly hair. Her brother, Yoav, sat completely frozen, and Dvorka clasped and unclasped her fingers. Only Jojo seemed to have taken it in, and after squirming in his chair and crossing his long thin legs, he put his hands on the arms of his chair and said, "I still don't understand why we have to do it. What do you do in other cases? Why all the secrecy?"

"If I may," Machluf Levy, who up to now had not uttered a word, suddenly intervened. He waved a hand in Michael's direction and then turned to the little group sitting in a semicircle facing the desk. "Let me explain," he said in a patient tone. "The fact of the matter is, whether you like it or not, there's a murderer loose on your kibbutz."

Dvorka shuddered, Moish lowered his eyes, and Michael suddenly realized that the understatement and restraint of his presentation were out of place, that what was needed here was shock treatment, and he asked himself why he was unable to speak with Machluf Levy's brutal frankness, which had given rise, for the first time, to the expression of open fear that now appeared on the faces of their audience. The fear had been there all along waiting for an opportunity to surface, and Levy had exposed it with his crude, spontaneous words.

"It's not like a thief," he continued, "not like those cases with drugs and volunteers that I've worked on in some kibbutzim. We're talking about a murderer, in cold blood, a poisoner, who's walking around your kibbutz now, at this very minute."

"Maybe it's someone from outside," suggested Jojo weakly.

"I hope it is," said Levy. "I really hope so. But the way it looks now," he continued in an authoritative tone, "it doesn't seem likely that someone from outside would have known where the bottle of parathion belonging to . . . to Moish here's father was. So it can't be someone from outside, unless he brought the parathion with him. Sorry, but it would take a miracle for it to be someone from outside." He stared at them dramatically, then moved his eyes from face to face, looking deeply into their eyes. There was a new strength in his face, and an awareness of his own power. Machluf Levy was definitely the right person to talk to them now.

"There's a cold-blooded murderer among you, and we don't know what his motives are. We don't even know yet if he's finished his dirty work. Because we don't know enough yet about the victim. But there's no point in burying your heads in the sand, as they say. What you have to do is, one, face the facts, and two, understand that if you want us to find this murderer, you have to help us find the parathion bottle first. You're on your home ground, you can go into all the rooms, sniff around, see what's up—*before* we tell everybody else on the kibbutz about the parathion." His voice rose: "And who knows? Maybe you'll succeed where we've failed. There are things that you know better than us without even knowing that you know them! And apart from talking to you one by one, which we'll come to in a minute, so we can ask you the questions that will help you to discover what you don't know that you know—apart from that, it's important for you to understand," now he dropped his voice to a whisper, as if there were someone listening behind the door, "how vital it is keep it a secret and to find the stuff quickly. So we can catch this guy before he does it again."

The grayish pallor of Moish's face now turned to a dark, muddy color, and he put one hand on his stomach.

"I'm not staying on the kibbutz," said Rickie in a shaky but determined voice. "I can't stand it, this is the last straw."

No one reacted.

"Don't you think you're exaggerating a little?" asked Dr. Reimer. From behind the lenses of his spectacles his intelligent eyes looked at Machluf Levy. He ran his fingers through his fair beard. Levy shook his head solemnly, but Reimer went on talking. "In any case, there are all kinds of people wandering around the kibbutz, volunteers from abroad, there are other possibilities—"

"We won't ignore any possibility," Michael promised, "but think about the bottle of parathion that has disappeared from the poison shed, and ask yourself who could have had access to it if he wasn't from the kibbutz, who could have known that Osnat Harel was in the infirmary, who in the space of twenty minutes could have taken the risk taken by the murderer, if he didn't have a legitimate reason to be there." He let it all sink in before adding, "Of course, the picture is still blurred. We still don't know enough about the victim, and naturally we still haven't got a clue about a motive, but perhaps we will by the next time we talk to you."

Machluf Levy turned to the doctor. "What I described was an understatement. I don't think you realize the danger you're all in."

"So what do you want of us?" Moish burst out. "Do you want us to start poking around in people's rooms?"

Levy was not shocked by the question, nor did he twist his ring around his finger even once during the conversation. He—unlike himself, thought Michael—appeared to feel quite as ease as he said, "Exactly. That's what you have to do. You have to suspect everyone and everything and keep your eyes open everywhere; you have to be careful and at the same time to watch out for the others." The last sentence was accompanied by an admonitory finger. The two young people stared at him open-mouthed; Shlomit stopped obsessively separating locks of her long hair into neat strands, and her brother, the soldier, continued to sit frozen in his chair.

Rickie wiped her damp forehead, hit her knee with her hand, and said, "I don't intend to get mixed up in it. I'm leaving tomorrow morning. People are already looking at me in the dining hall as if I did it." She stole an anxious look at the two young people and then glanced out of the corner of her eye at Dvorka, sitting beside her, who wordlessly laid a vein-roped hand on her arm.

Dvorka had said nothing all this time, only her eyes had grown redder. Her wide lips were clamped together in the expression Michael remembered from the first time he met her; now they drooped even more emphatically downward. Her hair gathered into a gray bun, the plain gray dress she was wearing, the stillness with which she sat on her chair—all spoke of a praiseworthy restraint, and not for the first time he asked himself whether such restraint was not indeed admirable, and what was really the advantage, what was the absolute value, of the ability to express your feelings directly? At the same time he also wondered about the nature of the society that produced people like Dvorka, people for whom restraint was the supreme value, the glue that kept the whole fragile, threatened, ramshackle show on the road. Even so, he had questions about this so-called Spartan culture, which taught its members not to bow their heads to the storm but to withstand its ravages and emerge the stronger thereby. Dvorka was the only person in the room, except perhaps for Jojo, who up to now had maintained a stiff upper lip, and Michael knew from experience that one small crack in this restraint would be enough to bring the entire edifice tumbling down.

"What do you say? Say something!" cried Moish in despair, looking at her expectantly. She did not reply immediately.

"I thought we'd already seen everything," she said at last in a hollow voice. "You were too young, perhaps you don't remember, but who could have foreseen what happened in 1951, when ideology and politics split kibbutzim right down the middle? Ever since then I've thought we'd seen everything. Families destroyed. The hatred. We've already seen hatred, but then it was open." She spoke monotonously, in a dirgelike rhythm, one word following the other with no change in the cadence of her voice.

"So what are you saying?" shouted Moish. "That we should be prepared for anything? Do you hear what you're saying? Dvorka! It's murder! They're talking about murder in our home!"

"We'll have to overcome it," said Dvorka, and her voice softened as she looked at the young people. Then she looked at Moish again. "What do you want me to say?" she said finally, a more human note creeping into her voice. "My own life is over, I haven't got many years left to live. It's your future and the future of our children that's at stake; what went wrong must be put right."

"Went wrong?" Michael pounced on the words as if he were hearing them for the first time.

"Went wrong!" Dvorka repeated firmly. "There's a slow and gradual process of decay! It didn't begin today. Hired labor . . . " her voice rose passionately, "hired labor on the kibbutz! All the kibbutzim are prostituting themselves today, they're prostituting themselves! They're renting the lawns in front of their dining halls to the public for weddings and bar mitzvahs, can you imagine?"

Moish sighed. "Dvorka," he said despairingly, "that's not what we're talking about now. Can't you see the difference? Nothing like this has ever happened before, not in my worst nightmares—"

"What difference?" Dvorka said, stressing every word. "There's no difference here. One thing leads to another, it's a process, can't you see that we're talking about a process here? Can't you see that it's a process of putting the individual above the group, putting the good of the private person above the general good, that it's the inability to postpone material gratifications? Can't you see," she extended a hand in front of her, "that's it's all one long process—you begin by speculating on the stock exchange and profiting from bank shares, and you end up having to give our own members credit points for picking the fruit off our own trees? For a long time now you've refused to examine yourselves," she said wearily. "For a long time now the members have regarded their private rooms as their homes instead of the kibbutz as a whole. There's a process here whose climax is your plans for family sleeping and for . . . " She fell silent. Her lips curved down, her hands trembled. She clasped them and squeezed her knuckles.

"I'm leaving, I can't stay here," said Rickie.

"Oh, stop it already," said Moish in a throttled voice.

"You'd better take me seriously," said Rickie, her voice growing hysterical.

"Okay, we hear you. Nobody's forcing you to stay," said Jojo impatiently. "What's the matter? You haven't been the center of attention for a few minutes in a row?"

Michael made a mental note to remember the open anger—along with the beads of sweat on his forehead—breaking out in the man who had kept himself under control up to now, and to investigate its causes.

"I'm leaving today, or tomorrow at the latest. I can't stand those looks anymore. I kept hoping you were going to explain it to everybody, and now it turns out we have to keep it a secret, so people will go on behaving as if I killed her." She burst into tears and Dvorka sighed deeply. "I swear it wasn't me!" she cried imploringly. "It wasn't my fault!"

"Nobody's accusing you of anything," said Machluf Levy. "The fact that you're here now should be enough to convince you." Rickie went on crying.

"We'll do what has to be done," said Jojo. "We'll keep quiet and look for the bottle, until we find it or until you tell us to stop. Whatever comes first."

"Things like that can't be kept a secret for long," said Moish despairingly. "Not with us, and not a secret like that."

"I don't know," said Michael quietly. "Maybe that's one of your myths too." And he knew that he wasn't directing his words only at Moish.

The words had been aimed primarily at Dvorka, who was now sitting opposite him as he alternately rummaged through his papers and looked at her. In other rooms the other members of the group were being interrogated, and the fact that Michael had referred to these interrogations as "personal interviews" did nothing to change their true nature. He had given Jojo to Machluf Levy, and Benny was shut up with Moish. The young people were with Sarit in the back room. "You can't talk to him now, he's conducting an interrogation," he heard Sarit calling from behind the door, as he asked Rickie the nurse to wait outside.

He was now alone in his office with Dvorka. Placing a glass of cold water in front of her, he looked into her blue, bloodshot eyes, which looked back with a piercing gaze that gave him an uncomfortable feeling, a combination of respectful awe and a determination not to evade her look. Finally he said, "It's very difficult to investigate a case of this nature without understanding the person involved." About the difficulties of understanding "the spirit of things" he said nothing, just as he had said nothing to his colleagues. NUSCI was not the place for lyrical flights, as Shorer had warned him: "Keep your philosophy and thoughts about life to yourself there." And when he began to talk to Dvorka, and perhaps even before, when he had sat looking into her eyes, he remembered the conversation he had with Nahari on the day he received the case.

"How old were you when you arrived in Israel?" Nahari had asked.

"Three," Michael had replied.

"And from the age of three you've never had any experience of a kibbutz?" Nahari had said with surprise. "How come? Quite a few kids from your school spent time on kibbutzim when they were in the army, in Nahal, and so on." And then, when Michael came up with some hollow phrases about his fear of rigid structures that stifle the individual, Nahari had smiled sarcastically and gestured at the room. "No one could say that you chose a flexible structure as your workplace. The dynamics here aren't exactly individualistic."

"Yes," Michael had admitted, "but at least the social aspect isn't affected."

Now Dvorka asked him in a hostile voice, "What do you know about the kibbutz movement? Have you ever lived on a kibbutz?"

Michael ignored the question and said, "Tell me about Osnat." He lit a cigarette and waited.

Dvorka lowered her eyes to the glass of water, and he watched her face with its faint twitches, its tightening and relaxing of the wide, narrow lips, and its eyes that looked straight into his and made him shrink. She looked right through him, as if he were transparent, as if he didn't exist.

Never in all his life, he said to Shorer later that night, had he felt as insignificant as he had facing Dvorka, even though she said nothing aggressive or contemptuous to justify the strong feeling she gave him that, as far as she was concerned, he simply didn't exist. Alongside the awe and respect she aroused in him, he began to feel resistance. "Look," he later explained to Shorer, "maybe it's natural to feel like that in the presence of a bereaved mother. You feel guilty because your life's going on as usual, because you've been spared," he said, knocking on the wood of the table between them, "for the time being."

Shorer grimaced doubtfully. "They can make you feel like that in any event," he said. "Those kibbutzniks, who built the country and drained the swamps, they've got God by the short hairs. Ask Nahari. If he hasn't already told you about it."

"About what?" asked Michael.

"What, he hasn't said anything to you? He hasn't waved his superior understanding of the kibbutz movement under your nose?"

"Yes, actually I've been surprised. He does seem pretty well informed," said Michael.

"Then let me tell you that he hates them too. He was on a kibbutz with a Youth Aliya* group. I thought he talked about it . . . " said Shorer. "You didn't ask him?"

"I didn't want to pry and—"

"Okay," said Shorer, "you're not the only one he wants to screw. He's got a score to settle with them, I don't know exactly what it's about."

Now Michael still sat facing Dvorka's seemingly unseeing yet penetrating gaze, drawn to her eyes like a bird to a snake's. Her eyes closed, and he waited patiently for them to open as her fingers interlaced and she said, "I don't know if it's possible to tell you about Osnat." Only now did he hear the echo of a Russian accent in the way she pronounced the *l*. He kept quiet, a firm believer in people's need, even Dvorka's, to talk, and listened attentively when she added, "I don't know what to say to you; she was a part of me, like a daughter, more than a daughter."

"Never mind if it comes out confused," he reassured her. "You can

---

*A branch of the Zionist movement, founded in Germany on the eve of the Nazis' rise to power, which organized the immigration of Jewish children and youth to Palestine, where many of them were absorbed on kibbutzim. Later expanded to include needy Jewish children in other countries, including Israel itself.

begin with her life history, with her personality, with the people around her. We need some sort of lead."

And while she turned her head toward the window and narrowed her eyes, Michael reconstructed his conversation with her in the kibbutz secretariat, on the night he conducted his search with Machluf Levy and Moish for the parathion bottle, when she had unprotestingly described her movements on the day Osnat died. Until twelve noon she had taught, and after that she had gone to the dining hall. Although it was late at night, he had noticed that she had not lost her tendency to be sidetracked by ideological issues. Even then she had made a little speech in parentheses, her emotion simmering under the skin of her restraint, about why she made it a rule to eat and cook in her room as little as possible.

"I'm opposed," he remembered the exact words, "to people shutting themselves up in their rooms and eating there. Taking meals together is also a value on the kibbutz." And even then, in the secretariat, he knew that there was nobody else better able to embody the spirit of things for him than Dvorka, but then as now, he had also felt uncomfortable, prompted by a strong urge to get through to her, to make contact, to earn her respect. And when he had asked her then, in the secretariat, about the dining hall, she had explained, in the way you explain something to someone you don't expect to understand you, "It's part of the general change kibbutz society is undergoing. Especially in the evenings, people are drifting away from the collective social experience in favor of the family cell."

And when she talked about herself, about the humdrum details of her daily life, he felt as if he were being included in something lofty, as if he were being allowed to participate in something of which he was unworthy. "I sometimes sin in that respect too in the evenings, when I'm too tired to move, and all I want to eat is a yogurt. Women of my age . . . " And she immediately roused herself: "But I make it a point to go and eat in the dining hall anyway, because that's when you can meet people and sit around the same table, discussing your day and keeping in touch on a daily level, which is really what it's all about . . . " She feel silent, as if she had just remembered whom she was talking to, and there was a skeptical look in her eyes as she said, "We're a nonalienated society, the last bastion of a lack of alienation in today's horror-ridden world. And you've seen our dining hall," she added suddenly.

"Yes, indeed," Michael said enthusiastically, "it's very fine, very modern, the marble and the ceramics and all the up-to-date appliances—"

In fact, he was responding to what he assumed were her expectations, and he was therefore overwhelmed with a feeling of failure when she looked at him angrily and snapped, "It's precisely because of that, precisely because there's no scarcity of anything, there's something corrupting about all that abundance. The curse of affluence." He looked at her in embarrassment, then resumed his questions about her movements on the day of the murder.

She had intended, she said to him, to visit the infirmary after lunch, but on the way she met Rickie, who told her about the injection and said that Osnat was resting, and so she had gone to her room.

"Your house?" asked Michael hesitantly.

"We call it a room," she replied in a patronizing tone, and realizing the depths of his ignorance, she went into more detail. Michael almost always made the people he was talking to feel as if he lacked the knowledge, but not the ability, to understand, and so they unconsciously supplied him with the information he needed. They dropped their guards when confronted with the expression of intelligent pupil that he adopted. With Dvorka, however, even now that she was sitting with him in his office in the NUSCI building, in what was supposed to be his fortress, the place where he should have had the upper hand, he was actually overwhelmed by a profound feeling of ignorance and incomprehension. When she had spoken then about the curse of affluence, he had felt that he was an integral part of the phenomenon being denounced, and that feeling grew even greater now.

"My room is situated between the dining hall and the infirmary, not far from the kindergarten children's house," she had said to him in the secretariat, "and I thought I'd drop in on the children's house on my way. The little one had a cold, and with Osnat sick—"

"And did you go there?" Michael had asked.

"No, it was already the rest period in the kindergarten, and it's important not to disturb the routine. Visits from parents interfere with the educational norm. According to my calculations, the housemother had already put the children to bed, and a visit from me would have upset the balance. I decided to wait."

That night in the secretariat he had already insisted on secrecy, in an authoritative tone and without giving any explanations, and even then she had reacted with a tightening of her lips. He thought of all this now as she sat before him, her eyes opening and closing, dropping and looking straight at him. She looked as if she was wondering if it was worth the effort, rather than as if she was searching for the right words, as if she was asking herself whether he would understand a word of what she said. On that night in the kibbutz, he had already asked her tactfully about her relations with Osnat, and now the words she had spoken sadly and honestly then echoed in his ears: "We had a disagreement recently. A severe ideological disagreement."

"Why don't you begin with that disagreement you had with her?" he said now.

Dvorka sighed. "It begins with the fact that Osnat wasn't born here, that she didn't enjoy the benefits of collective education, that she didn't sleep with the other babies in the infants' house. And because she didn't receive a solid foundation . . . " Dvorka fell silent for a moment, in the middle of her sentence, and taking him completely by surprise, she suddenly blurted out, "You know what her father was?" Then she looked as if she bitterly regretted what she had just said, as if the words had escaped her against her will. She intended, Michael saw, to return to the matter of principle, but he naturally pounced eagerly on her last words.

"Who was her father?" he asked, vividly remembering Moish's flat statement to the effect that her father was unknown, about her having no family outside the kibbutz.

"Apart from myself and my mate" (not husband, Michael noted, which, he supposed, was too bourgeois), "no one on the kibbutz knew anything about it. Nobody made the connection, and we kept it to ourselves, but the truth is that now it doesn't matter anymore." And breathlessly, as if announcing a catastrophe, she said, "He was a petty profiteer on the black market during the austerity period."

Michael froze the expression of surprise that almost rose to his face and bit back the words—"Is that all?"—on the tip of his tongue. But Dvorka was able to register his unexpressed disappointment, realizing that he had missed the point, and said rebukingly, "For you that's a small thing. Well, perhaps you're too young to remember." She paused for his reaction but refrained from asking him outright how old he was.

"They were the real scum, the lowest of the low, the profiteers during the austerity period, the black marketeers. And then too," she said, her eyes clouding over, "it was very hard not to sell to them, and I'm sorry to say the kibbutz sold eggs and chickens and so on, on the black market. My mate, Yehuda, was external secretary then, and we were obliged to deal with this man, this miserable wretch, the poorest of the poor, but not too poor to exploit the situation. A speculator. And later on, when Osnat first arrived on the kibbutz and the social worker who brought her whispered in my ear that the father had abandoned the family and refused to have anything to do with them, and she mentioned his name and described him, I realized immediately that it was him. But he never came to the kibbutz. He had left them right at the beginning, he took no interest in his daughter whatsoever, and as for the mother—she was no better than he was."

"Where is he now?" asked Michael.

"Dead," said Dvorka and closed her eyes. "On the mother's last visit she told me of his death." Dvorka opened her eyes. "You've made me remember things I haven't thought about for years. On the mother's last visit I had a talk with her. It was very hard." She took a deep breath and sipped some water. "Osnat refused to see her, and nothing helped. She forbade her to come to the kibbutz. None of the members knew about that either. She was only twelve then, at the beginning of puberty, and this woman turned up, and Osnat came to me, as she always did when she was in trouble, and said, 'Get rid of her,' and even I was astonished, even though I knew her so well. I was startled by the cruelty with which she, a child of twelve, said, 'As far as I'm concerned, she doesn't exist, she's dead. Tell her I never want to see her again, tell her to go away and never to come back.'"

Dvorka put the glass down. "As a teacher, an educator, I'd already had to deal with difficult situations, painful problems. But I'd never seen anything like Osnat's rages before. Or her willpower. She had that determination right from the beginning; it was impossible to budge her an inch from her position. God only knows where she got her strength from, if only . . . " She fell silent and clasped her hands.

"If only what?" Michael made bold to ask.

"If only she had channeled those powers correctly," whispered Dvorka, relaxing her fingers.

"But I understood that she, like you, was an educator, and that she was elected secretary of the kibbutz."

"Yes," said Dvorka without enthusiasm, "I don't know if I can explain it to someone from outside."

Michael was silent.

"So I had to explain to the mother," said Dvorka, and Michael realized that she was determined to tell her story in the way she saw fit, "that the child refused to see her, rejected her, and that it would be better if she left her alone. And that woman," Dvorka sighed and closed her eyes as if she couldn't bear the memory of the scene, "and that woman," she repeated, opening her eyes, "if you could have seen her." Suddenly she looked at him with new interest, as if seeing him for the first time. "You must see a lot of women like that in your surroundings."

Michael made an effort to ignore the anger that overwhelmed him at the patronizing arrogance of that "in your surroundings" and rested his chin on his hand. "She looked like a cheap floozie with her dyed hair and her tight-fitting floral dress. I remember the red shoes with the high heels; it was hard to believe, at the end of the fifties, that there were people like that here. The vulgarity! The makeup, in the middle of summer, her face painted like a doll, and she was so young, in that heat. We were all in short pants and sandals, at best." Her lips stretched, not exactly in a smile, but with the expression of someone looking at a picture from the depths of her past and examining its colors close up. In other circumstances he would have smiled.

"But at the same time," Dvorka continued, "it was difficult not to feel sorry for her. That poor creature, so lost and yet keeping her pride. I remember exactly that she pulled herself together and said, 'If she doesn't want to, she doesn't have to.' Not one tear did she shed. She had the hardness of someone who has lived in the gutter. And the astonishing thing was the resemblance to Osnat, in that stubborn determination too, only the direction was different, ostensibly."

"Ostensibly?" Michael repeated, taken aback. His voice sounded alien to him, artificial.

Dvorka was silent.

"And did Osnat go on confiding in you all those years? Did you talk to her about personal matters?"

"Nobody talked to Osnat directly about personal matters," stated Dvorka. "You had to read between the lines. Osnat never, but never, fully trusted anyone. Her inner world was something you could only deduce from how she behaved and what she did, but you could never have an intimate conversation with her. Not even when . . . " She fell silent, and a look of panic crossed her face.

"Not even when what?"

"There are some things that nobody knows about."

Michael said nothing. ("Subtle isn't the word," Nahari said later, as he was listening to the tape with him. "Those silences of yours, who taught you when to talk and when to keep quiet? That's what everybody said about you, that you are an outstanding interrogator.")

"When Osnat was fifteen—nobody knew about it, not even Aaron Meroz; to this day I don't know how she managed to keep it a secret—she got into trouble."

"How?"

"Somebody made her pregnant."

"Who?"

"What does it matter?" said Dvorka. "Someone. Someone nothing could be done about."

"Who?" insisted Michael.

"One of our members' sons, a very problematic boy, a year younger than she was. Just imagine, only fourteen years old."

"Is he still living on the kibbutz?"

"He's still living on the kibbutz, luckily for him; that's still one thing we've managed to hang on to, one of the wonderful things, accommodating ourselves to our deviant members. He's definitely deviant, and at the same time he has a place among us. Nobody ever dreamed of . . . getting rid of him."

"Who is he?" said Michael in a tone that demanded an answer.

"Fanya and Zacharia's son," Dvorka blurted out, "but that's not what—"

"She got pregnant, and then?" asked Michael, aware of the avidity with which he pounced on what seemed a possible lead.

Dvorka appeared to be weighing her words. "To illustrate the extent of her reserve, she kept it a secret for six months! Nobody knew, not even the girls she shared a room with. And we're talking about the intimacy of the communal showers, and getting dressed and undressed together, and a group of people highly sensitive to any change taking place in their companions. It simply didn't occur to anybody."

"And nobody knew that there was anything between them?" wondered Michael.

"There wasn't anything between them, except for brief sexual encounters, perhaps only one encounter. I couldn't get any details out of her even then; she clammed up completely."

"So what happened?"

"Our nurse at the time, Riva, she's no longer with us, noticed that Osnat's periods were irregular. She drew my attention to the fact that the girl had been accumulating sanitary pads for months, that her dates were irregular, I don't remember exactly. She should have spoken to Lotte, the housemother, about it, but when there were any problems with Osnat, people tended to come to me." She smoothed the folds of her gray dress and looked at him again through those slitted eyes in a way that made him feel like a cheap voyeur.

"So what happened?"

"As soon as Riva spoke to me, I remembered how much weight the girl had put on lately and . . . finally I asked her to come to my room, when there was nobody there, of course, and I didn't even ask her, I told her that she was pregnant."

"And?"

"We terminated the pregnancy," said Dvorka dryly.

"In the sixth month?"

"It seems that anything's possible if you're determined enough. And I was determined not to allow her to make the same mistake as her mother. It was what she wanted too, to get rid of the baby. Of course. But the only reason I'm telling you this is to show you how closed, how lacking in trust, and how self-destructive she was."

"And no one knew about it," Michael reflected aloud.

"No one. Except for Riva, the nurse, who's no longer with us. She passed away a few years ago. Not even the boy himself, not Fanya. No one knew."

"So it's possible?"

"What's possible?"

"For no one to know a thing like that on a kibbutz."

Dvorka was silent.

For the first time Michael felt triumphant. But then she said, a surprising note of cunning stealing into her voice, "I knew. It was impossible to hide anything from me."

Michael said nothing. She took a sip of water, and he lit a cigarette and thought about Nira, his ex-wife. "She's got eyes in the back of her head," Nira would say about her mother, Fela. "You'll see," she warned him before they got married, when he suggested she terminate her pregnancy without telling her parents. She became very pale, and for the first time Michael heard about her fear of her mother: "It's better to lie to her in advance, so that you can go through the whole process of exposing the truth with her. She knows everything, and she really knows nothing, but go tell her that and go tell me," she said miserably. "When she exposes all that wickedness in me, which I never even dreamed existed, finally even I believe the worst of myself."

"Osnat had a lot of energy," Dvorka continued, "but from that time on, she never let anyone touch her. She abstained from everything to do with sex, but it wasn't a question of trauma, because with my son, Yuvik, there were no signs of traumatization—there are four children, after all. It was more a question of will: She seems to have made a kind of decision to channel her energy into different directions."

"No wonder, if you were her model," said Michael to himself.

"And on the kibbutz, in the kibbutz movement in general and on our kibbutz in particular, we weren't conservative as far as sex is concerned. Even then it was permitted to talk about sex frankly and openly. Prophylactics were available, we gave the children sex education, and among the adults there was no lack of scandals of a romantic and sexual kind. We had a number of unmarried mothers here, long before it became fashionable, and nobody said a word in condemnation. And nevertheless . . . she . . . " Dvorka fell silent, and Michael waited, his heart still missing a beat whenever her eyes opened and fixed themselves on him with a sorrowful gaze. "Osnat was a force to be reckoned with. I don't know if you can grasp, if you can imagine the driving force of that energy, so instinctual in its source, when it was channeled into ideas. She was determined to renounce her parents' side of her personality, to put down roots here, to be part of everything, to exert an influence, to contribute. That was the source of her ideological campaign in recent years. She waged a powerful battle," Dvorka muttered and tightened her lips, "very powerful, but lacking a constructive vision. The foundations were flimsy," she argued as if debating some invisible presence in the room.

She began talking about Osnat's adolescence again, about the warm home Srulke and Miriam had tried to give her, about her bouts of depression and her uncontrollable outbursts. "When her mother died," said Dvorka, "I tried to persuade her, to influence her, to ask her to go to the funeral, to lay a wreath on the grave. With no results. She never mentioned her, not to the children either. And once . . . " her voice died down, and she looked at him in embarrassment and confusion. "It doesn't matter," she blurted out.

"What doesn't matter?"

"I don't want to go into the kind of petty little affairs you get on every kibbutz."

"I want you to go into them," insisted Michael.

Dvorka hesitated. "There's something misleading and sordid about details of that kind."

"There's something sordid about murder too," said Michael without knowing where the words came from.

"I wouldn't dismiss suicide so quickly," said Dvorka.

"We'll discuss that later. What happened once?"

"Not once," admitted Dvorka. "A few times, in the past year, too." Briefly, and with revulsion, she told him about alleged affairs, accusations of affairs with men on the kibbutz, about jealous outbursts from women. "The kind of power possessed by Osnat arouses strong instincts," she said in a low voice, "and naturally Boaz was attracted to her. And there were others too. But that's not the interesting point. If you don't allow yourself to get bogged down by insignificant details, you can see the overall process by which Osnat was transformed into a nun. Purely and simply, a nun. Fanatical, almost dangerous." Dvorka was breathing rapidly.

"Dangerous," Michael repeated.

"To herself. Dangerous to herself. Driven. She didn't have the real strength to lead. She wanted to change things, turn everything upside down, make her mark. A real mark. She aroused opposition, and she couldn't take it. For that she didn't have the strength. And her ideas aroused opposition."

"For example?" Michael requested.

"The matter of family sleeping has already been mentioned here, but in comparison to other kibbutzim, that's no longer a radical innovation—even the Kibbutz Artzi is contemplating a change in policy. What Osnat wanted to do was set up a kind of separate community for the elderly, an 'old-age home,' as Fanya calls it, and that aroused strong opposition."

"Why did she want it?" asked Michael, looking for details, names, for the specific incidents Dvorka avoided telling him about, not for the same reasons as Moish, but because she simply refused, he had the impression, to acknowledge their significance at all, wanting to raise everything to a plane of inevitable processes in which individuals were no more than incidental decor. This was the only way, Michael thought, that Dvorka could defend herself, protect herself from sorrow, from the things she didn't want to see.

"We saw what was happening. There are a lot of elderly members, and this holds up the implementation of the new processes, some of which are important and desirable, and we realized that the hidden aim of the plan was to transfer the old people somewhere else, like they were trying to do on kibbutz Beth Oren, and there were economic calculations too. Many members of my generation, the founders of the kibbutz, are tired, or not functioning, some of them are sick, but at the same time they all want to be involved in the decision-making process. To me it all seemed like nonsense, and I told her so, but in any case, that plan of hers would never have passed the vote." Dvorka pursed her lips.

Stubbornly Michael returned to Osnat's personal life.

"Yes," said Dvorka, "the position of kibbutz secretary can make enemies for the person who holds it, especially if she's not flexible, and Osnat wasn't flexible. But her personal life was unblemished, apart from her social isolation, which is something I've been talking to her about since she was nine years old." Dvorka smiled a pale, sad smile that was only a slight twitch of the corners of her wide lips and a faint tremor of her withered cheeks. "Even at that early age she was very anxious to guard her privacy. Apart from which," she shook herself, "your whole approach is misconceived. It's not a question of enemies in such vulgar terms."

"And she was married to your son," said Michael, daring at last to touch on the subject. It was then that he realized that part of the awe he felt for her stemmed from his guilt at her being a bereaved mother. Bereavement had always been a touchy subject for him, even in situations like these.

"Yes," Dvorka confirmed, "she was married to Yuvik. Psychologists would say it was a choice that enabled her to infiltrate even further and corrode the foundations of the kibbutz, but she wasn't conscious of it. And Yuvik was a special person." She said this in a matter-of-fact tone, as if speaking of some distant stranger. Michael held his breath. "All mothers say the same about their sons, but Yuvik possessed a rare awareness and openness. He was a true man of labor, a last remnant of purity; there was nothing dearer to him than this land."

Michael silently waited.

"We waited for him for so long. I lost two babies before he came," said Dvorka, looking out of the window. "Not even Osnat knew about it. Yes, it was a terrible time." Michael couldn't understand why he was so privileged; he wondered if this was the beginning of the crack. But she spoke as if in a trance. "Yuvik came to us after I lost two babies. They were stillborn." She sighed.

"Those were different times, hard times, you can read about them in the special brochure we issued on the occasion of the kibbutz jubilee, but you won't really understand even then. It's difficult to transmit what the first contact with the land was like. The hardship, the dryness, the water, the hunger. Especially the hunger, and the hard work. Twelve hours at a stretch sometimes, clearing and plowing and gradually building. And the heat in summer, the cold in winter, the poverty and the hunger. The men were weak with hunger and hard labor, all of us were. There were days," again the shadow of a smile, "when all we had to eat were two slices of bread and half an egg a day for a pregnant woman, and a few olives."

Michael lit a cigarette without taking his eyes off her. "And the disease, well, all the things that for you are history, literature, I don't know . . . " She looked around her vaguely. "When I lost the babies, people avoided me, like they avoid me now. In those days, when I walked down the paths, women would quickly cross the path and hurry off in the opposite direction, just to avoid meeting me. The feeling of identification was so strong that they couldn't stand the guilt. Especially," she sighed again, "women who had recently given birth. It's hard for people to confront the grief of others, that's understandable," she said simply. And then, with renewed energy, while Michael was trying without success to picture her as a young woman, walking down the paths in her short pants: "But we survived, and then came Yuvik. What you said about Aaron Meroz and Osnat came as a big surprise to me," she said suddenly, fixing him with her eyes.

"Aaron was an unusual boy, but his story too proves the point that you need a strong base in order to preserve your identity within our society. He was a withdrawn boy, very attached to Osnat, and when she moved in with Yuvik he suffered a severe crisis." Altogether, she added in embarrassment, she had felt guilty toward him all these years. "And the fact that he was so successful in the outside world didn't prevent me from feeling guilty for failing to give him a real sense of belonging on the kibbutz. Miriam . . . " her voice died away. "Srulke's Miriam," she resumed, "wasn't a sophisticated person. She was a simple woman, a loyal comrade, and a hard worker. All her life she worked in the kitchen, and it was hard work feeding the kibbutz in times of want . . . " Again he had the feeling that she was overwhelmed by images from the past, until her cracked voice made itself heard. "Until the economic situation improved, Miriam ran the kitchen on miracles performed with eggplant, as I suppose they did in town too during those years." she looked at him in expectation of a reaction, something that would betray his childhood, but she didn't ask in so many words, and he remained silent.

"You spoke about Miriam," he finally said, "in connection with Osnat and M.K. Meroz."

"Yes," she said reflectively, as if she had lost her train of thought and also her passion. "Miriam was unaware of the isolation of the two children, of their desperate attempts to belong. We succeeded with Osnat, and we failed with Aaron Meroz."

Michael thought of Osnat's photograph and wondered about her love life.

"As I said, she had a clear tendency to asceticism, and there was something unhealthy about her abstinence from sex," Dvorka said without embarrassment, "and from emotion too. I talked to her about it a few times, but she only looked at me and said, 'It's not a matter of principle, it simply doesn't come up,' and I was helpless in the face of that passion of hers, which gave her a lot of power when it was channeled into ideological issues, but at the same time there was something destructive about it, not only to her, but to all of us, to everyone around her, to the whole kibbutz, something unhealthy . . . "

"You were right; you can never tell how things will develop," said Michael to Machluf Levy as he peered into the crumpled package of Noblesse cigarettes and then rapidly collected his belongings. "Do me a favor, let him know that I'll be late," he added in order not to listen to Levy's silence. In his eyes he read the mocking look that seemed to say, "Calm down, I know my job." And at that moment, Michael thought as he hurried down the stairs and heard the clang of the big metal door closing behind him, he again reminded him of Uncle Jacques.

Michael phoned the Hilton again from the office of the police psychologist, Elroi. Aaron Meroz was in his room waiting. He did not protest when Michael announced that he would be delayed again, but sighed and said, "I, at any rate, am here."

Slowly stuffing his pipe with tobacco, Elroi weighed his words carefully, avoiding anything definite. Again and again he stressed the need to examine every assumption "and base it on facts." Despite his self-importance and the distant, formal manner he affected, Michael respected him and valued his professional opinions. There was always a matter-of-factness in their contacts that did not give rise to the wish for anything further, but it didn't alienate him either. "Politeness is worth something too," Michael had once said to Danny Balilty—when the latter was sneering at Elroi, imitating the way he cleaned his pipe and walking stiffly to the door and opening it with the psychologist's characteristically courteous gesture—"not to speak of professional competence." "That's true," admitted Balilty, his smile fading, "you can't take that away from him."

Elroi now mumbled something about the psychologist who worked with NUSCI and, without saying anything explicit, hinted that his services could still be called on. With uncharacteristic curiosity he questioned Michael about his new place of work and whether he felt comfortable there. The vague reply he received evidently satisfied him, and after listening to what Michael was consulting him about, he asked, "What's he taking?"

Michael took a note out of his pocket and read in a hesitant voice: "Two hundred milligrams of Mellaril daily and fifteen milligrams of Haldol. I don't have a clue what that means, I don't know these drugs, but she said that he was regarded as a patient under home hospitalization. They try not to exclude people in his situation from the kibbutz. What I'm asking is whether it's possible for someone like that to be violent."

Elroi put his pipe down at the edge of the desk and, stressing every word, as if to make sure of being understood, slowly said, "Yes, at least it can't be ruled out. You understand, the great majority of mental patients aren't violent. If you'd told me that he was a manic-depressive, for instance, I would have said you could forget about it. That type of patient is dangerous only to himself. But since you tell me that the diagnosis is paranoid schizophrenia, then if he doesn't take his medication—"

"But he did. Every morning and evening he came to her to take his medicine."

"Where did she get that diagnosis?" asked Elroi suspiciously.

"At the hospital. He was hospitalized for a short time twice. She sounded definite about the diagnosis."

"And did he get any treatment apart from the medication?"

"There was a period when he went to see a psychiatrist at the joint regional center—"

"Yes, I know them. And now?"

"For the past few years, she said, he's refused, he wouldn't cooperate in the sessions, and they had to be content with keeping an eye on him on the kibbutz. Why do you ask? Don't you agree with the diagnosis?"

"No, it fits the medication, but the question is whether he takes the medication. The fact that he goes to her to get it doesn't mean anything. All she has to do is turn her head away, and he puts the pills under his tongue but doesn't swallow them. They have all kinds of tricks; I've worked in a hospital, and I know all about it."

"Okay, so let's say that he didn't take the medication," said Michael impatiently.

"If he didn't take the medication, his condition could deteriorate into paranoid psychosis—he would feel that he was being followed, et cetera. The medication only remains in the body for forty-eight hours. If he doesn't take it for a few days, and he's under pressure, he could end up having a dangerous attack."

"And then, according to what you've described, a carefully planned parathion poisoning is the last thing you'd expect, right? He would assault his victim violently, no?"

Again the business with the pipe, the slow, deliberate gestures, the quiet voice, the careful, neutral pronunciation of the words, the wariness of committing himself. Elroi nodded and said, "In principle you're right, but in this case, with this diagnosis, you can't rule it out. I, at any rate, wouldn't rule it out. A paranoid on this kind of dosage is . . . has the potential of being a dangerous man. Sometimes I just don't understand them," he said after a brief pause, on a more emotional note.

"Who don't you understand?" Michael inquired.

"Those kibbutzim, with their insistence on keeping everyone at home. They're playing with fire. With the kind of medication he's taking, he should be hospitalized. Altogether, the whole case astonishes me."

"What astonishes you?" asked Michael.

"I happen to have done quite a bit of research in my time," said Elroi with an undisguised expression of self-importance he seemed completely unaware of, "on all kinds of subjects, but especially on the subject of aggression. I once conducted research for the army on aggression in kibbutzniks as compared to nonkibbutzniks. It was a big study, I can give you a copy of the conclusions if you're interested."

"I'm very interested in any material on the subject," said Michael sincerely, "but in the meantime just tell me what surprises you."

"We had three groups, and what characterized the kibbutzniks, the ones who hadn't left, the ones who were still living there, was the distinct tendency to turn their aggression against themselves. And that's probably the reason too why there aren't any murders on the kibbutz. I wrote an article about it for a professional journal; I've got a copy here somewhere . . . " He turned around to look at the stacks of books and papers behind the glass doors of the bookcase.

"There was an attempted murder once," Michael reminded him.

"Yes, but it was so transparent, so inept, that even there you can put it down to self-destruction, to aggression turned against the self. You're referring to that woman who tried to poison someone with Luminal? She too, by the way, was very emotionally disturbed. But one case in all the years of the existence of the kibbutz movement is quite astonishing. And there was another case, a psychotic breakdown that ended in murder, but nothing like what you've got here."

"So what do they do with their aggression?" asked Michael. "What does it mean to turn it against themselves? How does it express itself in practical terms?"

"Well, look at the suicide rate. They have a lot of suicides. It's a more acceptable solution to states of conflict, distress, aggression. Do you know that suicide is an act of aggression?"

"I've heard about that," said Michael, thinking of old Hildesheimer of the Jerusalem Psychoanalytic Institute and wondering what he knew about kibbutzim, and whether it might be possible to enlist his assistance again.

"Where did he work, your mental patient?" asked Elroi.

"In the factory. They've got a big cosmetics plant there, and he worked under some Canadian guy who's been in the country for ten years. He's apparently a bit of a weirdo himself, and they're friends. I haven't talked to him yet."

"I'd try to find out if the mental patient knows anything about parathion, and what kind of relationship he had with the murdered woman."

Michael told him about the pregnancy. Elroi listened attentively, nodded, and said, "Okay, as I said, you'll have to check it out. How the kibbutz managed to produce a paranoid schizophrenic in the first place is an interesting question in itself," he reflected aloud, tapping his pipe on the round tin ashtray. "You know, there was a big study of mental illness on kibbutzim, and they found that there's no difference between the incidence of mental illness on kibbutzim and in towns, except for one astonishing thing."

"What thing is that?" asked Michael.

"That on kibbutzim all the same disturbances appeared as in town, except one—there was no schizophrenia. Don't you think that's astonishing?"

Michael stretched out his legs and said thoughtfully, "Yes, I think that's very interesting. How do they account for it?"

"That's a subject for another discussion. Maybe it's because kibbutz members internalize the whole kibbutz as their family image. But that's only a superficial, off-the-cuff hypothesis. The study didn't deal with causes, only with findings, which are astonishing in themselves." Again there was the business with the pipe. "Paranoid schizophrenia—there has to be a genetic component. Who did you say his parents were?"

"I don't know much, only that his mother is a hard case too. She and her sister came to the kibbutz after the war in Europe."

"Ah," said Elroi, as if everything were now clear. "Second-generation syndrome. That explains a lot."

"What does it explain?" asked Michael.

"Well, all kinds of phenomena that were passed on to the children as a result of the trauma suffered by their parents. A lot's been written about that in recent years. There's also been a very interesting conference on the second generation. Lately there's been a lot of interest in the subject." (Michael swallowed the ironic comment that was on the tip of his tongue about the conference and the public interest in second-generation Holocaust survivors: "Look," he wanted to say, "we suffer too, we're all fellow sufferers, and we've got a label to prove it.") Elroi went on, "There are all kinds of burdens of guilt and anxiety that were transmitted to the second generation—there's a real syndrome. It could also lead to paranoia. And the father?"

"I haven't met him yet, but I know that he's a Yemenite who joined the kibbutz in the difficult years before the War of Independence. I don't have any details."

"Very interesting," Elroi said and went back to playing with his pipe. "I'd be glad of more details if it turns out to be relevant. Altogether, this whole case interests me. I'd like to go into the question of how they're coping with all these changes. Maybe the time's ripe for another study. And you should do a bit of reading on the subject yourself."

"What do you recommend?" asked Michael, suppressing a smile at the other's patronizing tone.

"I've got a few things right here," said Elroi. He rose from his chair, went over to the bookcase, with difficulty opened the creaking glass door, and came back with a book and a small pile of papers in his hand. "This is a little amateurish and perhaps too popular, but it's not bad for a start," he said, handing Michael a copy of Bruno Bettelheim's *Children of the Dream*. "But apart from what I'm giving you here, you should read the literature, the historical texts. After all, weren't you originally a historian?"

"European history," said Michael. "I don't know anything about the history of the kibbutz movement."

"Then start with Bittania, the commune established in the early twenties by Hashomer Hatzair* on a hill overlooking the Sea of Galilee," Elroi advised. "Start with *Kehilatenu,*† the published annals of the group, including a record of the daily so-called *sicha,* which was actually a prolonged session of public confessions and hysterical breast-beating. You can't imagine what went on there. Since you know how to read historical texts, you should read that stuff, it's absolutely fascinating." And then, as he led him to the door and Michael was thanking him, Elroi remarked, "You won't have an easy time investigating this case; there are too many things you don't know. You need an ally on the inside." He smiled unpleasantly.

Michael went on seeing that smile in his mind's eye all the way to the lobby of the Hilton Hotel, where Knesset Member Aaron Meroz was waiting for him in patient despair, with a brave and miserable expression on his face. He was more impressive-looking than on his television appearances. His hair was a nondescript shade of blond turning gray, his features sharp and clean-cut. His eyes showed all the anticipated emotions: tension, anxiety, and misery.

They sat in Meroz's seventh-floor room, which was reserved for him when he had to stay over in Jerusalem. Today he was there for an extraordinary meeting of the Education Committee. Michael handed him a photocopy of his letter to Osnat, and Aaron Meroz said, "Yes,

*A left-wing Zionist youth movement founded in Poland in 1916 and later affiliated with the Kibbutz Artzi movement.
†*Our Community.*

that's mine." He blushed and returned it to Michael without looking at him. "I never thought that this letter would come into anyone else's hands," he said finally, and after mentally circling the question, he shook himself and asked nervously, "What were you doing there? You said you were from the National Serious Crimes Unit—why were you called in the first place?"

"She didn't die of natural causes." Michael had chosen a formula that, although not completely satisfactory, allowed him to maintain a neutral tone, to reveal as little as possible.

Meroz looked at him in alarm. "What do you mean, not natural, you mean it wasn't from the injection? Because I was told, Moish told me, that an examination was being conducted to see if it was from the injection."

"No," Michael replied without taking his eyes off Meroz, "it wasn't from the injection or from the pneumonia or any virus."

"So what was it from?" asked Meroz.

Michael scrutinized his face and, thinking about people's acting ability, remembered that the man was a politician; how far could he believe in the expression of alarm growing in his eyes?

"From parathion poisoning," he said finally.

Meroz looked at him in disbelief. "Parathion? How come parathion? What possible contact could she have had with parathion? They haven't been spraying the fruit with it for years."

"It wasn't from sprayed fruit."

"So how did she come in contact with parathion?"

"I'll explain in a minute," said Michael, "but first I want to know when you saw her last."

Without a moment's hesitation, Meroz replied, "Saturday night, exactly a week and two days ago."

"And when did you send the letter?"

"That night. No, the Sunday morning after I saw her. I wrote it late at night and sent it first thing in the morning. I didn't know how sick she was."

"And after that you had no contact with her? After Saturday night nine days ago?"

"None. Not until Moish phoned me," said Meroz. His voice trembled.

"And what was this letter all about? If you don't mind my asking, what were your relations with the deceased?"

Meroz sighed. He looked at Michael and said, "What the letter implies. You must have read it, otherwise you wouldn't be here. Intimate relations. There's no point in my denying it, once you've read the letter. What else?"

Michael said nothing.

"What else?" repeated Meroz bitterly. "What else do you want to know?"

"Everything. The more the better. How long it went on, why you kept it a secret. Everything," said Michael without hesitation, in a firm, quiet tone.

Meroz sighed again. "What you hope to gain from it, I don't know," he said finally. "It's not connected to anything."

"Everything's connected to everything," said Michael, hoping they weren't going to get into a struggle about parliamentary immunity. ("Try not to rub him up the wrong way, try to get his cooperation," Nahari had advised him in a tone of would-be paternal guidance. "Otherwise we're going to be in for one hell of a hassle. They say you're an expert at gaining the confidence of the people you're interrogating. So go ahead and gain his confidence.")

"In the first place, I'm married," said Meroz without the embarrassment and apprehensiveness characteristic of men in his position. "But mainly because of Osnat, who didn't want her name on everybody's tongue. In all that kibbutz gossip." He fell silent and then burst out, "But I want to understand what she died of. Why did she die? Tell me the whole story."

"Why is a question that you may be able to help me answer. Of what, I've already told you."

"Yes, but how did she come to die of parathion? You have to explain to me."

"From what you knew of her," asked Michael, "do you think it would have been possible for her to commit suicide?"

He thought for a long time before answering. "Not now. Maybe once, but not now. She was too busy living now." With bitterness he added, "What she thought was living, anyway."

"When, once?" asked Michael.

"Maybe when we were children. But not even then, when I think about it seriously. She was full of rage, terrible rage, but even that was a sign of the life force, of that tremendous vitality of hers. No, she wouldn't have killed herself, I'm sure of it."

Again Michael heard the story of her life. Aaron Meroz had never met her mother. He dwelled at length on Osnat's beauty, and then slowly, as if formulating it to himself for the first time, explained her great fear "of being the kibbutz bimbo, a free mattress for the guys . . . She could have been so feminine, so sexy, I don't know . . . Well, you've read the letter," he said in a choked voice.

Michael said nothing.

"There's something tragic," said Meroz, "about this 'concept,' as she called it, that she was so involved with. It's as if she was setting out to avenge herself without any idea of what she was doing." He wiped his brow. "There's something tragic—maybe tragic's too strong a word—there's something sad about the fact that she and I couldn't really belong there. Especially for Osnat. You've always got that image of Dvorka haunting you, driving you to live up to some ideal of perfection. You always feel naked with Dvorka, transparent, as if you've done something wrong, even if you don't know what it might be. And if you haven't done it yet, you surely will, or it's enough to think about doing it, or just to think about yourself ahead of the others." He paused and then plain- tively asked, "So if she didn't commit suicide, what happened?"

The moment had arrived: Michael knew that he would be unable to get anything more out of him unless he said it now in so many words. "We think that someone poisoned her," he said as if releasing the pin of a hand grenade, then he waited.

Aaron's face reflected the same incredulity, fear, and all the other emotions he had seen on the faces of Moish and the others. But his expression very quickly gave way to one of thoughtfulness. Michael saw a new understanding dawn in his eyes, almost as if Meroz had been expecting something like this. Unlike the others, he reacted as if he could believe it, even accept it. The expression on his face after the initial shock was one of confirmation.

"You're not surprised," Michael stated.

"It seems unreal to me. I don't feel anything," confessed Meroz. "I simply don't feel anything. Not surprise or anything else. Apparently the fact that she's dead was devastating enough for me. Do they all know this?"

"Very little. Only Moish and the family, the people who needed to know," said Michael.

"And how did they react?" he asked, and without waiting for a reply, he let out a snort of bitter laughter. "Poor innocents. This is really the end." And he added maliciously, "I'd like to see Dvorka now. I'd like to hear what she's got to say now. Are you sure?"

Michael nodded. "I also want you to take a polygraph test," said Michael, looking directly into Meroz's pale, strained, and very tired face.

Meroz nodded. "No problem," he said. There was no indication that he was thinking of his status or parliamentary immunity. "No problem. I can also tell you where I was and what I was doing at every hour of the day. I don't have any secrets. Osnat was my only secret, and now she's not even a secret."

"I need your help," said Michael, having found the simple formula that seemed to him right for the man sitting opposite him. "Can you come up with anything that might give us a lead? Do you have any ideas?"

"What about? You mean who did it?" asked Meroz, wiping his brow. The air conditioning was on, and it wasn't hot in Jerusalem either, but he was sweating freely. "I still haven't taken in what's happened. But there's something I haven't told you." And only then did he tell Michael, allowing his mind to dwell on it for the first time, about the figure in short pants he had glimpsed in the dark.

"Do you have any idea who that might have been?"

Meroz shook his head. "Not the foggiest notion."

"Could it have been Yankele?" Michael shot at him.

Meroz froze. Then he recovered. "What Yankele? Fanya's son?" Michael nodded.

"Why Yankele? Where do you know him from?" he asked, gripping his left arm tightly.

Michael ignored the questions. "Think about the contours of his body," he said, "and that light-footed running you just mentioned."

Aaron Meroz bowed his head and closed his eyes. "Have you ever seen him?" he asked when he raised his eyes. Michael didn't answer.

"It might have been him, but when it comes to particular figures, real people, I don't like to think about it. After all these years, I still feel like a traitor to them; I don't even know why, because believe me, I worked very hard for what I received from them, and I suffered too. As far as I'm concerned, it could have been anyone there, man or woman."

"Why do you specify that it could have been a woman?" asked Michael.

"I don't know why I said that." Meroz stood up and walked out of the room. He came back with a glass of water, opened the window, and breathed deeply, holding his left arm with his right hand. It was only later that Michael saw that everything he had said and done during the interview had been leading up to this, but at the time he put it all down to anxiety, the fact of the interrogation itself, the presence of NUSCI, of the police.

"Now that I think of it," said Meroz suddenly, "the evil there really is concentrated in the women. The men somehow keep quiet or talk about principles, like Zeev HaCohen; or live their inner lives somewhere else, like Felix or Alex; or they're henpecked, like Zacharia; or work selflessly without understanding a thing, like Moish. It's a completely matriarchal society, when you come to think about it. That whole business of communal education, with the kids living and sleeping together in the children's house, was invented to free the women for work, to put them on an equal footing with the men. And on that kibbutz in particular, just look, Osnat was the secretary, for years they had a woman as the chairman of the education committee, the whole thing was like a beehive . . . " His breath grew heavier. "And if you think about Yankele's mother, Fanya, and her sister, Guta, then altogether . . . "

"Altogether what?" asked Michael.

"Well, they're the most terrifying people I've ever seen in my life," said Meroz unsmilingly. "You know what it was like working with them? There are some people who don't visit the kibbutz to this day because of them."

"What's so frightening about them?" asked Michael.

"First of all, they came from the Holocaust. I don't know if you can understand this," Meroz hesitated and looked at Michael, who thought of Yuzek and Fela, Nira's parents, "but that's already a source of pressure, of unlimited guilt. Not that they ever mentioned it themselves, but there was an atmosphere around them. Apart from that, they fixed work norms that made even Dvorka look pale next to them, even the pioneers of the early twenties. Then, at least, they sang; here they didn't sing and they didn't smile, all they did was work. I remember . . . " His voice died away and his face twisted in pain, which Michael attributed to the strain of remembering and the shock of Osnat's death. "I remember that once I was late for work, someone had forgotten to wake me up. I was on shift duty in the milking barn, with Guta. She's queen of the milking barn to this day. I swear, I was only five minutes late, no more, and I explained to her when I arrived running, really running, that they'd forgotten to wake me up because I hadn't slept in my room, and the whole story. She looked at me and said, 'Yes?' That was all. But I knew that all my explanations had fallen on the ears of a person who didn't believe anything, who knew in advance that it was all rubbish. And she's the better of the two."

Again the spasm of pain and the expression of intense anxiety. (Afterward, when Michael asked him why he hadn't complained at the time, he said that he didn't realize what was happening to him, that he'd experienced similar pains in the past, once having even gone to the emergency room, where they hadn't found anything wrong.)

"But if you've never lived on a kibbutz," said Meroz, and Michael knew that he was going to hear this sentence repeated ad nauseam, "you'll never understand anything. You don't understand the sanctification of work. Work is the supreme value. You can be a total nothing—but if you work well, they'll forgive you everything."

"And apart from Yankele, assuming that's who you saw, what else can you tell me?" Michael asked when Meroz fell silent.

"There's Tova and her story with her husband, Boaz, who was in love with Osnat and kept hanging around her room, especially after she was widowed, and trying to get her to go to bed with him." And Michael again heard the story of the scene in the dining hall.

"Who else comes to mind? Who do you think I should talk to?"

"To Alex. He was close to Osnat, even when Riva was still alive. Osnat didn't like Riva. To Dvorka, of course. I don't know. To everyone. To Moish. There's no point in wasting any time on Havaleh, although she's a champ at gossip. To Jojo, to Matilda, if you can stand the viciousness. So much spite and envy! What a load of rubbish it is—all that talk about the ideal society! Look what it turned into! But right from the beginning, the idea of a place or a society where people would be equal, from each according to his ability and to each according to his needs—what nonsense!" said Meroz. He sipped his water. "To each according to his ability and the strength of his elbows and the loudness of his yells—that's what really happened.

"And sleeping in the children's house. The kids still didn't like it even when they had reached the age of twelve; some of them were still wetting their beds at that age. Children would always be waking up during the night, and there were always arguments about which among all the parents would be watching over them, and as for the status of the parents in general—who ever asked them anything? Who cared what they thought?

"I remember when they built a pool, and there was a decision by the education committee about the age at which kids could go and swim without someone bringing them. I know because I was a lifeguard. Yes, yes," he said, answering Michael's look of surprise, "I passed the lifesaving course. You can't see me in that role now, but I was a lifeguard. Two little girls came to the pool one summer day, when I was already a student away from the kibbutz. The first few years, I used to come back on visits quite a lot, but as time went on, the less I visited. The two little girls had come to the pool alone, on a Saturday afternoon," he said smiling, as if contemplating a distant image, picture, "and I was sitting close to the gate. Then I saw Elka, she was the head of the education committee then, and you should have heard the bureaucratic speech she made to them: The education committee has officially decreed that fourth-graders are not to go to the pool unaccompanied by et cetera, et cetera. No one cared what the parents might have thought, no one asked them. They didn't exist. Only Lotte and Dvorka existed."

"Who's Lotte?" asked Michael.

"She was our group's housemother for a few years," replied Meroz. "If she'd been working with any other teacher, she would have ruled supreme. But because it was Dvorka, we had two goddesses instead of one. Going to your parents with questions or problems was unheard of, unthinkable. Everything went through Dvorka or Lotte. I think the mothers found about the onset of their daughters' menstrual periods a year after the event," he said without smiling. "The first to know were Lotte and Dvorka, and maybe Riva, the nurse. That whole idea of one uniform education for everybody, one standard design—you can see the product for yourself; it's nothing to write home about. On the kibbutzim, mediocrity and materialism are now having a field day. It's a society without challenges, except for the challenge of hanging on to your individuality.

"On second thought, it's the very *idea* of the kibbutz that I don't like," muttered Meroz, as if to himself. "It's giving too much credit to the human race to believe that it can attain true equality—and among Jews, besides. No wonder Osnat fought like a lion. If she'd had still more strength, she wouldn't have stayed there at all." Like Moish, he buried his face in his hands and said, "It breaks my heart, Osnat's story. It's a tragedy, whichever way you look at it. Even the four children. Marrying Yuvik, Dvorka's finest creation, who was a bulldozer in the fields but a block of wood at home. With his navy rank and all. He never confronted himself in his life. Not that I've ever confronted myself to God knows what extent up to now, but Moish's father Srulke's death and Osnat's death have done something to me, I don't know what. Maybe they drove it home to me that we've got so little time."

At this point, precisely when Michael was about to bring up various options and suspects, about to question him about Moish and Dvorka and others, the Knesset Member and chairman of the Education Committee groaned and said, "I don't feel so well."

His head fell back, coming to rest on the back of the chair, and he lost consciousness. Michael leaped to the telephone and asked for a doctor, then began giving Meroz mouth-to-mouth resuscitation until the doctor arrived with a mobile intensive-care unit and confirmed that Meroz had suffered a heart attack. "Although, of course, we won't know how severe until we examine him," he said when the resuscitation efforts had ended with regular breathing and the color returning to Meroz's face. By the time they arrived at the hospital (Michael being allowed to accompany them after identifying himself), he had fully regained consciousness.

"Do you know what you're asking for?" Shorer demanded rhetorically. "If it wasn't one o'clock in the morning now and I didn't know the kind of day you've had, I would really give you hell. What are you, crazy? Completely crazy. I can't possibly authorize it, especially these days, with all the problems on the kibbutzim. You know what a scandal we'd have on our hands? Just imagine the headlines in the newspapers, it would be the end of me if they got onto it."

Michael sipped his coffee, made a face, and looked around him. "And you, don't sit there as if butter wouldn't melt in your mouth," Shorer said angrily. "You're taking advantage of me. And what about the girl? What do you think it is, a joke? There's a psychopath on the loose there—how can you think of endangering her like that? And if they find out . . . Anyway," he suddenly roused himself, "it's not even in the hands of the commissioner; a decision like that has to be taken at the ministerial level." He finished his beer and wiped the place where his magnificent mustache had once been.

Michael said nothing.

"Wait a while at least," Shorer finally implored.

Michael looked into his eyes, and finally, as if he was determined to force the issue, he said quietly, "There's no point in putting it off. They won't catch on to her. I'm telling you, they won't catch on to her."

Shorer snorted and said, "What's this, are you a prophet now? You know as well as I do that these things are impossible to predict. We have to take it into consideration as a real possibility that the whole thing will blow up in our faces. It's not some theoretical danger."

"Give it to me in writing, and I'll take the responsibility. If they find out, I'll say that—"

"Don't talk nonsense," snapped Shorer. "Either I do it or I don't, and I'd have to be crazy to do it. Do you know what it means to be a nurse on a kibbutz? The Wailing Wall is nothing compared to her, there's nothing she doesn't know about, nothing!"

"That's what I understood today," said Michael. "I heard a few things from that nurse."

"Anything significant?" asked Shorer.

"How should I know? It's hard to tell. Maybe. There's someone there . . . How much do you want to know?"

"We're already sitting here, aren't we?"

"Right," said Michael, looking around him. They were the only people in the lobby of the Hilton, where Michael had returned and called Shorer after accompanying Meroz to the hospital. They were sitting on either side of a fancy corner table, with the whole lobby spread out before them. There was a sense that the hotel was humming with life, although no one was to be seen. On the floors above them, thought Michael, there were hundreds of people—happy and unhappy people, couples making love, cooks and bakers and dozens of other kinds of workers, and silence as well as the murmur of hidden life. And not far from here, not far at all, there was the Intifada with its stones and Molotov cocktails and Yuval in the alleys of Bethlehem, and everything about to explode in their faces anyway.

And having read Michael's thoughts, Shorer said, "Don't start worrying about the kid now, the kid's fine, everything's fine. All you need is a woman, a home, and everything will be fine. Stop looking so miserable."

"The nurse told me about some scandals from the past. Jealousies, infidelities. It's a small world: Everything happens there. She wants to leave right away, and I told her that as far as we were concerned, there's no problem. But I can't keep tabs on what's happening there without help from the inside. Try to understand my position. I'm asking you."

Shorer looked at him gloomily.

"How often have I asked you for something?" asked Michael pleadingly.

"This is blackmail," said Shorer.

"Call it what you like. I'm begging you," said Michael, undeterred.

"We'll talk about it later. What else did you learn from the nurse today?"

"Out of all the barrage of gossip, which children belong to which fathers, how many divorces, how many extramarital affairs, how many thises and thats, in the end it seems to boil down to this one guy . . . " Michael enlarged on the story of Osnat's teenage pregnancy. "This character, Yankele," he concluded, "is mentally ill. There are a few other cases on the kibbutz, but he's the only one who looks at all likely. Rickie didn't know about his relations with Osnat. She's only been there three years, and that story's ancient history. Meroz nearly had a fit when I told him. He was so close to her in those years, and he didn't know either. There's another girl there with big problems too, a teenager with anorexia nervosa. It's an illness where you stop eating until in the end you starve yourself to death. Have you ever heard of it?"

Shorer nodded and said, "Yes, crazy isn't it? I read an article about it in the paper. Well?"

"In any case, this guy, Yankele, his mother's not exactly sane either." Michael described Fanya's behavior at Srulke's funeral. "According to what I hear, she's quite terrifying."

"But you've got nothing new on motive?" Shorer asked Michael, who shook his head slowly, thinking of something else. "You're dying to see it as the work of some maniac, aren't you?"

Michael smiled. "Are you giving me permission or not?" he asked stubbornly. "I want her to be there by tomorrow. Just give me the go-ahead."

"I have to sleep on it," Shorer finally said.

Michael's face clouded. "You don't have to sleep on it," he said vehemently. "You know all there is to know already. If you don't let me go ahead now, we're not going to get anywhere fast. In any case, I don't know if it's possible at all—"

"I have to sleep on it," repeated Shorer.

Michael looked at him in silence.

Shorer sighed. "Come and see me in the morning," he said, "before you do anything. Give me a ring, in the morning things look different."

Michael said nothing.

"And don't you dare," warned Shorer, "don't you dare send her there without authorization and ask me to cover your ass afterward. Don't you dare. I'm warning you. There's a limit to everything."

"Just remember that I asked you, in person," said Michael at the door of Shorer's car, without blinking an eye.

"You've got no shame," Shorer said and started the engine.

11

For almost two days and nights Moish and Jojo made the rounds of the members' rooms, the children's houses, the laundry, the sewing shop. They visited the factory as well. They didn't always succeed in timing their visits for when nobody was there, but the pretexts they came up with went unchallenged, no one asking them why it was suddenly necessary to examine the electricity boxes and storerooms in the children's houses or why they were checking the sewing machines in advance of the technician's semiannual inspection of the sewing shop, where they were greeted, instead, with open arms. After a few hours on the job, they had already become skillful enough to convince even Fanya. Matilda too asked no questions when she was told that there was a malfunction in the main generator. It was tacitly understood that Dvorka and Osnat's children would take no part in the search. Moish understood Dvorka's need to shut herself off in her room in order to devote herself to the children and to avoid the necessarily deceitful contacts with kibbutz members.

It seemed to him that she had completely lost her feeling of togetherness. Her loss was greater than anyone's, and she knew something they didn't know. This extra knowledge, Moish was painfully aware, put her in the position of an outsider. And he was horrified when he realized that he too was separated from the others by knowing what he knew. That knowledge placed him in an ironic position vis-à-vis the members who spoke of the way Osnat had neglected herself.

"She took too much on herself," said Matilda, who was standing next to him in the storeroom of the kibbutz minimarket while he pretended to be examining the electric cable of the refrigerator unit. ("Where's Hilik? That's his job," she said, and went on talking without waiting for an answer.) He waited for her to leave him alone, and when she failed to do so, he started looking around openly while she went on talking.

"That's just what I say, there are a lot of parasites here, people who do nothing, and a few people who do everything for the parasites. You think it's easy for me to run the minimarket and manage the kitchen supplies and the storage and all the other functions I perform, that I took on myself, I'm not saying unwillingly. I don't have to rest, I'll rest in my grave, but look what happens in the end—snuffed out like a candle. Her of all people. Who dies today of pneumonia? They've got all kinds of medicines today. But when people neglect themselves because they haven't got time to breathe, because they're the secretary and the education committee, and they've got all kinds of newfangled ideas on top of it—then what's the wonder?" Matilda started when she saw his hand raised to one of the shelves. "What are you looking for?" she asked.

He took down a bottle and read the label. "What are you looking for?" she repeated suspiciously. "Do you need something?"

"No, I was just looking," said Moish, putting the bottle back and glancing at his watch. "I didn't know it was so late," he said and hurried out in order not to hear any more of Matilda's nagging voice, which never failed to make him, like everyone else, tired and nervous after a few minutes in her company.

Matilda's bulbous nose, and her little eyes sunken in her swollen face, haunted him when he left. As usual she was wearing wide, blue work pants, with a rubber apron over them. Each morning she washed the floor of the minimarket, which was closed until the afternoon. She only changed out of the blue work pants for supper in the dining hall, where she appeared in a floral dress. In the dining hall she would turn her head from side to side like a chicken, trying to see what was new, who was sitting next to whom. Ostensibly she didn't miss a thing, but actually, Moish suddenly understood, she was so obsessed with details that she never saw the forest for the trees. She never succeeded in fitting the details into the picture as a whole, and sometimes her distorted vision resulted in what Osnat called "poisoning the wells." ("She talks about things she doesn't understand and sows all kinds of suspicions in people's hearts," he remembered Osnat saying angrily.)

And when he mounted his bicycle he remembered a long-ago event during one of the peach-picking mobilizations. He could even hear the buzzing of the gnats. Matilda, in a white babushka and wide blue pants, short and squat, her face burning and her short, thick arms reaching for a branch, saying, "What's this, why are the irrigation pipes here in a pile? Yesterday I saw Yuvik going out in the jeep with that Swedish volunteer." In Yiddish she added, "The one with her tits hanging out." Then, continuing in Hebrew, "I was sure he was on his way to lay the pipes and her too." And only then did he see Osnat emerging from behind nearby trees, pretending not to have heard.

But as his mother had said long before that day, when he and Osnat were children, "You can't run away from Matilda, there's always some Matilda everywhere, just don't pay any attention." This had been when they had complained of the war Matilda waged when they came to get ingredients to bake a cake for Lotte's birthday. "Don't let her upset you," Miriam had said; "she's a good woman really. It's not that she's stingy, she's just careful of everything because it's her home. And think what a hard life she's had, alone for so many years."

Moish rode down the path and almost smiled as he recalled Osnat's reply: "If she wasn't so mean, she wouldn't be alone. Nobody dares to go near her. I don't understand how anyone ever came near enough to her to give her a child."

Miriam had looked around apprehensively, to make sure that no one had heard Osnat's words, which had been spoken loudly on the lawn in front of the room, and said, "Shh, Osnatileh, that's not nice, she wasn't always like she is now. When she came here after everything she'd been through, she wasn't like that in the beginning, and her intentions are good."

Now Moish could still see the expression of thoughtful contempt with which Osnat reacted to Miriam's never-failing tolerance.

He rode slowly from the minimarket to the sewing shop, holding on to the slack wire hanging from the handlebars, which was attached to the hand brakes of the old bicycle, and a feeling of depression took hold of him, slowing down his movements and making his thoughts stray. He looked around him without actually searching. There was something terrible, he thought on his way to the toolshed, about the mourning that had descended on the kibbutz. The deaths of Srulke and Osnat had been combined into one sorrow, one grief leading straight to the next. And this mourning, so intimate on the one hand and so anonymous on the other, suddenly made him feel that there was something false about the atmosphere of bereavement. There was something solemn and ritualistic here that the circumstances illuminated in a terrible light. He shuddered to think of the coming ceremonies, which people were already talking about, to mark the thirtieth day after their deaths. The labor of pain and grief that went into planning such memorial services now seemed to him artificial.

His sense of oppression grew when he thought of the diligent devotion that stemmed from a sincere desire to express the feeling of loss at the death of one of their own. But none of them had really known Osnat or understood her, and above all, none of them knew the truth. The whole kibbutz was shrouded in a sad, quiet, solemn gloom. A bar mitzvah celebration that should have taken place that week had been postponed for a month.

Dvorka had found a refuge in the company of Osnat's two youngest children, tightening her wide lips, which kept twitching, at them in a forced smile that found no echo in her eyes. From time to time someone would drop into her room, so as "not to leave her alone," but the presence of the children prevented them from referring directly to the tragedy.

The whole kibbutz devoted itself to organizing life so that the children would not suffer. On the evening of the day they returned from the interviews at NUSCI, an air-conditioned van was waiting to take the Squirrel group of kindergarten children, to which Osnat's youngest belonged, to a campfire. Moish stood looking at the van being loaded with the insulated picnic hampers containing the children's suppers and the people running around and checking the equipment to see if anything was missing. Only fourteen children and all this commotion, he thought; even the security precautions were exaggerated. These children, reflected Moish, wouldn't even have to look for twigs and branches for the fire: A bundle of specially cut firewood tied up with brand-new twine lay on the tractor parked behind the van. He noticed the glitter of the aluminum foil in which the potatoes were wrapped, peeped into the box containing the chocolate and fruit-flavored yogurt, overheard the housemother asking about the chocolate milk, and knew that the big insulated hamper was full not only of little plastic bags of cold chocolate milk but also of ice-cream bars that would be distributed at the end of the meal. And they would come back to the kibbutz, fourteen small children and seven adults, their hands sticky with ice cream and chocolate milk, but no traces of soot from the campfire and the baked potatoes would soil their clothes.

He remembered Aaron's joking remarks about how the kibbutz children were pampered and overprotected, when he had met him in a café on one of his trips to Tel Aviv. Despite the silences between them, which grew heavier with the years, and the meaningless small talk they exchanged, Moish felt a need, which he believed was shared by Aaron, to see their relationship as a close friendship that time could not destroy, that withstood all the changes in their lives, that existed independently of the family, and that would always be intimate (even though neither of them ever actually said anything intimate) because they would always understand what was left unsaid.

"They go out into the world with the feeling that everything's coming to them," Aaron had said, and now Moish remembered his angry, almost hurt reaction when Aaron went on to say, "You don't give them a chance to cope with the existential problems of life, and the end result is a kind of stunting of the capacity for suffering, for doubt; they take everything for granted, they know nothing except the need to accumulate material possessions. That covetousness, that acquisitiveness of theirs, it all stems from anxiety, from the fear of an independent life outside the kibbutz, and from the memory of deprivation transposed to a sphere where it didn't exist at all: The real deprivation had nothing to do with material things, it had to do with the stunting of individual growth." Moish thought now of Havaleh's greed for new clothes, of how she always wanted to buy something on their visits to town, the way her eyes lit up at the sight of every new rag, her never-ending hoarding of possessions.

Now he thought too of the trips abroad—to Africa, to South America, to Asia—taken by all the youngsters in search of themselves, thirsty for adventure, hungry for something else, however alien and threatening, as long as it was different. Some came home to the kibbutz defeated, withdrawn into themselves, more lost than they had been before setting out on this aimless adventure; only a few succeeded in readjusting themselves to kibbutz life, and then they looked at life there as the very epitome of compromise.

Dvorka once initiated a *sicha* to discuss what she called "the difficulties of the younger generation." She had spoken then, Moish remembered, about the loss of meaning as the main motive for those trips. She was not opposed to them, he recalled. Then too, as always, she had astonished him by her ability to see things in a different light from everyone else, by her unexpected open-mindedness. "These trips should be seen," she had said, "as a natural and constructive reaction to a spiritual quest. We should encourage them to travel as part of the process of apprenticeship in which a person learns that the meaning of life is to be found within himself. Think about how hard it is for them. They don't have any swamps to drain. They have nothing to protect them from emptiness. It's hard to live without a challenge, and we have to help them to find one."

Now, as he rode his bicycle down the path—passing Rachela, who waved a hand at him with obvious fatigue, at only twenty-four, he quickly calculated—he thought of Aaron's words and wondered if there was any truth in them. The pain of loneliness and questions about the meaning of life seemed to descend on the young people all at once, as soon as they left the stifling greenhouse they were so eager to escape in order to experience new things, disorienting and alienating them from the possibility of returning to that same greenhouse and bringing up their children as they themselves had been brought up, in the sincere belief that this was the very best of all possible ways. Moish now stood next to his bicycle allowing his thoughts to flood through him for once without fighting them, and suddenly, for the first time, he understood them. Osnat's death—and perhaps Srulke's too, however peaceful and inevitable it was—had cracked the protective wall that had prevented him from understanding what Aaron had been talking about.

That evening, when he went to Dvorka's to see if everything was all right, he found her sitting in a folding chair on the lawn, staring at the path. The scent of flowers was rising into the air. Moish had already passed that way earlier twice before, pursuing his search from room to room on one pretext or another, and both times she had been sitting there, motionless as a statue. Now, as he stopped and kneeled down beside her, she putting her wrinkled hand, its brown spots clearly visible in the glare of the lamp, wordlessly on his shoulder, he asked himself how she could possibly tolerate the unmasking of such violence, such destruction. Newly appalled, after a silent moment he stood up and went on his way.

Moish had spoken with Simcha Malul that afternoon, when he had gone, sweat-drenched, into the air-conditioned infirmary refreshingly dimmed by its half-drawn curtains. Fanya had made these curtains, when the infirmary was newly built, from fabric bought in the Old City. When he brought her the blue-and-purple striped material from Jerusalem—where she herself had refused to go, as she refused to leave the kibbutz to go anywhere—the verbal expression of her satisfaction was, "I think that will do." Fanya stayed up all night sewing the curtains, and the next day Zacharia hung them in the new infirmary.

Moish stood beside Simcha Malul as she washed the dishes and told him about her son. He scratched his head and said, "Bring him here, we'll see what we can do; maybe we can get around the formalities," and to his embarrassment he saw tears well up in her eyes before she turned her back on him and resumed her vigorous scouring. He opened the cupboards in the hall and then went into the rooms where the old people were lying, even peeking under the beds.

"What are you looking for?" Simcha asked. "Have you lost something? Can I help you?"

Moish calmly said, with apparent absentmindedness, "I think I left a silver bottle here on the day that Osnat . . . Maybe you saw it?" She hadn't seen it. If she had seen it, she would have put it away under the sink, she said, because how was she supposed to know what it was? But there wasn't anything like that, not anywhere, she cleaned everywhere, she knew every corner of the place like the back of her hand. Moish was embarrassed by her obvious anxiety, her fear of being accused of negligence. And even though he would have liked to ask her if she had seen anyone coming out of the infirmary that day on her way back from the secretariat—after he and Jojo had locked up and gone to the dining hall for lunch and she, as he had heard from the police, had left the patients unsupervised—he stopped himself at the sight of the naked fear in her eyes. "Leave it to the police," he said to himself, "that's their job."

Before leaving the infirmary, he looked in again at Felix, who was lying curled up with his face to the wall, and remembered with a pang the day he had painted a mural of fairy-tale figures on the walls of the children's house. He was so big and strong then, as he worked with the children gathered around. It was more than thirty years ago, Felix must have been about forty at the time, younger than he himself was now, thought Moish in dismay. He recalled Felix's warm smile twinkling in his dark eyes as he listened to the children's requests while he sketched in charcoal the figures of Snow White and the seven dwarves and Jack climbing up the beanstalk.

The mural was still there; Felix's murals still adorned the walls of all the children's houses on the kibbutz. Once every few years they had held a Felix Day in all the children's houses, when he would renew the faded colors and seat the kindergarten children on his knees and tell them old and new fairy stories full of dreadful details the children begged to hear. And Moish thought of his statues standing all over the kibbutz, statues all visitors wanted to see, and of the fact that—even though he was a sculptor of international renown, with his stone figures, radiating a power impossible to ignore, displayed in prominent places in Israel, and although the kibbutz allowed him to work as much as he liked in the vast studio that had been built for him not far from the cowsheds—he was scrupulous in observing the ordinary kibbutz work quota he set himself. Sometimes he worked whole days, sometimes half-days, but you could be sure that he would show up for every mobilization, that he would never shirk doing his share, and his wife, Nora, who had died a few years ago, was the same.

They both lived modestly, never complaining about the fact that they were still living in their old house, which had never been exchanged for a new one. They had four children, who took turns visiting Felix now. The three of them who remained on the kibbutz had inherited their parents' work ethic and modest way of life and the well-being and contentment that shone from their eyes. Gady, the second son, had also inherited his father's marvelous gift for whistling without a false note, and he whistled the tunes his father would whistle on the paths of the kibbutz. You could always tell where Gady was, just as you used to be able to tell where Felix was, by the sharp, clear sound of the long tunes—which Moish couldn't identify, knowing only that they were from operas—as in the days when Felix would whistle in the children's house as he painted on the wall and say, "Do you know what this tune is?" and when the children asked, "What?" he would tell them the story of the opera the tune came from.

Moish remembered his mother telling him that in his early years on the kibbutz, Felix was "a different person," possessed by some unruly spirit. Like Zeev HaCohen, he couldn't leave women alone, turning his room into a "satanic place" to which women, married and unmarried, came every night. Until Nora, who had a plain face and was a few years older than Felix, arrived on the kibbutz. It was she, Miriam recounted wonderingly, who "made him settle down." After Nora came into his life, the lecherous fire died down, and he never again looked at another woman. There were rumors about "a child he had fathered on a woman who had left the kibbutz," and the question of whether Yaela was Yedidya's daughter or Felix's was still unsettled, but it was no longer talked about. It was all forgotten. Only the founders' generation preserved these memories, bringing knowing smiles to the lips of some of them when they were brought up. Now Felix lay in the infirmary waiting for death.

Moish looked in at Bracha too. When her eyes opened wide for a moment, he saw the cunning, subversive look in them. There had always been something subversive about her. He wondered how aware she was of her surroundings. Then he thought about Rickie, the nurse, whose belongings were now lying packed up in the corner of her room, who had said to him, "I've turned the whole infirmary upside down, and there's nothing there. In my opinion you're wasting your time. They must have thrown it away somewhere; you'll never find it."

Behind the dining hall he met Jojo, who had searched the garbage bins there that morning. The dining-hall bins had already been emptied at the big dump outside the kibbutz, not far from the main road, where it was burned once a week. "This isn't the right way to go about it," whispered Jojo as they stood next to one of the big bins. "We need a general mobilization for something like this. Invent some story so we can rope everyone in, otherwise we'll never find it."

"We can't do that yet, you heard what he said there," said Moish despairingly. "If you believe what the detective said, then the minute we make the search general, somebody will know that we know about the parathion, and he'll hide it or do it again, if you believe what the detective said."

"Do we have a choice?" asked Jojo. "What choice do we have?" He turned to see Shula, the work-roster organizer. Though still pale, she had recovered from her gastric flu.

"We have a problem with the mobilizations," she said to Moish.

"What problem?" asked Jojo, and Moish, whose heart was beating wildly at the thought that she might have overheard part of their conversation, put on an interested expression and got ready to react.

"Let's move away from the bins," said Shula. "It stinks here. Why are you standing here of all places?" Shula had been chosen for the work-roster job because of her good nature, her even temper, her problem-solving abilities, and her inexhaustible sense of responsibility. Everyone knew that you could rely on Shula. She didn't want the job. "Only for six months," she insisted after she had been appointed, "and then I'm going back to the children's house." No one had ever been eager for the job, and it was generally understood on the kibbutz, although never explicitly stated, that no one would stay in it for more than a year. "It's an ungrateful job," Zeev HaCohen had said at the meeting years ago when Moish himself had been elected to it, "but nobody who's capable of doing it has the right to shirk it. Only a few people have the skills required for this delicate and complex task, and we obviously can't exist without it. Somebody has to do it."

Ever since her appointment, Shula had been dashing frantically about the kibbutz, and her previous expression of calm satisfaction had been replaced by one of strained exhaustion. Moish remembered the period when he had been responsible for organizing the division of labor on the kibbutz: People changed expression when he approached them in the dining hall, nervously awaiting what he had to say. Some of them would bristle in advance, glowering at him and saying such things as "Don't even think of it. I've already worked three Saturdays in a row," while others shrank in their seats and pretended not to see him. Sometimes he felt that the minute he walked into the dining hall, unseen currents turned against him and people avoided his eyes and averted their faces, hoping that he wouldn't notice them and would go and ask somebody else. He remembered how sick and tired he became of the arguments. Late at night there was always somebody knocking on his door to complain about the work roster for the next day or the next week.

"What's the problem?" Jojo asked Shula.

"Today Shmiel told me that he needs a mobilization three weeks from now to pick the plums, and on that same Saturday I need a mobilization for the factory because they've got a big order from Germany and need help with the packing. Do you feel all right?" she suddenly asked Moish.

"Yes, fine. Why?"

"You're awfully pale, look at your color," said Shula. "If Osnat was alive, I'd have gone to her; she would have known what to do. She had a real flair for fixing things. For instance, she knew who to put in what mobilization so that somebody else would want to be there. Like, say, to put two girls from the Palms group in the plum mobilization so that the boys from the Nahal unit would want to be there, or not to put Dana in the packing in the factory if I want Ahinoam there, and stuff like that. Well, what's the use of talking," said Shula, sighing. "What a tragedy we suffered with Osnat, eh Moish, what a tragedy!"

Moish looked away. A few years younger than they, Shula had not been close to Osnat, but she had always shown an admiration for her that bordered on hero worship. Moish now suddenly remembered a Friday night years ago: Shula standing in the doorway of the dining hall and saying to Osnat, with an expression full of childish admiration, "How beautiful you look, and how white suits you. How do you find the time to dress like that with all the work you've got, and how do you manage it on the allowance we get?" And the angry expression that crossed Osnat's face, and the look of suspicion that followed it.

Moish knew now that at that moment Osnat was asking herself what to do with these compliments, what Shula meant by them. Only now, remembering the scene, did he realize the extent of the aggression behind that innocent admiration. "I don't think about it, it isn't important," Osnat had unwillingly answered Shula, who was waiting stubbornly for a response. "That's beautiful too," said Shula with an admiration that only increased the expression of anger on Osnat's face.

"You can't think about all those subtleties in everyday life," Aaron had once said to him when he was trying to interpret a hurtful remark by Yocheved or Matilda. He couldn't remember the circumstances, but Aaron's words suddenly echoed clearly in his ears: "It doesn't matter," he had said aloud, but as if addressing himself, still a kibbutz member then, "you have to make yourself immune, grow a thick skin over your ears. You have to live with these people every day, so you can't spend all your time figuring out what's behind their words."

Osnat's death, Moish suddenly realized as he heard Shula's voice rising and falling without taking in what she was saying, had stripped off the thick skin covering his ears. "Cast out the beam from thine own eye," he heard Dvorka's voice quoting and then explaining the words. When Aaron had spoken of the thick skin he himself had not succeeded in growing, Moish had thought angrily of his endless complaints, and he had said so too: "Stop thinking so much, you're always digging." And now he himself couldn't stop digging. Everything he heard sounded different now, every sentence had a double meaning. Ugly things were hiding under every word.

"In order to live here, you need a special kind of character," Aaron had said to him one night. "That's what all the people here have got in common, a thick skin to enable them to survive, otherwise they wouldn't be able to survive here." They had gone to lay irrigation pipes with a girl whose name he couldn't remember, only that both of them wanted her and that Aaron, as usual with Moish, withdrew. But then Yuvik had appeared from somewhere and taken her away for himself.

Moish looked now at Shula's expression of responsibility and concern that reflected concentration and full awareness of the problem to be faced. With her protruding eyes and the two lines creasing her forehead she looked to him like a concentrated lump of malevolence. From the end of the path he saw Guta approaching, her lips pursed and a network of wrinkles around her mouth. She went into the dining hall, and he knew that it must be after two because Guta—due to her work in the milking barn—came to eat late, only after the chairs were already upturned on the tables and somebody was washing the floor. Shula stood next to her bicycle, holding the handlebars and fingering the rubber coating of the bell. "In other words, I need two mobilizations for three weeks from now, and I don't know how to organize it; what with the plums and the peaches I haven't got anyone left. I'll have to think of extra bonuses, and I thought that maybe we could get a work camp from the youth movement for the plums. But even if we can, that doesn't solve the problem of the packing for the factory. They won't agree to having a bunch of kids in there, and altogether ever since we decided against hired labor I'm at my wits' end and—"

"Okay, we'll think about it this evening," Moish interrupted her, hiding his impatience. "I'll come by, after putting the kids to bed."

"So you'll come? About what time?"

"I told you, after I've put the kids to bed."

"About ten?"

"Or before," said Moish.

At four o'clock Jojo said, "We'd better pack it in for now, the kids will be arriving in a minute."

Moish decided, "Before they burn the garbage—they're burning it tomorrow—let's go and take a look at the dump."

"We won't find anything there," said Jojo. "In all that pile, how could we find anything?"

"Who knows?" said Moish, sighing. "Maybe not, but what have we got to lose? A metal bottle doesn't burn so easily."

"You want to walk, or ride?" Jojo hesitated. "Or should we take the van?"

"Let's take the van," said Moish; "it's already late."

They drove toward the big, empty lot from which smoke was already rising.

"What's going on? Why are they burning it today?" said Moish in alarm.

"I don't know," said Jojo; "today's Monday. Maybe they brought it forward because of Children's Day. Now there's really no point in going. What makes you think we'll find it there anyway?"

"Because," said Moish thoughtfully, "if you think about it, the simplest way to get rid of that bottle, if you take into account that the person who did it never imagined that anybody would find out, that everybody would think it was the pneumonia, then the simplest way to get rid of the bottle was just to chuck it into the garbage bin, don't you think? And if he threw it into the dining-hall bins, or anywhere else, it would end up in the dump."

"Poking around in the garbage in this heat, and in the middle of all that smoke," muttered Jojo, who was bathed in sweat, as they stood next to the dump, which gave off a stench of burning rubber among all kinds of other waste. They started raking over the pile using the pitchforks lying there, pulling things out and pushing them back after examining them. "I hope nobody sees us," said Jojo suddenly. "What are we going to say if anybody sees us?"

"That we're looking for a part of a machine that broke down," said Moish without thinking. "A part that was broken and was thrown out and now it turns out that it's needed after all. What's the problem? Nobody knows."

"Except for the one who does know," said Jojo, sighing.

"Except for the one who does know," Moish agreed.

"I mean the one who knows."

"I know what you mean," said Moish angrily. There was no one else at the dump. They had set the fire and left. They would come back only after the smoldering fire had consumed everything. The job of burning the garbage was always given to the Nahal group, and despite the strict warnings that someone had to be there during the burning, they always slipped away. The matter had come up a few times in the *sicha*, where the danger had been pointed out in vain.

"It's already after four," said Jojo finally, "and I haven't seen the kids for two days, except for dropping in at the children's house this morning. And the twins, I haven't seen them for three days now. I think they must have grown in the meantime."

But then Moish said softly, incredulously, as if he had known all along that it was there and couldn't believe his eyes when it actually materialized in front of him: "Here it is," and with the help of the pitchfork he rolled a silver metal bottle, which was not even sooty yet, off the far end of the dump, which suddenly looked small and lost in the open space around them. Jojo was silent.

"It really is here," said Moish in a stunned voice. "That's what kills me. Just the way I thought the bottle would be here, here it is. How could I have known, how did I get inside the head of the person who did it?" And he sat down on the cracked, brown earth, the silver bottle lying next to his trembling foot. Jojo stood next to him without saying a word. His heavy, rapid breathing thundered in Moish's ears. He raised his eyes to Jojo, who had stopped sweating and whose breathing grew faster. Finally Jojo too sat down on the hard ground, next to Moish.

"What are we going to do?" whispered Jojo, and Moish did not reply. He was fighting a feeling of suffocation, of breathlessness. He sensed everything growing blurred and clouded around him. Jojo's voice whispering "What are we going to do?" over and over again reached him as if from a vast distance. Other sounds rang in his ears too—the sounds of cymbals and of a sudden drop in altitude. Jojo took off his spectacles and put them on the ground next to him. Finally he took a deep breath and said, "It's really true, Moish. It's one of us, someone who knows when the bins are emptied and everything. There's no getting away from it."

Moish couldn't say a word. He felt the sweat pouring down his back and the clamminess of his palms resting on the ground, and he saw the swarm around an anthill underneath his thigh. Looking at a long column of scurrying ants, he said in a cracked voice, "I don't know, if only . . . " He didn't finish the sentence; the words he thought but didn't say were, ". . . I could cease to be, disappear, crawl into that anthill and never come out."

Finally Moish found the strength to get up. He reached for the bottle, picked it up, and examined it. The cork was missing, and the bottle was empty.

"How much was there in it?" asked Jojo as if reading his mind.

"I don't know, it was the only bottle left. I know that because Srulke told me that the bottle was almost empty and that I should bring him some from Tel Aviv, or ask someone else to, because since the Intifada you can't go to the territories for it anymore. He wanted it for his flowers. This was his last bottle, and if I know Srulke, he must have spoken to me about it the same day he first opened it. He didn't like being without it."

"So let's say it was full," said Jojo. "What did they do with what was left, if the bottle's here? What did they do with what was left?" he asked anxiously and stood up.

"There are two possibilities," said Moish, looking at the horizon. "Either they threw it away half full or nearly full, or they transferred it to another bottle. That's not our problem. He asked us to find the bottle, not to invent theories for him."

"Moish," said Jojo, "understand what I'm asking. If there's more of it somewhere, then it can be used again. Do you understand?"

"I can't do anything about that!" said Moish in a burst of rage. "What can we do? Arrest the whole kibbutz, call a *sicha*? What do you suggest we do?"

"Eli Reimer's on reserve duty in the army, so we haven't got a doctor, we haven't even got a nurse," said Jojo in growing panic.

"Yes, we have," said Moish; "we've got someone coming tomorrow, with terrific recommendations. She'll be here tomorrow."

"So we'll have to talk to her, we have to be prepared," stated Jojo.

"I can't live like this," said Moish, "not trusting anyone. I'm telling you, I just can't cope with it. And when I think of Osnat, all I want to do is die. I feel as if I'm treading in darkness, in a kind of hell, that everything's suddenly different from what it seems. I can't cope with it." Moish buried his face in his hands and rubbed his eyes, which were stinging from the smoke. "Believe me, I don't know anything anymore," he said, and he sat down again on the dry, brown ground, breathing in the stench of the smoldering garbage. "Not anything. I don't understand anything anymore, I just don't understand."

A thin, scarecrowish silhouette in short pants, Jojo bent down and rolled a sheet of yellowing newspaper he had brought from the van around the silver bottle. "We can't share this find with anyone else. We have to think of the good of the kibbutz," he said with a serious expression, and after wiping the sweat from his face, he suddenly added, "We're the only ones who know about it." There was a note of excitement in his voice, and Moish sensed that it held something new that had not been there before. "We found it, we're the only ones who know," said Jojo. Moish looked at him in surprise. He waited for him to go on, but Jojo was in no hurry to respond to his questioning look. Only when he said, "It's something that's never happened before, nothing like this has ever happened," did Moish recognize something of Matilda's tone when she was announcing some sensation or other.

But he brushed the association aside and said, "Let's go back and get in touch with the police. At least we can tell them that *we've* found it. That's something too."

12

They had locked themselves into the secretariat as the technician from the mobile forensic unit who had been brought in from Ashkelon worked on the silver bottle. Machluf Levy stood looking over the shoulder of the technician, who finally said, "There's nothing, except for sand and soot and his fingerprints." He pointed at Moish, who couldn't stop wiping his hands on his trousers.

"I want to know what's going to happen now," demanded Jojo. "What are we going to do now?"

Michael Ohayon lit a cigarette, inhaled, and said, "We'll go on looking." His tone was matter-of-fact, as if he didn't understand the question.

"How long will we have to go on keeping it to ourselves, without telling anyone, not even our wives? It's impossible to go on like this!"

"Yes, it's difficult," Michael agreed, hearing the chill in his voice, "but we've got no other option at the moment: It's necessary for the investigation."

"And you won't even tell me how long it will take until . . . "

"I can't tell you what I don't know myself," said Michael. "You're not children. Obviously something terrible's happened here, but I would have expected two leading figures of a kibbutz like this to be able to cope with it." He himself didn't understand the hostility welling up in him. He said to himself, "Try to show a little sympathy," but he couldn't bring himself actually to do it. Something in Jojo's excitement, in his tone of complaint, in the dramatizing attitude that didn't fit a man who up to now had seemed calm and sensible, got Michael's goat, and he suddenly thought of the cars that kept stopping at the spot on the Tel Aviv–Jerusalem highway where the Number 405 bus had careened down the cliff in the recent terrorist incident. Day after day the cars stopped on the verge of the cliff, and people got out and looked down, reliving the catastrophe. He thought of the horror that seized hold of him when he saw them do this. Not all of them were grieving friends and relations. Some of them, he thought on recent mornings as he drove by on the way from Jerusalem to Petah Tikva, were people who just wanted to know exactly how it had happened, and not only in order to give concrete shape to their own abstract fears, but because of something else that Michael refused to think about, something that gave rise in him to the same rage and revulsion he felt now at the tone of Jojo's voice.

"You'll have to live with it alone for the moment," he said more sympathetically, looking at the signs of dread and suffering on Moish's face. "I'm sorry, but that's the way it is."

"But how will you find him? And what about the danger?" Jojo burst out. "And why did you take Yankele away? Where have you taken him?"

"We haven't taken him anywhere," said Michael patiently. "It seems that he's not had his medicine for several days, and in the light of the situation here, things might get dangerous."

"And what are you looking for in his room now?" asked Jojo. "You're lucky Fanya doesn't know yet, but she'll find out, she always finds out, and something like this, especially where Yankele is concerned . . . "

Machluf Levy shifted uneasily on his feet. "We've already finished our search there," he said to Jojo, "and there's no parathion. He," Levy pointed at the laboratory technician, "smelled every bottle because of what you said, and there's none there. But he could have thrown out what was left in the silver bottle, or maybe it's not in his room but somewhere else."

"You're crazy!" said Jojo, horrified. "You're completely crazy. Yankele would never do anything like that. Why should he do such a thing? You don't know him, you can't treat him like that. He's got problems, but he's not a murderer."

"Who is?" Michael suddenly shot at him.

"Who is what?" Jojo said, startled.

"Who is a murderer here?" asked Michael.

Machluf Levy sat down, twisted the thick ring around his finger, and said, "It won't make our job any easier, and we won't find the solution any quicker if you don't help us. Our only lead so far is Yankele."

"What do you mean?" asked Moish in a hoarse, cracked voice.

"I mean that apart from this Yankele, we haven't got any other suspects. We haven't even got a serious motive," he concluded plaintively.

Michael thought of the Special Investigation Team meeting he had headed this morning, where Nahari, who was sitting next to him, had said with a joyless smile after the facts had been presented: "What you're telling me is not only that you don't have a serious motive—apart from that woman Tova and the business with her husband and this Yankele with his obsession about Osnat—but you're also saying that everyone's got a great alibi. You don't even know who wasn't in the dining hall when it happened—who was at work somewhere or resting in their room or even away from the kibbutz. And you won't even let the polygraph people in."

"It's not a question of me letting them in or not," Michael protested. "You yourself understand the need for secrecy, and apart from the people who already know, you can't bring in a polygraph team without telling them why, and I'm telling you that our only hope of finding a lead is Avigail. I wouldn't even know what to ask in a polygraph test. What would I ask them?"

Sarit, who was a nail-biter, had already gone on to the skin around the nails, and Michael noticed blood on one of her fingers as she said, "There's plenty to ask. And we can begin right now with the ones who are already involved."

"Okay, we'll ask," said Michael angrily. "We already have, but my problem is that I haven't got a picture yet, something in that whole world there escapes me. I get the feeling that I don't understand something basic there, and that's what you're ignoring. There are romantic involvements on every kibbutz, and I've yet to hear of somebody being murdered as a result. What's new here? What's different?"

"Since when have you become an expert on kibbutzim?" asked Nahari sneeringly. "You've never had any experience of kibbutz life, as far as I know."

"First of all, I've already learned a few things, and second, I can read books," said Michael defiantly.

"Ah, books," Nahari said. "Yes, books are very important, but they're not life. Books are only books, you know."

"I don't think so," said Michael. "And you wouldn't be taking that line either, if you didn't feel that you had privileged inside information about this unique 'specimen,' as you call it. Mind you, I'm not saying it's not unique. What is this?" he said defiantly, feeling the anger surging up in him. "I can learn about some village or town in South America or about Leningrad and the Russian mentality from books, but not about the phenomena typical of kibbutzim? Have you ever read *Kehilatenu*?" he flung at Nahari, who admitted that he had not.

"Then read it. Let me remind you," Michael heard his voice rising to a shout, "that it's not as if I've never set foot on a kibbutz in my life, or as if I come from Lapland! I live here, after all. There's a limit, no?" He lit a cigarette, cupping the match in his hand although the windows were closed and there was no breeze in the room. The aggressively demonstrative superiority he had been encountering in everyone with firsthand experience of kibbutz life was driving him up the wall.

He was fed up, too, with Nahari's grudging assistance, which was given only in exchange for almost outright admissions of helplessness, and of the lack of any direction from him, unless it was made clear that some particular lack of progress stemmed from ignorance, from unfamiliarity with the values of kibbutz society. Then Nahari would deliver a series of pronouncements on the nature of the kibbutz, and when Michael once remarked that things had perhaps changed in recent years, he had said dismissively, "Ah, nothing's changed in principle.

Everything's the same. It makes no difference if they've got a factory now and didn't have one before."

"There are people there who think it makes a big difference, and also who think it's a serious matter of principle to consider opening a regional old-age home and maybe bring in old folks from town as well, for a hefty sum, of course, in order to solve the problems of social isolation, to recycle them in the community, to increase the options available to them. Don't you think that's a matter of principle?" asked Michael, chewing the end of his matchstick. Something in his own words sounded charged to him, even though he himself didn't know what it was. "I feel that I understand the principles of the kibbutz movement by now," he said without undue modesty; "that's not the problem. The problem is what happened here on this kibbutz because of these principles, and that I don't know. Not because nobody told me, but because they themselves don't know."

"I don't understand," said Nahari. "I've lost you now."

"There's something they themselves don't know because they're inside," said Michael.

"Who's 'they' when they're at home?" asked Nahari, and Sarit reached for the bottle of Coca-Cola standing in the middle of the table.

"The ones who know about it, Dvorka and the older children and Moish and Jojo and that nurse, all of them. They know something they don't know they know. That's the way it always is, but here it's more striking."

"Excuse me," said Nahari coldly, "don't you think you're being a little—how shall I put it?—enigmatic? Would you mind telling me what you're talking about?"

"Don't you understand? It's like conducting an investigation inside a family."

Sarit put her glass down. "You remember that case with the kid," she said in a thoughtful voice, "where the parents kept saying all the time how wonderful he was and everything, and in the end all that stuff came out, and it wasn't that they were lying, they just didn't read the signs right? Is that what you're getting at?"

"I think that people are trapped," said Michael as if he hadn't heard the question, "in their patterns of thinking and relating to other members of the family. They can't separate their own egos from the family ego, and any new angle seems to them impossible. Here it's the same thing, only with three hundred people. And I understand this," he went on after thinking for a moment, "from what I've read, not from what I've heard from people with firsthand experience of the kibbutz."

Nahari maintained a lengthy silence. "According to what you say," he said finally, without irony, "we have to tackle this case as if it were a family murder."

"Something like that," mumbled Michael, whose passion had cooled down, leaving him feeling embarrassed. "And the problem is," he continued in a more deliberate tone, "that I don't have any suspects. I simply haven't got a clue."

"What about that crazy guy?" asked Sarit, looking at the tip of the yellow pencil in her hand.

"Who, Yankele? He's not a serious suspect," said Michael. "He really did hang around her place at night, it was him, all right, but he didn't kill her. Even though you could say that he hated her, he certainly had a real obsession about her, too."

"Why?" asked Sarit with undisguised curiosity.

"It's complicated," said Michael vaguely, "and it's connected with his illness. He had some idée fixe about guarding her chastity, not allowing her to be sullied by sex and so on, but he doesn't have the foggiest notion about parathion, he didn't have any connections with Srulke, and he didn't have the opportunity to do it, because at the time he was in the plant with Dave, that character from Canada, whom I still have to talk to."

"But his mother . . . " said Avigail.

"Yes," Michael agreed, "his mother is apparently a different matter."

After that there were concrete questions about Avigail, who had returned from a meeting with the head of the C.I.D., the Lachish Subdistrict C.O., the police commissioner, and the minister of police—"all the bigwigs," as Sarit, not without envy, had said at the beginning of the meeting. There were also further suggestions to examine, and then the session began to expire, as SIT sessions sometimes did when nobody knew where to go from there, in an atmosphere of impasse and an attempt at a summing-up from Nahari: "Pull yourselves together. It's a case like any other case. We have to look for a motive. His mother. And talk to Meroz again. How did he do on the polygraph?"

"We haven't done it yet, because of his heart attack," Michael reminded them. "It was serious, and we'll have to wait another two weeks. He's not allowed to be excited." Nahari was silent.

At the door, on his way out—Sarit was collecting the papers and Nahari ceremoniously lighting a cigar—Michael suddenly said, "Or maybe we'll just have to rock the boat there, because we're really stuck."

Nahari looked at him over the cigar and carefully asked him, "How exactly do you intend to do that?" But Michael closed the door without replying.

The noises outside the secretariat door made the policemen lower their voices. Someone had a hand on the door handle and was pushing it violently up and down. Then came a shout: "Open up, open up!"

"Didn't I tell you?" whispered Jojo triumphantly. "Here comes Fanya."

Michael nodded, and the lab technician put the bottle in the plastic bag and sealed it. "We're off," said Machluf Levy, and Michael stood up to let them pass by him in the room that was too small to hold them all comfortably. In the treasury and accounts room next door, the telephone rang despairingly, but Fanya's yells as she burst into the secretariat—pushing Machluf Levy and the technician aside, ignoring Michael Ohayon, making a beeline for Moish and pouncing on him—drowned everything else out.

"What have you done to him? You bastard, what have you done to him?"

"Fanya," said Moish, standing up. "Calm down, Fanya."

"You said something to someone, and they took him away in an ambulance!" yelled Fanya. "And to me, his mother, nobody says anything!"

"It's only for tests," said Jojo. "They're not going to do anything to him."

"And where's that nurse? I can't find her!"

"She left. There's a new nurse," said Moish.

"You take me now to my child. Now, right this minute!" said

Fanya in a fiery voice, stepping over to Moish, grabbing his arm, and pulling him. "Now you come with me in the van to where he is! Where is he?"

Moish looked at Michael in a silent plea for help. "He's in the hospital in Ashkelon," said Michael in a soothing tone. "They'll send him home tomorrow. It's just for tests."

"Who's that?" asked Fanya, and without waiting for a reply, she went on, "You take me?" She let go of Moish's arm, turned to Michael and gave him a threatening look. "So you take me there now, now! Ashkelon! Where you took him!"

"There's no point. He'll be back tomorrow," ventured Moish.

"For me," said Fanya, "there's no tomorrow. Maybe you're so clever, you know what happens tomorrow. For me there's no tomorrow. If you don't take me now, now, I walk by foot. By foot I walk!" The last words were uttered in a scream as she approached Michael, standing on tiptoe to seize hold of his collar with both her swollen hands, with fingers misshapen by years of work. She shook him with all her strength and screamed broken, unintelligible syllables.

It was impossible to shake her off, impossible to silence her. He had to make a strenuous effort to pry her hands off his shirt collar, which began to make a tearing sound. He noticed the blue number tattooed on her arm, and uneasily aware of the false note in his would-be reassuring tone, he said to Moish, "No problem, take her to the hospital in Ashkelon, he's there in the psychiatric ward. Take her now and bring her back here. I want to talk to her when she comes back."

Fanya calmed down at once. Her body went limp, but her hands trembled. She sat down on a chair and clamped her lips together. "Come on," said Moish in a shaky voice, "I'll take you. Do you want Guta to come too?" Fanya did not reply. She stood up and went to the door, and Moish followed her out.

"Who's Guta?" asked Michael.

"Guta's her sister," said Jojo quickly.

"And are they very close?"

"They came here together after the war. Guta's older."

"Is she like that too?"

"No," said Jojo without asking what he meant. "She's much more normal. She's in charge of the dairy section. There isn't another one like it for miles around; she's won a lot of prizes for her cows. There are legends about Guta; they say that when her daughter was small, she walked on all fours and said 'moo' all day in order to get the same attention her mother gave the cows. She works like a demon."

Michael remembered Aaron Meroz's stories. "And is she communicative?" he asked Jojo, who again without asking what he meant, said, "She talks like a human being. Very good Hebrew. She learned Hebrew in the old country. She doesn't have an accent."

"The milking barn and the sewing shop," Michael reflected aloud, "both central places. The sewing shop is a hotbed of gossip, right?"

Jojo shuddered and whispered, "Not this one. They're both close as the grave. They don't tell anyone anything. Fanya doesn't talk at all. Guta sometimes talks in the *sicha*. But only sometimes. And when she does say something—boy oh boy!"

"You mean," said Michael slowly, "that her words carry weight?"

"Oho!" said Jojo. "And how!"

"I want to talk to her," said Michael, his mind made up.

"Now?" asked Jojo. "What for?"

Michael did not reply.

"You want me to take you to her?"

Michael nodded.

Jojo looked at his watch, sighed, and said, "Oh, well, all right."

They walked quickly, in silence, down the kibbutz paths. Once again Michael sensed the contradiction between the tempo of his movements and the surrounding serenity. Children rode bicycles on the paths, and three toddlers were being pushed in a mobile playpen with creaking wheels. The playpen was wider than the path, and the wheels were crushing the grass. The young man pushing it and the toddlers sitting inside were tanned and serene. One of the babies, with golden curls, stared at Michael and Jojo with her big eyes and stuck a plump thumb into her mouth. On the lawns, in front of the open doors, parents sat with their children. Sounds of clattering cups came from the rooms. Again Michael took in the cultivated landscape around him, the pruned, thick-trunked trees, the sign saying "Six-hundred-year-old sycamore" on one of the massive trunks, the greenness of the lawns, the merrily dancing sprinklers. Once or twice old women in golf carts forced them to step off the path onto the lawn. They passed the culture center, the sports hall, and the spacious playing field, from which they could hear cheering and a thudding ball; they passed playgrounds with jungle gyms and slides. People in bathing suits were returning from the pool on their bicycles.

"Is it far?" Michael finally asked.

"No, it's right here, in the founders' quarters," said Jojo, who was sweating profusely in spite of the increasing nip in the air. He walked as if it cost him an effort, and he stopped and bent down to fiddle with the buckle of his dusty, shabby biblical sandal. When he straightened up, his expression was very tense. He fingered the unfastened top button of his shirt, pointed to a row of houses, and said, "The second room is Guta and Simec's."

"You're coming with me," stated Michael firmly.

But Jojo shook his head, an expression of real fear on his face. "What should I say?" he asked. "That you're from the police?"

"No, you'll say that I'm from the psychiatric service, here from Ashkelon in connection with Yankele."

Jojo gave in with obvious unwillingness. "In the end she'll know the truth, they always know in the end," he said despairingly, "and she won't forgive me for it."

Michael thought about his first impression of Jojo, of the composure he had displayed in the interview in Petah Tikva, and he wondered what had made that calm composure, that rational behavior, give way to his present anxiety. Finding the bottle, he thought, which had verified everything he had resisted believing. And having to keep the secret probably hadn't helped either.

Jojo knocked discreetly on the door, which opened immediately, as if someone had been standing behind it waiting for the knock. Guta was at the door, and Simec was sitting and reading the newspaper, his feet resting on a small wicker stool. The floor of the room was wet. In the middle of washing it, Guta stood next to the pail, mop in hand, and looked at them unwelcomingly. "Wait a minute," she said to Jojo, "it'll be dry in a minute." They stood in the doorway, and Michael noticed a pair of big black rubber boots, the kind that children used to wear once, standing all muddy outside the door next to a big oleander bush. "That's the way it goes when your grandchildren give you joy; it's unavoidable," she said. And while she vigorously wiped the gray floor with a dry cloth, she asked after Jojo's children.

It was clear to Michael that she had noticed him, even though she took care to show no sign of interest. "That's it, you can come in," she said, again turning to Jojo—only to Jojo. "What would you like to drink? A cup of coffee?" Michael wondered how she would have behaved if he had not been accompanied by the kibbutz treasurer.

"I really haven't got time, Guta," pleaded Jojo. "I haven't been back to the room all day."

Guta looked at him with surprise. "I thought that this is the representative of the computer company, for the milking barn," she said, "and that we were going to go over the plans."

All this time her husband hadn't said a word. He had taken his feet off the stool and put the newspaper down, but he hadn't spoken. He had an unpleasantly ingratiating smile.

"No," said Jojo, "he isn't the computer man, he's . . . " and he looked at Michael, who said, "My name's Michael Ohayon, and I'm here about Yankele's condition."

Guta's expression changed immediately. The look in her eyes was now one of profound suspicion and alarm. She stood next to the sink with an electric teakettle in her hand, and her body froze. "He's from the mental-health services," mumbled Jojo, taking a step toward the door. "We had a problem with Fanya."

Guta put the teapot down on the tile counter; her hands were shaking, but she controlled herself.

"Nothing's happened to her," Jojo quickly assured her. "She's all right. She just wanted to see Yankele. They took him to Ashkelon because he hasn't been taking his medication."

Guta wiped her hands on the apron she was wearing over her floral dress and then took it off. "So where are they now?" she asked in a trembling voice, looking at the door as if she intended going to them directly.

"They're in Ashkelon," said Michael in a calm, reassuring voice. "They'll be back tonight or tomorrow. We just want to keep Yankele under observation for a while, to see how he's doing. I just want to talk to you, to ask your advice—about Fanya's outburst, too."

Guta's face relaxed, something of her anxiety dissolving, but her suspicions remained. "I have to run," said Jojo, "they've been waiting for me for hours, it's nearly seven already. When are you going to the dining hall?" he asked Simec, who was still sitting silently in his chair with the newspaper on his knees.

Simec smiled and said, "Later, afterward, the grandchildren have just gone."

As Jojo was leaving, Michael looked around the living room and, at one end of it, the kitchenette with its small refrigerator and oven. On the counter was a big baking sheet with two rolls of yeast cake on it. They gave off a marvelous smell of freshly baked pastry, which almost overcame the strong smell of the cleaning materials still hanging in the air. Leading out of the living room was a narrow hallway giving onto two doors—to the bedroom and the bathroom, he surmised. He sat down on an easy chair covered in a pale wool fabric unpleasant to the touch. Opposite him stood a matching couch, the upholstery covered with a starched white sheet, the likes of which he had only seen in his ex-wife Nira's parents' big salon, where Fela kept the furniture covered with such sheets, removing them unwillingly only for special occasions. Guta did just that with the sheet on the couch and folded it with nervous movements.

Between the armchair he was sitting on and the couch stood a dark, square wooden table, holding a bowl of fruit and a smaller dish of little sweets, whose very appearance gave rise to a sourish taste in his mouth. The fruit bowl stood on a crocheted doily with a lacy pattern and dangling tassels. When Michael looked around him he saw that every object in the room stood on such a doily: even the big television set gleaming on a bookshelf, the big Venetian glass fish next to it, and a big empty vase. On the armchair next to him, Simec sat smiling, his head, too, resting against a round doily. On the wooden shelves, supported by metal posts, Michael noted the two volumes of *Scrolls of Fire*, the memorial to the fallen in the War of Independence. There were only a few other books on the shelves. Around the yellow Formica table dividing the kitchenette from the living room stood six slender-legged chairs whose seats were upholstered in green plastic. Everything shone with cleanliness.

Unexpectedly, Simec broke the silence, "I'm going out to prune a bit, before it gets dark," he apologized to his wife as he rose heavily from his chair. There was something childish in his smooth face and in the eyes that looked at her for a moment in apprehension. Guta did not bother to reply. She sat on the wicker stool, her eyes fixed on Michael as if waiting for a judge to pass sentence.

When they were alone, she said suddenly in a restrained voice, "Now." Then she took a deep breath, and he shivered. "Now, tell me exactly what happened." He immediately noticed her rhetorical ability, so superior to her sister's, and in general there seemed to be no resemblance between them, apart from the blue number tattooed on the arm, to which Michael's eyes were drawn again and again, irresistibly, like a child looking precisely at the place where he has been forbidden to look.

"Nothing happened. He hasn't been taking his medicine, and Dr. Reimer was worried about his condition. He applied to us, and we took him in for observation. It's for his own good. Your sister, Fanya, heard that he had left the kibbutz, and she reacted with a hysterical outburst. I wanted to ask you what you thought, how she would react to hospitalization or something similar."

"Out of the question," said Guta, pursing her lips. "There's nothing to discuss. He's the son of a kibbutz member, he's a kibbutz member in his own right, and nobody but his parents will decide what happens to him."

"He's no longer a child," said Michael, "and he could be dangerous to himself and to others."

"He's a wonderful boy," said Guta. "Problematic, but a wonderful boy who wouldn't hurt a fly." Pursing her lips again, she said firmly, "And nobody's taking him anywhere. We look after him here ourselves, with the doctor and the nurse." She pulled a crumpled pack of cigarettes out of her pocket, lit one, took a deep puff, and saying, "Just a minute, please," got up, went outside, and called, "Simec! Simec!" Michael could see him emerging from behind the bushes through the mesh of the screen door, which she had taken care to close behind her, and he heard her saying something about supper. "So, three yogurts and six eggs?" asked Simec, and Guta nodded her head and came back inside.

"It's both insensitive and irresponsible, taking him away without consulting us," she said. "Why couldn't they say something? Sometimes I just don't understand. And some concern should be shown for Fanya too. She shouldn't be upset. Her health . . . " She fell silent, and her face clouded in an expression of distress.

"How long have you and your sister been on the kibbutz?" asked Michael.

"Since forty-six," said Guta, going into the kitchenette. Again she filled the teakettle and clattered cups. "You'll have a cup of coffee?" Michael murmured a polite thanks.

"Not long after the war," he said, and Guta sighed in confirmation.

"Why here precisely?" he asked, as she placed lace doilies on the table and set the containers of milk and sugar on them. She sighed again, went back to the kitchenette, poured the boiling water into the glass cups, and carried them in.

Only then did she sit down, remove the cigarette butt from the corner of her mouth, and say, "Well, what a question. We didn't exactly know where to go. It was because of Srulke that we came here. Srulke was a kibbutz member who passed away a month ago."

"And how did he come into the picture?"

Guta gave him a quizzical look. "How old are you?" she asked.

"Forty-four," said Michael. He knew when a straight answer was required.

"So you really can't be expected to know, especially since they don't teach these things at school in town. There's Holocaust Day and that's it. Over here we see to it that the children know exactly what happened, and what part kibbutz members played in the War of Independence and the Jewish Brigade and the rescue and escape organization, the Bericha."

"The Bericha?" asked Michael, and Guta cocked her head and looked at him mockingly. She passed a dark hand through her cropped gray hair. "It sounds to you like something out of a children's adventure story, doesn't it? You've never heard of it before, right?" And after lighting another cigarette, she asked, "What are you, a social worker?"

Michael confirmed her assumption with a vague gesture.

"In that case you should know such things," said Guta in a tone that made him feel like a rebuked child.

"What was the Bericha?" he finally asked explicitly.

"First of all, you can read about it in the literature if you want to. There's a book here by Avidov," she said, standing up and striding across to the bookshelf, where she pulled out a big book. "He was one of the organizers. It was an organization run jointly by the Jewish Agency and the Joint Distribution Committee. The entire Jewish population of Palestine took part in it, although afterward we heard that there were fights between the different component bodies."

"What about?" asked Michael.

"It was the organization that brought the refugees to this country," said Guta impatiently, "and as usual, they were interested not only in the good of the refugees, but also in their own jockeying for power. Human beings!" she said with contempt and blew her cigarette smoke sideways. "Instead of working properly, they get sidetracked and mess things up. If only everyone would just do his work properly, everything would be different."

"So the Bericha was an organization run jointly by a number of different bodies," Michael clarified to himself. "And you came to the country with them?"

Guta ignored his question. "There was a division of authority, there were power struggles. Eitan Avidov, Avidov's son, was killed in a fight between the Irgun and the Haganah over the Bericha operations in Italy."

"Killed? For that?" asked Michael in astonishment.

Guta did not reply, and Michael thought of Yuval running through the streets of Bethlehem.

"We were in Italy," she said suddenly in a different voice, away in a world he could not share, "in Milan, in a refugee center, and there too we fell between two stools. The American Joint were responsible, they paid for the food and transport. There were similar centers in all kinds of places—in Austria, in Italy, in Czechoslovakia. The best organized was apparently the one in Austria—in Milan it was terrible, nobody knew . . . and in Castel Gandolfo . . . if it hadn't been for Srulke, who stayed behind after serving in Italy in the Jewish Brigade, who knows what would have become of us? Fanya was so sick . . .

"What am I doing here?" Michael asked himself in a sudden panic. "Why am I sitting talking about such things, where will it all lead, why don't I get to the point?" But then he heard himself ask, as if against his will, without knowing why, "And how did you get here, what kind of a journey was it?"

"What do you want, the whole story? It's a long story," said Guta. The room was growing dark, and she stood up to switch on the light. Michael could see on her face the wish to talk, together with the resistance. He looked at her intently. Something told him to follow the inclinations of his heart, before her momentary serenity, this fragile trust he had managed to establish, was disturbed.

"It's a long story," repeated Guta hesitantly, and she suddenly smiled. The smile cracked her dry skin. There was something dreamy about it. The lines of her face softened, her beaky nose appeared less prominent in the sharp face whose wrinkles had blurred. "If I had the talent, I would write it, someone should write it." And after a minute, suddenly, without any further preliminaries or hesitation, she said, "We crossed into Italy on foot through the Alps, and we were smuggled over the border itself in closed trucks, like cattle. It was in forty-six; everything was corrupt, everyone took bribes, and the Italian police were no exception. They didn't even open the tarpaulins, and we got off at the railway station in Verona, and from there we were taken to Milan, where there was a kitchen that fed all the refugees. It was a transit point, and from there we were transferred to Castel Gandolfo. There we waited half a year for the ship to come and take us. And there we met Srulke. From there we went to Metaponto, where there was a camp for the insane."

"The insane?" asked Michael.

She looked at him as if she had forgotten his presence. "That's what they called it for the authorities," she said impatiently, as if he should have understood it by himself. "And there was no food and nothing to drink, and it was winter, and the ship was five kilometers from shore, and we waited there for three days, because of the militia. And all the time we pretended to be insane. I remember how they would say, 'Jump, jump, shout, they're coming to check, there's an inspection.' And after three days we embarked on that small old ship, which was no good for anything except transporting refugees. We made the journey in concentration-camp conditions. There was no room to lie down properly. There were metal pens and people vomiting on each other, and finally the ship sprung a leak and began to sink, and then three British cruisers arrived, and a few heroes in our group threw cans of food at them. The British surrounded us, they grabbed hold of people and actually threw them onto the battleships, and that's how we arrived in Haifa, on the night of the explosion of the refineries. That same night we landed, and they took us off the cruisers. It was night."

She took a deep breath, as if she saw the scene in front of her, and went on talking: "There was a guard there with a red beret, and they took us off one by one, and there was a British officer standing there, and I asked him if I could send a letter, and he said, 'Write it and I'll send it.' I wrote to Srulke, who was the only person I knew in the country, from the six months in Italy, and I wrote and told him that we were in Haifa and I didn't know what was going to happen to us. They took away what little we still had left and put us into some building with big rooms and told us to go to sleep, and they were the ships *Osher* and *Yagur*!" she said in a dramatic tone. "And he sent the letter, that officer, he actually sent it. Srulke showed it to me," she explained, shaking her head in wonder.

"What?" asked Michael, spellbound by the story. "Ships?"

"Yes, prison ships, there were two of them, acquired by the Haganah for bringing refugees to the country and later impounded by the British. And when we woke up we were in the middle of the sea. And from there a year and a half in a detention camp in Cyprus."

"That's terrible," Michael ventured.

"It was very hard," said Guta, who had not even mentioned the war that had preceded all this, "and some people went really insane. You could see the stuff people were made of by their reactions at sea. All the time, by all kinds of things, you can tell what people are. They're capable of anything, anything, but when they were in the middle of the sea, on the way to Cyprus, and realized what was happening, that after everything they'd been through they weren't in the land of Israel, they didn't care anymore. They didn't hide anything."

In the silence that fell in the room, the chirping of crickets and distant croaks became audible. Guta took a deep breath and broke the silence with a statement full of wonder at herself: "All these years I've never told anyone, I always said it was a long story. In our first years here nobody asked us anything either, they didn't want to remind us, but Srulke knew. He came to get us when we returned from Cyprus, and he knew the whole story. Maybe his death is what's made me talk." She looked at Michael with a friendlier look, perplexed, exposed, and vulnerable.

"So it must have been a grim voyage—with the way people were behaving and everything, I mean," said Michael in a reflective tone, covering up his agitation, alarmed by the thought of what he was going to say soon, when he would be relinquishing in a few moments, with great sadness, the sympathy and trust he had inspired with so small an effort on his part. He looked at her and thought that this woman would not be able to hide the facts for an instant, that arguments about expediency would have no effect on her. She's the person, he thought as he came to his decision to lance the boil, who would not be afraid of the pain, as long as it's out in the open.

"I want to tell you something," said Michael. "I'm not a social worker, I'm a policeman. I'm a chief superintendent, a section head in the Unit for Serious Crimes Investigation."

Guta choked, her face turned to stone, frozen in an expression of astonishment. And before it turned to one of betrayal, to anger at having been tricked, Michael hurried to add, "And I'm not here about Yankele. I'm here because of Osnat's death."

Guta sat rigid. The only thing she couldn't control was the trembling of her hands.

"Osnat didn't die of pneumonia but of parathion poisoning, apparently not accidental but deliberate poisoning. In short—there was a murder here on your kibbutz." The trembling of her hands was so terrible that he would have preferred her to scream. It was hard to see her like this. "Up to now," he continued, "we've kept it a secret. Except for a handful of people, nobody on the kibbutz knows. But I'm telling you because now I need your help, your advice. You have power. And you've given me an idea."

From somewhere in the distance Guta's voice emerged, faint and shaky, hoarse. She folded her arms, dug her big, broad-nailed fingers into them, and asked, "Does Dvorka know?"

He nodded.

"And she kept quiet?" She sounded stunned. "She didn't say anything?"

Michael was silent.

"Who else knows?" she demanded, her voice clearer. He listed the names.

"You're not surprised," said Michael. "What I've told you doesn't surprise you."

"It's very difficult to surprise me," said Guta, but her hand, which was lighting another cigarette, went on trembling.

"Yankele used to hang around outside her room at night."

"Don't talk nonsense!" shouted Guta. "There was nothing he had to do there."

"You don't know anything about his relations with Osnat?" asked Michael.

"There's nothing to know. He's never had any relations with girls. It causes Fanya a lot of pain."

"Nothing? You don't know anything about it?" insisted Michael.

"What, that he had a crush on Osnat?" said Guta dismissively. "I thought so when he was a child, but it was over a long time ago, and he didn't do anything to her. I'll give my right hand that he didn't do anything to her."

"But there's a possibility that he knows something we don't know."

"I find that hard to believe. Yankele's a good worker, but he doesn't exactly live in the real world. He never sees a thing."

"And Fanya?"

"What about Fanya?" Guta started, and the tremor in her hands, which had grown fainter, came back in full force.

"Did Fanya know that he . . . that he had a crush on Osnat?"

"We didn't talk about it, but what if she did know?" asked Guta indignantly.

"She's the younger sister?" Michael asked suddenly. "You see yourself as responsible for her?"

"She's my little sister," said Guta, her hands still trembling.

"I wonder," said Michael, "how she would have reacted if she'd known about his crush on Osnat."

"What's there to react about," said Guta in undisguised anger. "You're talking nonsense, she wouldn't have done anything to Osnat."

"But she didn't like her, she didn't like Osnat."

Guta said, "Leave Fanya alone. You're not going anywhere near

Fanya. You can talk to me. I told you that Fanya never did anything to anyone, and I don't know if she even knows what parathion is. There's obviously nothing to talk about." She spoke in an angry, threatening tone, and her hands had steadied.

Michael said, "We'll have to talk to Fanya. There'll have to be an investigation. There was a murder here. But we'll be as discreet as possible. It's for her own good." He thought about Maya and her anger at what she called "using people manipulatively."

"You won't talk to Fanya!" said Guta fiercely. "And don't talk rubbish about her own good. She's never done anything to hurt anyone, and your investigations don't frighten me." Her breath came in gasps, her face was alight with anger. "I'm going to talk to the other members about it, I'm going right this minute to talk to Dvorka and Moish and all the other people who think they're so clever. What do you think, you can just walk in here and talk to Fanya? Police? You think you can do what you like here?" And then, after taking a deep breath, she took a step toward him. She didn't touch him, but there was a threat in her voice when she raised her hand as if to slap him and said, "You can forget about secrets from now on!"

She made for the door, and Michael felt as if he had set a golem in motion. When she left the room he felt the terror filling him at the thought that he himself had released the brakes, that he was going to see an entire kibbutz seized by panic at a deed that had no precedent. He tried to calm his own alarm, to push it aside by saying things to himself like "Thank God people are sometimes predictable," but all the way to Dave's room he could not shake off the panic that gripped him at the thought of what was going to happen in this big family when they found out how Osnat had really died.

13

Sitting hours later with Shorer and Avigail in the small café on the main street of Jerusalem's Machane Yehuda market, he could still hear Dave's deep laughter. It seemed to resound through this place where, even though they were out of uniform, everyone knew but pretended not to know who they were. The pretense was maintained even when, as it was now, their marked car was conspicuously parked just outside the broad entrance to the café. Shorer sat on a little wooden stool, and Avigail—in the long-sleeved white shirt she was wearing despite the heat, with the blue jeans and the ponytail that made her look like a high school student—on an orange plastic chair, looking around alertly, as if she were determined to take in everything and remember her impressions.

At one o'clock in the morning even the main street of the market was quiet and dark, apart from the patch of light surrounding the small café, where people sat till dawn playing cards and filling in soccer-pool cards to the accompaniment of loud exchanges of views. A handful of boozers came there too, to get drunk in company. As they were entering the café, Michael had noticed, sitting inside, an elderly man with a thick gray beard and bloodshot eyes whose shabby clothes looked too warm for the hot, dry Jerusalem night. He gave off the stench of someone who slept in his clothes and whose body had not been washed for days, and even after sitting down with his back to him, Michael could not shake off the sight of that thick gray beard and those bloodshot eyes, which joined the sound of Dave's warm laughter still echoing in his head.

In front of Emanuel Shorer on the small, sticky Formica table stood a tall, full glass of beer. Avigail ordered mint tea and a *bureka*, which was served warm and fresh, and Michael, despite Shorer's snickers and sighs, ordered a tiny cup of Turkish coffee and a glass of cold water and shook his head to rid it of sights and sounds of the day still ringing in his ears: Fanya's shouts, Guta's parting whispers, and Dave's laughter, which was not in the least demonic. It was, in fact, warm, unrestrained, good-humored, without inhibition or pain, the laugh of a man who allows himself to see the picture and hear the words and lets the sounds escape freely from his throat.

"In a few hours, she'll be arriving for work there," Shorer said thoughtfully, "and the place will be a shambles." Then he straightened up on the little wooden stool, turned to Michael, and nervously asked him, "Have you spoken to Nahari? Does he know that you've let the cat out of the bag?"

"I have, and he does," Michael reassured him.

"And what did he say?" asked Shorer, curiosity overcoming his nervousness.

"He said that I could have consulted him first. Although," Michael added with a smile, "he also said that he had a feeling I was going to do it, but that it wasn't my job to do things on my own, and that I should have consulted a psychologist too, which is probably right. But it guess I wanted it to be spontaneous. Or maybe I just didn't think of it," he admitted; "the psychologist, I mean."

"You got off lightly," said Shorer, and he looked at Avigail, who was carefully fishing the mint leaves out of her glass and laying them on the empty *bureka* plate.

"How come?" asked Michael.

Shorer sipped his beer and said, "That he didn't yell at you, bawl you out."

"Who says he didn't?" Michael said with a little smile. "You didn't ask me exactly what happened. He made a big speech about the fact that I wasn't working alone, that I wasn't in the Jerusalem Subdistrict anymore, and that in his outfit everyone is at least as intelligent as I am. And hadn't I ever heard of teamwork, and if I had, why didn't I put it into practice and use the members of my team, 'exploit the resources at my command,' in his words?"

"Quite right too," said Shorer, giving him a hard look. "And if I were you, I wouldn't be so proud of what I'm doing."

"Who's proud of what?" Michael protested.

"You are," said Shorer mercilessly. "You're walking around feeling that you're carrying that whole kibbutz on your shoulders and you're going to save them and reveal the truth about themselves to them. There's a smirk on your face as if you've got the fate of the whole kibbutz movement in your hands—you, the man who dropped the bombshell and takes sole responsibility for the consequences. As if," he said, gulping down the last of his beer, "you're the only person in the world who understands anything."

"Why are you so angry with me?" Michael asked in surprise. After a moment's reflection, he looked at Avigail and said, "It's because of her, because I put you on the spot about her."

"Don't tell me what my motives are," said Shorer angrily. "Stay out of my head, please, if you don't mind." He looked around. The drunks looked in their direction, the soccer-pool players fell silent, and only the three men playing cards went on with their game as if they hadn't heard anything. He lowered his voice. "No, it isn't because of Avigail; it's because you worked alone without understanding the risk you were taking, and I'm not talking about the fact that now there's a poisoner loose there who knows that everyone knows and who could now be even more dangerous than before. That's not what I'm talking about, and don't tell me"—he held up his hand to stop Michael—"don't tell me that you left Machluf Levy and Benny from your team there, because you know very well that I'm not talking about physical dangers now. I'm talking about psychological dangers, about the implications of dropping that kind of bombshell. I don't have to remind you that no such thing has ever happened before. You didn't discuss it with anyone beforehand, the people there aren't ready for it, their reactions weren't taken into account, and you carry on blithely, wander around there, and talk to that spaced-out American freak . . . "

"Canadian," Michael corrected him.

"Okay, Canadian . . . and come to me with bright ideas. But you've left them there with the feeling that there's a murderer among them. Three hundred members and their families."

"Three hundred twenty-seven," Michael corrected him wearily.

He ignored the look Shorer gave him as he said, "Who am I, Ariyeh Levy, that you've begun talking to me like that? Maybe success really has gone to your head."

Avigail touched her empty glass and cleared her throat.

"And I'm purposely not waiting until we're alone," added Shorer furiously. "This is no time for discretion. Like an idiot, I gave you permission to send Avigail there, but I gave it to you before you made everything public. It's not the same anymore. You told me that only four people knew that the Harel woman was murdered. You didn't tell me you were going to reveal that to the entire kibbutz. And it's important for you to know too"— he turned to Avigail—"that you're going to a wounded place, a place in shock, and you'll have a lot of work to do. People who had felt a little out of sorts are going to be really sick, people who were always quiet and reserved are suddenly going to be hysterical. It's impossible to predict how they'll take it. They need a psychologist there now."

"They'll have one," said Michael. "I left a psychologist there too, I asked for one to be sent."

"Well, I don't know," Shorer said more calmly, sighing. "You have to stop working alone. Maybe now with Avigail you won't have any option but to work with her."

"Believe me," said Michael after a pause, "I know there's something in what you say, but we were completely stuck. It's not as if I decided on it during a team meeting and kept it to myself. The idea was simmering somewhere at the back of my mind, and finally it took on concrete shape when I saw Fanya and heard about Guta. It was only then that I knew I was looking for a way of doing it, of rocking the boat."

"Okay, let's leave it at that," said Shorer impatiently, "there's no point in talking about it anymore. Just don't think you're God. It's very dangerous when a man starts thinking he's God. Now let's get on to what seems the crux of the matter. What's your story?"

"Do you want the full-length version or the bottom line?"

"The bottom line first, and the rest later, if necessary."

Michael was silent. "I'm wondering," he said after long moments, "how to put it so it doesn't sound completely off the wall. Maybe I'll just say it straight out. The bottom line is that Srulke didn't die of a heart attack but of parathion poisoning."

"Srulke," Shorer pronounced slowly. "Who is Srulke again?"

"Srulke was Moish's, the kibbutz general director's, father. From the founders' generation, seventy-five years old, in charge of the landscape gardening. He died five weeks ago of a heart attack, as they thought, but the idea came up that it too might have been parathion, because he was the only one who still used the stuff. Dave, the Canadian, said that Srulke sprayed his roses the day they found him dead. I had a long talk with him after the business with Guta today, and he came up with the idea."

"Does Nahari know?" asked Shorer suspiciously.

"What is it about you and Nahari?" asked Michael irritably. "Why are you so concerned about him?"

"I'm not concerned about him, I'm concerned about you, about the right and proper order of things, about you not working alone. Nahari is your superior officer; you can't come and tell me things without talking to him. I'm concerned about myself as well—I don't need any trouble with him. You can't keep doing this, going above his head, coming to me to fix things up for you, as if I were your father or something . . . " He caught himself too late and looked in embarrassment at Michael, who dropped his eyes and turned the still half-full glass of water around in his fingers before taking a sip. Shorer took a deep breath and went on, ignoring the strained atmosphere with obvious effort: "And as I've already said, he's not Ariyeh Levy and he wasn't born yesterday. So does he know or not?"

"He knows," said Michael resentfully. "He knows."

Avigail rested her chin on her hand and said nothing. It sometimes seemed that they had forgotten her presence, but Michael was constantly aware of the delicacy of the slender wrists peeping out of her long white sleeves and wondered why she chose to wear them in such heat. What myth was she building around herself, what was she trying to hide? What lay beneath those long sleeves of hers? When he too ordered mint tea, he noticed the card players again, shouting and laughing. He looked out at the street, where a car occasionally sped past, its wheels screeching on the bend after the café. The street was dirty. Rotten fruit, squashed cardboard boxes, plastic bags, and empty cigarette packs littered the space in front of the café entrance. The smell of dust and garbage hung in the air, and he himself felt dusty and sticky after the long day, and exhausted by the drive from Jerusalem to Petah Tikva and from there to the kibbutz and then back to Jerusalem, and by the constant confrontations with people and the telephone conversations with Nahari.

Now he was sorry that he hadn't stopped at home, that he had only phoned to see if Yuval had arrived. Yuval was there. He had operated the washing machine by himself, he announced, and ironed his uniform. His leave would be over tomorrow morning, and by now he was already fast asleep. He would only be able to see him briefly in the morning, thought Michael as he recalled the telephone conversation with his son from the kibbutz before leaving for Jerusalem. There was no irony in Yuval's voice when he said, "Try to get here, Dad, if you can. It would be nice to see each other sometimes." He said nothing about the distress in which he was living, but Michael knew very well—precisely because there was no anger or bitterness in his voice, precisely because of the gentle, adult tone—something of the compassion only those who have experienced suffering can feel. Through this compassion Michael heard loneliness, and again he thought that the tour of duty in Bethlehem had matured him, aged him, and robbed him of his youth. But for the fact that Yuval had a girlfriend—thought Michael as the glass of mint tea was set before him, causing Shorer to fall silent and wait for the proprietor to leave them—he would probably be more worried about him than he was. Although there too things weren't exactly cheerful, since the girl now was in Military Justice in Aza, and they didn't have many opportunities to meet.

Michael often pictured the two of them when they had still been serving together: They had seemed so childish and innocent in their shy love and with her embarrassment on the weekends when Yuval brought her to his father's house, the seriousness with which she spoke of the "group"—the Nahal unit to which they both had belonged—and her awkwardness when she tried to explain her motives for leaving it. More recently she seemed to have lost her awkwardness and also her embarrassment.

"With your connections, you could have arranged something," Nira had said bitterly to Michael when they met at the basic-training graduation parade, "but why should you bother, it's only your son. I would have pulled every string there is to get him out of the paratroopers."

"I did," Michael had said in a rare moment of identification with her. "I pulled every string I could, believe me, and they promised me too, but he didn't want it. They promised me they would transfer him against his will. I don't understand what happened and how come he's there anyway."

"So go and pull some more strings," said Nira ruthlessly. "Today they send paratroopers to the territories. My son's not going to serve in the territories—it's dangerous; you can get killed there."

He hadn't answered. It had been a few years since he had seen her last, and despite the familiar tone of endless complaint, he was sad to see the gray in her fair hair and the net of fine lines surrounding her mouth. For the thousandth time he had asked himself whether things could have turned out differently.

"What did Nahari say about it?" Shorer wanted to know.

"About what?" asked Michael. "What did he say about what?"

"About the business with Srulke. What did he say about the possibility of there being another unnatural death there?"

"Nothing," said Michael absentmindedly, feeling tired and depressed and again noticing Avigail's slender, transparent fingers as she chewed a lock of her hair. "What could he say? He called Kestenbaum and asked him if it was possible to know after five weeks, because we couldn't find a precedent for exhuming a body after such a long time to check for parathion poisoning."

"Well?" said Shorer.

"Well, so Kestenbaum looked it up and said that it was possible." He grimaced. "It seems that after a month you can't see the percentage of cholinesterase in the blood, but you can still identify traces of parathion in the decomposition fluid, if you'll forgive the graphic detail."

"So do we have to dig him up for an autopsy?" asked Shorer. "In other words, I mean, are there sufficient grounds for it?"

"It depends on how you look at it. What I didn't tell Nahari is how he came to his conclusion."

"Who?" asked Shorer.

"Dave. How Dave arrived at his conclusion," said Michael, and again he saw the big body and completely bald head of the man sitting in his room on the outskirts of the kibbutz, in the singles' quarters, not far from the room belonging to Yankele, with whom, so he said, he had a close and special relationship.

"Could you tell me something now about this Dave, please?" said Avigail in her lucid voice, startling them both. "I'm quite nervous about landing there tomorrow after what's happened today, and altogether I'm not exactly delighted about the job. In any case, I'd prefer to know as much as possible beforehand."

"You needn't be so tense," Shorer reassured her in a paternal voice, emphasizing the word *so*. "You're not going to be all on your own there. He"—he nodded toward Michael—"will be in touch with you all the time."

"It's not going to be so simple," said Michael. "By now everybody knows who I am, and they've got a supermodern telephone exchange there—it registers every incoming and outgoing call—and we don't want NUSCI calls being registered to Avigail's phone."

"So steal in to her at night," said Shorer, laughing—but suddenly he stopped and looked thoughtfully from Michael to Avigail, a roguish twinkle gleaming briefly in his eyes, and then he said wearily, "You'll solve it somehow, I trust you."

"I remember what you've told us and what I've read in the file about the family and about Moish," said Avigail, "and I understood Yankele's story about Guta and Fanya and all that. But what about this Dave? Please fill me in wherever you can." Her gray eyes looked at Michael expectantly, intelligently inquiring. They were deep and narrow. He was sitting close to her, seeing her rather pale but long lashes and the faint line already evident, even when she wasn't frowning, between her eyes.

"I don't know what I'm doing sitting here," said Shorer, "or how you managed to rope me in like this. But the night's already over anyway," he sighed, "so keep talking."

In a few sentences Michael described the room, the strange cactuses growing beside the front door, the relations between Dave and Yankele. "He's been there for ten years," he said; "they accepted him after a two-year period of candidacy for membership." And as he was speaking, he again heard Dave's warm laughter and remembered the tolerant look in his eyes while he explained that he had been accepted as a member despite his weirdness because he had contributed so much during his time as a candidate: "things like improving the packaging machinery, but mainly this," he said, waving a cactus he fished out of a jar standing on the windowsill. "It's our greatest hit; we make our most expensive cream out of it." And at Michael's bewildered look he laughed again and said, "I invented it."

Then he explained that in his spare time he had grafted varieties of cactuses together (he had been involved with engineering patents by profession, but cactuses had become his hobby) and succeeded in creating amazing hybrids. In the greenhouse to which he took Michael, all kinds of cactuses were riotously blooming. Dave said of himself that he was a jack-of-all-trades—"a *kolboinik,* as they call that container for discarded food on the dining-hall tables"—and there was nothing he couldn't fix. Above all, Michael said, quoting Moish, he was a wonderful worker, even Shula saying that the only person who didn't give her problems on the work roster was Dave, who went wherever he was sent. During the second year of his candidacy, they had sent him to the dining hall, and for six months he had worked there cheerful and smiling, as if cleaning tables were the ambition of his life. He had not complained even once. And he was the only person who had ever worked in the milking barn with Guta whom she asked for again. Guta said, Michael quoted Moish, that he had a way with cows and they simply loved him.

Shorer snickered, and Michael smiled despite himself. "That's what she said," he said apologetically.

Avigail pushed her hair out of her face and said, "Well, you have to know how to treat animals, and cows are animals too, no? And it says something about a person if he knows how to get along with animals. Apart from which, I understand that he lives alone there." They both looked at her.

"So in spite of his being forty-five and a vegetarian and a Canadian and a bachelor, and in spite of the fact, as he himself told me, that there are all kinds of rumors about him because of his eccentricities, they accepted him as a member," said Michael, again hearing Dave's voice in his heavily accented but fluent Hebrew:

"At the beginning, they tried to fix me up with all kinds of single women on the kibbutz, and when that didn't work they tried to send me to all kinds of seminars and ideological weekends." Dave had grinned and then laughed his deep laugh, and finally he had become completely serious, saying with a thoughtful expression that what interested him—he had thought about it a lot—was that from everything he had read about the creation of the kibbutz movement, he would never have expected them to take the institution of the family so seriously. After all, kibbutz society was supposed to be one big family, Dave had said with a puzzled air, and the family cell was perceived as being inimical to society, and here he was, discovering every single day the conservatism of the kibbutz. In fact, he had said unsmilingly, it was such a bourgeois society that they hadn't succeeded in overcoming the family cell at all. And the kibbutz, like the rest of the country, was one big family when it came to coping with tragedy, like now with Osnat's death, but when it came to the joys of life, and celebrations were a public matter too, they were a lot less enthusiastic. Had he noticed this? he had asked Michael.

To Dave's credit, he hadn't asked Michael a single question about his personal experience of kibbutz life. He had brewed the herb tea with a serious, concentrated expression on his face—he never went to the dining hall for supper—and sliced the cake he had baked himself with whole-wheat flour and dried fruit. As far as Yankele was concerned, Michael told Shorer and Avigail, scribbling something with a burned match on the matchbox, Dave had said only that he was different, not like other people. "He said that all that medication they gave him causes cumulative damage, and that this too was a proof of the conservatism of the kibbutz, that in principle it didn't accept the deviant individual."

"What do you mean, in principle?" asked Avigail. "Why does he think it should be a matter of principle here?"

"Dave said that Yankele was completely isolated and that he was his only friend. It's true that they look after him, not only his mother but other members too, he goes to parties and everything, they treat him decently, with full equality, just as they treat Dave, but in principle," Michael stressed, "in principle they don't accept the deviant individual. There's even a lesbian couple there. They don't accept lesbians in principle, but they accept the individual case; as long as they contribute to the kibbutz and work hard, they accept them and look after them. But they also isolate them."

Again Michael withdrew into himself, selecting the details he would tell them, hearing Dave's voice saying, "You can condemn them for it, but you can also see the beauty in it—that, so to speak, the individual triumphs over the principle. If you think about the sanctity of equality here, and the conformist bourgeois attitude underlying it, it's a fine thing that they accept the individual in practice, above and beyond the principle. The human being prevails over the ideology, however unconsciously and unwillingly."

Dave had smiled and then grown serious. "And Yankele is a lonely person, emotionally he's lonely. And this contradiction between physical care and economic equality, on the one hand, and the social gap and isolation, on the other, is very hard to take. If you think about it," Dave had sighed as he refilled the little Chinese porcelain teapot with boiling water, "there's something primitive, threatened about such a conservative society. Somewhere or other they confuse Yankele's intelligence with his illness, and he's actually an intelligent guy, even wise, and very well informed; he reads a lot, and when he's not having an attack, when he's calm, he's worth listening to. He understands all kinds of things, and he's open to mystical subjects."

Dave had taken a sip of tea and added that he himself was always willing to try new experiences. One of the main advantages of living on a kibbutz, he said even before being asked about his motives for living there, was the freedom from all kinds of things that people outside enslaved themselves to. Here too you could be a slave to material standards of living—he could see it all around him—but you didn't have to be. Because the minimum you were provided with here was more than enough. But he was not only talking about material goods but also about other worldly vanities, status and so on. He wanted to live a clean life, he had declared as he set the little porcelain teapot and cups down on the table, and here you could live a clean life and also create and work, and there were good people here, they weren't all limited, and it was precisely the misfits who interested him, maybe because he was one himself. He himself wasn't bothered by being labeled a misfit; it was the price you paid for being different, and it didn't make him bitter, but one of the reasons he could handle it was because he was a free man, without family or pressures. He even had an adoptive family here—Dvorka, if he knew who she was (Michael didn't react), and he took part in the *sicha*, fulfilled his obligations, volunteered for mobilizations, and they didn't try to stop him from holding his study circles on mysticism and in general had so much faith in him that they had put him in charge of the volunteers, which in his opinion was quite a feather in his cap. There was something very comforting in knowing that everything was taken care of, that you were a little cog in a big, well-oiled machine. But he didn't have any illusions. This society had nothing to do with justice.

When Michael had asked him how he had ended up on the kibbutz, Dave explained, with absolute seriousness and no self-irony, that he had come here as a volunteer looking for meaning, after he had already been all over the world, in Africa and India and God knows where else, and he had liked the austerity of his life here, and their receptiveness toward his inventions—especially the interest and openness Srulke had shown toward his experiments with the cactuses. Altogether, Dave had said, Srulke had been a special person. It was an experience to meet him, someone who with his own hands had made this land bloom, and if you went outside the borders of the kibbutz, you could see what it had been like before.

"Srulke was a man of few words. He didn't pay himself compliments, but he knew exactly what he was worth, no more and no less." Dave had explained that he and Srulke had enjoyed "mutual esteem." "And by the way," he had added with stoic calm, as if speaking in all innocence about a well-known fact, "I don't think that Srulke died of a heart attack."

"Of what, then?" Michael had asked in alarm.

"His anima wasn't compatible with a heart attack," Dave had said in a matter-of-fact tone.

"I beg your pardon? What are you talking about?" Michael had then begun to wonder whether to take everything else Dave had said with a pinch of salt as well.

"I think that he died of parathion poisoning too," Dave had said in his deep, calm voice.

"What makes you think so?"

Then had come the explanation that Michael now set forth before Shorer and Avigail. Dave knew that Srulke sprayed his rare varieties of roses against pests with parathion, habitually diluting the chemical very carefully himself. But Moish had told him that Srulke had been in the midst of working with the roses when he was stricken, and that his hands were wet from the sprinkler when they discovered him. Moreover, Dave himself, who was at the jubilee celebration when Srulke died, said that just at that time he had the mystical experience of a loss of breath, a feeling of suffocation, and so he was certain that Srulke, whose death he had sensed in this way, had died of accidental parathion poisoning.

Shorer ordered another beer. He looked at Michael, averted his eyes, and said, "Whatever I say won't come anywhere near what I think."

"Okay, I told you. I warned you," said Michael. "I know it isn't logical. But logic doesn't seem to have gotten me anywhere so far."

"Explain that to the court when you apply for an exhumation order," said Shorer unsmilingly.

"Excuse me," said Avigail. "I don't want to argue with feelings, and I don't think that there's no such thing as telepathy in the world. What I'm asking is this: If Srulke died at work, in an accident, where's the bottle? Why did they find it in the garbage dump? It causes death very quickly, and he didn't go and put it in the garbage bin himself. Do you understand what I'm saying?"

"Yes," Michael answered her. "But I won't have an answer until we know the main fact. And I need the consent of the family too, in other words Moish, and I don't know exactly how I'm going to tell him because he's in terrible shape as it is."

"In other words," said Shorer in amazement, "you want to dig up a body because of what some lunatic says he felt?"

"What have we got to lose? At the moment, I'm completely

stuck," said Michael despairingly. "I haven't got a lead, I haven't got a motive. What Dave told me about Osnat is that there was a time when they were quite close, but he didn't shed any new light on her. I haven't got a motive, I haven't got a thing, I'm ready to dig him up. The dead don't feel pain, he won't feel anything. What harm will it do? What's the worst that can happen? The worst possibility is that we won't find anything. No?"

"But you can't give that as your reason," said Shorer aghast. "That some American brought the gospel here from India!"

"The reason's a technicality: They'll give it to me on the basis of Osnat's murder and Srulke's circumstantial connection with the parathion. The problem is that it could really have been an accident," said Michael, wiping his face with his hands and aware of the look Avigail was giving him.

"And so, as Avigail rightly asks, where's the bottle?" asked Shorer. "Why wasn't it found there? What have you got to say about that?"

"That somebody walked past and saw Srulke lying dead, for instance, and took the bottle and used it," said Michael quickly. "That's also a possibility, no?"

Shorer was silent. Then he asked, "What did Nahari say about the possibility of digging him up?" He finished the last of his beer.

"What he likes saying when he feels threatened," replied Michael.

"What's that exactly?"

"His favorite sentence in such situations is 'I'll have to think about it,'" said Michael bitterly.

"How long will he have to think about it?"

"I want to know by tomorrow."

"So you can explode that bombshell too on the kibbutz without consulting anyone?"

Michael was silent.

"You don't know exactly what you're going to do with this information, if it exists at all," said Shorer, giving Michael a look that combined impatience with affection.

"No," Michael admitted, "not exactly. But," he said, stretching his back, raising his shoulders, and looking down at the low wooden stool with a puzzled expression on his face, "I've learned something that you know too, that sometimes the craziest things are the ones that save the day. And we have to know the truth in any case, no?" After some reflection, he added, "And in my opinion, knowing the truth is worth any distress it might cause them."

Shorer paid the check. When they were in the car, he said, "Let me off first, please. At my age I should have been in bed long ago."

14

Avigail looked at herself in the mirror, smoothed her white smock, and sighed. Since she began to work in the police she had never imagined that she would ever go back to wearing a nurse's uniform. Now she found herself once more in a shining clinic, a one-story white-walled building among tall eucalyptus and poplar trees, with a broad lawn in front of it and a winding, concrete path leading to its entrance.

The two rooms and the kitchen gleamed. She didn't know when the clinic had been cleaned, and when she looked at the stainless steel sink, which gave her back a distorted reflection of her face, she remembered that in her day it was the Nahal group who had been responsible for cleaning the communal buildings on a kibbutz.

Avigail opened the medicine cupboard. They had searched it—three times they had searched the clinic, she recalled—and now there was no sign of it. She removed the key to the toxic-drugs cupboard from the hiding place Jojo had shown her and rummaged about among the containers of pills. The pills intended for Yankele were in a separate bag, next to the tranquilizers and sleeping pills and various other drugs she was not allowed to dispense on her own initiative. "You can hand out one sleeping pill or one Valium if the necessity arises due to the circumstances," she had been told by the psychiatrist from the clinic in Shaar HaNegev, a bearded man with spectacles and a grave expression, "but nothing massive. In the light of the situation there'll be a doctor from our clinic here every day after we leave, and in case of an emergency—straight to Ashkelon in the ambulance. For anything else, wait for the backup doctor to arrive."

It had been explained to her that the regular doctor, Dr. Reimer, had left a few days earlier for five weeks of army reserve duty in the Nablus prison. "That's how it goes with doctors," said a sighing Yoska, who had come to pick her up at home and drive her to the kibbutz. "They say that doctors are the only ones who do their reserve duty down to the last day—they don't let them off even a bit. There's only one thing that liberates a man from the ranks, as they say, and that's . . . " he braked and fell silent. They were at the last traffic light before turning onto the Ayalon freeway from Tel Aviv to Ashkelon, and he pretended to be concentrating on the traffic.

The air conditioning in the van was broken, and Avigail's skin felt sticky and sweaty. The newscaster's voice blared from the radio, giving the amount of humidity in the air on the coastal plain, and Yoska, to cover up his confusion, checked again to see if the windows were open. Words, thought Avigail as she glanced at his embarrassed face, that up to a few days ago were spoken unthinkingly, suddenly had taken on a different color and could no longer be uttered without exerting their new power.

She closed the door of the medicine cupboard. The clinic had its psychiatrist from the Shaar HaNegev Medical Center, but there were also social workers and psychologists from there newly scattered in the secretariat, the accounting office, the clubhouse, and elsewhere on the kibbutz. She had met them all at lunch, during a break in the group activities of what they called "crisis intervention."

It was Zeev HaCohen who had the idea of summoning them all to the kibbutz, announcing that this was the time to exploit these services, which were intended for precisely the kind of circumstances in which they now found themselves. He had had to struggle with the objections of Guta, whose shouts—Jojo told Avigail—could still be heard as far away as Ashkelon. Guta went berserk: "Crisis shmisis, there's no crisis here! It was somebody from outside, maybe one of the hired workers, one of the men working on the road or one of the volunteers." Yocheved had supported her: "We don't need psychologists," she said. "Where will it get us? Look where it got some of us, all that blah-blah." "There's too much blah-blah," Matilda had agreed. Avigail shivered as she recalled the three women swooping down on Zeev HaCohen like a flock of mother flamingos. She had once seen a television documentary about these ugly birds with the thick, scaly skin shielding their legs in the waters where they built elaborate nests for the protection of their eggs and the chicks to come. Suddenly she was filled with wonder at the complex mechanisms constructed by nature to enable survival.

The scene had taken place in the downstairs lobby of the dining hall, and Avigail, pretending to read the notices on the bulletin board there, had listened attentively to every word and to the various tonalities: Matilda's nagging resentment, Guta's fiery rage, and Yocheved's self-righteous complacency. Just as she was asking herself what it was going to be like to live with them, to see them every day in the dining hall—and shuddering at the possibility of being exposed by them—she heard a long "Shhh" and turned her head. Remembering what she had heard and read about her, feeling the strength of her presence in the power of the one syllable that instantly silenced the three women, Avigail knew that this could only be Dvorka.

"What's all this fuss about?" Dvorka had asked. "We don't know anything for sure yet, and the psychologists can help—they certainly won't do any harm. And if Zeev wanted to bring them in, he must have a reason for it. The education committee pondered it all night, and the education committee, as you know, is also authorized to deal with crises." Avigail had stolen a look at Dvorka, seeing her burning eyes exercise their power over the three women, who stood before her like bewildered children.

"Our role," Dvorka had explained in a quiet, authoritative voice, "is precisely to support people, to show that we can't be broken so easily and that life goes on as usual. Everyone will do their job and conduct their daily business, and together we'll surmount this too."

Standing in the lobby next to the members' post office boxes, Avigail had felt the atmosphere lighten, becoming purified of the angry currents that had been directed at Zeev HaCohen, whose face wore an expression of horror and disgust. "We'll get organized now," he had said, "we'll begin with the little children and find out what they've heard and what they know and how they're taking it."

Avigail had walked past the kindergarten after lunch and peeped through the window into the main room. Five women were bending over a little group of children who were busy drawing pictures. The women were exchanging significant looks as they scrutinized the children and their drawings, but Avigail quickly saw enough to know that the children's colorful drawings merely revealed what children's drawings usually reveal: nothing but houses and tractors and flowers and skies.

For the two days she had been on the kibbutz, the place had been buzzing with policemen politely but lengthily interrogating people (some on the kibbutz itself and others back in the Serious Crimes Unit headquarters, and searching for the remainder of the parathion. Uniformed policemen visited the rooms in the morning with the members' permission, the cooperation of the entire kibbutz being such that the words "search warrant" never had to be used.

Avigail was under no illusions that the search would uncover anything, "if anything exists at all," she had said to herself as she and Machluf Levy ignored each other outside the accounting office, where he was explaining something in an undertone to two policemen. She wondered whether the murderer had simply spilled what remained in the bottle on the ground at the garbage dump, or down the toilet in his room, or anywhere else, or even if there was nothing left to get rid of after he had poisoned Osnat. But they had to continue the search, she agreed to herself. Early in the afternoon, when she had opened the clinic and noticed—smiling the pleasant smile she used on such occasions—a few people waiting outside the door, she suddenly saw in her imagination the parathion in a scent bottle and a manicured feminine hand spraying it onto the bare skin of a body lying in bed, and she was filled with horror.

Avigail realized that she had been infected by the fear she saw on the faces of the people in the dining hall, outside the infirmary, in the clinic, in the secretariat, and on the kibbutz paths, which she knew from her own experience should have been full of children and their bicycles but were now deserted.

On her two nights there, tossing and turning on her bed, she too had become victim to the fear fathered by the thought that any one of the people she met on the paths—on her way to her room, on her way to the dining hall, on her way to the children's house to inspect heads for lice at the request of the housemother (who took it for granted that the nurse's role, among other things, was to stand beside her as she wielded the close-toothed comb), on her way to take blood pressures, on the way to pretexts she devised to be everywhere and look and listen for some telltale sign—that any one of these people she had never met before could be a murderer.

How did she imagine, Shorer had asked her, that she could be of help there? How did she plan, he pressed her, to get the measure of such a large group of people who were strangers to her? "It would take a year to get to know the characters in this case," he had said, but Ohayon had reminded him that Avigail would be there as the kibbutz nurse, and "the information would come to her." But patients did not stream to the clinic as they had assumed they would. Their predictions had been wrong, thought Avigail as she filled little pieces of paper at night with notes about everything she had seen and heard and waited for Michael Ohayon to make contact with her so that she could hand over the information she was so carefully collecting.

It was years since she had left the kibbutz where she had once been a member of a Nahal group. In those days, when she was a young soldier, she had been oblivious to her surroundings; her thoughts had been on other things. But of all this she had said nothing to them—to Ohayon, Shorer, Nahari, the police commissioner, to all those who had briefed her and warned her repeatedly to beware of any attempts at intervening, reminding her that "if he had done it once, he could do it again," and cautioning her over and over to be careful. The words "be careful" had come up so many times that Avigail had finally reminded them that she had been a nurse for years, that she wasn't pretending to be anything she wasn't, and that there was no reason why she should be exposed.

"Just report back immediately if you notice anything suspicious," they had told her during the last telephone call she had made from her

Tel Aviv apartment, before she locked the door and got into the van that was to take her and her two suitcases to the kibbutz.

All the way there she had responded pleasantly to the shameless questions put to her by Yoska, who also told her his own life story without being asked.

He had asked her how long she had been a nurse, where she had worked before, and why she wanted to work on a kibbutz. He asked her if she was married, if she had ever been married in the past, and reacted to her negative replies with a sigh. Yoska was on his way back to the kibbutz after a "big order" he had been dealing for the cosmetics plant, where he was in charge of the bookkeeping. In reply to her polite question, he had explained that the plant was indeed big enough to require a separate accounting department of its own, and after he had listed all the countries to which they exported their products ("thirteen countries!" he had proudly exclaimed), he had gone on, without being asked, to describe his other activities. He did other things too in his spare time, he had announced with a grin that broadened his mustache and revealed his white teeth, and he patted his sagging paunch.

Looking at his shorts and the broad foot in the big sandal on the gas pedal, Avigail had thought about the tragedy of the Palmach generation growing old even as they refused to grow up. Even though, she had said to herself as she passed her finger over the rubber gasket of the open window, Yoska didn't exactly belong to the Palmach generation—she had correctly estimated his age before he told her that he was "fifty-three, but well preserved. I don't feel a day older than fifty-one," he had said, laughing at his own joke, which sounded pathetic to her. He hadn't therefore fought in 1948, she calculated, but he did belong to the generation that had hero-worshiped the Palmach fighters and tried to emulate them. She knew that he must walk around in winter in army boots with socks rolled over the tops, the lining of his pockets sticking out of his shorts. The whole phenomenon, Avigail had thought, was pitiful, but she had to overcome her revulsion because she was wrong to feel it. "He's a good man," she had suddenly said to herself as he went on talking and, like some old gossip, asked her, "How come a pretty girl like you never got married?"

"His intentions are good," Avigail had thought, subduing the surge of anger welling up in her, and instead of telling him to mind his own business, as she would have liked to, she again reminded herself of his good intentions and told herself that he was only chattering in order to fill the void created in all of them by the unbearable tidings. But the rage surged up in her again with every new question and every stale joke she knew he had already told innumerable times before.

Once, a long time ago, Avigail had stood outside the doctors' room in the internal-diseases ward where she was working and heard the voice of the head nurse saying, "Maybe she's a snob, as you say, maybe she's stuck-up and keeps to herself, but one thing you have to say for her is that she knows how to listen, and people sense it. They want to talk to her because they know that she pays attention, and that's an important quality in a nurse." Avigail could still see the embarrassed faces when she opened the door and went quickly inside, putting an end to this conversation, one of many, she was sure, that took place behind her back in response to her attitude of reserve.

Yoska had rattled on, and by the time they reached Yavne, he had already made some remarks about his married life and given her a sideways look, as well as saying something about how the previous nurse, Rickie, had left them in the lurch in this time of crisis. "But you don't know anything about the crisis," he had said, proceeding to tell her about Osnat's death. Avigail had waited for him to say something about the murder, about the deliberate poisoning, since she already knew, as they all knew, that the news about the way Osnat had died had swept through the kibbutz like wildfire, but Yoska hadn't said a word about it. He had used the word *tragedy,* and she had made a mental note to tell Michael Ohayon about this good-natured chatterbox, with his mustache and his paunch and his rivers of sweat and humming of Hebrew tunes, about this gossip who knew how to keep his lips sealed. She had tried, there in the van on the way to the kibbutz, to imagine a member of the kibbutz telling her how Osnat had died—what had killed her. But she understood that even the barrier to this revelation would be hard to break through.

Yet Yoska had spoken without any inhibitions about his wife's difficulties in becoming pregnant, about the infertility treatments and the side effects of the drug Pergonal, about the triplets and two more children his wife had borne after the treatments, about the stammer of one of the triplets and the lingering childhood illnesses of his youngest child—and even about the mental problems of his elderly mother-in-law, who had come with her husband, who had Alzheimer's disease, to live with them on the kibbutz, and the difficulty of caring for the two of them. "You're a nurse. You know," he had repeated several times during the course of the journey, while she had listened to every word, uttering only a few encouraging and sympathetic sentences as she waited patiently for the moment when something would be said about Osnat. But all he had said about Osnat was, "We suffered a tragedy."

In the clinic on her first day at the kibbutz, listening to the chirping of the birds and looking around her, she realized that there had been no solid foundation for her fears of returning to her nurse's uniform. Here everything was different, as expected: There was nothing to remind her of the miserable internal-diseases department at the Ichilov Hospital in Tel Aviv, where she had worked for nine whole years in one of the hospital's eight departments that had decayed from year to year, and whose smell—like the smell of an old man's mouth in the morning—seemed to cling to the rooms with their dozens of geriatric patients. But although she recognized the differences, she now again felt the weariness stemming from despair that had overcome her every morning during those last days in the hospital. "It's a conditioned reflex," thought Avigail, "because there's no reason to feel like that now; it's not the same thing at all. It's three hours' work, easy as pie, easier than a night of interrogation at the unit, being here three hours a day, dealing with people's problems, dispensing medicines and taking things in without anyone knowing that I'm not what I purport to be." But nevertheless the old weariness returned, spreading through her as she buttoned her white smock.

When Avigail had started studying at the nursing school, she imagined herself—in spite of everything she had heard, which should have been enough to disillusion her—clad in white, an angel of mercy saving and healing people.

She could not in advance have guessed at the extent of the erosion, at the weight of the stony heart that would grow heavier and heavier inside her, at the weariness that would numb all feelings in her on the nights when she—sometimes alone and sometimes with another nurse—would be responsible for the entire ward, forty-two patients when all the beds were occupied, and sometimes even more, lying in the corridors degraded and humiliated. She didn't know, although she should have known, how she would be haunted by images of women wrapping themselves in their bedclothes to cover pajamas that never matched or fit properly, or of frantic night searches for a pillow or a sheet. What was described by the media as "the distressed state of the hospitals" and "the crisis in the health system" became for Avigail an experience to which she awoke each morning, a source of increasing despair paralyzing her initiative and will and even her ability to feel compassion.

"Why nursing school?" her mother had fumed. "With grades like yours you could have taken up something more serious and easier too, you could even have studied medicine. We always thought that you would have a serious career." But Avigail wanted to be a nurse. Probably because of Esther, her father's younger sister. Esther had been a nurse. She died alone in Tel Aviv, in her small, old apartment on Ben Yehuda Street crammed with mementoes and photographs inscribed with words of thanks by former patients, some of whom she had treated for nothing. There were times, Avigail remembered, when Aunt Esther had sat up all night long at the beds of dying patients, giving them painkillers, soothing them, holding their hands, waiting with them for the night sky to grow pale and their fears of loneliness and death to subside.

Esther had often explained to her that there was nothing more noble than the act of accompanying a person to his death and blunting his loneliness. When Avigail visited her at the hospital where she worked—sometimes she was even asked to help—the patients would say, "Is she your mother? Are you her daughter? She's an angel," and they would remark on the resemblance between them. Avigail had heard about Florence Nightingale, Esther's childhood heroine, when she herself was still a little girl, uncritically absorbing her aunt's naive, old-fashioned adoration. It was only after Esther's death, when Avigail thought about her life, that she asked herself why her aunt had chosen to live alone, in a solitude without bitterness.

Esther was the youngest of six children, of whom only she, the only daughter, and the oldest son, Avigail's father (who escaped to Russia before the German invasion), had survived the Holocaust.

About that, Esther was only prepared to say that one day she left the house to accompany a friend (a "goy," she remembered her aunt saying), and when she returned "they were all dead." This story too she told unwillingly, in response to her niece's pleas one winter night. About her parents and her dead brothers, she never spoke at all. And then, when she spoke about the day the war broke out, she said, "You only love once in a lifetime, and that's only when you're sixteen."

When Esther died, Avigail was seventeen. She died suddenly. For two days the body lay in the Ben Yehuda Street apartment and nobody knew. And only after two days, when they received a phone call from the hospital, did Avigail's father reach for the rusty nail behind the refrigerator, for the key kept there for emergencies, and stride resolutely out of the house, keeping his anxiety to himself. After that they buried Esther, and Avigail never forgave herself for having no premonition of the disaster, and for the fact that when Esther died, of a stroke ("Thank God," said her mother, "it ended like that. God knows what would have happened if she'd remained an invalid for the rest of her life"), she herself had been at the movies, watching *The Passenger*, with the only thing troubling her the question whether Ohad would take her hand in his or not. He was her first boyfriend, and also—as things turned out—her last. Even then she had already begun to think that all the talk about intimate ties and soul mates was nonsense without any basis in reality.

For nine years Avigail worked as a nurse. By the time she was thirty-three, she felt burned out. The figure of Esther, which had accompanied her in many difficult hours, began to fade, and with it the enormous significance she had bestowed on her niece's daily labors. There were days when Avigail could not even remember Esther's face. She no longer saw her before her eyes as she wiped the sweat from the brow of a suffering patient at night, and she no longer saw her warm smile when she covered a body with a sheet. When Esther's spell disappeared, Avigail's world changed. People seemed crueler to her, more distant, colder and harder. There was no more room for Esther's romanticism, which had been so right in its time.

First came the backaches. The pains had already begun in her fourth year at work, when she had left the internal-diseases department at the Levinson Hospital for the children's ward at Ichilov and later the internal-diseases ward there. She had withstood the pressures to specialize as a surgical nurse, refused to take the road leading to the position of head nurse, and also declined to take a course in midwifery, because deep in her heart she was seeking direct contact with suffering, with no practical purpose and no happy end. Suffering that had nothing beyond it. And when the psoriasis began, she knew that she had to escape.

It appeared suddenly. One day she discovered a red patch on her right elbow and then on her left elbow too. The itchiness and scratching began after the patches thickened and deepened and ugly scales spread over the reddish surface and changed its color to a silvery purple. After that came the pain. She realized what the patches were at once, although she pretended to herself that it was only a passing allergy, and she began to wear long-sleeved uniforms, or to roll the sleeves up to just below the elbow. When the first patches appeared behind her knee, she went to see a dermatologist, and when his diagnosis confirmed what she already knew, she burst into tears.

The doctor was of the older generation and about to retire. His hands trembled as they felt her skin, and she recalled the rumors of an illness. He lacked the cruel efficiency characteristic of the younger doctors, as well as the callousness that made them send people for exhausting and complicated tests simply to reinforce what they knew already, and with an eye to using the results for still another medical journal article. He did send her for a couple of tests, but they both knew there was no real need for them, and standing at the door as they parted, he said to her, with a sad, fatherly smile, "Young nurse, you should know that this is a disease with psychological causes, and if you're under stress for some specific reason, you should try to reduce it, and I wouldn't rule out a visit to a psychologist."

Avigail didn't see a psychologist. She requested a year's leave and wondered what she should do to earn a living while she studied criminology. A friend in the police described the conditions of her employment and talked in glowing terms of the interest she took in her work, and Avigail announced, ignoring her mother's sour face, that she was joining the police force. At the end of her first year she was invited to an interview where words such as "a special aptitude" and "impressed by your work" were spoken, and she was co-opted onto a team in the

Serious Crimes Unit, the only woman at the time (Sarit joined the team later) among eleven men. The police work blunted her chronic, everyday malaise, but the psoriasis did not improve. And in the summer, when the condition was supposed to get better, she discovered the patch on her breast.

Ever since her affair with Ohad, which had lasted throughout their military service and also during the period when they stayed with the Nahal group on the kibbutz after being discharged from active duty, she had not had another boyfriend. The wound, others may perhaps have explained, from which she had never recovered when he left her had taught her to be careful, and she did not again allow anyone to come close to her.

Once her literature teacher had quoted Freud's saying that the ego was built of patches, and that every working through of a separation was a new patch that strengthened it, but Avigail thought that for her separations were not reinforcing patches, and she had never succeeded in elaborating them into ego-building material. For her separations were only additional tears in the garment. She felt naked in her sadness whenever anyone came close to her. She never told anyone about the psoriasis, and despite all medical advice, she never went to bathe in the Dead Sea or exposed her body to the air and the sun. She knew that there was something self-destructive about her behavior. Aunt Esther had died when she was forty-six, and Avigail wondered whether this was what she wanted for herself as well.

Although she sometimes felt lonely and longed for a man to embrace her, for a man's voice in her own room, and too for the intimacy and affection of close conversation with a woman, and although there were women who sometimes aroused her interest or sympathy and sometimes even a wish to come closer to them, against her own inclinations Avigail clung tightly to the sentence of chastity and renunciation she had wordlessly imposed on herself, and she allowed no one to invade her privacy. She read a lot. She absorbed herself in her work, which provided her with action and sometimes interest too, and in her studies, to which she related with a curious mixture of seriousness in the fulfillment of her obligations and irony with regard to the contents. When she came home to her one-room apartment, she was tired to death.

Sometimes she woke from her dreams inflamed with desire, dreams centered on Ohad, whom she had not seen since they split up thirteen years before, after he had spent months finding excuses for his need for freedom, talking about his fear of commitment, and his inability to connect with "another person." She herself knew that Ilan was not to blame for the way she lived, that he was not the reason for her present loneliness, or even the pretext for it, but rather something deeper. Nevertheless, she sometimes said furiously to herself that it was all his fault. On nights when she woke up with her body on fire and his figure before her eyes, she would get up and go out, to wander the streets of Tel Aviv and stoically contemplate the emptiness of wasting her life away without being able to change it in any essential way.

The summer nights were particularly hard to bear; the windows open to the street let the laughter in, and the uninhibited, spontaneous voices coming from outside illuminated her self-imposed punishment in a light that was almost grotesque.

That April the road to Petah Tikva had been flooded with the scent of orange blossoms and acacias. The scents tormented her, and she began frequently waking up at night from the dreams that threatened the equilibrium of her solitude. The face of the man in her dreams was now sometimes that of Michael Ohayon. They had never exchanged an intimate word, and she knew nothing about his private life.

This was the situation when Avigail arrived on the kibbutz, the day after Ohayon had "dropped the bombshell," as Jojo said to her in a trembling voice while accompanying her from the secretariat—where Yoska had left her after helping with clumsy chivalry to carry her luggage into the room she had been assigned—to the clinic. Jojo, too, did not mention the way in which Osnat had died but mumbled something about a crisis on the kibbutz and the assistance and crisis intervention being provided by the authorized agencies and the police who were still there "making everybody nervous."

When Avigail arrived on the kibbutz that morning ("What have you got here, stones?" Yoska had asked, laughing as he put down the suitcases filled with books along with her six pairs of jeans and six loose white men's shirts), she had sensed her elbows burning, and even before rolling up her sleeves, she knew that the situation had deteriorated. The patches behind her knees too, in the place where her mother used to say, when Avigail was a child, "potatoes will start growing there if you don't wash with soap," seemed worse to her. She didn't know whether it was the thought of the white smock that was irritating her skin or the fear instilled in her by Shorer's talk the night before about having to cope with an entire kibbutz in shock.

Now, as she looked into the medicine cupboard, she began to itch again. She took off her smock and rolled up her sleeves. The patches were scarlet, and the scaly skin looked horrifying in its ugliness. She opened her bag and took out a blue tube of cortisone ointment.

A woman burst into the bathroom as Avigail was standing in front of the mirror soaping her hands with disinfectant soap to get rid of the traces of the ointment, and she made haste to roll down her sleeves. She noticed the muddy marks left by the woman's black rubber boots on the gleaming tiles and heard the muffled voices coming from outside the open door.

The hefty, elderly woman stood in the bathroom doorway and almost shouted, "She has to take something and she won't take anything!"

Avigail tried to look over the woman's shoulder and said "What happened?" covering up her alarm in a professional voice. If the woman had burst in a moment earlier, she would have seen the patches on her elbows.

"My sister's in trouble," said the woman, grabbing Avigail by the hand. "Come, come!" Avigail went outside with her. A shorter elderly woman was standing in front of the door with her hand clenched on her chest. She was sobbing and grunting and panting for breath. "Get the ambulance," shouted the hefty woman, "Fanya can't breathe."

And now, even in the midst of the turmoil, Avigail somehow had the presence of mind to realize who the two women she was dealing with were. Later, too, Avigail didn't know where she had found the authoritative voice that enabled her to get Fanya inside the clinic and make her lie down on the narrow bed, where she took off her work boots and woolen socks. Guta trod heavily in their wake. Her red hooked nose stood out in her pale face, and her short gray hair bristled every which way as she pushed her big fingers through it with a compulsive movement. Afterward, Avigail told Michael that they had looked like a pair of witches from the illustrated book she had as a child. She raised Fanya's feet and put them on a big pillow. Fanya did not complain of pain or nausea. Her blood pressure was normal and her pulse rapid but regular. But she had difficulty breathing.

"Is it her heart?" asked Guta respectfully as Avigail measured her blood pressure.

Avigail looked at her and said, "I don't think so, but perhaps you should have something to drink—there's cold water in the refrigerator—and then why don't you tell me what happened." The end of the sentence was addressed to Fanya, who closed her eyes and grimaced.

"Does something hurt you?" asked Avigail gently.

"What hurts you?" yelled Guta, breathing fire. "Fanya, tell us what hurts you! It's all because of those hooligans!" Avigail said nothing. "Because of the police!" yelled Guta. "First they take Yankele away, and then they dig up Srulke's body."

"Take it easy," said Avigail. "One thing at a time. Tell me exactly what happened." Guta took a crumpled pack of cigarettes out of the pocket of her blue housedress.

"They called me from the milking barn in the middle of work. Maybe twice in my life I've been called away in the middle of work, and Fanya was in the sewing shop. When they told her about Srulke, she almost fainted."

"What happened to Srulke?" asked Avigail, looking at the second hand of her watch as she held Fanya's wrist. The pulse slowed down.

"Srulke . . . " Guta looked at Avigail as if she were seeing her for the first time. "Srulke died a month and a half ago. He died suddenly on Shevuoth. Of a heart attack. Srulke . . . " Guta fell silent and suppressed her sobs with a deep drag on her cigarette. Fanya opened her eyes and looked at her sister with a stunned, frightened look. The sound of her breathing weakened, and the expression of pain on her face gave way to one of shock. The fear Avigail had felt when Guta burst into the clinic returned, struggling at once with the nurse competently taking a patient's pulse and with the policewoman who only wanted to know.

"You know there was a death here on the kibbutz? A murder?" said Guta. "You've already heard that somebody poisoned Osnat?" Avigail was silent. "Someone gave her parathion, and she died," said

Guta, looking at the white wall against which the narrow bed was standing. She stared at the drawing of the Jerusalem hills by Anna Ticho that was hanging there. Fanya moaned. Avigail tightened her grip on the wrist and felt the pulse accelerate. "Last night they dug up Srulke's body and saw that him too. This morning they came to tell her in the sewing shop," said Guta, looking at her sister.

"And what happened?" Avigail asked. "What did they tell her?"

"That him too," Guta said and inhaled smoke.

"Him too?"

"They found parathion in him too. And now they've started their interrogations again, and they're talking to Yankele again."

Fanya closed her eyes. Again her mouth twisted in an expression of pain and her rapid, shallow breathing became audible in the room.

"They're holding him as a suspect even though he wouldn't hurt a fly. Excuse me," said Guta, pulling a piece of toilet paper out of her pocket. She blew her nose. Her eyes were dry. "It's too much for us. That and Srulke too." Fanya began to grunt. The grunts grew louder, and there was something terrifying about the sounds emerging from the depths of her throat.

"Hysteria," Avigail said later to Michael. "Pure hysteria. I knew it from the beginning."

Guta looked at her sister and said, "For us Srulke was like . . . " again she inhaled and coughed. "Like family," she finally said. "He brought us here. He saved us. He always took care of Fanya. Of Yankele too. And now they told Fanya that because Yankele wandered around there at night he . . . They're taking him away for questioning. And there's nobody to talk to, not even Moish . . . And I want . . . " Guta looked at the narrow bed. "Are you feeing better now?" she asked Fanya. Fanya did not respond. She lay there with her bare swollen feet like two red lumps on the white sheet. Her arms, thin and wrinkled, stuck out of the wide sleeves of her faded dress. Her hair, white threads among the chestnut curls, was longer than her sister's. The lines of her face were soft. There was no resemblance between her and Guta. "They dug Srulke up, they took him out of the ground," whispered Guta, "and they made her sick." Her hands trembled. "They say that he died of parathion too. And now they say that Yankele took the parathion from Srulke and that he, and that he . . . "

Fanya again began grunting half-words in Yiddish. "We have to be strong," said Guta to herself, and she bent over the white wastebasket and ground the butt of her cigarette out on its side. "We thought . . . what did we ask of life? All we wanted was a little peace. That's all. And they don't let us live in peace, and that's all we wanted."

Avigail shot out the questions. No, said Guta, there had been no heart attacks and no illnesses. They had never been sick, except for when they arrived in the country, when Fanya had tuberculosis, but that passed and all the chest X rays were fine, and that was from the war and the hunger, she said apologetically, because of what they had been through. Apart from the tuberculosis, there had been no other illnesses.

Avigail put a little yellow pill in Guta's hand and said, "You take one too now." Then she supported Fanya's head, and she swallowed the water obediently. "This is a difficult time for you, everyone's reacting badly," she said to Guta, who put the pill on her tongue.

"What is it?" Guta asked after swallowing.

"Just a tranquilizer," said Avigail.

"She had foam on her lips," said Guta, "I saw foam on her lips, all because of the talk in the sewing shop and because that tall policeman took Yankele for questioning. Just because he used to wander around there at night he thinks he would kill Osnat. And he wasn't even there," added Guta as if she had just remembered, "he was with Dave all the time. How could he have done it?"

"Perhaps they only want him to assist them, perhaps he saw something," said Avigail.

"And on the holiday, when Srulke died, Yankele was with us all the time, and afterward he was in the kitchen, on shift duty."

"Everything will be all right," Avigail said reassuringly.

"And now that policeman with the mustache told Fanya she had to go with them to talk to them. And I won't let her go. She can't go anywhere."

"When the doctor comes, I'll ask him to look at her," said Avigail.

Fanya sat up on the narrow bed. "No need," she said in a dull voice. "I don't need a doctor."

"You understand," said Guta to the Anna Ticho drawing, "we're the easiest ones to pick on. They're not questioning Jojo. Even though he knows all about parathion. Only Yankele, who never touched it in his life."

"Jojo knows about parathion?" asked Avigail.

"He's even got a diploma, I know," said Guta to the room at large. "He was a licensed sprayer when he was still a *pisher,* and nobody's asking him anything. Not about other things either. They have to pick on Yankele."

"They're only questioning him," Avigail reassured her. "It doesn't mean anything."

"All our life we sit here and work our fingers to the bone for them to come and take us to the police," grumbled Fanya as she began slowly pulling on her woolen socks.

15

It was late at night, as Shorer had predicted, when Michael stole into Avigail's isolated room at the edge of the kibbutz, in the row of houses before the ones inhabited by the Nahal group. A shaft of yellow light broke through the drawn curtains and was absorbed by the light of the full moon, which gave the path a silvery, metallic sheen. When he knocked on the door and looked around him at the deserted landscape, he felt ridiculous, but he was also aware of his excitement, his racing pulse, and he was as embarrassed as a boy.

"No one saw me," he said to Avigail when he was inside the room. He had dismissed out of hand the idea of meeting outside the kibbutz: "Intifada," he pronounced, and described the dangers lurking at night in the fields bordering the kibbutz, on the dirt roads, in the uncultivated lands. "Those places are too dangerous. Things aren't what they used to be, when a boy and a girl could go for a walk in the fields," he said, and Avigail blushed. "Someone should study the effects of the Intifada on the romantic life of the homeless," he added in order to break the embarrassed silence that reasserted itself between them as they stood facing each other in the room.

Michael had spent the whole day again in lengthy interviews with kibbutz members, which he had tried to conduct in as friendly a spirit as possible. They had decided not to bring them to the NUSCI building for questioning: "Three hundred people is a bit much," Nahari agreed. But the forensic people had refused to bring the polygraph machinery to the kibbutz, and so some of the members had been obliged to travel to Petah Tikva.

"You were taking a chance, talking to Benny like that on the path next to the dining hall," said Michael now as Avigail looked at the little gray document he was holding. He described waving it at the treasurer, who had paled and said, "I'd forgotten all about it, it dates back about thirty years."

"Twenty-four," Michael corrected him, "and you never said a word about it. In the present circumstances your forgetfulness seems strange."

"I swear to you I forgot," said Jojo. "It's from the time when I was a cotton sprayer. I've even forgotten that I ever sprayed the cotton," he pleaded in confusion. "Why should I hide it?" The polygraph test showed that he hadn't been lying. The license authorizing the bearer to spray with parathion led nowhere.

After their visit to the clinic, Fanya and Guta had been unwilling to take a polygraph test. "You have to prove that there's a reason for us do it," Guta had said, raising a threatening arm at him, and Fanya had grunted in agreement. "Not willing?" Nahari had said. "What's that supposed to mean, not willing? Arrest them. They'll be willing then, I promise you." "I'd rather wait," Michael had insisted. "In any case there's nothing there for us." "You know who the gift of prophecy was given to?" Nahari had asked rhetorically before resuming his perusal of the papers in front of him.

Boaz's Tova, too, it soon turned out, wasn't lying when she declared that it would never have crossed her mind to murder Osnat: The shame she had caused her to suffer in the dining hall was quite enough. "If I had to poison everyone Boaz ran after, there wouldn't be too many women left alive here," Tova had said to Machluf Levy, who quoted her with undisguised enjoyment.

Between one interview and the next, between the thousands of words he had been listening to for the past three days, Michael occasionally caught a glimpse of the stunning tranquillity of the landscape surrounding him. The serenity radiating from the neat paths and lawns, from the playgrounds and the plaza fronting the dining hall, from the cemetery with its separate section for those who had died on military service, seemed to him absurd. It made the whole case seem somehow unreal, and sometimes, looking around him when the place seemed deserted—at night or early in the afternoon—when the heat was unbearable, he wondered whether there had been a murder here at all.

Late at night he slipped into Avigail's room, and she opened the door silently and locked it as soon as he was inside. He watched her as she carefully stirred the Turkish coffee in the finjan, in the ceremony she seemed to have picked up from the kibbutz members. He looked at her slender silhouette and the hair that swayed with her every movement, at her delicate hands. She was wearing a black Japanese robe whose tiny buttons were fastened to the neck and whose wide sleeves were gathered around her wrists. The air conditioner hummed comfortably, and the sound of the crickets chirping outside was inaudible inside the room. He sighed deeply as he sat down.

"For the first time I feel I'm getting somewhere here," he said suddenly, and she looked at him with a questioning, concentrated expression. He felt surprisingly comfortable in her presence. She gave rise in him to a strong desire to make her happy, to see her laugh. "You want to make an impression on her, to make a conquest of her," he said to himself without affection. The jealousy with which she guarded her privacy made him curious. He sensed her vulnerability too, and her uncertainty, and they aroused a wish to protect her, to be kind to her. She did not threaten him, she gave off no signals of expecting something to happen, of the anticipation of a relationship, but at the same time he felt sure that he interested and attracted her. He thought of her clear, fair complexion, and he wanted to touch her cheek. Above all he wanted to peep at the arms under those long sleeves. But he stretched out his legs and held the cup of coffee and looked at her as she stirred her tea and waited. She too waited.

"Have you got something for me?" he finally asked, wondering as he spoke at his choice of words.

"I have and I haven't," said Avigail. "I can tell you in general what you must have seen for yourself during the past couple of days, that everyone here seems quite shaken. But I haven't got anything concrete, I can't see any leads. Except for what I've already said about Guta and Fanya."

"Then tell me about what you can see; go into detail," requested Michael. She took two small and closely written pieces of paper out of the sideboard. He reached out and took them from her.

"They won't help you much," said Avigail, bending over the notes. "You won't understand anything, they're just for my own use."

"In general," she said after a pause, "nobody who came into the infirmary mentioned it. Not only that, but even in the dining hall, even when they showed me around the kibbutz, when I went to the children's house to inspect them for lice, wherever I went, you could tell if they'd been talking about it or not from the way they fell silent. When I approached a group of people in the dining hall, you could have cut the silence with a knife."

"Nobody?" asked Michael.

"Nobody said anything specific. At the most they said something like 'in view of the situation'—like that girl, what's her name?" and she leaned over the little piece of paper. "Ronit. She asked for something to help her sleep at night 'in view of the situation.' I gave her Valium. It was this afternoon, and she was pale, with black rings under her eyes, she looked as if she hadn't been sleeping. After that someone called Zvika came, he's already been to my room too, and said something about a project he was organizing for the children, and it seemed a little strange to me."

"How strange?"

"He was short of breath and full of energy, and it didn't seem appropriate. He also said, 'in view of the situation,' and I repeated his words with a question mark: 'In view of the situation?' but he didn't give me any information. I only noticed that he was very busy with this project for the children, organizing a treasure hunt for them, and he wanted to use the clinic for it. By the way, last night that guy from Ashkelon was here, the one with the dogs, and he turned the place inside out. There's no parathion here."

"I've given up on that already," said Michael, staring at his coffee cup.

"Apart from that, there's a kind of quiet here," Avigail went on, stirring her tea over and over again. "Apart from that," she said thoughtfully, "I can tell you that quite a lot of people were watching the cable television they've got here until late at night, and there's someone called Matilda who talks your ear off whether you like it or not. I heard her when she was waiting outside for some medication she gets on a regular basis. She's a real character."

"Yes, I know, the one who works in the minimarket."

"So she said something about some other woman watching television all the time, and Moish—in my opinion he's got a bleeding ulcer, and after the exhumation and the whole business with his father it's probably going to get worse, and in the end we'll have to send him to the hospital. In any case," said Avigail, looking down at her hands, "there are all kinds of things here that I'm sure are connected with each other, and the fact that it was in the paper today doesn't help either, and I've already heard that they turned some reporter away today. It's a good thing I arrived when I did."

"Yes, we told him about his father," said Michael, "and he took it very badly. We also told him that it's impossible to tell whether it was an accident or murder, not like with Osnat, but that didn't help much."

"Some of the people here have gone into a kind of coma: They don't talk to anyone. And then there are others, like one of the women, the treasurer's wife—"

"Jojo's wife," said Michael.

"—who seems to be having a wonderful time, as if she's in her element, going from one person to the other and talking without stopping. I saw her in the dining hall, and I heard people talking at the table behind me, and one of the women shouted, 'It wasn't one of us,' and another one joined in, I don't know who it was, but I can show her to you, and I heard them talking about Yankele, and how his mother, Guta, is prowling round like a wild animal, and she hardly leaves the milking barn, which is where she works."

"Avigail," Michael said, rolling her name around his tongue, "Guta isn't Yankele's mother. Fanya, the dressmaker, the one I told you about, is Yankele's mother."

"She's a sick woman," said Avigail. "I meant to say aunt. Both of them are frightening, but they're suffering." She wiped her lips with the back of her hand. "The long and the short of it is that I haven't got a single lead, like I said, but perhaps I could write an essay on a kibbutz in shock, and I can tell you that it's quite contagious, and quite alarming too. And not only that . . . " She fell silent and they both stiffened at the sound of footsteps and the rustle of dry leaves trampled underfoot, followed by a hesitant knock at the door.

Avigail held her breath and looked at the lock, and Michael rose carefully, went into the next room, and closed the door as Avigail said in a shaky voice, "Just a minute," and without asking "Who's there?" opened the door.

Michael sat down on the double bed and looked at the open clothes closet. He took in the white shirts hanging in a row and the pile of folded jeans, the two white smocks and the few cosmetics, the books on the bedside cabinet, and he tried to identify the muffled male voice on the other side of the door. He heard Avigail's voice clearly, and it was trembling with an emotion he could not pin down. He stood up and put his ear to the door. The voice belonged to a man he did not know. He heard the words, "afraid to be alone," and Avigail's voice, full of an anger she made no attempt to disguise: "It doesn't bother me in the least, and at an hour like this you should be with your wife. As far as I know, you're a married man. Don't you think it's a little out of line to come to my room at two o'clock in the morning on such an idiotic pretext? Couldn't you wait until tomorrow morning for the aspirin? And isn't there someone a little closer you could have awakened in the middle of the night?" Again he heard an indistinct mumbling in a male voice, and then Avigail: "No. I'll decide whether to talk about it to anyone or not. Just don't come to me again without an invitation, even if you think you can see a light on." He heard the sound of the door slamming and the key turning twice, and then she was standing in the bedroom doorway and saying, "He's gone."

"Who was it?" asked Michael.

"Someone, it doesn't matter. He's showing signs of shock too. His name . . . I've forgotten his name, but he spoke to me today in the dining hall. I think his name's Boaz, and I think he's Matilda's son, and he fancies himself a Don Juan—or no, not Matilda's, Yocheved's son, and it seems to me that he was the one who tried to come on to

Osnat and his wife made a scandal in the dining hall, I've lost track—a tall, thin guy."

"A middle-aged glamour boy?" asked Michael.

"Yes," Avigail said and suddenly smiled. "A middle-aged glamour boy. He's been working in the dining hall since I arrived."

"He's between jobs," said Michael. "Up to now he was in charge of the orchards. It's aberrant, his behavior, exaggerated. After all, you've only been here for three days."

"He asked me if I was alone in life," said Avigail, "and I told him that I wasn't alone in life, I was only living alone here, and apparently even that wasn't enough. I didn't say they weren't upset. This evening in the club two people fell asleep in front of the closed-circuit TV. And I overheard Yocheved saying that one of the women, I don't know who, didn't even go to work, she spent the whole day watching television, and I actually saw two fathers going to work in the fields today with small children. But on the surface you can't see anything. As if nothing's happened. Except that the dining hall's half empty. People stay in their rooms. Ah," she suddenly said, "I completely forgot, there was one woman who demanded an urgent *sicha*. She stood next to Dvorka and she said, 'I want a *sicha* on the subject,' and Dvorka didn't answer her, but Moish, who was standing next to her, said that it wasn't the right time for a *sicha*. 'What do you want, Hila, for us to hold a *sicha* and ask the murderer to come forward? It's in the hands of the police now.' And she shouted, 'No, no, it isn't one of us, in my opinion it's somebody else, somebody who left and came back now to destroy us, and everybody should be told.' And Moish said that there was no point in having a *sicha* on the subject until after it was all over and the murderer had been caught, and in the meantime she should get help from the group set up by the psychologists."

"And Dvorka?" asked Michael. "What did Dvorka have to say about it?"

"She said, 'Why? There's no need for a special *sicha*; life goes on as usual. It's something we have to cope with just like any other tragedy.'"

"That's what she said?" said Michael in surprise. "That it was like any other tragedy? Interesting."

"She's behaving," said Avigail thoughtfully, "to judge by the little

I've seen, as if nothing happened. She's got that business-as-usual expression on her face. You know what I mean? I know the type from my work in the hospital. In any crisis situation, when there's a tragedy in a family, there's always one person who undertakes the role of maintaining the norm. One member of the family who says life must go on and sees to it that nobody else gets carried away. The type of person who keeps going with the help of a self-control that may not seem abnormal, but now that you seem so taken aback, I think there may really be something pathological about it."

"No, not pathological," said Michael, "there's something surprising here. I thought, I was sure . . . " His voice died away, and then he explained. "The picture I had in my head was that she was restraining herself as long as it had to be kept a secret, and after that I thought she would break down. But she's apparently made of sterner stuff. And Zeev HaCohen?"

"He looks impressive," said Avigail, "but he's full of himself. He takes himself seriously, like all those founder-generation types, but with him it's also a pose. I haven't seen anything unusual in his behavior."

"And Dave?"

"Dave." Avigail smiled. "Dave suggested intensifying the mysticism study circles, increasing the number of meetings. But did you know that he's got mescal?"

"What's mescal?" asked Michael.

"A cactus with hallucinogenic properties, a kind of narcotic."

"How do you know?" he asked suspiciously.

"I know because I once read up on Central American drugs, and somebody showed it to me. And he doesn't even bother to hide it. I asked him what the name of that round cactus growing outside his door was, and he said, quite shamelessly, 'mescal.'"

"What were you doing outside his room?" asked Michael, astonishing himself by the aggression in his voice and the sudden stab of jealousy he felt.

"I went to their study circle. And yesterday I went to a literature study circle, and the day before to a music circle. I've only been here three nights, and I've already been to three study circles, and I even dropped into a course on ceramics for adults. They're a big thing here, these study circles. Everybody on the kibbutz takes part in some study circle or other, and Dave's circle on mysticism and the history of mysticism meets in his room, over cups of herb tea. There were more people than usual there, so I understood from what he said, and nobody mentioned the reason, but you could see from their eyes that they were feeling terrible.

"I thought about Fanya," Avigail said suddenly, "that she may have done it to protect Yankele; and about Guta, that she might have done it to prevent Fanya breaking down over Yankele; and about Aaron Meroz too. I hear he's being interrogated again."

"But he was in Jerusalem," said Michael, "and it's a little difficult to poison someone from there in the space of half an hour, and Fanya was in the sewing shop with ten other people, and Yankele was in the plant with Dave, and Guta was in the dining hall, she was seen. We're talking about half an hour, three-quarters of an hour during which someone disappeared without anyone noticing, and the milieu presents a special difficulty. Because people say, 'I was here and there,' or 'I was on my way to somewhere or other.' Apart from which, I need a motive."

"And there is no motive," said Avigail.

"That's what's driving me to despair," confessed Michael. "I've gone over her life with a fine-tooth comb. I've read every letter, every piece of paper, I searched Meroz's house too, with his permission. Nothing. Not a thing. The most exciting thing I found in Osnat's room was the kibbutz news bulletin, *Times and Tides,* they call it—they've got a name for everything here," he said, grimacing, "and in fact I took the back copies for all of the past year, in the hope that I might learn something from them, but it's a daunting task—they put one out every week."

He spread his hands out in a helpless gesture and brought them down on his knees. "I've glanced at them every opportunity I get, apart from the fact that Sarit is going through them all systematically. I thought, I had the feeling, that I'd find something there that nobody took the trouble to hide because they didn't consider it significant. The only thing that came out of the search of her room was a reinforcement of Meroz's argument that she was dedicated to public affairs, to ideology."

"Ideology?" Avigail echoed skeptically.

"Yes," said Michael. "What do you think about it?"

"It's a little romantic to talk about ideology in connection with murder," said Avigail. "After all, we know why people commit murder."

"Yes?" said Michael. "Why do they commit murder?"

Avigail was silent.

"So we shouldn't look for what we don't know?" He looked at her. "What do you say, Avigail, that we should stop looking? Have you got any practical suggestions, ideas for motives that aren't romantic? What do you think, Avigail?"

"I don't know. I haven't the faintest idea."

16

On the threadbare carpet of the old secretariat where Ohayon had set up shop, copies of the kibbutz weekly news bulletin, *Times and Tides*, lay scattered. One of the legs of the shabby armchair Michael Ohayon was sitting in was missing and had been replaced by a red brick. He leaned back, touched his cup of cold coffee, and looked at the copy he held in his hand.

Again and again he had run his eyes over the mimeographed pages. And finally—between a recommendation for changing the point system crediting work accomplished and a review of forthcoming closed-circuit video programs—he found the article that had made him push aside all the other issues. In this copy, he had started with a report on the completion of the annual cotton harvest, "an occasion marked by the traditional ceremony with the cotton pickers, draped in the blue and white of the national flag and the red flag of the working class, being driven in formation with their lights on for the picking of the last rows and emptying the cotton into the bins in unison. . . ." The forced humor in the account of misadventures during that year's cotton picking ("Mickey's hand was in the wrong place and consequently caught in the blades") deeply irritated him. And the same kind of humor combined with self-righteousness, in a dramatic description of the heroic last-minute repair of one of the machines, made him grind his cigarette butt into the cracked clay plant pot he was using as an ashtray.

After leaving Avigail's room, he had spent all night reading back issues of the kibbutz bulletin. He had read even the announcements and the messages of thanks and congratulations. When the pale light began to break through the slats of the broken blind at five o'clock, his temples were pounding rhythmically in time to Nahari's voice inside his head. He tried to suppress the spasms of pain that made him grit his teeth, in turn producing a familiar pain in his jaw. His throat felt raw and dry. Suddenly he imagined Yuval's reproachful and disappointed voice saying, "How could you, Dad, how . . ." The last word was repeated several times, and then Michael saw a sorrowful expression in his son's eyes as his mind turned to what he would do if one of the kibbutz people were to commit suicide. Michael thought of Yankele's haunted face, of Fanya's grunting sobs when she returned from the hospital in Ashkelon, after standing outside the room where the mainly silent Yankele was being questioned. And of Guta's fury, of the yellow-gray tinge on Aaron Meroz's face, of the dark circles around Jojo's eyes. Dvorka's eyes pursued him wherever he went, suspicious and accusing. He suddenly thought, too, of Osnat's soldier son, and asked himself how he would be able to face the hysterical outbursts, the shock and the pain and the sorrow of the kibbutz members.

The air was cold and clean, but not even the deep, slow breaths he took next to the open door at five o'clock in the morning could dispel what he knew to be an attack of panic.

"Why did you shake the trees like that?" Nahari had upbraided him, and the question came back to nag at him now as he glanced again at this bulletin from the end of February.

"So that the rabbit would come out." Michael had used this banal metaphor without thinking of the meaning of the words.

"And what makes you think that it will?" Nahari had asked. "Because it would suit you?"

Ignoring the sarcasm, Michael had explained seriously, "Perhaps to protect itself. Maybe, for example, out of fear that somebody knows."

"In that case," Nahari had warned, "you'd better give some serious thought to the implications. I don't know if it's occurred to you, for example, to organize some serious protection for the people who were close to Osnat. Because when the rabbit comes out, and it's more like a tiger than a rabbit, it can be dangerous to others."

Michael had said nothing.

"I'm talking about the fact that you'd better keep a sharp eye on Dvorka and Moish and the rest of them."

The exchange had taken place at the same meeting where the question of the time limit was discussed. Unlike the grumbling of Ariyeh Levy, the Jerusalem Subdistrict chief, it was impossible to dismiss Nahari's strictures as a nuisance you had to live with. "I don't give a damn for what people will say," Nahari had explained calmly. "In principle, I don't care if it takes a few more days in order to build a case that will stand up in court, but in this case, with its special dynamics and the unusual risks we're taking, the time factor is crucial. You can't leave policemen in a kibbutz for long without putting the backs of the whole kibbutz movement up and getting questions asked in the Knesset. And that's by the way. I'm a lot more worried about the fact that if your rabbit-tiger doesn't jump out of the forest in a week or two, you'll have a whole kibbutz in a state of stress on your hands. If you don't get a move on in this case—and I'm not talking about the Kibbutz Artzi and the Knesset and Meroz and the scandal, I'm talking about the good of the people concerned—you'll start getting the backlash within a few days: They won't be able to take the tension, they'll break down. Think about it: It's like walking around with the feeling that somebody in your family is a murderer. We can't tell what it might lead to. What will you do if one of them commits suicide? It's happened before."

Michael had opened his mouth, but Nahari raised his hand and said, "I know, I know that you've got all kinds of mental-health people down there, but there are things that we've got no control over. Apart from which, prolonged stress makes rabbits dangerous. You have to come up with something soon, if not a solution, then at least a lead. They say you're a clever fellow, that you perform miracles." Here Nahari had interrupted his long speech, which he was delivering in the conference room of the section Michael headed, in order to moisten his fat cigar with his tongue, resuming only after ceremoniously lighting it.

"I'm not talking about the fact that you planted Avigail there. How long will it take before somebody remembers meeting her somewhere? In a country this size, you can't keep things hidden for long. Someone must have sat on the potty with her mother or seen her on the way to Petah Tikva, someone must have bumped into her in the corridor at the university. Someone will see you visiting her at night, overhear you talking."

Michael now put the news bulletin down and walked heavily to the toilets outside the old secretariat building, where he put his head under a stream of cold water at a cracked sink. When he dried his hair on the checked army-issue towel Moish had left for him on one of the beds in his room, he thought of Avigail and of the vulnerability hiding behind the silky hair falling over her face, and then he was flooded by a piercing pain, almost abstract but still very much alive, for Maya, and again he was overcome by a wave of anxiety, and Nahari's words came back and hammered in his head like drums. He saw Moish's tense, white face, and Jojo, who lowered his eyes whenever Michael spoke to him, with the color fading from his freckles, and Osnat's soldier son, with his bitten fingernails.

Osnat's article in the bulletin, headed "From the Secretary's Desk," was squeezed in between a photo of the cotton harvest and congratulations to Deddi on graduating from his flying course. It was a report on a seminar attended by the secretaries of dozens of agricultural settlements, on the subject of "Mutual Liability on the Kibbutz." Once more he read the next-to-last paragraph, as if to learn the words by heart:

Among many other questions that were discussed (such as whether mutual liability exists in all circumstances, including, for example, the embezzlement of public funds, or alternatively, the sale of public property for what is purported to be the good of the kibbutz, as in the case of certain office-holders who have behaved as if they were a law unto themselves and acted according to a private agenda of their own), there was a general sense that we were facing a profound and significant crisis, which could not be resolved merely by amending this or that article, but only by a courageous and intelligent reexamination of first principles.

Then his eye again fell on the secretariat report concerning "loans granted to kibbutz sons/daughters leaving for a year outside." Mechanically he took in the words "a sum of money for initial settling-in arrangements, as a loan to be returned during the first four months," and then returned to "From the Secretary's Desk."

The last paragraph in Osnat's column read:

The kibbutz must restructure itself as a society in which the individual is the goal and the collectivist-egalitarian community is only the means (superior to others) toward his development and the realization of his aspirations. Such a kibbutz will have the power to compete against its rivals in the market for the "good life," which has become even more relevant in the wake of the declining attraction of the ideology and praxis of Zionist pioneering values. The atmosphere is far from gloomy or despairing, we see a movement with vast human potential standing at a historical crossroads and considering which road to take. And once the way becomes clear, it will have the strength to race full steam ahead.

All this was a series of bombastic cliches and lofty generalizations reading more or less like a word-for-word transcript from speeches made at the seminar. What riveted Michael was the passage in parentheses in the preceding paragraph, with its concrete, businesslike tone.

His anxiety was overtaken by a sense of urgency, a need to act quickly. He carefully folded the news bulletin and set off in the direction of the dining hall. Moish wasn't there, and he poured himself a cup of coffee from the big urn, added warm milk, spread a roll with cheese and olive paste, and sat down at an empty table in the corner of the large room. There were only a few people there at a quarter past seven in the morning. Someone nodded to him without smiling. The four men sitting at the table behind him in working clothes ate without speaking. At the far end of the hall, he caught sight of Guta in her black rubber boots, absorbed in cutting up vegetables for a salad. After looking at his empty coffee cup, he pushed his roll to the end of the table, unable to bring himself to throw it into the receptacle for discarded food standing in the middle of the table, and left the dining hall. On his way to the secretariat building, he remembered the double meaning of the word for this disgusting kibbutz object. *Kolboinik* was used to describe not only this slop bowl but also someone, like Dave, who had golden hands, knew how to fix everything. He asked himself how they had come to use a word for a garbage receptacle to describe human skill and ingenuity. And especially, he wondered, what did it say about them?

Moish was already in his office. Michael heard his voice through the open door, and when he looked inside he saw his back. The office chair was turned sideways, and Moish was looking out of the big window as he spoke into the gray telephone. Michael too looked at the green lawn and the tall cypress trees outside the new, white building housing the kibbutz secretariat. Only when he said "Excuse me" and knocked on the open door did Moish swivel his chair around and indicate the chair opposite with a nervous, irritable gesture. His face was pale and his expression tense, and he concluded his conversation by saying abruptly, "Let me know when you've got an estimate of the damage." He turned to Michael, who asked if there was anything wrong. "Nothing new," said Moish with a sigh, "a jackal got into the henhouse again and had himself a ball."

Michael took the folded bulletin out of the brown envelope he was holding and spread it out in front of Moish on top of the papers piled neatly in the center of the desk.

Moish leafed through it and raised his eyes questioningly. "What?" he finally asked. "What's the problem?"

"There isn't anything there that bothers you?" asked Michael. He idly took a black felt-tipped marker from a penholder made of a cardboard toilet-paper cylinder thickly painted blue and glued onto a base made of a thick cardboard rectangle on which was printed, in multicolored letters: "TO DADDY, IN HONOR OF HIS NEW JOB."

"No," said Moish in a tone of weary bafflement, and with an expression saying, "I don't have the strength to play games," he added, "Why don't you just tell me what the problem is? When's it from?" He turned the page and looked at the picture of the cotton harvest. For a moment his eyes clouded as he looked at the boy in the corner of the picture. "My oldest son, and that's Osnat's boy next to him," he sighed. Then the glint of pain in his eyes was covered over again by incomprehension. "What have you found here?"

"Why don't you read it yourself?" suggested Michael laconically, pointing with the felt-tipped pen to the column "From the Secretary's Desk."

Moish raised the page, held it away from his eyes, and began to read. Michael noticed that his lips moved as he read. Then he put it down and passed his hand over his eyes. "I've read it. I can't see anything special, unusual, out of the ordinary," he said impatiently. "What are you getting at?"

Michael put his hand down calmly on the page and said, "There's something odd in parentheses here." Moish reread the sentence silently, and then aloud, pronouncing the words separately, one by one, as if they were items on a shopping list. Then he closed his eyes, shook his head, and said, "I don't see what you're getting at."

"How do you understand that sentence?" asked Michael.

"How should I know? I have no idea. I wasn't at that seminar."

"Was anyone else from the kibbutz there besides Osnat?"

"I don't know," replied Moish hoarsely. "How long is it since then? This is from the end of February, so it's about six months ago. How do you expect me to remember?"

"And nobody noticed anything?"

"Do me a favor," said Moish, pushing a few papers aside. "A news bulletin like this comes out every week; people don't read it so closely. I don't remember, I didn't hear anything. I don't remember hearing anything. If you tell me what you have in mind, maybe it'll give me a clue," he said with growing annoyance, and finally he burst out angrily, "All these questions all the time, it's driving me crazy! When is it going to end?" And then, "Sorry, I'm a bit tense, I'm not sleeping well; it's not exactly easy, what's going on here. And the business with my father, that hasn't helped either."

"Even though we said that in his case it was probably an accident?"

"Okay, an accident, but where's the rest of the parathion? Who's got it? And where's it going to end up?"

Michael was silent.

"When will you have an answer to *that*?" asked Moish. There was more despair than anger in the question.

"What I want to know," said Michael slowly, "is if Osnat composed that sentence herself, or if she was quoting something said by someone at the seminar. How exactly did it come up?"

Moish made a face as if to say "Search me," and Michael, again feeling the sense of urgency and the need to act quickly, said, "How can I get hold of the minutes of the seminar?"

"I don't know if there are any, I don't think there are. It's held every year, and there are scores of people there, secretaries of all the kibbutzim."

"Okay, so who else was there?"

"People from other kibbutzim around here. From the north; I wouldn't really know."

"She never said anything about it to you?"

"Not to me, but maybe she spoke to someone else, maybe to Dvorka, maybe to . . . I don't know."

"Maybe to whom?"

"I don't know, I tell you. Why don't you try Dvorka?"

"Okay, I'll try Dvorka, but I'd also like you to put me in touch with the secretary of a neighboring kibbutz, if you don't mind," Michael insisted.

"Who would remember a thing like that?" asked Moish with a sigh, but he reached for the telephone and pressed one of the buttons on the sophisticated instrument. Then he said, "Who is this, Misha?" and then, "No, it's Moish Eyal," and after a silence, "Yes, it's very difficult, it isn't easy with this invasion we've got here . . . " His voice died away as his eyes fell on Michael. "Tell me, Misha, do you remember the seminar for kibbutz secretaries last February? . . . Never mind, there's something I need to know. Were you there? . . . And was Osnat the only one there from here, or was there someone else as well? . . . Just Osnat," he repeated and looked at Michael, who lit a cigarette, stretched out his legs, and stubbornly gazed back at Moish. "There's somebody here who wants to ask a few questions about what happened there," said Moish hesitantly into the receiver. "Never mind, not over the phone. Can you come here? . . . Yes, I know, but it's connected to . . . It's urgent, it would be better if you came here than if he came to you, and I don't want to say anything more over the phone. How long will it take you to get here?"

"Twenty minutes," said Moish, "and I think he knows it's about . . . that it's connected to . . . " His voice died away, and he began rummaging in the desk drawers until his hand emerged holding a roll of toilet paper. He tore off a piece and blew his nose loudly. "Allergy," he explained. "Every year I get this allergy." He rolled the paper into a ball and threw it violently into the wastepaper basket. "Dave gave me some cactus that's supposed to help, but I don't believe in all that nonsense," he said in embarrassment.

"How does that kibbutz secretary know?" asked Michael.

Moish let out a sound between a laugh and a snort. "From the minute the news got out over here it was impossible to stop it going farther. Our kids go to the same regional school, we've got projects in common, cultural activities, all kinds of connections . . . . And people talk on the phone. I'll bet there isn't a kibbutz in the country that isn't buzzing with the story. I can't understand why the place isn't swarming with reporters yet."

Michael remembered Shorer's mocking words: "How long do you think it will stay a secret? You're not God, you know, not even now that you're in NUSCI." He had taken a noisy gulp from the beer can and smiled. "How long do you think you'll get away with your bluff? Your smoke screen? And let's say you manage to maintain radio silence, someone from the *Cockamamie Women's Journal* or the *Scientific Bullshit News* will get onto it. What do you think, that nobody on the kibbutz has an aunt in town whose son moonlights as a 'crime reporter' for some local rag? How long do you think you're going to be able to hold them off with the kind of double talk you gave out yesterday?"

Moish's voice penetrated the drumbeats that were again hammering at Michael's temples: "You have to be really naive to think you can keep it a secret; every minute that passes without a phone call from some newspaper seems to me like a miracle."

Michael suddenly broke the silence that had fallen between them: "Do you know about anything like that happening here?"

"Anything like what?"

"Embezzlement or theft or selling kibbutz property—any of the things Osnat mentioned in her column?"

Moish thought for a long time and then said, "Not really. There was a period when some members' rooms were burglarized, a sudden spate of burglaries, but we didn't involve the police, we found the culprit and dealt with it ourselves. Osnat wasn't involved at all. It was one of the volunteers who was into drugs, never mind the details. And then there was a very unpleasant business with stealing that our security liaison officer discovered."

Michael raised his eyebrows curiously, and Moish looked at him in embarrassment. "It was a good many years ago, when Alex was in charge of security. Such things happen on every kibbutz. Suddenly some member goes crazy, I don't understand how it happens . . . " he said without addressing Michael, looking down at his hands. "It's like stealing from your parents. You can take what you like, so why steal? In any case, it happened, and Alex got some bloodhounds from the border police, and they led straight to the door of one of our members. A veteran member. What could he do? He said thank you very much to the dog handlers and went home to sleep. I heard about it not from Alex but from someone in the border police. To this day I don't know who the thief was."

"And the border police kept quiet?"

"Well, there's a kind of unspoken agreement, they let kibbutzim solve things like that themselves," said Moish, tearing a long strip of toilet paper off the roll. "They understand. Like it says here—mutual liability." Then he added firmly, "We never had any embezzlement here, but I know of a kibbutz not far from here where they accused the woman in charge of the sewing shop of taking clothes out of the stock and sending them to her family in town without paying. And I also know of a kibbutz in the north where there was a big embezzlement: Someone was transferring funds to a private account in town, and they didn't bring the police in either. The kibbutz dealt with it."

"How?" asked Michael.

"Well, there are all kinds of ways," said Moish uneasily. "In the case I just mentioned I know that they made the guy leave and he gave them back the money down to the last cent, and it ended in a tragedy, because the wife and kids stayed on and they were completely ostracized. It happened two years ago; they're still getting the cold shoulder from everybody, and they're still there. They don't want to leave."

"And how about here, on your own kibbutz?"

"I told you. We've had a few little problems, but we took care of them ourselves. If you can call it 'taking care,'" he said bitterly. "But we never had anything like that here, and I don't really understand what she means about 'selling.' I don't think it's anything concrete, she just got carried away. She had a tendency to get carried away like that."

"Like that? What do you mean 'like that'?" asked Michael sharply. "Where else do you see anything 'like that'?"

"So not exactly like that, but you can see how seriously she took everything. Read all the other stuff she writes there."

"I've read it," said Michael. "And I haven't seen anything else 'like that' anywhere."

"In the other numbers of the bulletin you'll see that every week she's goes on about things like that, and she often actually stresses that it's not concrete, just hypothetical."

"Okay, so let's take the hypothetical case in question—what could have inspired her to write precisely this?"

"Search me," said Moish after a long pause for reflection. "I don't have a clue. I don't know at all what she's getting at with the business about 'selling public property.'"

At this point there was a knock on the door, and a middle-aged man walked into the room, passed his hand over his perspiring bald pate, and said, "Here I am. What's up?"

"Coffee?" Moish asked the man, who sat down heavily on a chair he pulled up from a corner of the room.

"Why not? I'm standing in a corner of the room, a round, old kettle always a customer for coffee," Misha said, smiling and exposing a gap in the teeth at the side of his mouth. "Black, no sugar." Moish got up and went over to the old electric coffeepot whose cord was held together with a fraying piece of insulation tape.

"That tape's no good, you need a new cord," said Misha, walking over to the coffeepot. "You'll get a shock. You'd better get it taken care of. I don't understand you, with your automatic phone exchange and cordless phones, couldn't you organize an automatic coffeemaker?"

"I had one and it broke down," said Moish apologetically as Misha took his seat again. "It's been fixed, but I forgot to go get it."

In a hesitant, embarrassed voice, Moish introduced Michael Ohayon to Misha, who couldn't conceal the gleam of sensation-seeking excitement in his eyes, contradicting the serious expression on the rest of his face.

"So what do you want to know about the seminar?" he asked quickly, after muttering some words about "the tragedy for all of us, for the whole kibbutz movement."

Michael learned that Osnat had been the sole representative of the kibbutz at the seminar, and after hearing about the program and its format, to make sure that he had understood, he asked, "In essence, then, it was a forum to discuss general questions of principle and their application to particular cases on various kibbutzim?"

Misha nodded and went on to relate it, as well, to the social aspect: "It's healthy to exchange ideas and methods. For all our disagreements, it's one of the ways we can feel we're all part of one movement, and it's fun, too, you can imagine, having lunch together and meeting everyone."

"And you'd remember if there was anything special, anyone you spoke to in particular," urged Michael.

"Look, it isn't exactly the kind of event where you remember every word that was said," Misha said apologetically. "I wrote something about it for our news bulletin, and I remember something about mutual liability, but I'm not a young woman like Osnat, I've been to a lot of seminars and I don't take it all as seriously as her," he said with an embarrassed smile. "I'm more in favor of getting on with the job, which is difficult enough as it is, and on that particular day I was busy talking to some old friends from the north. I hardly had a chance to talk to her, and we didn't travel home together either." He looked at the hissing coffeepot. "It's still not boiling, that piece of junk," he said, then quickly wiped the smile from his face in favor of an expression showing responsibility. "All I can tell you is that if she had said something—how can I put it?—out of the ordinary or dramatic, I would have remembered." He sighed. "How beautiful she was!" he said suddenly.

"What bothers me," said Michael, "is the article in here." He handed Misha the mimeographed news bulletin.

Misha tugged at the black cord around his neck with an exaggerated flourish and extracted the small reading glasses that had been hidden inside his big blue shirt, whose long sleeves were untidily rolled up to his elbows. When he had finished reading, he put the bulletin carefully down on the desk, closer to Moish than to Michael, and took off his glasses. He didn't say anything.

"What do you say?" asked Moish.

"I don't know what to tell you; I'm trying to remember. There was so much talking there."

"You don't remember if things like that came up?" asked Michael with surprise.

"Yes, there was something about crimes on kibbutzim and about how we protect our members too much, and I remember now that Osnat got very excited about something, but the details . . . " Here he delivered a long sentence in Yiddish, which Michael didn't understand, but he did catch the words *alte kop*—"old head"—which were repeated a number of times. Finally he shook his head slowly and solemnly from side to side and said, "I can't help you."

Then, with grandmotherly concern, which he tried to disguise, he asked Moish, "How are things here? How are you coping with all this?" After a few attempts at polite civilities, he smiled and said, "Nu, the coffee will have to wait for another time, I have to get back, Uri's waiting for the van." And only then did the old coffeepot begin to make bubbling sounds and the lid begin to jump, and Moish carefully pulled the plug out of the socket and said, "Are you sure?"

"Yes," said Misha.

"I'll see you to the car," said Moish, following him out and closing the door gently behind him. Michael heard their lowered voices growing fainter and dying away. A few minutes later Moish returned and said, "That's it. I can't tell you anything more. Talk to Dvorka."

His conversation with Dvorka, too, in the reading room next to the library, produced no results. She studied the mimeographed page at length. Then her piercing blue eyes, sunk into deep hollows, glittered as she looked at him over the pile of books and papers on the broad table in front of her. Although they were alone in the big room, she whispered, "I have no idea. I remember vaguely that she came back from the seminar preoccupied, and she said that it had been very illuminating. But even at the time, when I read her report, I didn't notice anything out of the ordinary. But now that you draw my attention to it, I agree that there's something odd about it. However, I don't imagine for a moment that she was referring to anything specific."

"I really can't say," she said in an offended tone when asked who Osnat might have shared her preoccupations with, and put her hand down on the pile of books. Once again Michael felt the tension this woman aroused in him. He looked at her aged hands, ringless and almost masculine in appearance, noticing the brown spots on their backs, and then he felt his eyes irresistibly drawn to her eyes with their riveting power. He asked himself again if she had been beautiful when young, and how she had coped with her bereavements and loneliness. And what it was that she was hiding from him, because she was clearly watchful and on her guard. But this thought only occurred to him on the way to the parking lot, before they began to serve lunch in the dining hall, where everyone avoided him like the plague. Although he had been invited several times to make himself at home, he went there as little as possible, preferring to share the pita and stuffed vegetables prepared by Machluf Levy's wife, which reminded him of the snacks Balilty would sometimes bring from the old man in the corner kiosk next to the Russian Compound in Jerusalem.

Aaron Meroz had been transferred from the intensive-care unit to the internal-diseases ward, where he lay in a room containing only one other bed. He smiled wanly at Michael and pushed aside the tray holding the leftover mashed potatoes that filled the room with their smell. Shifting the newspapers lying on his bed onto the black visitors' chair, he said, "Wait for me a minute outside. I'll get up and join you there."

While he was waiting, Michael thought, as he already had several times, about the special relationship that had grown between himself and Aaron Meroz. Even though he was recovering from his heart attack, had not yet regained his strength, and although he had both the reason and the means to avoid him, he willingly cooperated and showed an interest in everything Michael said. Perhaps too much interest, thought Michael as he waited tensely in the visitors' waiting room next to an ashtray affixed to the marble wall. A big window looked out at the enclosed garden in the courtyard of the Hadassah Hospital in Ein Karem. Meroz emerged wearing a striped robe over his blue pajamas, walked slowly over to him, and pointed to two seats in the corner.

"Isn't there a private room here for a member of the Knesset?" asked Michael, and Meroz replied that as a rule there was, "but yesterday they asked me if I was willing to share, because of the overcrowding. So what could I do? Make a fuss?" And with his characteristically forced smile he added, "Noblesse oblige, you know, except that in this case it's the opposite. I'm supposed to be a public *servant*, after all."

Aaron Meroz smiled again as he held the news bulletin in his hand. "Once upon a time I was the editor of this thing," he said with a dreamy expression. "Nothing's really changed," he added wonderingly, "it's the same old things. Here, look at the summary of the *sicha*: So-and-so has been accepted as a kibbutz member, so-and-so has been granted a year's leave, and so-and-so's housing problem has been solved. The changes are only apparent; actually it's all the same."

"Not exactly," said Michael.

"No," agreed Meroz, "not exactly, not in our case anyway. Soon you'll be able to give me a polygraph test, too. I told the officer who was here today—what's his name? Levy, the one with the ring—that I'll be out of here in a week and I have no objection to taking a polygraph test." Michael nodded.

"I'd be very suspicious of his consent," Nahari had warned. "He could get out of it very easily if he wanted to; why doesn't he use his prerogative?"

"And what's his motive, in your opinion?" Michael had asked.

"Look," Nahari had said in a didactic, philosophical vein, "when it comes to an affair between a man and a woman, nobody besides the two of them knows what's really going on. Even if they talk about it to other people, and especially when it's clandestine. What do we really know about him?"

"I've got a lot of time to think here," Meroz said now. "About life in general, and about Osnat and what happened. Whichever way I look at it, it seems more and more inexplicable. It's crazy. I can't even imagine how they're taking it on the kibbutz. The thing itself, and your presence there. How are they coping with it?" he asked in a voice that had more than one tone, including a tone of satisfaction he had already heard from him before, the same as in Nahari's voice when he had said, "So they're not immune to everything."

"But that's not what you want to talk to me about. You want to talk to me about the bulletin. What's so special about this bulletin?" asked Meroz, turning the pages. "Ah, the end of the cotton harvest. So they're still making a big deal out of it?" And now there was sadness and longing in his voice, reminding Michael of the way he had talked about Osnat. He glanced through the bulletin until he came to the place marked with the black felt-tipped pen, where he stopped and read with concentration. Finally he sighed and refolded the mimeographed pages.

"What do you see there?" he asked Michael. "I see that you've marked it." The soft afternoon Jerusalem light coming through the large window illuminated the dusty corners of the room and painted the metal rims of the plastic tables with gold. A young woman in an elegant pink suit hit the public telephone with a manicured fist in the hope of retrieving her lost token. From somewhere or other came the sound of a television set.

"You came all this way because of that?" asked Meroz, wrapping himself more tightly in his robe, whose belt was too short to go around his waist. "What do you see there that's so important?"

"I don't really know if it's important," said Michael, "but it's odd. The sentence in parentheses."

Meroz reread the sentence.

"I thought that maybe she had spoken to you about it. She was close to you recently, and I thought that maybe something was bothering her."

Meroz sighed. "She had all kinds of bees in her bonnet," he said, "questions of principle. I'm sure you'll find more of the same in other numbers of the bulletin."

"Yes, I did, but not like this. This is different. There are too many assumptions here. What public property could she be referring to, in your opinion?"

"I don't know. What do they have there that someone could sell without the others noticing?"

"Nothing material," Michael reflected aloud, "only something like knowledge, information," he said, hearing the note of surprise with which he ended the sentence. "Did she ever talk to you about the cosmetics plant?" he suddenly asked.

"No," said Meroz, "she hardly ever mentioned it, except in the context of hired labor and the problem of shift work. But how does the plant come into it?"

"Think for a moment," said Michael, standing up in order to take the pack of cigarettes out of his trouser pocket. "What could you sell without anyone knowing about it, on a kibbutz? On your kibbutz."

Aaron Meroz scratched the gray stubble glittering on his chin in the yellowing light. "Once," he said thoughtfully, "there was a business about a special sprinkler that Felix invented and a manufacturer stole his idea. But that was years ago, and it was impossible to prove that Felix invented it; he never showed it to anyone outside the kibbutz. He built just the one model of this special sprinkler drip, and we tried it out. It was years ago; there was no awareness then of industrial potential on the kibbutz, he only did it to solve a particular problem we had with the irrigation pipes . . . " Gradually his voice died down, and he looked suspiciously at Michael. "What are you thinking about?"

"About the plant. About your factory."

"Don't say 'your,'" said Meroz sharply. "In my time there wasn't any cosmetics factory on the kibbutz."

"Do you know how much the formula for an expensive face cream is worth?"

"No," admitted Meroz, "I don't know, but the whole thing sounds too American to be true, and even if it is, if there was industrial espionage, nobody from the kibbutz would . . . " he himself realized the irony of his words. "Okay, it's impossible, after what's happened, to talk about something that nobody from the kibbutz would be capable of doing," he admitted, "but it sounds too sophisticated to me."

"Have you ever seen the plant's profit figures?" asked Michael, and Meroz said no, he'd never taken any interest in the subject.

"But I have, and you'd never believe the size of the numbers," said Michael. "I thought only huge companies dealt in terms of that kind of money. Last year, when industry in the rest of the country was in the doldrums, that plant flourished and made huge profits because of patents invented on the kibbutz. The face cream Dave concocted from cactuses—and even the packing machine he invented."

"Okay, so the plant's doing well," said Meroz, a look of suffering appearing on his face.

"Do you feel all right?" asked Michael with sudden concern.

"Yes," said Meroz, "I feel fine. I just have these attacks of weakness, especially when I sit up for a long time."

"She never said anything to you about the plant? About industrial espionage?"

"Nothing," Meroz assured him.

"Can you guess who she might have meant by the reference to 'officeholders?'"

"You don't have to be a genius to guess," said Meroz. "How many high offices are there on a kibbutz? The secretary, the treasurer, the general director, and the members of a couple of committees. And if you insist on following the line you're taking, it's the economic positions you should be interested in."

That same night, after a long talk with Dave, Michael knocked on Jojo's door and asked him to come outside. Jojo looked hesitantly over his shoulder back into the room, where the blue light of a television screen flickered, and said, "I'll be back in a minute." Outside, he asked apprehensively, "Are you sure you don't want to come in?"

"It would be easier if we went to my place," said Michael, looking at Jojo's thin legs and wide, short trousers. Even in the dim light of the lamp shining at the end of the path, he could see the beads of sweat breaking out on his companion's forehead. "I've just come back from a meeting, I'm rather tired," said Jojo, but Michael took no notice and strode off in the direction of the old secretariat.

Jojo couldn't control the trembling of his hands even when he put them on his knees. He read the mimeographed page Michael placed before him and carefully put it down next to him on the bed. Michael had sat down in the armchair after straightening the red brick, which wasn't broad enough for its task.

Jojo was silent.

"So what have you got to say?" asked Michael, with an effort to keep his voice calm.

Jojo shrugged his shoulders. When he tried to reply, only a hoarse croak emerged from his throat. He looked at the floor, and Michael had to suppress an urge to shake him. "Maybe it wasn't a good idea to talk to him now, after such a long day," he said to himself, but the drumbeats that had returned to reverberate between his temples reminded him that he had no time to dawdle or rest. "So do you want someone else to do it?" Sarit had asked him when he put through a call to NUSCI from the hospital in Jerusalem. "Or do you intend to drive back there tonight? Machluf Levy's there now, in the area, and there are other people too, you don't always have to—"

Here he had interrupted her firmly with the statement that he was on his way back to the kibbutz. Now he thought about his preference for working alone. "You can't be a loner here, the way you were in Jerusalem," Nahari had warned him, "and if you want to get this case over quickly, before there's another catastrophe, you'd better change your methods. There's something screwed up about your dynamics with people. We heard about you before you got here," he said without smiling, "and you can't get away with it here."

"Look," said Michael, leaning toward the bed where Jojo was sitting withdrawn into himself, his eyes fixed on his fingertips, whose trembling he was trying to hide, "there's no point beating about the bush, it would be better for you if you said whatever you've got to say right way, believe me."

"What about?" asked Jojo. In the light of the naked bulb dangling from the ceiling, Michael could see his freckles growing paler.

"What about?" Michael repeated sharply. "You know exactly what it's about—what's the point of pretending? And I know too, especially after my long talk with Ronny, the manager of your cosmetics plant."

"What do you want to talk about?" Jojo persevered.

So tired he couldn't control his voice properly, Michael heard himself almost shout, "Not about the weather! I want you to talk about the confrontation you had with Osnat about the plant!"

Jojo kept quiet.

Michael lit a cigarette and looked at his watch. "We're going to sit here until you talk," he said angrily. "We should have talked about it long ago, three days ago."

But Jojo still kept quiet.

"Look," said Michael as if in one last spurt of patience, "I even know the name of the face cream you gave to the Swiss firm, and I also know how the kibbutz recovered from the crisis with the bank shares after that. I already know most of the details, so why don't you just tell me how Osnat found out?"

"By accident, the same way you did," Jojo said finally. "She didn't know the details, and I persuaded her how right I was, and in the end she was only angry about the principle."

"When did you talk about it?" asked Michael in a businesslike voice, as if he were filling in a form.

"After she wrote this article. I didn't initiate the conversation, and I hadn't even seen the article. I was supposed to go with her to that seminar, and in the end I didn't go because of . . . " Jojo tried to control the violent trembling of his body.

"Because of what?" Michael asked.

"Because of some tests I had to have on the same day, which I couldn't put off," he said unwillingly, "at Barzilai Hospital . . . about my eyes," he added with evident difficulty as Michael observed him silently. "They suspected a tumor behind the eye," he burst out, "if you want to know," and when Michael didn't change his expression, Jojo went on: "In the end everything turned out all right."

Michael kept quiet.

Jojo looked as if he were groping for the precise words and then hesitantly said, "I don't know what Ronny told you, but it isn't what you think."

Michael kept quiet. It was Shorer who had taught him this, early on, saying, "You also have to know how to shut up. And the right way to do it. There are all kinds of ways of keeping quiet, but that's something you'll learn to sense for yourself." And now Jojo had to talk: At the stage they had reached, there was no way he could any longer keep quiet.

"After that article came out, she was sitting with me in her room, we were going over the accounts. By then I'd seen the article, but I didn't want to ask her directly. I only said something about the seminar, and then she said, 'I was waiting for you to come and talk to me, what I wrote in that column was addressed specifically to you.' Have you got a drink of water?"

Michael hesitated. He didn't want to interrupt the rhythm of the interview. He would have to leave the room for the water, and he was afraid that a break in the face-to-face session would make Jojo clam up again. On the other hand, he identified almost completely with the treasurer, whose mouth felt so dry that he kept licking his parched lips with a dry tongue.

"In a minute," he finally said, "I'll get you some water in a minute."

"The details aren't important . . . " said Jojo, looking at Michael inquiringly.

"We'll have to see if they are or not."

"In the end I understood that she'd spoken to Ronny, and that he had told her about the competition with the Swiss. We already knew about that from the plant report a year and a half before, it also came up in the kibbutz *sicha,* because Ronny brought it up in connection with the hired labor, never mind that now . . . " Again there was inquiring look and the quick flick of the tongue over the lips.

Michael kept quiet.

"Anyway, to cut a long story short, she put two and two together and came to the conclusion that I'd gotten hold of the formula and sold it to the Swiss to get the kibbutz out of that mess with the bank shares."

"And it never occurred to her that you did it for personal gain?" asked Michael in surprise.

"What personal gain?" asked Jojo in confusion. And then he waved a hand angrily and yelled, "What the hell are you talking about? So where's the money?"

"I really don't know. I've heard that kibbutz members have private bank accounts now, here too."

"Well, I haven't," said Jojo furiously. "No inheritances and no presents and no reparations money from Germany—and Osnat knew that too."

"How much money was involved?"

"Nearly a million and a half dollars," whispered Jojo, "but I had no choice. If I hadn't done it, everything would have gone down the drain, and this way we still came out with a profit when the bank shares collapsed and all the other kibbutzim lost their shirts."

"And she didn't have any suspicions about a private account?"

"No. I told you, she knows me."

"It turns out that a lot of people think they know other people, and they're sometimes wrong."

Jojo kept quiet.

"And then," asked Michael.

"What? Then what?"

"After she confronted you with what she knew, what happened after that?"

"Well, we had a long talk," said Jojo with an effort. "I can't say I enjoyed it."

"When was this?"

"A few months ago. I don't know exactly, three or four."

"And how did the talk end? In what spirit?"

Jojo said nothing.

"You've got nothing to say," said Michael.

"Perhaps I could have a drink of water now?" asked Jojo.

Michael went out to the toilets and returned with a glass of water. Now the break was possible and even necessary.

"Yes, so how did that conversation end?" Michael asked again after Jojo put the glass down on the floor, beside the bed.

"We disagreed."

"In other words?"

"She thought it was a crime to do something like that without consulting anyone else."

"And what did she intend to do about it?"

Jojo kept quiet.

"Listen to me, my friend," said Michael impatiently, "in the end we'll find out everything, and it's already past midnight, and let's not forget that you've got a license to use parathion. So how much pressure do I still have to put on you?"

"She wanted to bring it up at the *sicha*," said the treasurer, passing a trembling hand over his damp forehead.

In the silence of the room, Michael could hear the crickets chirping and the frogs croaking. For the first time he noticed a spider web in the corner of the ceiling above the bed in which he had tossed and turned the past two nights.

"So," he said at last, lighting another cigarette.

"But I didn't kill her," said Jojo.

Michael kept quiet.

"Even if she had brought it up at the *sicha*, what could have happened?"

"I don't know," said Michael. "You tell me."

"What could have happened? There would have been some shouting and a bit of a scandal, but nothing would have happened to me. The kibbutz is like a family, they wouldn't have thrown me out for it."

"But?"

Jojo kept quiet.

"What would they have done?" insisted Michael. "Maybe they would have appointed a new treasurer?"

"I wish," whispered Jojo. "Do you think it's a lot of fun being the treasurer of a kibbutz?"

"I really don't know," said Michael.

"Well, I do know. It's no fun at all. I would have gone back to the cotton; I would have been much better off there," said Jojo in a choked voice.

"And what about the disgrace?" asked Michael. "I thought that was a factor here, no?"

"Yes," whispered Jojo.

"And why didn't she bring it up at the *sicha*?" asked Michael.

"She was waiting for me to agree."

"What?" said Michael in astonishment. "For three or four months she waited for you to agree?"

"Yes," said Jojo, and for the first time he raised his eyes and looked directly at the policeman, with pain and rage in his eyes. "I begged her, and she said she wouldn't do it until I understood for myself how vital it was."

"It was hard for you," Michael stated, and Jojo burst into dry sobs and buried his face in his hands. They too were strewn with freckles, noticed Michael, whose heart was now as cold as ice, and he went back to listening to the drumming in his temples.

"Who else on the kibbutz knew about it?"

"No one," said Jojo, wiping his nose on the back of his hand like a child.

"Not even Ronny?" asked Michael.

"No, Ronny suspected Dave; he told me so himself, but I told him, even before Osnat found out, that I was sure it wasn't Dave, because I didn't want . . . "

*   *   *

At three o'clock in the morning, after leaving an obscure note for his wife, Jojo sat down in the Ford Fiesta next to the driver's seat.

Neither one spoke until the outskirts of Petah Tikva, when Jojo said, "You drive like a lunatic. All the way I've been hoping you'd have an accident."

17

At noon they were waiting for him in the conference room. "The whole kibbutz is on the phone, and there are people outside too," said Sarit nervously, "and we'll have the press breathing down our necks soon, and I don't know what to say." She had met him at the big metal entrance door of the building, which clanged shut when she let it go. "What have you found out? Is it true, what we came up with?" she asked eagerly, but Michael didn't answer. He bounded up the stairs to the conference room, where Nahari was sitting at the head of the long table with smoke rising from the fat cigar in the ashtray next to him.

"One thing I'm glad about," said Nahari when they were all seated. "I couldn't get over the fact that he didn't take anything for himself. 'How come he's such a saint?' I said to myself. He got himself into such a mess just to save the kibbutz? It didn't make sense to me. Saints scare me. Now it all seems more logical."

"I think it would be a mistake to assume it was all due to personal motives," said Michael carefully.

Nahari grimaced and said, "Embezzlement on kibbutzim is nothing new. We've had to shelve three cases, because they decided not to press charges. Almost all kibbutz crimes are about monkey business with kibbutz funds, with the culprits opening bank accounts in town and depositing the money there. Which is what I hoped to find here. And that's exactly what we did find."

"Yes, but the account's not in his name," Sarit reminded him. "It's in Osnat's name."

"We have to put all the facts together," said Nahari, "from all the angles. And we'll begin from the end. Have you seen her? Is the story about his sister true?"

Michael nodded. Even after sipping the hot coffee Sarit had given him, even after sitting for long moments in the conference room, he couldn't rid his mind of the images and the voices: "Hello, gorgeous, you're so gorgeous, have you got a cigarette?" asked the fat woman who was touching him in the elevator. She fingered the buttons of her checked robe and opened her mouth, exposing a few teeth in the black hole of the grotesque smile she evidently imagined to be sweet and seductive. When Michael got out of the elevator on the third floor and strode rapidly toward the doctor's office, she was still following him. "What a gorgeous hunk of flesh, I want one like him. So tall, with those nice brown eyes. Why are you running away from me?" She trailed behind him, not running, asking alternately, "Want to fuck?" and "Got a cigarette?"

Now, as he looked at Nahari's deeply tanned face and bright blue eyes and the cropped Roman cut of his gray hair, the image from the psychiatric hospital seemed remote and unreal. He didn't describe the place, only saying, "It's all true. His twin sister. Even before they were brought to Israel he had asked to be separated from her. She was already sick then. And nobody, apart from Srulke, knew about it."

"And how did Srulke know?" asked Sarit. Nahari kept quiet and looked out the big window.

"Srulke brought him to the kibbutz," replied Michael.

"To each his own," said Benny without smiling. "When was this?"

"In forty-six," said Michael. "He was six, and we'll never know how they came to separate the twins and if it was really he, as he claims, who demanded it."

"It isn't clear how they survived the war either," said Sarit.

"There are a lot of things that aren't clear," said Nahari, "but one thing is: A year ago he looked for her and found her and transferred her to an institution that costs ten thousand shekels a month."

"And no one on the kibbutz knew," said Sarit.

"Nobody even knew that he had a sister," marveled Benny. "All those years nobody knew he had a sister."

"I think they thought he had a sister who died," said Michael, "together with all the rest of his family, and he had been left alone."

"Ten thousand shekels a month," muttered Nahari. "Human beings!"

"Why couldn't he just bring her to the kibbutz? They would have taken care of her there," said Sarit. "I don't understand the whole thing."

Michael Ohayon took a deep breath. "Look," he said, staring at the big, shining glass surface of the table. "What I'm about to say may be personal, but maybe it'll help us all to understand him." There was a silence in the room. They all looked at him expectantly. "How old was I when we arrived in this country? Three years old. That's all. What can a baby of three understand, what can he remember? Who knows? But one thing I do remember from the beginning." He raised his eyes and saw Nahari looking at him with a serious, concentrated expression, without a trace of irony. "I remember that all those years I was haunted by the wish to be like everyone else—an Israeli, a sabra. I would have done a lot for people not to know that I wasn't born here. We always imagine that this is a problem particular to the Jews from Arab countries, to the Moroccans. But in fact we know very well that the people who came from Poland and everywhere else also had the very same wish, the same problem."

With a steady hand Michael lit a cigarette. He blew out the smoke and looked at Sarit before going on, and she lowered her eyes. "It's the wish to obliterate the past, to enter what in the early years of the state they liked to call the 'melting pot.' But if you think about it, what happens to a person if you put him into a melting pot is that he gets burned—or at least he gets burned among other things that happen." Nahari sighed but didn't change his expression of intent attention. "It isn't hard to imagine what happens to a child of six or seven when he's put into a children's house on a kibbutz, and he's got a sister, a crazy twin, from there, from the Diaspora, from the Holocaust. Her and nobody else in the world. What do you think he'll do in order to survive? Look at Jojo, even that name of his—since when is a little boy from Poland called Jojo? It's not even an Israeli name, it's a Moroccan name, and not a name that Moroccans are proud of either. How could he have agreed to a nickname like that?"

"The whole business of nicknames on the kibbutz is fascinating," said Nahari. "How they come into being and so on—you could write a book about it. I could tell you a lot about it myself, but go on, go on." Again he cupped his chin in his hand.

"Think about him, this foreign orphan child on a kibbutz who wants to build up his image. He grows up there, he's a fighter in the army, he wears shorts and sandals, he's in charge of the cotton crop, he's everything he's supposed to be, he gets married on the kibbutz . . . "

"His wife's waiting outside," said Sarit. "A real dyed-in-the-wool kibbutznik."

"Yes," said Michael, "you see? A kibbutznik with a pedigree. What did you expect, for him to tell her about his sick-in-the-head sister? I saw her just lying there. A big vegetable. She doesn't talk or function. She has to be fed, washed, everything. Sometimes they have to feed her artificially."

"So what got into him all of a sudden?" asked Benny. "Why after all these years did he suddenly get a conscience about her and put her into a private institution?"

"He can't explain it himself. I think age is a factor here. He has no past without her, he says."

"So why not tell them in the kibbutz and get help?" asked Sarit. "They would have helped him, no?"

"And tell them about how he neglected her all those years? Only Srulke knew, Jojo told me that the only one who knew was Srulke. And Srulke, who was apparently a serious person, kept it to himself. He didn't tell anyone, and he didn't bring regards from her to Jojo. Nothing. And Jojo couldn't even tell his wife, let alone the rest of the kibbutz."

"But what did he think?" said Sarit in an agitated voice. "That he would be able to keep her there without anyone knowing, and pay ten thousand shekels a month? What did he think?"

"This is what he thought," said Nahari, pronouncing every word coldly and distinctly. "That he would take a tiny little piece," and he demonstrated with his fingers on the cigar, "a tiny little piece of the million and a half dollars he got from the Swiss, and keep his sister in a good place. That's what he thought."

"And the only problem was that Osnat found out."

"Let's go over it again," said Nahari, spreading the papers out in front of him.

"I've transcribed all the conversations from the tapes, it's all there," said Sarit. "I don't know how I managed it, I worked like a lunatic." Michael looked at her and smiled. She blushed.

"Good for you," said Nahari, glancing at the typed pages. "His real name is Elhanan, Elhanan Birenbaum, and God knows how that turned into Jojo. He changed his last name to Eshel. So your theory seems to be right," he said, turning to Michael, who only now felt shame at what seemed to him to have been a personal, private revelation. "Pearls before swine," Fela, his former mother-in-law, used to say whenever she described to her daughter the long, very personal process of preparing her gefilte fish.

"According to what's written here, it all happened by accident," said Nahari. "According to what you got out of him, what happened is that he received a million and a half—more than a million and a half, it says here—dollars from the Swiss in order to get the kibbutz out of trouble when the bank shares collapsed. With most of the money—apart from the little piece we discovered in the bank account—he bought gilt-edged government securities, no risks but no big profits either."

"But how did he get hold of the formula in the first place?" asked Benny impatiently.

"It's all written here," said Michael. "We brought the chemist from Pathology in too. Jojo has a degree in chemistry from the university, and after that he studied agriculture at Rehovoth. He got the formula from Dave. It didn't occur to Dave to be suspicious of him, and he explained it all to him in detail. And he had the keys to the safe too; we're talking about a man who had access to everything and who could understand what he was reading. He knew how to read a formula. They had a liaison man in Switzerland who helped them in the beginning when they first set up the plant. The Swiss made them offers and tried to tempt them all the time. But we won't go into that now. We haven't got the time at this stage to discuss industrial espionage."

"I can't get over how you found everything out so quickly," said Sarit to Michael.

The embarrassment and tension in the room were palpable before Nahari said in a reserved tone, "Yes, it's an impressive performance. But that's why you're here. We haven't got just anybody in this unit."

Michael cleared his throat. "It's a matter of luck, too," he said finally. "I'm not trying to be modest, but a lot of it was luck. Especially the business with the broker. We couldn't find anything irregular in the bank accounts. And then I thought of that broker I brought in for questioning two months ago, remember?" he asked Nahari, and Nahari nodded. "So I went back to him to find out about the procedures involved in selling shares and so on."

"You made a study of the subject," said Nahari with undisguised irony. "You became an expert in stocks and bonds."

Michael leaned back in his chair. The wooden back creaked. He stretched out his legs, and when Sarit quickly looked at him, he glanced under the table and said "Sorry." And they both blushed. "I thought it was the leg of the table," he apologized.

Nahari cocked his head. "I've heard you're a terrible ladies' man," he said with a sneer. "So that's how you do it? Underneath the table?" He was the only one to laugh at his joke.

"Maybe I should remind you again," said Michael, "that his main aim was to save the kibbutz from the mess he'd gotten them into with the collapse of the bank shares they were in up to their necks with, like most of the other kibbutzim. He needed one and a half million dollars. He got it from Switzerland. He didn't tell anyone, and he bought safe securities with the money. On the kibbutz, he said that he'd gotten out of market before the fall of the bank shares. He told me that he didn't want them to know that he'd messed up, and that he didn't have the time to wait for permission to sell the formula, especially since he knew that he wouldn't get it."

"Okay, we've already got his signature on that," said Nahari, pointing a short, manicured finger at the paper in front of him. "We're waiting for your story about the broker," he reminded Michael.

"Two months ago I spoke to this broker, who was being detained about something else. Yesterday I went back to him, and he put me onto another broker, who turned out to know Osnat. In fact, he had known her in the past and been after her. As you can see from your transcripts, Osnat, too, found out completely by chance. She got a phone call from this guy who had once been after her, and he asked her to meet him. She went and he said something like, 'I didn't know you'd become a rich woman.'"

"And then she confronted Jojo with it," said Nahari.

"Yes. She went to him after she saw the size of the sums involved."

"When I was typing the interviews, I didn't really understand all that about the money. I don't have a head for figures," said Sarit coyly.

"What's there to understand?" asked Nahari aggressively. "Jojo and Osnat were both empowered to sign checks for the kibbutz. He bought the shares by himself, on his own initiative, forging her signature. The money he took for himself he put into an account that he opened in her name, making her a party to the whole affair. What's there to understand?"

"And the rest of the interrogation, with the bit about how she skewered him . . . " said Sarit to nobody in particular.

"You could put it that way," said Michael, again glancing at the typescripts.

"She wanted him to go and confess to Moish and everybody," said Benny, "but she didn't know that he'd taken money for himself too; that simply didn't enter her mind. How naive can you get?"

"It's not so much a question of naivete," said Michael, "as of ignorance. She didn't know the story of his life; I'm not sure she even knew that he was a refugee who came to the country with the Youth Aliya. He was a few years older than she, and by the time she came to the kibbutz he had a whole new identity. He told her that he'd invested all the money for the benefit of the kibbutz, and she believed him. What got her goat was the fact that he decided and acted all by himself, without consulting the kibbutz, the financial committee, and so on. He managed to keep it a secret for a whole year. He managed to pull the wool over the eyes of the kibbutz accountant too. Everybody thought that he'd gotten out of the stock market before the crisis and bought the safe securities and saved the kibbutz from the bank-share crash."

"Once a year they publish a financial report there," said Benny. "Every member of the kibbutz gets a copy, and there's a special *sicha* where the treasurer presents the report and explains everything."

"And a ghastly bore it is too!" said Nahari. He stuck his cigar between his teeth. "It's the most hellish *sicha* of the year. Nobody goes except for a few fanatics. I remember."

"Yes, and hardly anybody actually reads the report either, at most they glance through it," said Michael.

"So how come nobody smelled a rat in the annual report, at the meeting where they discussed the budget?" asked Sarit. "Somebody goes to the meeting, somebody reads the report." She pointed to the booklet lying partly under the cardboard file.

"Because," said Benny with a serious expression on his face, "when the kibbutz treasurer tells the accountant or the bookkeeper, 'Leave the shares to me, don't touch that. I'm taking care of it,' that's what happens. And that's what happened here." Nahari pushed the mustard-colored ceramic ashtray aside. "That was the least of his troubles. His real troubles began when Osnat made him sign a letter saying that he would bring the matter up at a kibbutz *sicha* by the end of the year. That's what I see here in the transcript of last night's interrogation."

"Yes," said Michael with a sigh, "she had a letter from him to that effect. She didn't want to be an informer. He said that she had decided to make it into an educational issue."

"Don't make me laugh," said Nahari. "Sometimes you . . . What she really wanted was to clear herself of all suspicion. She wanted the drama at the *sicha* in order to prove her innocence. And he had that bank account in her name to blackmail her with."

Michael took a deep breath. "You have to think of the characters involved. Think of Osnat. It's not so simple. It's true that he implicated her to protect himself, but if you think about her, you'll see that she wasn't the kind of person to give in to blackmail, and she is the kind who would want to bring it up in front of everybody."

"Don't get carried away," said Nahari, looking at him through half-closed eyes, "and don't flatter yourself that you're the only one who understands anything. Where's the letter, for instance?"

"I went through all her papers and haven't found it anywhere. Maybe she kept it outside the kibbutz."

"Don't be surprised if it turns out that she had a safe-deposit box," said Nahari, smiling to himself. He took a cardboard box out of a drawer in the table and opened it. It contained slender cigars, different from the ones he usually smoked. He put it down in front of him and selected one. Michael watched him. "Does anybody want one?" Nahari offered, indicating the box. Michael took a cigarette out of his Noblesse pack. "Maybe it's time for another round of coffee?" Nahari wondered aloud, looking at the telephone. Sarit dialed and whispered something into the mouthpiece. Her hand left a damp mark on the gray phone.

"So what was that article she wrote in the kibbutz bulletin all about?" asked Nahari.

"Maybe she wanted to scare him, who knows?" said Benny, sniffing.

"Is the air conditioning working at all?" complained Sarit querulously. "How long can we go on sitting here in this heat?"

"Two things have been bothering me ever since we've gotten onto all this," said Michael. "First, the fact that it doesn't fit in with her personality to behave with such discretion, not to talk to anyone else about it, and, in general, to give in to that kind of blackmail. And second, the letter. It said that if by a certain date he failed to bring it up at the kibbutz *sicha,* she would show them the letter."

"What date?" asked Nahari.

Benny and Sarit looked at him questioningly, but Michael said quickly, "Two weeks from now. The *sicha* in two weeks' time was the deadline."

"A safe-deposit box, I'm sure of it," said Nahari.

"She didn't have a safe-deposit box anywhere, at any rate not in her name," said Michael. "In my opinion there are two possibilities: Either she gave it to somebody to keep, or Jojo destroyed it. We haven't given him a polygraph test on that yet, but he claims that after he signed the letter and gave it back to her, he never saw it again."

Benny sighed. He passed both his hands over his shining bald head and said, "But that's not the main problem."

"What is the main problem?" asked Sarit. "After doing all that typing I can't see the whole picture, only a lot of details and words."

"The main problem," said Michael, "is that although he's got a motive, he's also got a watertight alibi."

"He was with Moish the whole time," Benny reminded her.

"Maybe Moish is involved too," said Sarit doubtfully.

"We checked," said Benny. "There are witnesses and everything."

"So what we've got is a suspect with a motive, keys to the poison shed, a license to use parathion. The only problem is we don't know how he could have done it," Nahari summed up and looked at Michael. "Well, what has your lordship got to say about it?"

"That I'm looking for someone who could have gone past Srulke's place and taken the bottle. I've questioned a lot of people about it, and I haven't come up with a thing."

"What you're saying," said Nahari deliberately, "is that you're not confining your inquiries to Jojo?"

"What I'm saying is that I think we should keep Jojo in detention and go on working on both fronts: looking for anyone who had the opportunity to take the parathion from Srulke after he was dead, and looking for the letter. That is, going back to the kibbutz and continuing to stay there."

"Whom did you ask about their movements?" asked Nahari impatiently.

"Since the autopsy and since we found the empty parathion bottle, I haven't stopped searching," said Michael.

"Yes, yes, I've heard all about it," said Nahari, blowing out blue smoke. "But I want facts, not stories."

Michael replied without anger. "You know it's not simple," he said, leaning forward. As he spoke he saw his reflection in the glass top of the long table. His brows looked dark and tangled, his eyes sunken. The rolled-up sleeves of his white shirt were too tight on his arms. And the way Sarit was staring at him didn't make him feel any more comfortable. His height and leanness suddenly seemed grotesque to him; he felt gawky and stringy. "We found nine people who actually left the dining hall after the first half of the artistic program, all for reasons of their own. Their signed statements are there in the file, you've already seen them. But there are also elderly people who stayed in their rooms, and a housemother who stayed with two sick children, and Simcha Malul," he said with an effort.

"What about Simcha Malul?" said Nahari, stiffening.

"They invited her to the ceremony, and she was there; then, in the middle of it, she went to the infirmary to check up on Felix. She said . . . what did she say?" Michael paged rapidly through the papers in the card-board file. "Here we are," he said, pointing to one of the pages, "have a look," and he passed the file to Nahari. "She felt sorry for Felix, because he couldn't be there on a day like that, and when the ceremony outside was over, she went back to the infirmary to see him."

"And what have you got to say about it?" asked Nahari. "Perhaps you feel the need to protect a poor working-class woman too, like our Florence Nightingale?"

"I don't have anything to say about it," said Michael, shrugging his shoulders. "I believe her and the polygraph believes her too."

"You made her take a lie-detector test about that too?" asked Nahari. "I take my hat off to you. What can I say? You've got an answer for everything. Every angle covered."

When they brought in the tray with the cups of coffee and bottles of soft drinks and sandwiches, which smelled of hard-boiled eggs, Michael forced himself to keep quiet. "Just keep calm," he said to him-self, "and don't let him get to you. He's the poor jerk with an inferior-ity complex, not you."

"Everyone we interviewed either had a good reason not to be at the ceremony or else had no motive."

"And did you search their rooms, the ones who weren't there?"

"What do you think? We searched, all right, but we didn't find a thing."

"And there's only one way out?"

"Of the dining hall?" asked Sarit before she swallowed the last bite of her sandwich. "No, there's a back entrance through the kitchen, with stairs at the back of the building."

"But there are always people on dining-hall duty there before they serve meals," Benny reminded her, "and they were there all the time, and nobody saw anyone leave through the back."

"Who was on kitchen duty that evening?" asked Nahari.

Michael looked at the smoke rising from the cigarette he held between his fingers and listed four names.

"Yankele?" asked Nahari. "Crazy Yankele? What's-her-name's son? He's popping up too many times for my liking."

"Yes. I've got a funny feeling about it too," Michael agreed. "But he's not talking. Not to me or anyone else. Not even to the profession-als, the psychiatrist or the psychologist."

"After all that trouble with the exhumation and everything!" said Nahari with an expression of disgust on his face. "What have you done with the information about the parathion in the old man's body? Not a thing, as far as I can see."

"The parathion found in Srulke's body isn't evidence of murder," said Michael. "In this case there's no motive whatsoever. And our assumption has been—owing to the circumstances and everything we've already agreed on—that he wasn't murdered, that it was some kind of accident. All the signs point in that direction: He was spraying with parathion, and he was careless. No one murdered him; someone just took his bottle." He was silent for a minute. "And part of the problem here is precisely that we can't find answers to the most ele-mentary questions. But you're right, we shouldn't have neglected that direction."

"You don't have much time left. It's only in the movies that crimes are solved in twenty-four hours. And although your report on what happened last night is very interesting, it doesn't get us anywhere."

"If you can see this for yourself," said Michael, "then how about releasing us from the time limit? It's completely arbitrary, and we can't force things."

Nahari kept quiet.

"We don't have enough people to police the whole place," Michael continued, "and it's clear that something's going to happen, and I've got a gut feeling that every minute I'm not there somebody's in danger." Michael looked at his watch again.

Nahari grimaced and sucked silently on his cigar.

"I don't care if I sound melodramatic," said Michael dryly, "but every minute that I sit here people's lives are in danger. Every minute. I have to be there and you know it. Something terrible's going to hap-pen. You can cut the air there with a knife. I can't sit here and confine myself to following up the lead on Jojo."

"And you don't have to either," said Nahari, slamming the drawer shut after pushing the cigar box into it. "Let me remind you that you've got twelve people in your section, in case you've forgotten, and there's no reason for you to work alone. She"—he pointed at Sarit—

"is perfectly capable of taking care of Jojo, or else you can redelegate people who you've put on other cases."

"I'm off," said Michael, sweeping his papers up into a pile. He noticed that Nahari didn't get up until he was standing at the door. And until he closed the door behind him, not one of the others moved from their seats.

Avigail looked around her and covered the mouthpiece of the public telephone with her hand. Although the dining-hall lobby was empty and she was hidden behind a big concrete column, she could feel the fear turning to a cold sweat and collecting in the small of her back. When she began talking again, she dropped her eyes and noticed a yellow stain on the hem of her white nurse's smock.

It was cool in the lobby, where the floor had just been washed. In areas not exposed to the Sabbath sunshine, patches of wetness remained, and the marks left by the rubber mop with which the young girl, with very brief, cutoff shorts clinging tightly to her tanned thighs, had swept up the streams of water flooding the expanse of marble floor. Avigail looked at her watch and whispered into the phone that this was the dead hour before lunch and that in a few minutes people would begin streaming into the dining hall, stopping her from saying any more. "I thought he wasn't going to budge from here," she said into the receiver. "I thought there was no time to waste, that we were working against time." She was astonished to hear the note of grievance in her voice. "You're leaving me here all alone to cope with the hysteria about Jojo and—"

"Forget about it," she responded angrily to the soothing murmurs on the other end of the line. "What did you think? That there wouldn't be rumors about it? Are you crazy?"

"I'm under a lot of pressure," she apologized to the telephone receiver, making an effort to restrain the complaining tone she herself hated. "It's been two days since I spoke to anyone, and you can cut the atmosphere here with a knife. People come to me all the time with headaches and stomachaches, and the kids are doing all kinds of crazy things, the fact that Jojo's been with you, I mean us, for two days already doesn't help, and now, of all times," she said with growing bitterness, "he has to disappear."

"He's not the only one who can interrogate suspects, there are other people on the force," she said, and breathed deeply. "I can't put somebody new into the picture every five minutes; he already knows the people and everything. Let Nahari or somebody interrogate him."

"What are you talking about—Machluf Levy? There's a limit, no?" With her free hand she wiped her brow. Her elbows had been hurting her all day, and now she could feel the itch burning her skin. Through the glass wall separating the lobby from the plaza outside she saw the first people arriving for lunch, some of them coming up from the pool and hanging their towels on the hooks next to hats and bags. She saw a group of people approaching, a family being shepherded by Shula into the dining hall, saw a woman's clothing and makeup and the embarrassment with which she teetered next to Shula on her high-heeled shoes, and the affected ease with which the husband walked next to Shula's husband, Arik, and the noisy giggling of the two teenaged girls bringing up the rear immediately revealing their identity as visitors from town. Only Shula and Arik's little boy, his thumb in his mouth and a dreamy expression on his face, showed no signs of excitement.

From upstairs, smells began to waft toward her, some of which she had no trouble identifying: yesterday's chicken, sausages in pastry, meatballs, and boiled cabbage. She almost smiled at the thought that she could describe the menu sight unseen, but the receiver was wet from the sweat on her palm, and there was something almost grotesque about the calm, slow movements with which the middle-aged man leaned his bicycle on the contraption intended for this purpose and waited for the two children vigorously turning the pedals of their tricycles. He waited for them to park their tricycles next to his bike, and with an expression of observant interest, which included a didactic awareness of the importance of developing independence and self-reliance in those of tender years, he did not rush up to the smaller of the children, who bumped into a protruding bicycle pedal and fell, but allowed him to get up by himself. Only when the toddler, who must have been about three years old, burst into loud wails did the father say soothingly, "Come here, Avishai, let's see what happened to you." And Avishai, dressed only in underpants, beat his hands on his plump, brown thighs, and his face, which was also brown, crumpled in tears under his very fair hair, and he remained standing where he was. The father did not go up to him, but stood waiting at the entrance to the dining hall next to the glass partition.

Avigail took in the scene with a precision that surprised her. She couldn't hear the sound of the crying, only the words of the father, who went on standing and watching at the door. The little girl, also dressed only in underpants, was standing next to him now, her arms plump and firm, her tanned, dimpled face half-hidden under a shock of straight, crudely cut blond hair. Avigail looked at the little boy, who finally wiped his tears with the back of his fist and joined his father and sister, and when the three of them entered the lobby and walked past Avigail, she heard little Avishai say, "I always know how to do it, only this time I didn't," and his father reply with the same didactic patience, "I'm sure you always know how to do it, but you also have to get used to the fact that sometimes you don't succeed."

On her other side she heard a man's voice explaining to the young girl who emerged from behind the pillar, "You can't go into the dining hall barefoot," and beyond the glass she saw a group of three Scandinavian volunteers, one of them with a bad sunburn and the other with blisters on her hands, whom she had attended to yesterday, and they smiled at her sweetly.

Now she turned her back and stood facing the glass partition as she whispered into the receiver, "Look, what I have to say is this: In my opinion he should be here for the *sicha* today, and he knows it. . . . No," she shouted in a whisper into the black mouthpiece, "that's impossible and he knows it. I'm not allowed to go either, we can only watch on the closed-circuit TV. I can't record it, how do you expect me to record it, let him bring recording equipment, let Machluf Levy. I don't know, but none of us can go in. Of course," she whispered angrily, "he can do what he likes here, ostensibly, but their meeting wouldn't be the same if he were there in person."

"No, I'm not caving in or anything like that," she said in a tough whisper into the phone. "You don't have to feel sorry for me, I'm just pressured, and so would you be in my place. I've got the feeling that things are going to blow sky-high."

"Nobody's going to harm me," she said, sighing. "I know nobody is, but maybe they'll harm somebody else. Tell him that I want to remind him that there's a kibbutz *sicha* today and that he has to drop everything and be here. He hasn't even seen the agenda yet, and it's worth seeing.

"Not on the phone," she said. "People are beginning to come, I have to go now, just tell him."

Michael Ohayon looked intently at the small screen and almost smiled as he saw Guta sitting next to Fanya, who, as expected, was rapidly clicking the two knitting needles she held stiffly in her hands. He noted her pursed lips and sunken mouth before the camera moved on, and he glanced at Avigail, who was sitting next to him curled up in a heavy, brown armchair that gave off a smell of dank wool. She was wearing jeans and a loose white shirt with the sleeves buttoned at the wrists. He was holding a coffee cup in both hands, and from the white plate next to him smoke rose from the cigarette that was turning to ash before he smoked it.

Avigail didn't say a word, and the tension radiating from her infected him, too. As they waited for the meeting to begin, he thought again of Jojo sitting pale and sweating in the air-conditioned room in Petah Tikva and again and again repeating—of the little gray card with the wavy black line framing the words saying that Elhanan (Jojo) Eshel was licensed to use parathion: "It's only a coincidence: Lots of us had one, and it was years ago, *years*..."

Avigail's muteness marred Michael's concentration. He asked himself what had happened to her since their last meeting, before he brought in Jojo. Machluf Levy had filled her in on everything that had come out during the interrogation, the initial one and the ones that followed it, and Machluf Levy had also demonstrated to him the face she had made the several times she had said, "We have no case against him." But when he asked her, as soon as he walked into her room, why there was "no case," she had just shrugged her shoulders and said, "Never mind," and it became clear to him that he wouldn't get another word out of her until she decided to talk. Her longest sentence since his arrival was when he was still standing near the door (after she had carefully locked it) and she was reading him the agenda for the kibbutz meeting from a printed sheet in her hand. He interrupted her to ask, "How are you, Avigail?" and he was well aware of the effect the warmth in his voice had on her.

At first she only said, "The anxiety and tension here are contagious, and on Monday your time's up, and it's already Saturday night."

He shook his head understandingly and said, "It's hard on you, Avigail." Her eyes grew moist, and he couldn't avoid a feeling of victory, of having breached the fortress walls. He wanted to touch her, but he couldn't take his eyes off the screen on which the *sicha* was about to begin, and he was brought up short, too, by her vulnerability, whose like he hadn't seen in a long time, giving rise to pangs of conscience alongside the triumph of his little victory. As he spoke words he knew to be effective on people in distress—especially lonely people, especially those who hid their distress, proud people resigned to their loneliness—he could hear Maya's voice saying, "Sometimes you show a kind of empathy that seems to people who don't know you as if it comes from the heart, but to me it sounds like an exercise, an exercise in sensitivity intended to soften up your listener. And what will you offer him afterward?" But in fact—he sighed as he looked at the book lying facedown on the floor at her feet, *Chronicle of a Death Foretold*—Avigail really did give rise in him to strong feelings, which had been dormant for a long time, and it was precisely something about her suffering that attracted him. To express these feelings in words, however, was still beyond him.

He asked if she had anything new to tell him. "If there was, I would have told you already," she said crossly.

"Hasn't anything happened?" he heard himself ask.

"No, the only things that are happening are in my head. And the pressure of having a time limit—"

"Avigail," said Michael firmly, "it's not your responsibility, you can let yourself off the hook. The only one who undertook to keep to a time limit was me, and who knows what might happen by Monday? Anything can happen."

"Only in books," said Avigail.

He looked at his watch. "It's already nine o'clock. Why don't they start?"

"They're probably waiting for more people to arrive," said Avigail, sniffing. "The whole week long they've been talking about how to get more than twenty people to come to the *sicha*. I overheard Moish telling someone in the dining hall that if more than thirty-five people came, he would regard it as an achievement."

"That's a very small percentage," Michael reflected aloud. "I saw in their bulletin that some kibbutzim offer members bonuses for attending kibbutz meetings."

"I read that too," said Avigail, "and also that on one kibbutz they suggested having special refreshments to attract people."

"I don't understand them," said Michael in bewilderment. "Do they have some other home? This is their home, after all, and the *sicha* is where they decide things."

"I don't know how many kibbutz meetings you've been to," said Avigail, "but from what I hear, it's not pleasant."

Michael kept quiet and looked at the screen.

"Not just unpleasant, sometimes revolting," said Avigail with all the intensity the word demanded.

"You needn't take it so seriously."

"Wait and see, you can see everything there, and I mean *everything*," she stressed. "Settling personal scores, people's need to dominate, everything."

"Here's the guy who came on to you, no?" said Michael when the camera focused on Boaz, with Tova sitting next to him and Yoska on her other side.

Avigail kept quiet.

"Is he still bothering you? Knocking on your door at one in the morning and so on?"

She shook her head. "But there's somebody else," she said.

"Who?" asked Michael with seeming indifference, then lit another cigarette.

"The accountant at the plant. Ronny."

"I know him," said Michael with hostility. "I spent the whole of yesterday talking to him."

"Ah, about Jojo, I suppose," said Avigail. "When are you going to tell me what's happening?"

"When this is over," said Michael, pointing at the blue screen.

"He keeps track of all my phone calls; you know they record the numbers and everything?"

Michael nodded.

"He wanted to know if I had a boyfriend in town and all the rest."

Michael pulled the plate toward him and ground out his cigarette.

"They want to know everything, they have no shame. On the one hand, they don't ask me to their rooms—although they do ask me to join their study circles, and on the other hand, they ask me, Yocheved for instance, what my problem is. "A pretty girl like you . . . " and so on. The only person who invited me to their room was Moish, and that was only once. Ah, yes, and Dave."

"You've only been here a week," Michael reminded her.

Avigail made a silent calculation. "Yes," she said, "but it seems much longer, and there's so little time left. I have to find someone or something, and I can't come up with anything; everything's wrong, and I can't put my finger on it. And I feel as if I'm in a horror movie with something awful about to happen, and I don't know where it's going to come from."

"Aren't you hot?" Michael was astounded to hear himself ask.

"No," said Avigail, and her face assumed a hard, cold expression that put him in his place when she heard him say—the words slipping out of his mouth against his will—"Always with long sleeves."

And Avigail remained silent. There was something withering in her silence. It bespoke strength. Avigail knew how to keep quiet without embarrassment. She didn't fill the room with the sound of her own voice in order to cover up the oppressive silence, in order to make the moment easier for him. There was something constraining about this strength when added to her vulnerability, something inhibiting. But it attracted him, too.

Michael looked at the screen and thought—not for the first time—about Balilty and the surveillance possibilities that would have been available to him if the Jerusalem policeman had been involved in the case instead of the intelligence officer from the Lachish district, an uninspired character who had produced nothing so far, apart from his connection with the stockbroker.

Dave was sitting in the front row, not far from Tova and Boaz. Yankele sat beside him, and in the row behind them Michael caught a glimpse of Dvorka, with Zeev HaCohen and Yocheved next to her, and behind them other old people, their faces full of a tension and disquiet so obvious that even the amateurish cameraman could not fail to convey them. The camera jumped, but one brief shot was enough to show Dvorka's pursed lips, her scraped-back hair, her flashing eyes. Again he thought that she reminded him of someone, but he couldn't remember who. For a moment he thought of telling Avigail, but one look at her, huddled up in the armchair with her arms crossed on her chest, was enough to shut him up. Zeev HaCohen crossed his legs and shook one foot in its biblical sandal rhythmically to and fro. In the row of chairs facing the audience sat Moish and the members of the kibbutz committee. Moish whispered something to Shula, sitting next to him, and then she began.

"Good evening, everyone." She said that she was pleased to see forty-three members present, that this was "a significant improvement, and we hope that it's only a beginning and not a flash in the pan." She looked questioningly at Moish and then said that "in spite of everything that's happened, we have to go on running our lives as if . . . " she searched for the right word, and someone from the audience shouted "as usual." "Jojo isn't here today," said Shula in embarrassment, "so we'll put off the financial questions till next time." The agenda was read out, including the question of a mobilization for the peach picking, and Shula said her piece, concluding, "Comrades, the peaches have to be picked; do you want hired labor here? We'll have one work camp from the scouts, and I'm appealing for your cooperation, things are hard enough as it is."

Michael looked at Moish, who was chewing the end of a pencil and biting his lips whenever he removed it from his mouth in order to make a note on the pad in front of him, and at the row of old people— at Yocheved's face shiny with perspiration, at the deeply lined face of Matilda, who was crumpling in her hand a flimsy handkerchief, whose like he had not seen for years. Shula presented the next subject: Should Ilan T. be allowed three days a week off from work to paint? "More precisely," she said, glancing at the page in front of her, "two days a week to paint in the room we gave him next to the old cowshed, and one day a week to travel to Tel Aviv to study?"

"Now you'll see what a kibbutz is," said Avigail. "Now you'll see."

There were mutterings in the dining hall, and sudden movements of people shifting position in their chairs. "He received a negative answer from the higher education committee," said Shula in a louder voice, "and we decided to bring the matter up for discussion at the *sicha*."

Avigail went over to the television set and pointed to the young man sitting at the end of the second row—in shorts and with long hair and a cigarette between his fingers—who was looking around and shaking his head.

Five people spoke. Matilda was the last to speak, saying, "We don't have enough manpower, and we won't take on hired labor, and he already got time off last year. What else is there to say?" Guta, who was sitting not far from her, nodded her head vigorously.

"If everybody here decided that he was an artist . . . " cried Yocheved, and then Ilan T., his face flushed, burst out with restrained fury.

"You make me laugh. I've already held exhibitions in town, and the whole world recognizes that I'm an artist, except for you. This is the only place in the world where a person has to be ashamed of being an artist." In the uproar that now broke out, he shouted, "This is the only place in the state of Israel where being an artist isn't just not an honor, it's a disgrace, because it isn't productive labor. I don't need to ask your permission for anything."

"Just a minute," Zeev HaCohen said, standing up and turning to face Ilan. "Calm down, Ilan, please!" And turning to address the audience, he said, "I've got a suggestion. Let's try to be constructive and think logically here," and Dvorka nodded her head. Ilan T. kept quiet and passed a trembling hand through his long hair. The woman sitting next to him touched his knee, and Avigail said, "That's Ditza, his wife, she's from Haifa. They were both part of a Nahal unit, and they stayed on; they've been here for twelve years."

"I propose," said Zeev HaCohen in the silence that had fallen, "that we do what we've already done before in another case: invite a committee of experts from the Kibbutz Artzi to come and look at Ilan's work and advise us about the steps we should take. Let the experts decide if he deserves the special status of an artist."

"I know which other case you're talking about," Ilan burst out, "and there your brilliant committee of experts decided to send the artist to therapy. They said that, judging from his work, he was mentally unbalanced. And let me tell you," he said, the veins standing out on his neck, "that he's a famous, successful artist today is only due to the fact that he left the kibbutz. And that's what we'll do, too. I don't want to make any threats," he said in a calmer tone, "but that's what we'll do, because you're not giving us any choice; if those idiots who don't have a clue about art or anything else come here and say about me what they said four years ago about Yoel, whose work is recognized today by the whole world, I won't stay here."

"Comrades," said Dvorka calmly as the commotion raged and ebbed around her, "I want to say something." She stood up. "This isn't the only way to prevent injustice, to insure the equality we strive for, the synthesis between private and communal needs. Let's try to think if there isn't a better way of sustaining a society like ours." The camera showed the astounded expression on Guta's face. Fanya went on knitting as if nothing had happened. "We need artists," said Dvorka firmly but quietly, "we need artists here, and art too. We mustn't be rigid. There's no reason for us to set up obstacles in the path of a talented comrade. Our financial situation is good, there's no need to save money by denying a request like this. And perhaps," she said, looking at the group of young people sitting behind Tova, "perhaps instead of thinking about family sleeping and the allocation of resources to projects in the spirit of the times, we should change our attitude to the individual."

"So what do you propose, Dvorka?" asked Shula with a confused expression.

"I propose that we think about it again in a different spirit," said Dvorka calmly. Matilda sat up, and Zeev HaCohen put his hand soothingly on her arm.

The kibbutz members voted in favor of postponing the vote, and

Shula was about to present the next item on the agenda, when Ilan T., looking at Matilda (who kept up a steady muttering), burst out, "Osnat was the only person here who had any respect for artists, who appreciated art, who knew what it was all about."

"We are all grieving for her," said Zeev HaCohen, "but there are plenty of other people here who respect artists, and we must try to maintain a fraternal spirit in the *sicha*. There are other subjects to discuss. Don't say things you'll be sorry about later, Ilan; this is your home."

The blue screen did not convey Ilan's verbal retort, only showing him getting up, with his wife following, and walking toward the door while everyone else pretended that nothing had happened as they made short work of voting on the Yaffe family, who for a year and a half had been candidates for kibbutz membership. The family was widely considered to have been successfully absorbed by the kibbutz, an opinion reflected by a decisive majority in their favor, Shula announcing only ten against and two abstentions.

The last item on the agenda had now been reached. Shula turned to Moish and gave him the floor. Avigail changed her position in the armchair, shifted about nervously, and finally crossed her legs, straightened her back, and sat up tensely. Michael lit another cigarette. The growing tension in the dining hall conveyed itself to them in the little room, where the closed and dark-curtained windows created a cavelike atmosphere.

"Almost two weeks ago," began Moish, whose face was even more pale than usual, "we lost Osnat." There was a heavy silence in the dining hall. Zeev HaCohen and the other members of the kibbutz committee sitting alongside Moish bowed their heads. Dvorka didn't bat an eye, only tightening her lips for a moment and again relaxing them. "Osnat's death was a blow from which we have not yet recovered," said Moish, and Michael saw him peeping at a sheet of paper on his knee, "nor will we recover until a long time has passed after we have found . . . but that's not what I wanted to talk to you about tonight," Moish resumed after he recovered his voice, "but about what I will call, for the sake of brevity, 'her life's work.'"

The dining hall was completely still. Only Moish's voice and the sound of his breathing were audible. "Before going on I just want to say that we have complete faith in Jojo and no doubts about his innocence of any crime whatsoever, until proved otherwise."

Yocheved whispered something to Matilda.

Michael looked at Avigail, whose eyes were fixed on the screen. He knew that she sensed his eyes on her. When he began listening again, he heard Moish say, "Forgive the phraseology, but how can I put it? . . . For me, Osnat's death suddenly made all that about the transience of life and so on more concrete. And then the heart attack suffered by Aaron Meroz, whom many of you remember. As if our generation is about to vanish from the scene before we've accomplished anything of our own here."

Someone shouted something, and Moish said, "Please let me speak without interrupting me in the middle, it's hard enough for me as it is." In the ensuing silence Moish looked as if he was gathering his strength. Michael saw that his broad hands were completely steady. Only his pallor and rapid, heavy breathing betrayed his tension. "Naturally, Srulke's sudden death didn't do anything to relieve this feeling. I'm not saying that we haven't accomplished anything at all, but the time has come for us to leave our mark here, like our parents' generation did. As long as Osnat was here, I didn't feel it as strongly as I do now. Now that she's gone, I want to explain that I have an acute sense of what in fancy words you could call a mission. I feel that Osnat . . . that we have to continue what she began."

Moish fell silent and touched the piece of paper on his knee. Michael noticed the vicious movement of Fanya's knitting needles and Guta's frowning brow. Dvorka rested her chin on her hand and kept her eyes fixed on Moish. Zeev HaCohen uncrossed his knees and set his feet side by side on the floor in front of him. He crossed his arms and listened with his head tilted to one side, in a pose Michael thought must have been very charming once, but now looked too youthful, almost grotesque. Yocheved listened with an expression that grew increasingly sour as Moish went on talking.

"I feel that we now have to reexamine the question of the reorganization of life on the kibbutz from the point of view of the relations between the family and the community. I'm quoting from what Osnat wrote, and perhaps I'm not as good with words as she was, but I understood the picture she had in mind, just as most of you understood it. I don't want it all to come to nothing," said Moish in a voice full of embarrassed pathos, "just because Osnat is dead."

"What do you mean, 'come to nothing,' why nothing?" said Tova from the audience. "We've got a committee to deal with the development of the kibbutz, and that's exactly what we set it up for. Anyone would think that without Osnat—"

"Yes, I know," Moish interrupted her, "but I want us to discuss the whole thing also as a way of paying tribute to Osnat's memory." He cleared his throat. "In recent years, Osnat was one of the pillars of the kibbutz. I want us to discuss an immediate solution to the problem of family sleeping, and also to discuss from a positive, serious—I don't know—yes, deep, that's the word, deep point of view, the question of a communal facility for our older members."

Now Matilda rose to her feet, her round paunch sticking out, waving her arms, and shouted, "Are you starting on that again?"

Dvorka stood up too. Her lean, upright figure as she rose to her feet produced an immediate effect. Matilda fell silent and sat down. Dvorka's face, too, was pale. Her lips parted, and in a deliberate, didactic tone, unemotional and authoritative, she said, "Look, Moish, we've already spoken about it several times. The subject is a complex, complicated one and not to be taken lightly. We won't erect a memorial to Osnat by creating situations destructive to the group and the individual. Osnat herself didn't have any answers to all kinds of questions, even trivial ones, such as who would stay with sick children without the framework of a children's house. You sometimes forget that we created a productive, egalitarian society here a long time before the feminists burned their bras. This is the only place where a woman can work like a man, thanks to the solutions that were originally created to enable her to fulfill herself in meaningful, pioneering work.

"But these are side issues, and Osnat was in the habit of saying that we would solve them in the same way they were solved in other places. That's not the main point; the question that bothers me is the question of equality. We created an egalitarian society thanks to uniform education. Family sleeping will destroy that. And I have a lot more to say on the subject from the point of view of the principles involved, and this is not the time or the place to discuss them."

Guta's face, Michael saw, was distorted with hatred and rage as she began to speak, directing her words at Moish, "Why don't you say anything about the old-age home they want in order to solve the housing problem? Why don't you talk about that? The last time I complained about the new housing we weren't getting, Osnat told me that the housing committee was planning a new project, in other words, this old-age home, where they also want to sell places to people from town, as if we're short of money!"

"Guta," said Moish, "please, I ask you."

"Ask as much as you like, you won't shut us up!" shouted Matilda. "It's not just the housing, she also thought of it as a social solution, she told me so herself, how lonely older comrades would be able to meet new people in that old-age home, or whatever fancy name she called it."

"You just want to get rid of us for no good reason!" yelled Guta. "That's all your great new vision amounts to."

"So we won't be here to stop them from introducing all their modern changes," said Yocheved. Now she too was standing.

"And what will happen to the institution of the housemother? How do you see that? What will we need housemothers for?" asked a well-groomed young woman from the center of the dining hall. Michael didn't recognize her, and Avigail responded to his question with a shrug.

Dvorka bent over, pulled a dark-covered book out from under her chair, and said, "Comrades, comrades, please allow me." Gradually silence fell, and they all sat down again except for Dvorka, who remained standing with the open book in her hands. "In difficult moments like these, we should listen to what the early pioneers had to say, those communards who shared their innermost thoughts with each other so that we could derive comfort from them in moments such as these. I want to read something to you now from *Kehilatenu*. These are the words of David Kahana, here called David K. As you see, they felt no need to immortalize their names, and even today, comrades writing in our news bulletin don't sign with their full names but only with their first names and the initial of their family name, because the important thing is what we say and not who says it. We are living the highest ideal to which man can aspire: the happiness of the individual achieved by means of the integrity of the collective, as David

Kahana says." Dvorka now removed a pair of reading glasses from the pocket of her black trousers, bowed her head over the book, and began to read:

I tell you, brothers, even if I knew that in the end we would be drowned in the mire of life, I would not move from my place; perhaps I would pause for a moment to search for comrades in suffering and boldness, but I would not renounce the vision. Sometimes I come home from the quarry despondent and despairing, and it seems to me that everything around me has suddenly turned into a terrible tangle. Then I begin to unconsciously pass before me all the days of my life, from the Viennese Inferno—through the meetings and external events and through the inner struggles on board ship—until the 'purifying crucible' of the Galilee and the kibbutz, and the memories of the defeats and failures burn my flesh like fire and darken my eyes with thoughts of my decline in the Land. . . . But can I give up? No, brothers, I will not move from my place, for I make no distinction between the days of struggle and doubt and the days of the realization of the vision itself. Eternal seeking and endless struggle are our lot. They will accompany us all the days of our lives—from recovery to recovery, from task to task, from sacrifice to sacrifice; and to the extent to which the enterprise grows, the inner struggle will become harder, and to the extent to which the hand of fate presses more heavily on us—doubt will become more corrosive among us.

Dvorka shut the book, put it down on the chair, and then slowly took off her glasses.

"I don't believe it," said Michael. He was breathing hard and sweating. "That woman . . . she's showing her true colors at last." He stood up and went over to the sink, bent down, and drank from the tap.

"Has she gone off her rocker or what?" Avigail inquired of the room at large. "What was all that about?"

Michael returned to his chair and stared at the screen. The camera focused on Dvorka. "You don't understand," he said hoarsely, "she doesn't walk around with *Kehilatenu* in her pocket; she had to have come prepared. In fact, now that I think of it, she staged the whole drama, she knew what was going to happen here tonight."

"She has frightening eyes," said Avigail, "and I don't like her."

Michael tried to steady his breath. He lit a cigarette and stood up without taking his eyes off the screen. He was flooded with anxiety, almost with horror. At that moment, Dvorka looked different to him. He felt his face burning, as if he were witnessing something very threatening.

"I read you that passage mainly for the last sentence," said Dvorka now, stressing every word, "but also to show you that once upon a time people weren't afraid to express their feelings, and that within the family, the kibbutz family, it was legitimate to speak out frankly. The last sentence, which speaks of struggles, is the essential one. We have to examine ourselves endlessly, over and over again, in order to ascertain if the world we have built is the right one, and if it is, we have to preserve it." Dave stared at her wide-eyed, and shook his head from side to side like someone hearing words of wisdom from the master or like someone gazing at a rare species of animal.

The dramatic, passionate tone changed to a businesslike matter-of-factness as she said, "As far as family sleeping is concerned, I can't see any disadvantages in the present arrangements. Think of your own generation for a moment—is there anything wrong with you? And the memories, the experiences you have in common? And the involvement of all the members of the kibbutz in the development of every single child? Our involvement was so intimate, we all knew when the first tooth came, when each of you took his first step. And you're the living proof of the success of the experiment we carried out with such dedicated faith and devotion."

But Matilda, with the spiteful smile Michael had come to recognize, said, "We'll have to wait and see just how successful you are, but in the meantime you can enjoy the compliment."

"What about the old-age home?" said Guta. "That's what I want to know."

"It's impossible to talk about both subjects at the same time," pronounced Dvorka.

"Osnat thought it was possible," said Moish. "She thought it was necessary."

Dvorka clamped her lips into a wide, narrow line and then parted them to say, with an evident attempt to control herself, "And you know that I disagreed with her."

"There'll always be disagreements," said Zeev HaCohen in a conciliatory tone, "and there's no need to be hasty. Personally, I can't see any objection to a communal facility for older members, as long as it doesn't deprive us of the right to vote and participate in the life of the kibbutz, and as far as family sleeping is concerned, I think we should be open-minded about it."

"In any case," Dvorka broke into his words with uncharacteristic impatience, "it's clear that in the eyes of the majority these plans are completely unacceptable, because they undercut the whole idea on which the kibbutz was based." After a deep breath, she added, in a voice filled with contempt, "And don't quote other kibbutzim to us as examples. The idea of advancing with the times and following ruinous fashions won't guide our footsteps here. In the United Kibbutz Movement they're already talking about salaries, about paying kibbutz members for their work. In the light of such talk, I may sound anachronistic, but I know in my heart that the meaning of our lives won't be found in material rewards, but in inner realization."

"Only a minute ago you were talking about the need for dynamism and change," Zeev HaCohen reminded her.

"What's wrong with the way we brought up our children?" shouted Dvorka.

Moish's hands were trembling when he stood up and looked at Dvorka and the row of old people with a new, hard, unapologetic look in his eyes. "I'll tell you exactly what was wrong. There were a lot of things wrong. The first thing wrong is that we never talked about it. You didn't allow it, you didn't want to hear. I remember vividly how Srulke used to take me back to the children's house when I ran away to their room at night. The main thing that happened to me after Osnat died the way she died is that I have to talk. And I'm going to have my say, and you're going to listen to me. We'll have the kind of session here they used to have in *Kehilatenu*. I've read that collection of soul-baring monologues too, and my main thought was how things have changed since then, how the *sicha* has turned into a rubber stamp that grants or refuses requests or debates this or that organizational problem. What do you know about us? Maybe you know when we began to walk or talk and when our first tooth arrived, but about what goes on inside us you know nothing at all. We never had a chance to talk, only under cover of the jokes and skits we wrote for kibbutz celebrations and bar mitzvahs. I'm not saying there wasn't anything good about the way we grew up, but what about the misery, the nights when we woke up to a nonmother instead of a mother and a nonfather instead of a father, and to all kinds of other substitutes like the guy from the Nahal group who put talcum powder on Noga's vagina when it hurt her? On the kibbutz, that was a big joke."

Michael heard Avigail's heavy breathing and was aware of the movements of her hand up and down her arm.

"My mother, Miriam," said Moish in a choked voice, "who you all knew, was a simple, straightforward woman. I don't have to describe her here," he said, wiping his forehead. "She worked hard all her life, and she never spoke in the *sicha*, and there wasn't a more loyal member of the kibbutz." He looked around him. Nobody spoke, nobody moved. All eyes were fixed on him, some in amazement, some in shock. "My mother, Miriam," repeated Moish, "used to tell me, she told me often, about how you threw out our first housemother, Golda. I remember her name only from my mother's stories because, as people who understand about psychology have told me, we don't remember anything from before the age of eighteen months, and you threw her out when I was eighteen months old. But what about before I was eighteen months old? What about what happened then?"

There was nothing restrained or inhibited about him when he shouted, "Where were you before I was eighteen months old, when Miriam told me that the memory she had of me as a baby was of a little toddler walking behind his housemother with his nose and eyes streaming, tugging at the housemother's dress while the woman keeps pushing the little hand away? Where were you then?" His yell was directed at Dvorka, who did not lower her eyes. She was so still that Michael was afraid she would stop breathing. "That's what I want to know: Where were you? What were you thinking about then, on the nights when we were afraid? How did you come to agree to let mothers see their babies for only half an hour a day? Where did you get the nerve to decide that the family cell was inimical to society, and at the same time to make jokes about it and laugh at yourselves at kibbutz celebrations? That's what I want to know today. And what Osnat said to me was right: She said that you're opposed to change because of your own guilt, that's what she said. That in order to protect yourselves and justify yourselves you want to perpetuate that abuse!"

Someone muttered something, but Moish dismissed it with a wave of his hand. "Don't tell me to calm down," he yelled, "that's not what's important now, if I calm down or not. I'm telling you that it's enough! It's gone on long enough! Maybe you had your reasons, I don't know, you must have—the hardships of your lives and so on—but we don't have to continue your craziness now. I want to tuck in my children at night myself, the ones that still need tucking in. I want to hear them when they cough, in the room next to me, and when they have a nightmare I want them to come to my bed, not to some intercom, and not to make them to go out at night in the dark looking for our room, stumbling over stones, thinking that every shadow is a monster, and in the end standing in front of a closed door or being dragged back to the children's house. They'll be with me, and nothing else matters a damn."

He swallowed, and then his eyes met the eyes of the people sitting in the front row. "You'll come to terms with your own mistakes, like they've done on all the other kibbutzim," he said in a quieter voice. "I want you to feel guilty, why shouldn't you feel guilty? Lotte's no longer with us, but if she was here I'd have something to say to her about the years when my mother was allowed to come and see me only half an hour a day, and about the nights. You arranged things so it would be convenient for you. For the sake of the ideal of equality you organized things so we would have a group ego, but you destroyed our own, our personal egos. How healthy and secure do you think kids can be who've got only each other to turn to at night? And I'm not even talking about the beginning of adolescence and the communal showers and all your other brilliant ideas! I'm fed up! I'm fed up with being forgiving and understanding the hardships of the past. I want to understand what went on in your heads when you locked the doors of the children's house from the outside and told the night watch to check up on us twice a night! Two whole times! And we would sometimes stand there the whole night long banging on the door and crying and nobody came! I explode every time I think about it! It drives me crazy!" He leaned forward and burst out again, "Think of the little kids of this generation standing and crying at the door!"

"Well, well, well!" said Michael, lighting another cigarette. "Look at what's going on there!"

Avigail kept silent.

"And when we were bigger and ran away to you in the middle of the night, you took us right back to the children's house. I remember vividly how Srulke got out of bed and took me back. Twice I slept outside, at the door to my parents' room, so that I wouldn't be taken back."

Zeev HaCohen stood up, but Moish yelled at him, "You can sit down. I'm not through yet. Now that I've begun, I'm not going to shut up. You can wait until I've finished, you can wait until I've finished." Zeev HaCohen sat down, with a frightened expression on his face. "I don't give a damn about your equality," shouted Moish, "we're not the glory of the state of Israel or of anything else. What, I ask you, what came of it all? People accuse our kids of being materialistic and all kinds of things. What's the wonder? How else can they compensate themselves for the deprivations of their childhood? You at least had ideals that you could hide behind. What can we hide behind? What can we hide behind today? Work? Is work all our lives? Is that what you created the kibbutz for? The kibbutz: the glory of the state of Israel! Yes, sure!"

Moish stared at the ceiling and then fixed his eyes on the first row and shook his finger at them. "One of our members has been murdered; we don't know who did it or why. But what Osnat wanted to do I'll do now: There's no reason on earth why our children should be brought up by people who aren't their parents, and to hell with everything else!" He looked straight ahead of him and said spitefully, "No, Matilda, I haven't gone mad. On the contrary, up to now I've been mad. Nearly all the other kibbutzim have already done it, we've got the money to do it, and we're dragging our feet and messing around as if it's some trivial matter. My Asaf is going to be tucked in by me at night, you hear, Dvorka? Me and not the housemother, me and not the night watchman, me and not the intercom, me and nobody else. Because all you thought about was our first tooth, not our first fears, which we didn't even know how to put into words because we were so young. And I'm asking you, Dvorka, what ideal you can wave at me that's worth the fear and the loneliness of a child who doesn't know how to talk yet—why am I saying 'child'? a baby! I see my sister bringing up her children in town, and I'm not saying they've got everything they want, or that they go on picnics with insulated hampers and ice-cream bars or get clarinet lessons from the age of three, but they don't have the kind of fears I still suffer from to this day. And that's what I've got to say to you: We're going to have family sleeping here and everything else that Osnat wanted. An old-age home too, if that's what we decide."

"Over my dead body!" Guta's voice rose loud and clear, and then the storm burst and the TV screen blacked out.

19

"He agrees," said Guta, pushing Yankele into the room. "But do you • remember what we talked about?"

Michael nodded.

"Without Fanya. Leave Fanya out of it," she said grimly, and then she looked at him, softened, and said, "Only on account of her health, Yankele's already upset anyway." She talked about him in his presence as if he weren't there at all, thought Michael, as adults talked about small children. He looked at her expectantly. Guta ran her hand through her hair and looked back at him stubbornly.

"I want to talk to him alone," said Michael.

"Do you have secrets?" asked Guta, pushing her fists into the pockets of her smock. "I'm not leaving him alone with the police," she said in a determined voice.

"Guta," pleaded Michael. "I'm not the police. I'm me. We've already been over it. If you want the truth to come out, you have to help me."

"I'm not going," said Guta quietly. "And you won't make me. And you can stop looking at me with those pretty eyes of yours. I'm responsible for him. I'm not leaving him alone."

Michael sighed. "It's more for your sake than for his that I'm asking you to leave," he said finally.

"You don't have to worry about me," said Guta, averting her eyes. "I can hear anything. Nothing's going to happen to me."

Yankele sat on the edge of the ramshackle bed. He still hadn't said a word. He stared at his sandals, and suddenly he began to tremble. "I didn't do anything to her," he said. "I didn't do anything."

"But you were there at night, and you saw Aaron Meroz coming and going."

"I was looking after her. I had to look after her," said Yankele. He spoke heavily, as if there were stones in his mouth. His thin body trembled violently. Guta remained standing next to the closed door and lit a cigarette. "Why are you treating them with kid gloves," Nahari had scolded him recently. "What's all this pampering? We've got enough evidence to arrest all three of them, and that's it. What are you playing games for? Arrest them and you'll get whatever you want out of them. After a night in the lockup they'll answer all your questions."

"If they don't cooperate within the next twenty-four hours, I'll arrest them," Michael had said, "but I've learned that with people who've got nothing to lose it's better to try it my way."

"Nothing to lose," Nahari had grunted. "What's that supposed to mean? How do you know they've got nothing to lose?"

"I know. I know them, those two sisters. I've met people like them."

"What do you mean 'like them,'" Nahari had persisted, "in what sense?"

"Like them." Michael had refused to elaborate.

Now, looking at Yankele, who appeared terrified and withdrawn into himself, he wondered which of them was right. Guta stood at the door without moving. Even her breathing was inaudible. Out of the corner of his eye, Michael saw the cigarette sticking out of her mouth.

"I don't want to talk to you about the nights," said Michael. "The only thing I want to talk to you about is the kitchen duty."

Yankele looked at him in surprise. Suddenly he stopped trembling. He had long, dark lashes and a sad, frightened look in his eyes. "What kitchen duty?" he asked haltingly. "I'm not on kitchen duty anymore, the last time was on the holiday."

"That's exactly what I want to talk to you about. Dave told me that during the meal and the artistic program you were at the back entrance."

Yankele shuddered. "Dave told you?" he whispered. "He promised me he wouldn't say anything without asking me."

"That's all he told me," said Michael soothingly. "He didn't say anything else, only that."

Guta crushed her cigarette stub into a broken plant pot in the corner of the room and lit another. Michael didn't take his eyes off Yankele. "You're the only one who can tell me who left through the back entrance in the middle of the party," he said. "You're the only one."

Yankele was silent for almost an entire minute. Michael held his breath.

"She left," he said finally. "From the back entrance, quietly. Quickly. Nobody saw her leaving."

Now Guta's breathing was clearly audible. She didn't say a word.

"And what did you do?" asked Michael. He laid his hand on Yankele's arm, which was wet with perspiration. "Tell me exactly," he said, in the tone he had used with Yuval when he was a child, trying to convey the promise of total protection, of the power to understand and endure anything.

"I followed her halfway, and then she turned around, and I ran back to the dining hall," said Yankele. He dropped his eyes. "I thought that she . . . that she . . . was sad or something."

"And you wanted to look after her," said Michael.

"I didn't want anything to happen to her," said Yankele. "I wanted . . . I don't know," he stammered and raised his eyes to Guta. She didn't move. Her eyes were burning, and she held on to the doorpost with her back against the wall next to the door. Her face was pale.

"Only halfway?" asked Michael. "You didn't go any farther?" Yankele shook his head.

Guta opened her mouth, but Michael, alert for any movement on her part, gave her a warning look. "So why did you talk about bottles?" he asked suddenly, in a different tone. "If you didn't follow her all the way, you didn't see her next to Srulke."

Yankele began to stammer. He was trembling all over. "I know all about Dvorka," he said. "I know all about her."

Guta groaned and then began to cough. "He's talking about Dvorka!" she whispered. "All this time he's been talking about Dvorka?"

Yankele buried his face in his hands.

"You can go now," Michael said gently.

Neither of them moved. Then Guta came over to the bed and sat down on it. After waiting a moment, Michael left the room, closing the door gently behind him.

After only one knock on the door a voice inside the room said, "Yes."

She wasn't surprised to see him, but she didn't invite him in and looked at him with an inquiring air.

"I want to talk to you," said Michael, and he walked into the room.

She switched off the television and pointed to an armchair. The air conditioner was off, and it was hot in the room. She pulled her trousers straight and laid her hand on her knee. She looked at him in what appeared to be calm expectation, but the silence in the room was electric. A few seconds passed before he said, "You didn't tell me that you left the dining hall during the jubilee celebration; you didn't say anything about seeing Srulke."

"If I didn't say anything," said Dvorka calmly, "perhaps it's because nothing like that happened."

Michael studied her face. She maintained a frozen expression. "But you did leave the dining hall," he said finally.

"I left the dining hall," Dvorka agreed. "And what does that tell you? Why do you think I went to see Srulke?"

"I don't think," Michael assured her. "I know."

Dvorka looked at him without fear. "I can only say that you're mistaken," she finally said.

"Why, then, aren't you prepared to take a lie-detector test?" he asked quickly. "Anyone with nothing to hide takes a lie-detector test."

"I'm not accustomed to subjecting my statements to simplistic tests," said Dvorka stiffly. "In all my life no one has ever doubted my word. I'm seventy-two years old, young man, you should remember that."

"There's something else I want to ask you," said Michael suddenly. "About something else entirely." He saw a flicker of interest in her eyes. "I'd like to know why you prepared that passage from *Kehilatenu* for the kibbutz meeting, for the *sicha* last night."

In the seconds that passed before she recovered, Michael saw the flash of surprise and the wave of anxiety in her eyes, until the curtain came down again. "I don't understand your question," she finally said.

"One doesn't go around carrying that book like a Bible," said Michael. "Maybe nobody else noticed, but I realized that the whole thing was staged."

"Young man," said Dvorka, "I don't know where you got your information from about our *sicha* last night, but I presume you've got all kinds of devious methods . . . " There was an expression of revulsion on her face.

"That's not the point," said Michael, "that's not the point at all, and don't change the subject."

"You're impertinent. I'm not interested in nonsense like changing the subject," said Dvorka. "I went to the reading room on my way to the *sicha* to pick up the book. I often read it to my students, if you must know." She looked at him critically. "I don't know why I'm answering you at all, perhaps because I'm not in the habit of treating people rudely. Perhaps your impertinence can be excused against the background of the tension of the past few days. Not everybody can behave with restraint. Perhaps I'm even sorry for you," she said without emotion.

"It's a pity you weren't sorry for Osnat," said Michael.

Now she was flabbergasted. "Are you out of your mind?" she demanded. "What are you talking about?"

"About the poisoning," said Michael dryly. He had to remind himself that only he knew how rapidly his heart was beating, that no one else could feel it racing.

"You apparently understand nothing," said Dvorka as if she were reprimanding a pupil. "You apparently don't realize that I brought Osnat up, that I . . . " She fell silent.

"Yes, yes, I'm well aware of your status here on the kibbutz," said

Michael. "You think that you're above suspicion, that's what you counted on."

"Young man," said Dvorka, and her eyes bulged but she didn't raise her voice, "I think that you're getting at something that is so ridiculous it's beyond my comprehension, and there's a limit to the nonsense I'm prepared to tolerate. This conversation is pointless and ridiculous. You're behaving with shocking irresponsibility. Apart from everything else, think of the difference in age between us—how dare you?" For the first time she raised her voice. "Please leave at once," she said after gaining control of her breath, "at once! I have nothing more to say to you!" She pointed to the door without taking her eyes off him.

There was no point, Michael sensed, in trying to threaten her, to reach her in other ways. Simcha Malul's voice echoed in his ears: "I didn't see anybody," the woman had repeated miserably. "If I did, I would tell you." She had sworn on her children and touched his arm with her hand. She had seen no one, neither on her way out nor on her way back. "I'll begin to cry," she had said when he asked her to pretend. "I always cry when I tell a lie, or else I laugh. I can't do things like that. You want me to say I saw her coming out of the infirmary when I didn't really see anything?"

Simcha Malul had stood next to the sink in the infirmary kitchen, her hair wrapped in a white kerchief, scrubbing and scouring a perfectly clean dish and speaking in half sentences. Finally she had said to him, "You're one of ours—how can you ask me to tell a lie like that about a woman like her?" Michael gazed at her imploringly. She finally let go of the green plastic bowl and sat down at the little kitchen table. "Look," she said to him in Moroccan Arabic, "I would help you if I could, but to tell a lie?" And in Hebrew again, "She's a lady, I can't say a thing like that about her. They give her a lot of respect here. She never did me no harm, and I don't know how to lie, not even to my husband."

He looked at Dvorka's outstretched arm. It was perfectly steady as she pointed silently at the door. Michael stood up and left the room.

20

"Are you still here?" the switchboard operator asked Michael in surprise as he was walking to his office. "Some woman was looking for you, and I thought that you'd already left."

"And . . . ?"

"She didn't leave a message. Are you going to be around? In case anyone else asks for you—"

"I've got a few calls to make myself," said Michael, waving as he hurried down the corridor. He didn't even hear her last remark. When he opened the door to his office, he looked at the pile of papers on his desk and placed the cardboard file on top of it, and then he stared through the window overlooking the treeless backyard and felt homesick for the dusty ivy framing the window of his office in the Russian Compound. He thought about how he was making less and less of an effort here to cultivate the switchboard operators and the secretaries. What used to be easy, part of the day's work, now seemed mechanical and lifeless. He thought of Gila, Ariyeh Levy's secretary in Jerusalem, and glanced at his watch. In his mind's eye he saw her long fingernails running over the keyboard of the word processor that had recently replaced the electric typewriter. He missed her too.

"It's the feeling of transience," he said to himself, "which you've developed in order not to become attached to anything here. What have you got against this place?" he asked himself, and the answer, which remained unformulated, was connected to a feeling of wounded self-esteem. Not only were his skills always being called into question here, but they didn't even give him the credit that Ariyeh Levy gave him, however grudgingly.

He sat in the padded chair behind the desk in a room at least twice the size of his room in the Russian Compound and paged through the papers in the cardboard file. After reading and rereading the transcripts of Jojo's interrogations, he dialed the switchboard operator, and after hearing his request, she said, "Yes, right away." During the ten minutes that passed before the phone rang, Michael smoked two cigarettes and nervously wiped the dust off the desk with his finger. He tried to look through the pile of papers, but he couldn't concentrate. The words didn't add up to sentences. Only when he heard Aaron Meroz's voice on the other end of the line did he realize how tense he was.

In a distant, indistinct voice Meroz said that he felt better, and Michael heard the depression in his reserved tone as he said, "I have to be here for another week, and then we'll see."

"I'm speaking from the nurses' station," he said hesitantly in answer to Michael's question. In the background cries and murmurs were audible, and Meroz said, "If you can't come here . . . "

"Ask them to transfer the call to the doctors' room," said Michael persuasively, and the voices grew muffled as Meroz put his hand over the receiver.

"They're transferring the call," said Meroz finally.

Michael waited on the line for three minutes. He looked at his watch and counted the seconds. While he waited, he jotted his questions down on the back of an envelope in a wildly erratic hand.

"How did you know?" asked the M.K. from the doctors' room. Michael ignored his rapid breathing and restrained his rage, saying, "Why didn't you tell me? During all our talks?"

"Because I promised her that I wouldn't open it until a date in about two weeks' time. It's in my safe-deposit box at the bank. I haven't opened it, I haven't got a clue as to what's in it, I swear."

"So what if you promised her?" shouted Michael. "She's dead!"

"Sometimes it works that way," said Aaron Meroz after a long silence. "When we make promises to people and they die, the promise becomes more binding. She told me it had nothing to do with anybody. It was a personal matter."

"It doesn't matter now," said Michael. "I only hope it's what we're looking for. I'll be coming to talk to you myself, but first I'm sending someone to get your authorization to open your safe-deposit box." He listened for a moment and before putting the phone down said, "Don't worry, he'll bring a lawyer and the right papers for you to sign."

The feeling of uneasiness grew inside him as he went into the corridor and almost ran to Benny's room. As he dictated his instructions to Benny, who stood and wrote them down in a slanting, curly, surprisingly feminine hand, Michael felt as if inner voices were signaling to him with words like "danger" and "beware." Benny finally raised his head from the paper and, after passing a hand with a thick wedding ring on it over his smoothly shaven cheek, looked at the hand and said hesitantly, "Wouldn't it be simpler with your connections in Jerusalem . . . never mind."

"Too much depends on it," said Michael with a sense of urgency. "I can't start looking for people and connections now. I need it today."

"I thought you were in a hurry," said Nahari, glancing at his watch. "It's already half an hour since you told me, yet again, that every minute here means danger there."

They were standing in the broad corridor next to Nahari's office. Michael said, "It's true, we really can't afford to waste any time, but Benny's already on his way, and he'll bring it back here today. I don't know when I'll be able to talk to Jojo myself, but if you can find the time, maybe you could check with Sarit about how the interrogation's going. "

"I won't find the time today," said Nahari in a pompous tone. "I won't find the time today because in fifteen minutes I have an appointment with the attorney general, but I don't think anything will happen if you speak to her this evening."

Michael waved his hand in despair and ran out to the parking lot.

When his eye fell on the speedometer and he saw the needle wavering between 130 and 140 kph, he tried to lighten his foot on the gas pedal, to silence the inner voices that sounded like Avigail. When he felt the familiar pain in his jaw, he lit another cigarette. His uneasiness grew as the car approached the kibbutz. When he parked it next to the dining hall, he had to stop himself from running to the clinic. "Why do you think something's going to happen to her?" he asked himself almost out loud as he strode rapidly to the secretariat. There he saw the words "Back in a minute" in big, handwritten letters on a note pinned crookedly underneath the bronze sign saying SECRETARIAT.

He could hardly breathe as he stood in the doorway of the treasurer's room next to the secretariat. The woman who was sitting there talking on the phone raised her eyes inquiringly. She ignored the urgent looks he gave her and the question he began to formulate out loud and calmly completed her conversation. He asked her where he could find Moish, and she said, "He went somewhere for a few minutes. He didn't say where, only that he'd be back right away."

Against all the precautions he himself had insisted on, he asked for the internal phone book and dialed the clinic number. He kept his back to the woman as he dialed. She seemed absorbed in her own affairs. She didn't ask him who he was, and from the expression on her face—lips pursed, eyes averted—when she handed him the phone book, and the way she pointed to the phone, he knew that she knew who he was, that all her business with the papers on the desk was only a pretense. But even this wasn't enough to stop him. When he heard Avigail's voice saying a nervous "Hello," he could only say, in a throttled voice, "Good morning."

"It's almost afternoon," said Avigail, and there was something so reassuring in this dry reply that he sat down on the chair opposite the woman, who went on rustling her papers and listening to every word. He could feel the trembling of his limbs as his muscles suddenly relaxed.

"I just wanted to know if there's anything new," he said, weighing every word.

"Not exactly," said Avigail carefully. "There's someone with me now, but I'll be glad to talk to you in about half an hour."

"I'll come there," said Michael, in the face of all the alarm bells ringing in his head warning him to be careful. There was silence on the other end of the line. He saw her vulnerable face in front of him, and he knew that she was brushing her hair off her neck, he could see the delicate hand under the heavy fall of hair lifting the silky brown skeins with that characteristic gesture.

"Is that wise?" her cautious, reserved voice said at last.

"I can't consider that at the moment," he admitted. "But under the circumstances, you could call it natural."

He looked at his watch and saw that it would be twenty past twelve before he could be in the clinic. When he no longer heard her voice, anxiety again took control of the rhythm of his breathing. He tried to calm down and heard himself saying to the woman, in words that echoed hollowly, "So he'll be back soon?"

"In another few minutes," said the woman, and then she shrugged her shoulders and added, "That's what he said. But that other man was here too, the one with the mustache; he asked about him and then he went away."

Michael thanked her and walked toward the old secretariat building. Machluf Levy wasn't in the room they had been allocated. Nor was the intelligence officer from the Lachish Subdistrict anywhere to be seen. Michael felt lost. He tried to control his growing feeling of dread, to mobilize helpful voices, and he wondered where Moish could have gone, in the middle of the day, before lunch.

He heard Machluf Levy's heavy tread before he saw him standing in the doorway. He looked grave and was twisting the thick ring around on his finger. "What's the matter?" Michael heard himself asking with the same panic in his voice that he would hear in his then mother-in-law's whenever he phoned her. "What's the matter?" he tried again, but the anxiety was still there.

"Nothing's the matter," said Machluf Levy, "except for the fact that he suddenly went to talk to Dvorka in the middle of the day. First he talked to Dave, you know the one I mean."

"Yes, yes," said Michael impatiently. "What's he been doing since he got up in the morning? From the minute you changed shifts?"

"During the night he didn't leave his room. His wife made a

scene, but he didn't answer her. After that he couldn't fall asleep. I think," said Levy with a worried expression, "that he doesn't feel well, that ulcer must be giving him hell. I didn't see, but Itzik, who was on the night shift, told me that he was pacing around the room. The blind wasn't shut; there was no problem seeing inside. We could hear everything, but there was nothing to hear. In the morning he went to the dining hall, but he hardly ate anything. And then he went to work in the secretariat. I spoke to him there. He could hardly talk. I don't know what's bugging him, or what new thing's bugging him. But ever since you told me not to let him out of our sight, I can see that he's going off the rails, like they say."

"When did he go to see Dave?"

"That's just it, he went when Dave was in the plant. He rode there on his bike, and I had a problem, but he's so out of it, like they say, that he didn't even notice that I was following him. Finally I grabbed a bicycle; I haven't worked so hard for years."

"Well," said Michael, "what happened?"

"He rode to the plant, like I said."

Michael gave Machluf Levy a hostile look. The tension was making him speak slowly. Michael felt like shaking him. As if he had heard him gritting his teeth, Levy raised his eyes to him nervously and rapidly said, "He went inside and came out with Dave. We've got bugs in his room, and the other rooms, but nobody's wired, there's no way we could have overheard what they were saying. And everybody's where you said for them to be. Nobody's budged. And Itzik was outside his room all night." He looked at Michael expectantly, but Michael said nothing. "Dave didn't look any different from usual. Moish took him like this," Levy said, putting his arm around an imaginary shoulder, "and they walked away, and then Dave went back in and came out with Yankele."

"I didn't hear what they were saying," he said in reply to Michael's questioning look. "I stood behind that green fence they've got there, and I saw everything, but I couldn't hear a word."

"And you didn't speak to him afterward?"

"When afterward? He rode on his bike from there to Dvorka's."

"To Dvorka's?" repeated Michael.

"Yes, that's where he is now."

"So what are you doing here?" Michael asked sharply.

"They were already standing at the door on their way to the dining hall, and I didn't want them to see me hanging around there in the middle of the day. And anyway, we've got Baruch staked out next to Dvorka's room. He's there now."

"We should have brought more men in," said Michael regretfully.

"That's what I said, too," said Levy, shifting his weight from foot to foot.

"So what's the matter with you?" asked Michael. "What's bugging you? Something's bothering you, that's obvious."

The anxiety in Machluf Levy's eyes grew stronger as he said, "Well—I don't know how to put it—first of all, you made me nervous with all your warnings—don't let him out of your sight here and don't let him out of your sight there. Anyone would think we were playing some kind of game . . . and I don't even know what it's all about, what's in your head. What am I, a little kid to ride around on a bicycle in the middle of the day on a kibbutz?"

Michael looked at Machluf Levy's gabardine trousers and pressed shirt, without a tie this time, and nodded slowly. "And second," said Machluf, fingering his shirt collar, "I don't know, he looks in terrible shape to me, that Moish, and after the way he talked, too . . . There's one of our guys there, and Dvorka's room's bugged; we can listen to what they said afterward."

"Afterward?" said Michael sharply. "Why afterward? Now!"

"Good," said Levy. "I'll go there now, if you like. In any case, I know that he cried, he cried like a baby. And he said, 'How could you?' That was when I walked past the room on my way here. I could hear him at the door."

"What else did you hear him say?"

"I was on my way here to look for you," said Levy. "That's all I heard: 'How could you? How could you not tell me?' He kept repeating the same thing."

Michael looked at his watch and saw the big hand approaching three. "I have to go to the clinic for a minute," he said. "Do me a favor, go to the dining hall and tell Moish that I want to talk to him after that, let's say in half an hour. Tell him to wait for me at his place—at his room, where he lives. And then go and hide outside his room. Don't take your eyes off his room."

"Me personally?" asked Levy, twisting the ring on his pinkie.

"You personally, and don't let him see you. Behind the big bush, where Itzik was last night."

"What is this," grumbled Levy, "a movie? A detective story for children? Why can't we just sit in the van and listen in to what they say? What have we got the equipment for? What's the point of hanging around in the bushes? And in broad daylight, too."

"Machluf," Michael said, mobilizing all the patience at his command. "Do me a favor now, Machluf. Just go and stand there and keep out of sight, I don't know how. I know we're not properly organized, but there's no time now, believe me, Machluf, there's no time." He touched the broad shoulder of the man, who was at least a head shorter than he.

The clinic was empty except for Avigail standing at the sink and washing a test tube. The first thing he noticed was the flash of terror in her eyes when he opened the door. She wiped her wet hands on the spotless white smock and quickly turned down the cuffs of her shirt sleeves and buttoned them.

"Leave those buttons alone, Avigail," said Michael sternly.

"Why did you come here? Now somebody will know, they always know in the end," said Avigail.

"Because I want to ask you two things that can't wait," said Michael, and to his own surprise he found himself touching the hair reaching halfway down the nape of her neck. He looked into the gray eyes and saw fear and distress. There was no joy in them at all. With a quick, graceful movement she eluded his hand and stepped back.

"Avigail," said Michael, "listen very carefully to what I'm going to say to you now, and do what I tell you and don't move from the telephone. Here, take Dr. Kestenbaum's number, ask him again about the antidote and the amount of time it takes for—"

"There's no need," said Avigail in a dull, hard voice. "I know exactly, and everything's ready."

"So be ready next to the phone and wait. Don't move. If you're not here, then be in your room and don't leave it. So I can let you know at once."

"I don't understand what makes you so sure that we're close to a solution," said Avigail as she rummaged in a big cupboard and took out a disposable syringe in a plastic envelope. He watched her graceful movements and suppressed the urge to go up to her.

"I spent half the night talking about it. I thought you understood what I was talking about."

"What was the meeting like?" asked Avigail, putting the syringe and a little bottle into the big pocket of her smock.

"Is it safe there in your pocket?" asked Michael.

"What do you mean, safe?"

"It won't fall out?"

Avigail shook her head. "I'm not going to run and jump," she said without smiling. And then, hesitantly, she added, "I think you've worked yourself up into a state and you've decided that it's going to happen quickly because you need it to happen quickly. There was a reporter here to see me today."

"From where?"

"Does it matter? From *The Voice of the Negev*. She wants a scoop. When the news blackout is lifted and the story breaks, she wants to be the first to interview me." Avigail giggled.

"Why you?"

"Oh, because I'm a nurse and she knows that the nurse on a kibbutz knows everything."

"What did you tell her?"

"That I had a lot of patients this morning and I was busy and she should leave her phone number. I was nice to her because I didn't want to put her back up, I was afraid she might start snooping around and find something out."

"Who was here this morning?"

"Nobody special, apart from Dave, who was here when you phoned. He said that Yankele was on the point of an attack. What happened at the team meeting?"

Michael glanced at his watch and described the meeting in a few sentences. Avigail looked thoughtful, and when he was already at the door on his way out, she said, "Actually, I think there are grounds for your suspicions about Jojo."

"Now you remember?" said Michael. "That's already old hat, passé, water over the dam."

"You don't tell me anything about what's happening with the interrogation," said Avigail in a hurt tone.

Michael took his hand off the door handle and said, "Why do you think that about Jojo?"

"Because he knows too much about antipsychotic drugs, and I thought he must have some connection with a mentally ill person even before it came out, when we were talking about Yankele a couple of days ago. And I asked myself how come a kibbutz treasurer knows so much about antipsychotic drugs?"

"Why did he suddenly get careless?" asked Michael suspiciously.

"When people come to the clinic they . . . they get mixed up—they really want people to know about them," said Avigail thoughtfully.

"You're not moving an inch from here," said Michael, "or from your room."

"But now I'm going to eat," said Avigail. "And then I'll go to my room, and at three I'll be back in the clinic. But just because it's Monday doesn't mean that everything's going to happen the way you want it to."

Michael walked quickly to the secretariat. The air was blazing, and the soles of his feet felt as if they were on fire. The concrete paths and even the lawns gave off a palpable heat. There was nobody outside. Only at four, Michael knew, the first children would begin arriving at their parents' rooms, and at five people would begin disporting themselves on the lawns, where sprinklers were now revolving and spraying out drops of water that were quickly absorbed by the dry air.

Moish was sitting at his desk. He looked at Michael with a despairing, devastated expression.

"What's up?" said Michael. "Tell me now, without beating about the bush. We don't have any time to lose."

Moish looked at him and opened his mouth, but nothing came out.

"You're having a hard time," said Michael, looking at the hands covering half his face.

"I don't know," said Moish, trying to speak.

Michael tried another tack. "This is no time to break down. You know that Jojo's still in detention? We won't let him go so soon."

Moish kept quiet.

"Perhaps I should be more specific," said Michael. "Why don't you tell me what you talked about with Dave today?"

"Dave isn't important," said Moish.

"So who is important?" asked Michael. Moish didn't reply.

"So who is important?" Michael repeated stubbornly. "We don't have any time to waste, can't you see there's no time to waste?"

"You can't scare me anymore," said Moish. "I don't know anything anymore."

"What did you want from Yankele?"

"He was on kitchen duty when my father died."

"But we've already questioned him several times about that evening. He didn't see anything. What made you think now that he saw something?"

"Dave made me," said Moish in a broken voice, pushing his gray hair off his pale forehead.

"What about Dave? What did he say?" Michael asked and lit a cigarette.

With a trembling hand, Moish poured water from the jug into the blue plastic cup standing next to him. "It's hard for me to swallow," he said to Michael, "and this allergy's killing me too. Even the water's got no taste. Do you want some?" He filled an empty cup and handed it to Michael.

"What did Dave say?" asked Michael, taking the cup and putting it down.

"It all began after the *sicha* on Saturday. On my way back to the room I talked to Dave. He told me that Yankele's been talking strangely lately. That something was troubling him again. That after the *sicha* he was expecting him to react very badly. That sort of thing. I was hardly listening. But something stuck in my head. Dave said that Yankele kept talking about bottles all the time."

"Bottles? He spoke to you about bottles? Did he tell you anything?" asked Michael sharply.

"That's it. I didn't understand either. But suddenly in the morning I remembered, and then I understood, and I went to the plant. Not everybody knows how to talk to Yankele. I knew that I wouldn't be able to get anything out of him that you didn't get out of him. But I asked Dave to help me after explaining to him what it was all about.

And Dave asked him, and finally he said that Dvorka had left by the back entrance to the kitchen that evening, the jubilee celebration evening."

Michael looked at him and asked, "And how does that connect to the bottles?"

"Yankele followed her, that's what he told Dave this morning. He followed her halfway. As far as . . . as far as . . . in the direction of my father's room."

"And then?"

"That's it," said Moish, staring at his hands.

"That's it?" said Michael."Come on, that's not all."

"That's all I'm telling you now," said Moish.

"It's too late," said Michael. "You've already said too much to suddenly begin protecting people now."

"On Saturday night we had a very traumatic *sicha*," said Moish, "and ever since I . . . I haven't had any peace since then. Suddenly I realized that I have to rethink everything."

"What did Dvorka say to you?" asked Michael.

Moish looked at him in horror. "When?" he asked finally.

"Now, just now when you spoke to her," said Michael.

"She didn't say anything. How do you know that? Have you been following me? That guy with the mustache? What's the matter with you people? Have you lost your senses?" Now he was shouting.

"What did Dvorka say to you?"

"She didn't say anything. It was me who did the talking," said Moish in a different voice.

"And what did you say? What do you think? Tell me what you think."

"I don't feel so well," said Moish, shivering.

"Tell me what you think."

Moish put his hand on his stomach. His face was gray.

"Do you think that Dvorka went to your father's place?"

"I don't know what to think anymore," said Moish with an effort. "You don't understand what this is doing to me."

Michael said the words he had said so often before in similar circumstances: "Explain it to me."

"She didn't tell the truth. You asked her twice in my presence.

And you asked her alone too, I know, just like you drove everyone else here crazy with your questions. I asked her. My father was her friend. She didn't tell anyone that she knew he was dead. She didn't say if there was a bottle there or not. Who's she trying to protect? I don't understand why she had to hide a thing like that from me. For me Dvorka telling lies is like . . . it's like . . . for Dvorka to hide things like that . . . " Moish wiped his forehead. "I can't go on like this," he said finally, "I'm falling apart. And my medicine's in the room. I have to go back to my room."

"You've always got a bottle here in your briefcase," Michael reminded him.

Moish rummaged in his briefcase and took out the familiar plastic bottle. He looked at it and shook it. "Empty," he said and threw it into the wastepaper basket. "I'm going to my room."

"I'll come with you," said Michael, noticing the effort Moish was making to stand up. "Do you want to go to the clinic?" he asked. "Should I call the nurse? The doctor? Do you need a doctor?"

"No doctor," said Moish, "no doctor and no nurse and no nothing. I just want to lie down on my bed. After I take my medicine I feel better. It's just that I left it in the room."

They walked slowly. Michael suppressed his sense of urgency. To a casual observer they would have looked like two men going for an innocent stroll, but there was nobody outside to see them. The sun blazed in the sky, and in the glaring light Moish's gray face looked almost yellow. Outside the door of his room Moish stopped and said, "I'll be fine. Really. You can leave me alone."

Michael nodded and said, "We'll talk later, after you rest."

But before returning to the old secretariat he turned his head and glanced toward the corner of Moish's building. Then he went up to the big oleander bush and pushed the branches aside. A wasp darted out of the dusty branches, but Machluf Levy wasn't there.

Something stopped him in his tracks. He sensed eyes staring at him and wondered if he was losing his grasp of reality. He was about to move away when it seemed to him that he heard sounds from inside. He went up to the window. Moish was lying on the floor and vomiting. His body was convulsed. Michael opened the door. There was nobody there but Moish, who let out a groan. On the carpet next to him lay the plastic bottle, oozing the white liquid that always gave off a smell of peppermint. Now it had a different smell, and the same smell was coming from Moish's mouth.

Michael felt the sense of cool efficiency he had not felt for a number of days now flooding him. There was a note of certainty and command in his voice when he said into the phone, "Come immediately. Moish's room."

Then he bent over the tall man lying convulsed on the floor. He was conscious. "Do you recognize the smell?" Michael asked him, and he heard his own voice, gentle and reassuring, as if he were talking to a child, the voice in which he had spoken to Yuval when he was a small boy burning with fever at night.

"I can't smell anything," said Moish with an effort.

"Is it parathion?" asked Michael.

"It was in the bottle, I know. And I'm going to die."

"It isn't so easy to die," said Michael. "You won't die."

Moish vomited again. His face was white, and his body convulsed again. He let out a rattling sound, and Michael counted the seconds.

"It's always the same," said Avigail as she wrapped up the bottle. "It took me four minutes to get here, but to you it seemed like forever because you weren't sure I'd make it in time."

"If you hadn't come right away, he would have died," said Michael.

"In another five minutes, probably, if I hadn't given him the atropine, he would have died."

Michael shivered.

"But there's something else, which you may not have realized, which scared me just as much," said Avigail.

"What?" asked Michael, suppressing the shivering that had seized hold of his body.

"If you give someone the antidote to parathion and he doesn't need it, if he isn't suffering from parathion poisoning, it can be equally dangerous. Especially with his ulcer."

"But he was quite sure. And I remembered what you just said from Kestenbaum, he warned me about it a hundred times on the phone, but I trusted my sense of smell."

"Perhaps we shouldn't have taken such a chance," said Avigail.

"What choice did we have?" Michael retorted bitterly.

There were voices outside. The phone rang.

"Where the hell are you?" said Michael angrily into the receiver. "Just tell me where you are." He listened to the reply, with an occasional "Aha." The medical crew summoned by Avigail from the hospital came into the room.

"It took us fifteen minutes," said the doctor, and after examining Moish he added, "Lucky you had the atropine. Without it he would have been dead as a doornail."

Michael put down the phone. "I have to go," he said to Avigail. "You stay here until the people from Forensics arrive; what we've got here is a crime scene by any definition. And it's a miracle that it's not a murder scene."

"Where will you be?" asked Avigail.

"In Dvorka's room," said Michael.

Machluf Levy was waiting for him in the room. He sat opposite her in the slender-legged armchair and didn't take his eyes off her.

"He nearly died," said Michael.

"I stood there like we said. I saw her go in. I heard her through the bathroom window. I thought to myself, what business has she got in his bathroom? Dirty business is all. I stood there on the big stone we put into position yesterday. She was careless, she left the bathroom window open, and I heard noises but I couldn't see exactly what she was up to. I couldn't catch her in the act because I was afraid she'd see me through the window when she lifted her head. But here it is! I took it from her in the room. She isn't talking. I took it from her by force, it was in her pocket. A little bottle with a dropper, like nose drops. Here it is," and Machluf Levy handed Michael a plastic bag with a small plastic bottle in it. "I thought he was with you all the time. That's why I stuck with her."

When he saw the anger in Michael's eyes, he said, "I thought he was with you and he was safe and I had to stay on her tail." And then, when the rage still did not fade from Michael's eyes, he went on, "How was I supposed to know that you were going to leave him alone there? Did you tell me to arrest her? Did you tell me to follow her? You didn't tell me anything. And on top of everything," he added, lowering his eyes, "Baruch's radio stopped working, and he didn't hear a thing that I was saying to him. I couldn't contact him at all. I was afraid he wasn't there, and that she would slip out of our hands. That she would do something to herself. But we caught her red-handed," he said with satisfaction. "And she didn't kill Srulke, she just took the parathion."

Michael took the little bottle. Suddenly he realized who she reminded him of. It was Livia in the television series *I, Claudius*, the ruthless, scheming grandmother who poisoned members of her family right and left and wanted to be deified after she died. He was no longer afraid of her. Dvorka dropped her eyes.

Only after they had taken her away—Machluf Levy gripped her arm tightly and didn't let go—did the people from the mobile lab enter the room. From there they went to Moish's room. "Lucky the place is empty," said a woman Michael didn't know from the pathology team. "Where's the family?"

"They all went on an outing to the beach this morning," said Michael. From his position by the door he saw Avigail walking slowly down the concrete path. She was still wearing her nurse's uniform.

"I'll walk you to your room," he said when he caught up with her. "You can start packing, unless you want to stay on until the new nurse comes."

"Not even for half an hour," said Avigail. "I'm through here."

"How is he feeling?"

"He'll be all right, they've pumped his stomach and everything. She really sloshed it in."

"Moish knew," Avigail added thoughtfully. "He knew it was her."

"Yes," said Michael, kicking a pebble on the path.

"It must have driven him crazy," said Avigail. "And is it definite that Srulke's death was an accident?"

"That's what it looks like," said Michael.

"I don't understand why Moish didn't say anything," said Avigail.

"He wanted to protect her, too," said Michael. "It's a very difficult situation, when everyone around you is like your family. And especially Dvorka."

"I still don't really understand why," said Avigail. She looked at him. "Do you understand why?" she suddenly asked. "Why did she do it to Osnat?" Michael kept quiet. "Why don't you answer me?" complained Avigail. "Do you understand why?"

"Yes, I think so," said Michael.

"So say something," said Avigail. "Explain it to me."

"I think that Osnat, and then Moish, threatened the basic meaning of her life, and she hated them for it. We'll talk about it later. We'll talk about it a lot," said Michael. They approached the room.

"Do you need any help?" asked Michael uncomfortably. Avigail seemed so efficient. As if she could cope with whatever came along.

But inside the room the last light of the day brought the expression of vulnerability back to her face, the expression that made him catch his breath. He laid his hand on her arm, and she didn't evade his touch.

"Avigail," said Michael.

"What?"

"Will you do something for me?"

"What?"

"Will you show me your arm?"

Avigail looked at him for a long time. Then with an unsteady hand she unbuttoned the sleeve of her shirt.

"Is that all?" said Michael with a feeling of relief. "And I thought that you . . . I didn't know what to think, I just couldn't understand. It will pass, Avigail," he said and smiled. "In comparison to what I imagined, it's nothing," he assured her and took her head in his hands.

The phone rang. Avigail looked at him questioningly and picked up the receiver. She looked at him again and handed it to him. "It's for you," she said without surprise and went into the bedroom. Michael heard the closet doors opening, and after that he had to sit down to stop the panic. "It's nothing," said Sarit at the other end of the line, "it's not serious, someone threw a stone at him."

"Who told you?" Michael heard himself ask.

"His mother phoned. She said to tell you that it's not serious. His arm's broken, and a stone hit him near the eye. He's in Hadassah Ein Karem, and she just wanted us to let you know."

Avigail stood in the bedroom doorway and put her suitcase down.

"I have a son," said Michael in a shaking voice.

"Yes?" said Avigail, looking at him. "Has something happened to him? You look as if something's happened. What's happened? Where is he?"

"Hadassah Ein Karem," said Michael, trying to control the trembling of his hands.

"Who notified you?" asked Avigail as she took the burning match from between his fingers, blew it out, and put it carefully into the ashtray.

"His mother. I was married once, and I have a son. He's almost finished with the army, he'll be discharged soon."

Avigail took a deep breath. "I'll come with you to Ein Karem if you like," she said finally. "I'll wait for you outside."

The telephone rang again, and Avigail looked at him. Michael leaped for the phone. "Yes," he heard himself say. And then a few more times "Yes," and "As I thought," and in the end: "Take a signed statement from him and let him go."

Avigail picked up her suitcases. A few moments passed until he put out his cigarette and took them from her. "What have you got in here? Stones?" he asked. Then he closed the door behind them with his shoulder.

"What was that phone call about?" asked Avigail when they were already in the car.

"Benny. Osnat's letter really was in Aaron Meroz's safe-deposit box."

"I can't stop thinking about Jojo. Carrying a secret like that around with him and not telling anyone. What a way to live." And after a silence she added, "Well. He's not the only one."

As they approached the hospital, Michael said, "People imprison themselves in the reality they invent. They make up secrets, and afterward they don't know how to get out of them."

Avigail looked at her hands and didn't say a word. But when Michael parked the car at the hospital entrance, she smiled at him anxiously and whispered, "He'll be all right, your son. You'll see. What's his name?"

"Yuval," said Michael. "His name is Yuval."